About the Authors

Stacy Connelly dreamed of publishing books since she a kid writing about a girl and her horse. Eventually, made it onto the page as she discovered a love of ance and the promise of happily-ever-after. In 8, that dream came true when she sold *All She nts for Christmas* to Mills & Boon. When she is not in the land of make-believe, Stacy lives in Arizona her two spoiled dogs.

Barbara Hannay lives in North Queensland where she and her writer husband have raised four children. Barbara loves life in the north where the dangers of cyclones, crocodiles and sea stingers are offset by a relaxed lifestyle, glorious winters, World Heritage nforests and the Great Barrier Reef. Besides writing, rbara enjoys reading, gardening and planning ensions to accommodate her friends and her extended family.

Anne Oliver lives in Adelaide, South Australia. She is n avid romance reader, and after eight years of writing r own stories, Mills & Boon offered her publication 2005. Her first two published novels won the nance Writers of Australia's Romantic Book of the Year Award in 2007 and 2008. She was a finalist again in 2012 and 2013. Visit her website anne-oliver.com

Seasons in Love

COLLECTION

One Winter Wedding

STACY CONNELLY

BARBARA HANNAY

ANNE OLIVER

MIX
Paper from
responsible sources
FSC
FSC C007454

This book is produced from independently certified FSC™ paper
to ensure responsible forest management.

For more information visit: www.harpercollins.co.uk/green

Printed and bound in Spain
by CPI, Barcelona

MILLS & BOON

First Published in Great Britain 2020
By Mills & Boon, an imprint of HarperCollins*Publishers*
1 London Bridge Street, London, SE1 9GF

ONE WINTER WEDDING © 2020 Harlequin Books S.A.

Once Upon a Wedding © 2009 Stacy Cornell
Bridesmaid Says, 'I Do!' © 2011 Barbara Hannay
The Morning After the Wedding Before © 2012 Anne Oliver

ISBN: 978-0-263-28070-8

0120

ONCE UPON A WEDDING

STACY CONNELLY

To all my friends—
Thanks for being as excited about my dream
coming true as I have been.

Chapter One

I can't believe I'm doing this, Kelsey Wilson thought as she hurried through the airport as fast as possible in her straight skirt and low-heeled pumps. Her oversized purse thudded against her side with every step. The shoulder strap caught a lock of red hair that had escaped her sensible bun, and she felt as though someone had reached out and grabbed her. Holding her back from the job she had to do.

The family is counting on you, Kelsey. Her aunt's voice rang in her mind. *You know what can happen when a woman falls for the wrong kind of man.*

Kelsey hadn't needed Aunt Charlene's reminder. She had her mother as an example. Olivia Wilson had thrown away everything for a man who left her with nothing. Olivia had been eighteen when she met Donnie Mardell—Kelsey's father, though she never thought of him in those terms. Donnie had promised Olivia a love of a lifetime, as well as freedom from her too-strict parents, and she fell for every word. When her father made her choose between Donnie and her family, Olivia chose Donnie. But while Olivia may have had stars in her eyes, Donnie had dollar signs in his. When the Wilsons offered him money to leave town, he took it without a glance back at his girlfriend or unborn child.

But Kelsey's cousin Emily hadn't fallen for the wrong man. She was engaged to Todd Dunworthy. The only son of a wealthy Chicago family, he'd come to Scottsdale to start his own company and add to his already considerable fortune. Todd was handsome, charming, and Charlene couldn't have handpicked a better son-in-law.

Kelsey had worked nonstop for the past two months to put together the perfect wedding. The dress, the flowers, the music, the cake, everything wove together like the hand-stitched Irish lace in Emily's veil. But Kelsey knew how delicate that lace was. One wrong pull, and it could all fall apart.

She refused to let that happen.

She *needed* this wedding to be amazing. She'd staked her reputation on the success of the ceremony, certain her cousin's wedding was the spotlight that would make her business shine. She'd been so sure of that she'd put most of her savings into a down payment for a small shop in Glendale. Kelsey had felt confident making the huge step. After all, her aunt and uncle were wealthy, influential people with wealthy, influential friends. Once the guests saw the job she'd done, Weddings Amour would flourish.

Even more important, her aunt and uncle would see that she, too, could succeed, that she was more than the poor relation they'd taken into their home. She'd been sixteen when her mother died, sixteen when Olivia finally admitted she was not an only child as she'd led Kelsey to believe. Olivia had an older brother, a sister-in-law and two nieces…total strangers who became Kelsey's only family.

Hold your head high, Olivia had whispered to Kelsey only days before passing away. Her face pale and gaunt, her blond hair long gone, her mother's eyes still blazed with the pride that empowered her to walk away from her family when she'd been pregnant at eighteen. *You may not have been raised as one of the wealthy Wilsons, but you're going to show them what an amazing young woman you are.*

Tears scalding her throat like acid, Kelsey had promised. She'd had no idea how difficult—how *impossible*—keeping that promise would be.

Finally, though, after eight years, she would have her chance to make good on her word. As a wedding planner, Kelsey had found her niche. She was organized, efficient, detail-oriented. Lessons learned as she scheduled her mother's doctor appointments, oversaw her medications and dealt with the insurance company served her well as she juggled caterers, musicians, photographers and the occasional Bridezilla.

Every wedding that ended in *I do* was a tribute to her mother's memory, and Emily's walk down the aisle would mean more than all the previous weddings. But before Emily could say her vows, Kelsey had to deal with one serious snag.

A sudden attack of nerves cartwheeling through her stomach, Kelsey swung her purse off her shoulder. She unzipped the center pocket and pulled out her day planner where, along with every detail of the wedding, she'd written the flight information. According to the listed arrivals, the plane from Los Angeles was on time.

Connor McClane was back in town.

Kelsey flipped to the front of the day planner and pulled out a photograph. Her aunt had said the picture was ten years old, which could account for the worn edges and creased corner. Kelsey feared there might be another reason. How many times had Emily stared at this photograph and wondered what might have been?

Kelsey had never met her cousin's ex-boyfriend, the bad boy from the wrong side of the tracks, but the snapshot said it all. Connor McClane leaned against a motorcycle, dressed head-to-toe in black—from his boots, to the jeans that clung to his long legs, to the T-shirt that hugged his muscular chest. His arms were crossed, and he glared into the camera. A shock of shaggy dark hair, a shadow of stubble on his stubborn jaw and mirrored sunglasses completed the look.

Kelsey could tell everything she needed to know from that picture except the color of Connor McClane's eyes. The man was trouble, as bad a boy as Donnie Mardell had ever been. Kelsey knew it, just like she knew Connor was better looking in a two-dimensional photo than any living, breathing man she'd ever meet.

Stuffing the picture and her day planner back in her purse, she hurried to the waiting area, where she focused on every man headed her way. He'd be twenty-nine by now, she reminded herself, four years her senior. Kelsey didn't suppose she was lucky enough that he'd aged badly or gone prematurely bald.

A beer belly, she thought, mentally crossing her fingers. A beer belly would be good.

But at the first glimpse of the dark-haired man sauntering down the corridor, her heart flipped within her chest and her hopes crashed. No signs of age, baldness or overhanging waistline…just pure masculine perfection. Her mouth went as dry as the surrounding desert.

Connor McClane had stepped to life from the photograph. From his form-hugging T-shirt, to his worn jeans and boots, to the sunglasses covering his eyes, every detail remained the same. A plane took off from a nearby runway, and the low rumble reverberating in her chest could have easily come from a motorcycle.

Kelsey tried to swallow. Once, twice. Finally she gave up and croaked out, "Mr. McClane?"

"Yes?" He stopped to look at her, and Kelsey's only thought was that she still didn't know the color of his eyes. Brown, maybe? To match the mahogany of his hair and tanned skin. Or blue? A bright, vivid contrast to his coloring.

A dark eyebrow rose above his mirrored sunglasses, a reminder that she had yet to answer him. A rush of heat flooded her cheeks. "Uh, Mr. McClane—"

"We've already established who I am. Question is, who are you?"

"My name's Kelsey Wilson."

He flashed a smile that revved her pulse. His head dipped, and she sensed him taking in the red hair she struggled to control, the freckled skin she tried to cover, and the extra pounds she sought to hide beneath the khaki skirt and boxy shirt. She saw her reflection in his mirrored glasses, a much shorter, much wider version of herself, like a carnival funhouse distortion.

Kelsey didn't feel much like laughing.

Had she known her aunt was going to assign her this mission, she would have worn something different—like full body armor. The image of what Emily might have worn to meet her former boyfriend flashed in Kelsey's mind. She shoved the pointless comparison away. Too much like trying to force Strawberry Shortcake into Barbie's wardrobe.

"Well, what do you know?" Connor stood in the middle of the corridor, mindless of the sea of people parting around him. "The Wilsons sent out a welcoming party. Heck, if I'd known I'd get this kind of reception, I might have come back sooner."

"I doubt that," Kelsey muttered.

Connor McClane had planned his return perfectly, coming back to ruin Emily's wedding. Aunt Charlene was certain of it. Kelsey knew only one thing. Her cousin had nearly thrown her future away once for this man, and she could see how Emily might be tempted to do it again.

"Don't underestimate your appeal," he told her, and though she couldn't see beyond the reflective sunglasses, she had the distinct impression he'd winked at her.

Kelsey straightened her spine to the shattering point. "My appeal isn't in question. I'm here to—"

Keep him away from Emily, Kelsey. I don't care how you do it, but keep that man away from my daughter!

"To do what, Kelsey Wilson?"

His deep voice made her name sound like a seduction, and suddenly she could think of all kinds of things to do that had nothing to do with her aunt's wishes. Or did they? How far would Aunt Charlene expect her to go to keep Connor away from Emily?

"To give you a ride from the airport," she answered with a saccharine smile. "Baggage claim is this way."

Connor patted the duffel bag slung over one shoulder. "Got everything with me."

Eyeing the lumpy bag, Kelsey wondered how dress clothes could survive such careless packing. Maybe he planned to ride his motorcycle up to the church in leather and denim, the same way he'd ridden out of town ten years ago? Unless—

"You didn't bring much with you. You must not plan to stay long."

Something in her voice must have given away her hope, because Connor chuckled. He adjusted the duffel bag and headed down the corridor, his strides so long Kelsey nearly had to jog to keep up.

"Oh, I'll be here as long as it takes," he told her with a sideways glance, "but I won't need more than a few days."

A few days. Did she really want to know? Did she really want to throw down the verbal gauntlet? Kelsey took a deep breath, partly to gather some courage, partly to gather some much needed oxygen. "A few days to what?"

"To stop Emily from marrying the wrong man."

Connor hadn't known what to expect when he stepped off the plane. He'd given Emily his flight information with the hope she might meet him at the airport. He'd wanted a chance to talk to her away from her family and her fiancé. He was realistic enough to know the whole Wilson brigade might be lined up at the gate like some kind of high-fashion firing squad. But he hadn't expected a petite redhead. He'd never imagined the Wilson genes could produce a petite redhead.

"So who are you anyway?" he asked, only to realize the woman was no longer at his side.

He glanced back over his shoulder. Kelsey Wilson stood in the middle of the corridor, her brown eyes wide, her lips adorably parted in shock. She didn't look anything like the other Wilsons, and curiosity stirred inside him. He couldn't picture her at the elegant country-club settings the status-conscious family enjoyed any more than he'd imagined himself there.

A Wilson misfit, he thought, *on the outside looking in.* Their gazes locked, and the momentary connection rocked him. Shaking off the feeling, he circled back around and asked, "You coming?"

The flush of color on her cheeks nearly blotted out her freckles. "You don't actually think you can come back here after ten years and expect to take up where you left off? You weren't right for Emily back then, and you aren't right for her now!"

As far as insults went, the words were pretty tame, especially coming from a Wilson. And it wasn't as if he had any intention of taking up where he and Emily had left off. He'd made his share of mistakes, and some—like thinking he and Emily had a chance—didn't bear repeating. Emily had been looking for someone to rescue her from the life her parents had planned for her, and he'd been young enough to think of himself as a hero.

Connor knew better now. He was nobody's hero.

Still, Kelsey's reminder stirred long-buried resentment. *Worthless. Good for nothing. Troublemaker.* Gordon Wilson had shouted them all when he'd discovered his younger daughter sneaking out to meet Connor. After being knocked around by his old man during his childhood, he knew a thing or two about male aggression and had arrogantly faced down the older man.

But Charlene Wilson's clipped, controlled words had managed to pierce his cocky facade. "From the moment Emily was born, she has had nothing but the best," Charlene told him with ice practically hanging from her words. "We have given her the world. What could *you* possibly give her?"

He'd tried to give her her freedom, the chance to live her life without bowing to her family's expectations. If someone had given his mother that same chance, things would have been different, and maybe, just maybe, she would still be alive. But when Emily made her choice, she didn't choose him. She took the easy way out—and in the end, so did he, Connor thought, guilt from the past and present mixing. But he wasn't going to fail this time. He was here to help Emily, no matter what the redhead standing in front of him like a curvaceous barricade thought.

"Look, whoever you are," he said, since she'd never explained her relationship to the Wilsons, "you didn't know me then, and you don't know me now. You don't have a clue what I'm good for."

He ducked his head and lowered his voice, not wanting to attract attention, but the words came out like a seductive challenge. He stood close enough to catch a hint of cinnamon coming from her skin. The color faded from her complexion, and her freckles stood out clearly enough to play a game of connect-the-dots. He shoved his hands into his pockets rather than give into the urge to trace a five-point star over one cheek. He tried to imagine Kelsey's reaction if he touched her. Would she recoil in shock? Or would he see an answering awareness in her chocolate eyes?

Right now, sparks of annoyance lit her gaze. "I know all I need to know. You're no good for Emily. You never were— What are you doing?" she demanded when Connor leaned around to look over her shoulder.

"Amazing. You can't even see the strings."

"What strings?"

"The ones Charlene Wilson uses to control you."

"Aunt Charlene does not control me."

Aunt Charlene, was it? He didn't remember Emily talking about a cousin, but they hadn't spent time discussing genealogy. "Funny, 'cause you sure sound like her."

"That's because we both want to protect Emily."

Protecting Emily was exactly why he was there. Adjusting the duffel bag on his shoulder, he started toward the parking garage. "So do I."

"Right." Kelsey struggled to keep up with him, and Connor shortened his stride. "Who do you think you have to protect her from?"

"From Charlene. From you." Before Kelsey could voice the protest he read in her stubborn expression, he added, "Mostly from Todd."

"From *Todd?* That's ridiculous. Todd loves Emily."

Yeah, well, Connor had seen what a man could do to a woman in the name of love. Seen it and had been helpless to stop it from happening… Shoving the dark memories of his mother and Cara Mitchell aside, Connor said, "Todd's not the golden boy the Wilsons think he is. The guy's bad news."

"How would you know?" Kelsey challenged as they stepped out the automatic doors and into the midday sunshine. Exhaust and honking horns rode the waves of heat. "My car's this way."

Connor followed Kelsey across the street to the short-term parking, where the fumes and noise faded slightly in the dimly lit garage. "I could tell from the second we met."

She stopped so suddenly he almost crashed into her back. When she turned, he was close enough that her shoulder brushed his chest, and the inane thought that she would fit perfectly in his arms crossed his mind.

Her eyes narrowed in suspicion. "You've never met Todd."

"How do you know?"

"Be-because," she sputtered. "Emily would have told me."

Despite her words, Connor saw the doubt written in her furrowed brow as she walked over to a gray sedan. The car nearly blended into the concrete floor and pylons. Between her plain vehicle and sedate clothes, he had the feeling Kelsey Wilson was a woman who liked to fade into the background.

But he was trained to notice details. He'd bet the brilliant hair she kept coiled at the back of her neck was longer and wilder than it looked, and try as they might, the shapeless clothes did little to hide some amazing curves.

"If Emily tells you everything, then you know she and Dunworthy spent a weekend in San Diego a few weeks ago, right?" At Kelsey's nod, Connor added, "Well, I drove there to meet them, and we had dinner." Keeping his voice deceptively innocent, he asked, "Emily didn't mention that?"

"Um, no," Kelsey grudgingly confessed.

"I wonder why. Don't you?" he pressed.

Not that there was much to tell, although he wasn't about to admit that to Kelsey. When he left town, he never thought he'd see Emily again. But after hearing through the long-distance grapevine that she was getting married, calling to congratulate her seemed like a good way to put the past behind him. The last thing he expected was Emily's invitation to have dinner with her and her fiancé while they were vacationing in California. But he'd agreed, thinking the meeting might ease his guilt. After all, if Emily had found Mr. Right, maybe that would finally justify his reasons for leaving Scottsdale.

But when Connor went to dinner with Emily, he didn't see a woman who'd grown and matured and found her place in life. Instead, he saw in Emily's eyes the same trapped look as when they'd first met—a look he could not, would not ignore.

Kelsey kept both hands on the wheel and her gaze focused on the road, but she was far too aware of Connor McClane to pay much attention to the buildings, billboards and exit signs speeding by. The air-conditioning blew his aftershave toward her heated face, a scent reminiscent of surf, sand and sea. His big body barely fit in the passenger seat. Twice now, his arm brushed against hers, sending her pulse racing, and she nearly swerved out of her lane.

She'd been right in thinking the man was dangerous, and not just to Emily's future or her own peace of mind, but to passing motorists, as well.

"I can't believe how much the city has grown. All these new freeways and houses…" He leaned forward to study a sign. "Hey, take this next exit."

Kelsey followed his directions, wishing she could drop him off at a hotel and call her familial duty done. Unfortunately, playing chauffeur wasn't her real purpose. Connor had flat-out told her he planned to ruin Emily's wedding. If she didn't stop him, her own business would be destroyed in the fallout. Who would trust a wedding planner who couldn't pull off her own cousin's wedding?

Panic tightened her hands on the wheel. "Where are we going?" she asked.

"My friend Javy's family owns a restaurant around here. Best Mexican food you've ever tasted."

"I don't like Mexican food."

He shook his head. "Poor Kelsey. Can't take the heat, huh?"

They stopped at a red light, and she risked a glance at him. He still wore those darn sunglasses, but she didn't need to look into his eyes to read his thoughts. He was here to win back Emily and show the Wilsons and the rest of the world they'd underestimated him all those years ago. But until then, he'd kill some time by flirting with her.

Kelsey didn't know why the thought hurt so much. After all, it wasn't the first time a man had used her to try and get to her beautiful, desirable cousin.

The light turned green, and she hit the gas harder than necessary. "Let's just say I've been burned before."

A heartbeat's silence passed. When Connor spoke again, his voice was friendly, casual and missing the seductive undertone. "You'll like this place." He chuckled. "I can't tell you how many meals I've had there. If it hadn't been for Señora Delgado…"

Kelsey wondered at the warmth and gratitude in his words. Something told her Connor wasn't simply reminiscing about tacos and burritos. An undeniable curiosity built as she pulled into the parking lot. The restaurant looked like an old-time hacienda with its flat roof and arched entryway. The stucco had been painted a welcoming terra-cotta. Strings of outdoor lights scalloped the front porch, and large clay pots housed a variety of heat-tolerant plants: pink and white vinca, yellow gazanias, and clusters of cacti.

Still checking out the exterior, Kelsey remained behind the wheel until Connor circled the car and opened the door for her. Startled by the chivalry, she grabbed her purse and took his hand. As she slid out of the seat, she hoped Connor didn't guess how rare or surprising she found the gesture.

She thought he'd let go, but he kept hold of her hand as he led her along red, green and yellow mosaic stepping stones that cut through the gravel landscape. His palm felt hard and masculine against her own, but without the calluses she'd somehow expected.

When he opened the carved door, he let go of her hand to lay claim to the small of her back. A shiver rocked her entire body. His solicitous touch shouldn't have the power to turn on every nerve ending. And it certainly shouldn't have the inexplicable ability to send her mind reeling with images of his hand stroking down her naked spine…

Full body armor, Kelsey thought once again, uncertain even that extreme could shield her from her own reactions.

Desperate to change her focus, she looked around the restaurant. A dozen round tables stood in the center of the Saltillo-tiled room, and booths lined each wall. The scent of grilled peppers and mouthwatering spices filled the air.

"Man, would you look at this place?" Connor waved a hand at the brightly colored walls, the piñatas dangling from the ceiling and the woven-blanket wall hangings.

He removed his sunglasses to take in the dimly lit restaurant, but Kelsey couldn't see beyond his eyes. Not brown, not blue, but gorgeous, glorious green. A reminder of spring, the short burst of cool days, the promise of dew-kissed grass. Without the glasses to shield his eyes, Connor McClane looked younger, more approachable, a little less badass.

"Has it changed?"

"No, everything's exactly the same. Just like it should be," he added with a determination that made Kelsey wonder. Had someone once threatened to change the restaurant that was so important to his friends?

A young woman wearing a red peasant-style blouse and white three-tiered skirt approached, menus in hand. "*Buenas tardes.* Two for lunch?"

"*Sí. Dónde está Señora Delgado?*"

Startled, Kelsey listened to Connor converse in fluent Spanish. She couldn't understand a word, so why did his deep voice pour like hot fudge through her veins?

Get a grip! Connor McClane is in town for one reason and one reason only. And that reason was not her.

The hostess led them to a corner booth. Kelsey barely had a chance to slide across the red Naugahyde and glance at the menu when a masculine voice called out, "Look what the cat dragged in!"

A good-looking Hispanic man dressed in a white button-down shirt and khakis walked over. Connor stood and slapped him on the back in a moment of male bonding. "Javy! Good to see you, man!"

"How's life in L.A.?"

"Not bad. How's your mother? The hostess says she's not here today?"

"She's semiretired, which means she's only here to kick my butt half the time," Javy laughed.

"I didn't think you'd ever get Maria to slow down."

"This place means the world to her. I still don't know how to thank you."

"Forget it, man," Connor quickly interrupted. "It was nothing compared to what your family's done for me over the years."

Modesty? Kelsey wondered, though Connor didn't seem

the type. And yet she didn't read even an ounce of pride in his expression. If anything, he looked…guilty.

"I'm not about to forget it, and I *will* find a way to pay you back," Javy insisted. "Hey, do you want to crash at my place while you're here?"

"No, thanks. I've got a hotel room."

Finally Connor turned back to Kelsey. "Javy, there's someone I'd like you to meet. Javier Delgado, Kelsey Wilson."

Javy did a double take at Kelsey's last name, then slanted Connor a warning look. "Man, some people never learn."

Still, his dark eyes glittered and a dimple flashed in one cheek as he said, "Pleasure to meet you, *señorita*. Take care of this one, will you? He's not as tough as he thinks he is."

"Get outta here." Connor shoved his friend's shoulder before sliding into the booth across from Kelsey. "And bring us some food. I've been dying for your mother's enchiladas." He handed back the menu without opening it. "What about you, Kelsey?"

"I'm, um, not sure." The menu was written in Spanish on the right and English on the left, but even with the translation, she didn't know what to order.

"She'll have a chicken quesadilla with the guacamole and sour cream on the side. And we'll both have margaritas."

"I'll take mine without alcohol," Kelsey insisted. Bad enough he'd ordered her lunch. She didn't need him ordering a drink for her, especially not one laden with tequila and guaranteed to go right to her head.

"Two margaritas, one virgin," Connor said with a wink that sent a rush of heat to Kelsey's cheeks. With her fair complexion, she figured she could give the red pepper garland strung across the ceiling a run for its money.

"I'll get those orders right up."

As his friend walked toward the kitchen, Connor leaned

back in the booth and gazed around the restaurant. Nostalgia lifted the corners of his mouth in a genuine smile. "Man, I've missed this place."

"So why haven't you come back before now?" Kelsey asked, curious despite sensible warnings to keep her distance.

He shrugged. "Never had reason to, I guess."

"Until now," she added flatly, "when you've come to crash Emily's wedding."

Losing his relaxed pose, he braced his muscled forearms on the table and erased the separation between them. His smile disappeared, nostalgia burned away by determination. "First of all, there isn't going to be a wedding. And second, even if there was a wedding, I wouldn't be crashing. I'd be an invited guest."

"Invited!" Surprise and something she didn't want to label had her pulling back, hoping to create some sanity-saving distance. "Who…" She groaned at the obvious answer, and the confident spark in Connor's emerald eyes. "What on earth was Emily thinking?"

"Actually, she summed up her thoughts pretty well."

Connor reached into his back pocket and pulled out an invitation. He offered it up like a challenge, holding a corner between his first and second fingers. She snatched it away, almost afraid to read what her cousin had written. Emily's girlish script flowered across the cream-colored vellum.

Please say you'll come. I can't imagine my wedding day without you.

Good Lord, it was worse than she'd thought! The words practically sounded like a proposal. Was Emily hoping Connor would stop her wedding? That he'd speak now rather than hold his peace?

"Okay," she said with the hope of defusing the situation, "so Emily invited you."

"That's not an invitation. It's a cry for help."

"It's—it's closure," she said, knowing she was grasping at straws. "Emily has moved on with her life, and she's hoping you'll do the same."

He frowned. "What makes you think I haven't?"

"Are you married? Engaged? In a serious relationship?" Kelsey pressed. Each shake of his head proved Kelsey's point. He wasn't over Emily.

Kelsey couldn't blame him. Her cousin was beautiful, inside and out. And experience had taught Kelsey how far a man would go to be a part of Emily's life.

Connor slid the invitation from her hand in what felt like a caress. "There's no reason for me not to be here, Kelsey."

Here, in Arizona, to stop the wedding, she had to remind herself as she snatched her hand back and laced her fingers together beneath the table. Not *here* with her.

The waitress's arrival with their drinks spared Kelsey from having to come up with a response. Connor lifted his margarita. "To new friends."

Rising to the challenge this time, she tapped her glass against his. "And old lovers?"

If she'd hoped to somehow put him in his place, she failed miserably. With a low chuckle, he amended, "Let's make that old friends…and new lovers."

His vibrant gaze held her captive as he raised his glass. Ignoring the straw, he took a drink. A hum of pleasure escaped him. The sound seemed to vibrate straight from his body and into hers, a low-frequency awareness that shook her to the core.

He lowered the glass and licked the tequila, salt and lime from his upper lip. "You don't know what you're missing."

Oh, she knew. The taste of a man's kiss, the scent of his aftershave on her clothes, the feel of his hard body moving against her own. How long had it been since a man had stolen her breath, her sanity? How many weeks, months? She'd probably be better converting the time into years—fewer numbers to count.

Odd how Kelsey hadn't missed any of those things until the moment Connor McClane walked down the airport corridor. No, she had to admit, she'd suffered the first twinge of—loneliness? Lust? She didn't know exactly *what* it was, but she'd first felt it the moment she'd looked at Connor's picture.

"Aren't you having any?"

Her gaze dropped to his mouth, and for one second, she imagined leaning over the table and tasting the tequila straight from Connor's lips.

"Kelsey, your drink?" he all but growled. The heat in his gaze made it clear he knew her sudden thirst had nothing to do with margaritas.

Maybe if she downed the whole thing in one swallow, the brain freeze might be enough to cool her body. She sucked in a quick strawful of the tart, icy mixture with little effect. Frozen nonalcoholic drinks had nothing on Connor McClane.

Still, she set the glass down with a decisive clunk. "You can't come back here and decide what's best for Emily. It doesn't matter if *you* don't like Todd. You're not the one marrying him. Emily is, and her opinion is the only one that matters."

Connor let out a bark of laughter. "Right! How much weight do you think her *opinion* carried when we were dating?"

"That was different."

"Yeah, because I was a nobody from the wrong side of the tracks instead of some old-money entrepreneur with the Wilson stamp of approval on my backside."

A nobody from the wrong side of the tracks. Kelsey schooled her expression not to reveal how closely those words struck home. What would Connor McClane think if he learned she had more in common with *him* than with her wealthy cousins?

Kelsey shook off the feeling. It didn't matter what they did or didn't have in common; they were on opposite sides.

"Did you ever consider that Emily's parents thought she was too young? She was barely out of high school, and all she could talk about was running away with you."

"Exactly."

Expecting a vehement denial, Kelsey shook her head. "Huh?"

One corner of his mouth tilted in a smile. "I might have been blind back then, but I've learned a thing or two. Emily was always a good girl, never caused her parents any trouble. She didn't smoke, didn't drink, didn't do drugs. No tattoos or piercings for her."

"Of course not."

From the time Kelsey had moved in with her aunt and uncle, she'd lived in her cousin's shadow. She knew all about how perfect Emily was—her fling with Connor the sole imperfection that proved she was actually human.

"Emily didn't have to do those things. She had me. I was her ultimate act of rebellion."

Kelsey listened for the arrogant ring in his words, but the cocky tone was absent. In its place, she heard a faint bitterness. "No one likes being used," she murmured, thoughts of her ex-boyfriend coming to mind.

Matt Moran had her completely fooled during the six months they dated. With his shy personality and awkward social skills, she couldn't say he swept her off her feet. But he'd seemed sweet, caring, and truly interested in her.

And she'd never once suspected he was secretly in love with her cousin or that he'd been using her to get closer to Emily. So Kelsey knew how Connor felt, and somehow knowing that was like knowing *him*. Her gaze locked with his in a moment of emotional recognition she didn't dare acknowledge.

The question was written in his eyes, but she didn't want

to answer, didn't want him seeing inside her soul. "What was Emily rebelling against?"

Connor hesitated, and for a second Kelsey feared he might not let the change of subject slide. Finally, though, he responded, "It had to do with her choice of college. She hated that exclusive prep school, but Charlene insisted on only the best. I suppose that's where you went, too."

"Not me," she protested. "I had the finest education taxpayers could provide." One of Connor's dark eyebrows rose, and Kelsey hurried on before he could ask why her childhood had differed from her cousins'. "So after Emily survived prep school…"

He picked up where she left off, but Kelsey had the feeling he'd filed away her evasion for another time. "After graduation, Gordon wanted Emily to enroll at an Ivy League school. She didn't want to, but her parents held all the cards—until I came along. I was the ace up her sleeve. Guess I still am."

The bad-boy grin and teasing light were absent from his expression, and Kelsey felt a flicker of unease tumbling helplessly through her stomach. Did Connor know something about Todd that would stop the wedding? Something that would tear apart all Kelsey's dreams for success and her chance to prove herself in her family's eyes?

"Emily invited me because her parents are pushing her into this marriage. She's pushing back the only way she knows how. She *wants* me to stop the wedding."

"That's crazy! Do you realize Emily is having her dress fitting right now? And we're going to the hotel tomorrow evening to make final arrangements for the reception? She loves Todd and wants to spend the rest of her life with him."

Leaning forward, he challenged, "If you're right, if Emily's so crazy about this guy, then why are you worried I'm here?"

A knowing light glowed in his green eyes, and history told

Kelsey she had every reason to worry. After all, on the night of her senior prom, after spending the day having her hair artfully styled and her makeup expertly applied, and wearing the perfect dress, Emily had stood up her parents' handpicked date…to ride off with Connor on the back of his motorcycle.

Having met Connor, Kelsey could see how easily he must have seduced her cousin. With his looks, charm, his flat-out masculine appeal, how was a woman supposed to resist?

And Kelsey wondered if maybe Emily wasn't the only one she should be worried about.

Chapter Two

"Honestly, Kelsey, why are you ringing the doorbell like some stranger?" Aileen Wilson-Kirkland demanded as she opened the front door. She latched on to Kelsey's arm and nearly dragged her inside her aunt and uncle's travertine-tiled foyer.

"Well, it's not like I still live here," Kelsey reminded her cousin.

Aileen rolled her eyes. "You probably rang the doorbell even when this *was* your home."

"I did not," Kelsey protested, even as heat bloomed in her cheeks. Her cousin might have been teasing, but the comment wasn't far off. She'd never felt comfortable living in her aunt and uncle's gorgeous Scottsdale house, with its country-club lifestyle and golf-course views. Before moving in with her relatives, *home* had been a series of low-rent apartments. And, oh, how she'd missed those small, cozy places she'd shared with her mother.

"I didn't want to barge in," she added.

"You're kidding, right? Like I haven't been dying to hear how things went! Did you pick up Connor? Does he look the same? Do you think—"

Ignoring the rapid-fire questions, Kelsey asked, "Where are Emily and Aunt Charlene?"

"Emily's still having her dress fitted."

"Oh, I'd love to see it." A designer friend of Kelsey's had made the dress for her cousin, but so far Kelsey had seen only drawings and fabric swatches.

For such a gorgeous woman, Aileen gave a decidedly inelegant snort as they walked down the hall. "Nice try. Do you really think you can escape without going over every detail from the first second you saw Connor right up to when you left him—" Emily's older sister frowned. "Where *did* you leave him?"

"At a restaurant."

"By himself?"

"What else could I do, Aileen? Follow him to his hotel and ask for an invitation inside?"

"Well, that would make it easier to keep an eye on him."

"Aileen!"

Waving aside Kelsey's indignation, Aileen said, "I'm just kidding. Besides, he doesn't have a car, right?"

"Like that's going to slow him down! Don't you remember the time Connor got busted for joyriding in a 'borrowed' car?" She hadn't been around then, but her aunt had remarked on Connor's misdeeds long after he'd left town. In fact, Connor's name had come up any time Emily threatened to disobey her parents. Like some kind of bogeyman Aunt Charlene evoked to keep her younger daughter in line.

Her cousin's perfectly shaped brows rose. "You don't think he's still involved in illegal activities, do you?"

"I have no idea," Kelsey said, ignoring the internal voice yelling *no*. Her automatic desire to rush to Connor's defense worried her. She was supposed to stop him, not champion him.

"You should find out," Aileen said as she led the way into the study. The bookshelf-lined room, with its leather and mahogany furniture, was her uncle's masculine domain, but even this room had been taken over by wedding preparations. Stacks of photo albums cluttered the coffee table.

"Why me?" Kelsey groaned.

"You want to help Emily, don't you?"

"Of course I do!" she insisted, even if she had to admit her motives weren't completely altruistic.

"And you want the wedding to be perfect, right?" Her cousin already knew the answer and didn't wait for Kelsey's response.

"I know Mother exaggerates, but not when it comes to Connor McClane. I wouldn't be surprised if he tried kidnapping Emily again," Aileen added.

Kelsey fought to keep from rolling her eyes. "She took off with Connor on prom night and didn't come back until the next day. I think your parents overreacted."

"Maybe, but I guarantee he'll try to stop the wedding somehow." Aileen pointed an older-therefore-wiser finger in Kelsey's direction. "But don't let him fool you."

He hadn't bothered to try to fool her. Was Connor so confident he could stop the wedding that he didn't care who knew about his plan?

Walking over to the coffee table, Aileen picked up a stack of photos. "Here are the pictures Mother wants to show during the reception."

"Thanks." Kelsey flipped through images of her cousin's life. Not a bad-hair day or an acne breakout in the bunch. Even in pigtails and braces Emily had been adorable. As

Kelsey tucked them into her purse, she noticed a stray photo had fallen to the Oriental area rug. "Did you want to include this one?"

Her voice trailed off as she had a better look at the picture. At first glance, the young woman could have been Emily, but the feathered hair and ruffled prom dress were wrong. "Oh, wow."

From the time Kelsey had come to live with her aunt and uncle, she'd heard how much Emily looked like Kelsey's mother, Olivia. Kelsey had seen similarities in the blond hair and blue eyes, but from this picture of a teenage Olivia dressed for a high school dance, she and Emily could have passed for sisters.

Reading her thoughts, Aileen said, "Amazing, isn't it?"

"It is. Everyone always said—" Kelsey shook her head. "I never noticed."

"Really? But they look so much alike!"

"My mother, she didn't—" Laugh? Smile? Ever look as *alive* as she looked in that photo? Uncertain what to say, Kelsey weakly finished, "I don't remember her looking like this."

"Oh, Kelse. I'm sorry." Concern darkened Aileen's eyes. "I should have realized with your mother being so sick and having to go through chemo. Of course, she didn't look the same."

Accepting her cousin's condolences with a touch of guilt, Kelsey silently admitted Olivia Wilson had lost any resemblance to the girl in the picture long before being diagnosed with cancer. What would it have been like had her mother retained some of that carefree, joyful spirit? Kelsey immediately thrust the disloyal thought aside.

Olivia had given up everything—including the wealth and family that now surrounded Kelsey—to raise her daughter. Emily's wedding was Kelsey's chance to live up to her promise. To hold her head high and finally show the Wilsons how amazing she could be.

With a final look at the picture, Kelsey slid the photo of her mother back into one of the albums. "It's okay," she told Aileen. "Let's go see if Emily's done with the fitting."

"All right. But be warned," Aileen said as she led the way down the hall toward Emily's bedroom. "The photographer's in there."

"Really?" Kelsey frowned. "I don't remember pictures of the fitting being included. Was that something Emily requested?"

She had long accepted that her ideas and her cousins' differed greatly, but a seamstress fretting over her measurements would have been a nightmare for Kelsey, not a photo op.

Aileen shrugged and opened the door just a crack. "The photographer said it was all part of the package."

A quick glance inside, and Kelsey immediately saw what "package" the photographer was interested in. Emily stood in the middle of the bedroom, with its girlish four-poster bed and French provincial furniture. Her sheer, lace-covered arms were held out straight at her sides while the seamstress pinned the beaded bodice to fit her willowy curves. Dewy makeup highlighted her wide blue eyes, flawless cheekbones and smiling lips.

"What do you think, Mother? Will Todd like it?" Emily leaned forward to examine the skirt, testing the limits of a dozen stickpins.

The photographer, a man in his midtwenties, started snapping shots as fast as his index finger could fly. It wasn't the first time Kelsey had seen slack-jawed amazement on a man's face. Too bad she saw the expression only when her cousin was around.

"Of course he will. Audra is an amazing designer, and she created that dress just for you. It's perfect," Aunt Charlene insisted, keeping a narrow-eyed glare on the photographer.

Charlene Wilson didn't share her daughters' beauty, but she

was a tall, striking woman. She could instantly command a room with her timeless sense of style and demand for perfection from herself and those around her. Today she wore a beige silk suit that wouldn't dare wrinkle and her brown hair in an elegant twist at the nape of her neck.

Glancing down at her own clothes, a map of creases that spelled fashion disaster, Kelsey knew her aunt would be horrified by the sight. Fortunately, Charlene was far too busy to notice. Kelsey slid the door shut and walked back down the hallway with Aileen.

"I know all brides are supposed to be beautiful," Aileen said with a mixture of sisterly affection and envy, "but that's ridiculous."

"Please, I've seen pictures of your wedding. You were just as gorgeous."

Aileen gave a theatrical sigh. "True. Of course, I wasn't lucky enough to have you to plan everything. I ran myself ragged, and you make it look so easy."

Kelsey laughed even as her cheeks heated with embarrassed pleasure. "That's because I'm only planning the wedding. It's far more stressful to be the bride."

"Still, you're doing an amazing job. Mother thinks so, too, even if she hasn't told you. This wedding will make your company."

That was just what she was counting on, Kelsey thought, excitement filling her once again. "I know." Taking a deep breath, she confessed, "I put down first and last month's rent on that shop in Glendale."

Aileen made a sound of delight and threw her arms around Kelsey in a hug that ended before she could lift her stiff arms in response. After eight years, Kelsey should have anticipated the enthusiastic embrace, but somehow, both her cousins' easy affection always caught her off guard.

"That is so exciting, and it's about time! You should have opened a shop a long time ago instead of working out of your home."

"I couldn't afford it until now."

"You could have if you'd taken my father up on his loan," Aileen said.

Kelsey swallowed. "I couldn't," she said, knowing Aileen wouldn't understand any more than her uncle Gordon had. Starting her business was something she had to do for herself and for her mother's memory.

Wilson women against the world... Her mother's voice rang in her head. Opening the shop wouldn't have the same meaning with her uncle's money behind the success.

Aileen shook her head. "Honestly, Kelsey, you are so stubborn." A slight frown pulled her eyebrows together. "But something tells me you're going to need every bit of that determination—"

Kelsey jumped in. "To keep Connor McClane away from Emily. I know, Aileen. But if Emily's so crazy about Todd, what difference does it make that Connor's in town?"

Ever since he'd posed that question, Kelsey couldn't get his words out of her mind. Okay, so in her opinion, Todd Dunworthy didn't hold even a teeny, tiny, flickering match to Connor McClane. But if her cousin truly loved Todd, shouldn't he outshine every other man—including an old flame like Connor?

"Kelsey, we're talking about Connor McClane. I know you've sworn off men since Matt, but please tell me that idiot didn't rob you of every female hormone in your body!"

Even after two years, the thought of her ex-boyfriend made Kelsey cringe. Not because of the heartbreak but because of the humiliation. Still, she argued, "I'm not discounting Connor's appeal." If anything, she'd been mentally recounting every attractive feature, from his quick wit to his sexy smile and killer bod. "But if I were a week away from getting married and madly in love with my fiancé, none of that would matter."

Aileen sighed and slanted Kelsey a look filled with worldly wisdom. "It's cold feet. Every engaged woman goes through it. I called things off with Tom three times before we finally made it to the altar. You'll see what I mean when you get engaged."

The idea of Kelsey getting engaged was in serious question, but if that time ever did come, she was sure she'd be so in love she'd never harbor any doubts. "Okay, so you called off your engagement. Did you run off with another man?"

"You know I didn't."

"Well, that's my point. If Emily and Todd are right for each other, Connor's presence shouldn't matter."

"It shouldn't, but it does. You weren't here when Emily and Connor were together. He's the kind of man who makes a woman want to live for the moment and never think of tomorrow. When Emily was around him, she'd get completely caught up in the here and now of Connor McClane. But her relationship with Todd is something that can last." Aileen flashed a bright smile. "Look, you've handled prewedding problems before. All you have to do is keep Connor away. You can do that, can't you, Kelsey?"

What else could she do but say yes?

Connor scrolled through his laptop's files, going over the information he'd compiled on Todd Dunworthy. He had to have missed something.

Swearing, he rolled away from the desk in his hotel suite and pushed out of the chair. He paced the length of the room, but even with the extra money he'd paid for a suite, he couldn't go far. From the closet, past the bathroom, between the desk and footboard, to the window and back. He supposed he should consider himself lucky not to have

Kelsey Wilson shadowing his every step. An unwanted smile tugged at his lips at the thought of the woman he'd met the day before.

He'd finally convinced her to leave him at the restaurant, telling her he had years to catch up with his friend, Javy. The words were true enough, but he'd seen the suspicion in her brown eyes. He chuckled at the thought of the atypical Wilson relative. She was nothing like Emily, that was for sure. Compared to Kelsey's fiery red hair, deep brown eyes, and womanly curves, Emily suddenly seemed like a blond-haired, blue-eyed paper doll.

But no matter how much curiosity Kelsey Wilson provoked, Connor couldn't let himself be distracted.

After his relationship with Emily ended, Connor had drifted around Southern California. Different state, but he'd hung out with the same crowd. Busting up a fight in a club had gotten him his first job as a bouncer. He'd worked security for several years before taking a chance and opening a P.I. business.

Up until three months ago, he would have said he was good at his job, one of the best. That he had a feel for people, an instinct that told him when someone was lying. Listening to his gut had saved his skin more than once. Not listening had nearly gotten a woman killed.

From the first moment he'd met Todd Dunworthy, Connor had that same hit-below-the-belt feeling. And this time he was damn sure gonna listen. So far, though, his background check had merely revealed Dunworthy was the youngest son of a wealthy Chicago family. Numerous newspaper photos showed him at the opera, a benefit for the symphony, a gallery opening. And while the events and locales changed, he always had a different woman—tall, blond and beautiful—on his arm.

No doubt about it, Emily was definitely Todd's type.

"You sure you don't hate the guy just 'cause the Wilsons

love him?" Javy had pressed on the ride from the restaurant to the hotel.

Connor couldn't blame his friend for asking. And, okay, so maybe he would dislike anyone who met with the Wilsons' approval, but that didn't change his opinion. Todd Dunworthy was not the man they thought he was.

He'd spoken to several of the Dunworthy family employees and none of them were talking. It wasn't that they wouldn't say anything bad about their employers; Connor expected that. But these people refused to say a word, which told him one important thing. As well paid as they might be to do their jobs, they were even better compensated to keep quiet.

Most were lifers—employees who had been with the family for decades. But there was one woman he hadn't been able to reach. A former maid named Sophia Pirelli. She'd worked for the family for two years before suddenly quitting or getting fired—no one would say—two months ago. The silence alone made Connor suspicious, and figuring an ex-employee might be willing to talk, Connor wanted to find her.

A few days ago he'd found a lead on Sophia's whereabouts. As much as he longed to follow that trail and see where it ended, he couldn't be in two places at once. He wanted to stay focused on Todd, so he'd asked his friend and fellow P.I., Jake Cameron, to see if the former maid was staying with friends in St. Louis.

Grabbing his cell phone, he dialed Jake's number. His friend didn't bother with pleasantries. "You were right. She's here."

Finally! A lead that might pan out. "Have you found anything?"

"Not yet. This one's going take some time."

Frustration built inside Connor. Although he trusted Jake and knew the man was a good P.I., Connor wasn't used to relying on someone else. "We don't have a lot of time here."

"Hey, I've got this," Jake said with typical confidence. "I'm just telling you, she's not the type to spill all her secrets on a first date."

Connor shook his head. He shouldn't have worried. His friend had been in St. Louis for all of two days, and he already had a date with the former maid. "Call me when you've got anything."

"Will do."

Snapping the cell phone shut, Connor hoped Jake worked his cases as quickly as he worked with women. But he wasn't going to sit around waiting for Jake; he wanted to find something on Dunworthy, irrefutable proof that the guy wasn't the loving husband-to-be he pretended.

Scowling, he resumed pacing, lengthening his stride to cross the room in four steps instead of eight. Connor had never been one to back down from a fight, but some battles were lost before they'd even begun. Gordon and Charlene Wilson would never take the word of the kid from the wrong side of the tracks over their handpicked golden boy.

Dammit, he needed an insider. He needed someone the Wilsons trusted to break the bad news. He needed one of their own. He needed…Kelsey.

Connor laughed out loud at the idea, but damned if he didn't think it might work. Kelsey hadn't played a part in his past relationship with Emily. She was as unbiased a witness as he could hope to find. She had nothing at stake with Emily's wedding, nothing riding on her cousin saying "I do."

No doubt about it, Kelsey was his best shot.

The following evening, Emily twirled around the hotel's atrium, her arms outspread like Sleeping Beauty. "You were right, Kelsey. This is the perfect place for the reception. Don't you think so, Mother?"

She looked so beautiful and happy Kelsey half-expected cartoon animals to surround her at any moment. Smiling at her cousin's unfettered happiness, she breathed a sigh of relief. Connor McClane was wrong, dead wrong. Emily and Todd were meant to be.

"It's lovely," Aunt Charlene commented without looking up from her mother-of-the-bride notebook. "I knew we could count on Kelsey to find the perfect place."

"Um, thank you, Aunt Charlene," Kelsey said, surprised and pleased by the compliment. Even after eight years, Kelsey and Charlene had a tentative, tightrope relationship that had yet to get past a disastrous beginning.

When Kelsey had first come to live with the Wilsons, she'd been overwhelmed by their obvious wealth, and her cousins' beauty and grace had left her feeling outclassed. Especially when Charlene took one look at her and declared, "Someone must take this girl shopping."

Looking back now, Kelsey realized her aunt had been trying to relate to her the same way she did to her own daughters, who loved nothing more than a day spent raiding Scottsdale boutiques. But back then, as an intimidated, awkward teenager, Kelsey had suffered the pain of being seen as an embarrassment by her new family.

She'd survived the multiple fittings and outfit changes—a living, breathing, *silent* mannequin—as her aunt and a shopkeeper went back and forth over which colors, styles and accessories best suited Kelsey. But when she stood with her aunt at the register, when she saw the *hundreds* of dollars a single item cost, a sick sense of disbelief hit her stomach.

How many weeks' rent would that pair of shoes have paid for when she and her mother were living in tiny one-room apartments? How many months of food? How much better might her mother's medical have been with that kind of money?

In a quiet, cold voice, Kelsey had told the saleswoman to put every item back, before marching out of the store.

Later, once Kelsey had calmed down and realized how ungrateful her actions must have seemed, she tried to apologize to her aunt. Charlene had declared the matter over and forgotten, but never again did she offer to take Kelsey shopping.

Their relationship had yet to recover from that day. By asking Kelsey to coordinate the wedding, Charlene had helped breach the gap, but Kelsey knew this opportunity didn't come with second chances. This was her one shot.

"I've always thought this was an amazing place for a reception," Kelsey said, hearing the dreamy wistfulness in her own voice. The glass ceiling and towering plants gave the illusion of being in a tropical paradise, and from the first time she'd seen the hotel, Kelsey had known it was perfect.

Perfect for Emily, she reminded herself.

Although between having so many of her friends working the wedding and Emily's willingness to let Kelsey make so many of the decisions, the entire event was feeling more like *Kelsey's* dream wedding.

Except the choice of groom...

The insidious thought wove through her mind along with images of Connor McClane... His rebellious saunter, his too confident grin, his...*everything.*

"I hope Todd likes it." Emily lowered her arms, a small frown tugging at her eyebrows. "Do you think he will?"

"It's a five-star hotel, one of the finest in the state," Charlene said imperiously.

"I know, but Todd's family is from Chicago. They have all those historic buildings and...Todd can be particular."

Kelsey's hand tightened on her day planner at her cousin's hesitant tone. Suspicions planted by Connor's too-pointed comments threatened to sprout into tangled choking weeds, but

Kelsey ground them down. Finger by finger, she eased her grip before she left permanent indentations on the leather book.

Her cousin was a people pleaser. Of course she worried what Todd would think. "He agreed to let you make all the decisions about the wedding," Kelsey reminded Emily, who had in turn, left most of the decisions up to her. "So he must trust your choices."

"I know, but…" Emily took a look around the atrium without the excitement she'd shown moments ago. Trying to see it through Todd's particular eyes?

"But what?" Kelsey prompted gently.

"It's—it's nothing." Emily shook her head with a laugh. "I just want everything to be perfect. You understand, don't you, Kelsey?"

Yes, she knew all about trying and failing again and again. But not this time—not with Emily's wedding. "Of course I do. And your wedding will be perfect," she insisted, before an already familiar masculine voice filled the atrium and sent shivers up and down her spine.

"Hey, Em! How's the blushing bride?"

"Oh, my gosh! Connor!" Emily squealed her former boyfriend's name and ran to meet him. A broad smile on his handsome face, he caught her in his arms and spun her around. "What are you doing here?" she asked.

Keeping an arm around Emily's shoulders, Connor glanced at Kelsey. "When Kelsey said you'd be here, I had to see you."

Heat rushed to Kelsey's face. Bad enough Connor had out-maneuvered her. Did he have to rub it in in front of her aunt?

Connor McClane had been in town less than twenty-four hours, and she could already feel the familiar undertow of failure dragging her under.

"You told him we'd be here?" The words barely escaped the frozen smile on her aunt's face. Charlene would never make a scene in public. Even if it meant smiling at the man out to ruin her daughter's future.

"No! I didn't." Except she *had* told Connor Emily was making final arrangements for the reception that evening, and he would know where the reception was being held. After all, he'd been invited. "I didn't mean to," she almost groaned.

Charlene straightened her razor-sharp shoulders, taking charge of a situation that had gotten out of control. Out of *Kelsey*'s control. Interrupting Emily and Connor's conversation, she said, "Mr. McClane, you'll have to excuse us. Emily has a wedding to plan."

"Mother!" her daughter protested. "Connor's come all this way to see me. We have so much to talk about. Can't this wait?"

"This is *your* wedding we're talking about, Emily! The most important day of your life."

The most important day of your life. Kelsey understood the sentiment. Every bride wanted her wedding day to be perfect, and she was doing everything in her power to see that this affair was the type every girl dreamed about, but Emily was only twenty-eight years old. Shouldn't she have something to look forward to?

Why Kelsey chose that moment to meet Connor's glance, she didn't know. He flashed her a half smile as if he could not only read her thoughts but agreed one hundred percent.

"You're right, of course, Mother." Emily turned to Connor with a smile. "I'm sorry, Connor. We don't have much time before the wedding, and there's still so much to do."

"Don't worry, Em. We'll have plenty of time to talk before then. I'm in Room 415."

"You're staying here?" Kelsey blurted the words in horror. At the hotel where not only the reception was taking place, but also the rehearsal dinner.

Connor's grin was maddening—and disturbingly enticing. "Thought it would be convenient."

"Convenient. Right." That way he could *conveniently* intrude on every event she had planned for the location and drive her insane!

"Kelsey, Emily and I can take things from here. You have…other matters to attend to now."

Her aunt's pointed look spoke volumes. Charlene could handle the final wedding details. Kelsey's job was to handle Connor McClane. She desperately clutched her day planner to her chest like a leather-bound shield. There were some things in life she could not control, but everything else made it onto a list. A methodical, point-by-point inventory of what she needed to accomplish, making even the impossible seem manageable. Nothing beat the satisfaction of marking off a completed task.

And although Kelsey certainly hadn't counted on Connor when she prioritized her checklist for Emily's wedding, as long as she kept him occupied for the next week and a half, Kelsey would be able to cross him off once and for all.

Catching a touch of her aunt's righteous indignation, she straightened her own shoulders and nodded imperceptibly. Satisfied, Charlene marched Emily out of the atrium.

Emily cast a last, longing glance over her shoulder, and the uncertainty Kelsey saw in her cousin's gaze strengthened her resolve. Aileen was right. Emily was suffering from cold feet. Her worries about her future as a wife and eventually a mother had her looking back to simpler times. Back when she could lose herself in Connor's live-for-the-day attitude.

But her cousin would only regret it if she threw away her future for a man of the moment like Connor McClane. And Kelsey could not allow Emily to make the same mistake her own mother had.

Chapter Three

"You know, Kelsey, I've never been *attended to* before."

Even with her back turned, as she watched Emily and Charlene walk away, Connor sensed the determination rolling off Kelsey in waves. Shoulders straight and head held high, she looked ready for battle. And yet when he took a closer step, his gaze locked on a curl of hair that had escaped the confining bun. The urge to tuck that curl behind her ear and taste her creamy skin nearly overwhelmed him. He sucked in what was supposed to be a steadying breath, but the air—scented with cinnamon and spice and *Kelsey*—only added to the desire burning through his veins.

Struggling to hide behind the cocky facade that had served him so well in his youth, Connor murmured, "Gotta say I'm looking forward to it."

"I don't know what you mean," she said stiffly.

"You think I don't know I'm those 'other matters' your aunt was talking about?"

Kelsey opened her mouth, looking ready to spout another unbelievable denial, only to do them both the favor of telling the truth. "You're right, Connor. My aunt wants me to keep you away from Emily."

"Charlene wants me gone and Emily happily married. There's just one problem."

"That would be you," Kelsey pointed out. "A problem easily solved if you were actually gone."

"If I leave, Emily's problems will have just begun."

"That's your unbiased opinion?"

"Yeah, it is," he agreed. "And not one your aunt and uncle are gonna listen to."

"Can you blame them?" Kelsey demanded.

No, and that was the hell of it. Connor knew *he* was the only one to blame. He knew what the Wilsons thought of him and he knew why. He could still see the look in Gordon Wilson's eyes when he offered Connor money to break up with Emily. Not a hint of doubt flashed in the older man's gaze. He'd been so sure Connor—a dirt-poor loser from the wrong side of town—would take the money.

Connor had longed to shove the money and his fist into the smug SOB's face. But he hadn't. He *couldn't.* And the pride he'd had to swallow that day still lingered, a bitter taste on his tongue.

He'd let Emily down, although from what he'd gathered during their recent conversations, she didn't know anything about the payoff. She thought their breakup had been her idea…just as she thought marrying Todd Dunworthy was her idea. But Connor knew better, and this time he wasn't going to be bought off.

"The Wilsons aren't going to listen to anything I have to say," he acknowledged. "That's where you come in."

Kelsey frowned. "I *am* a Wilson."

He hadn't forgotten…exactly. "You're different."

Drawing herself up to her five-foot-nothing height, shoulders so straight Connor thought they just might snap, Kelsey said, "Right. Different." Hurt flashed in her chocolate-brown eyes as if he'd just insulted her, when nothing could be further from the truth.

"Hey, wait a minute." Pulling her into a nearby alcove, out of the way of nearby guests, Connor insisted, "That was *not* a put-down. Your aunt and uncle turned their noses up so high when they met me, if it rained, they would have drowned. I was trailer trash, and no way was I good enough for their little girl. So when I say you're nothing like them, you can say 'thank you,' because it's a compliment."

There were a dozen words he could have said, compliments he could have used, but the stubborn tilt of Kelsey's chin told him she wouldn't have listened to a single one. Someone— her family, some guy from her past—had done a number on her.

No, words wouldn't do it, but actions… How far would he have to go to show Kelsey how attractive he found her? A touch? A kiss? The undeniable proof of his body pressed tight to hers?

"In case you've forgotten," Kelsey pointed out, her voice husky enough to let him know she'd picked up on some of his thoughts and wasn't as immune as she'd like him to believe, "according to my aunt and uncle you *kidnapped* their daughter."

"It was not kidnapping," he argued, though he'd had a hell of a time convincing the police. Fortunately Emily had backed his story, insisting that she'd left willingly. Eventually the charges had been dropped; Emily had been eighteen and legally an adult, able to make her own choices. Not that her parents had seen it that way. "But that's my point. Your aunt and uncle won't listen to anything I have to say. Which is where you come in."

"Me?"

"Right. We'll be partners."

"Partners?"

"Sure. After all, we're on the same side."

"Are you crazy? We are not on the same side!" Kelsey argued.

"I want Emily to be happy," he interjected, shaking her thoughts as easily as his sexy grin weakened her composure. "What do *you* want?"

Challenge rose in the lift of his eyebrow, but Kelsey couldn't see a way out. The trap was set, and all she could do was jump in with both feet. "Of course I want her to be happy."

"That's what I thought. Kelsey, this guy won't make her happy. He's not what he seems, and I want to prove it. The Wilsons won't believe *me,* but with you to back me up, they'll have to at least listen."

Kelsey longed to refuse. She didn't trust him. Not for a second. Oh, sure, his story sounded good, but finding dirt on Todd wasn't just a matter of looking out for Emily—it played perfectly into Connor's interests, as well.

If Connor did find some deep, dark secret to convince Emily to call off the wedding, not only would he be the hero who saved her from a horrible marriage, he'd also be there to help pick up the pieces. But if Connor couldn't find anything in Todd's past, what was to keep him from making something up? Working together, he wouldn't be able to lie. Not to mention, he'd given her a way to keep an eye on him.

Connor held out his hand. "Deal?"

Sighing, she reached out. "Deal."

Connor's lean fingers closed around her hand. Heat shot up her arm, and a warm shiver shook her whole body. Like stepping from ice-cold air-conditioning into the warmth of a sunny day.

"All right, partner."

"Not so fast." She hadn't lived with her businessman uncle for as long as she had without learning a thing or two about negotiation. "You might want to hear my terms first."

"Terms?"

Kelsey nodded. As long as Connor thought he needed her, maybe she could get a few concessions.

Instead of balking, Connor grinned. "Let's hear 'em."

"First, we're equal partners. I want to be in on this every step of the way. No hearing about anything you've found on Todd after the fact."

"No problem. From this point on, we're joined at the hip. 'Course, that will make for some interesting sleeping arrangements."

"Second, this is strictly business," Kelsey interrupted, as if cutting off his words might somehow short-circuit the thoughts in her head. But they were already there: sexy, seductive images of hot kisses and naked limbs slipping through satin sheets in her mind. She could only hope Connor couldn't read them so clearly by the heat coloring her face.

"And third?"

"Thi-third," she said, clearing her throat, "you stay away from Emily. *If* we get any dirt on Todd, *I'll* break the news to her. Until then, I don't want you filling her head with your 'bad feelings.'"

Expecting an argument, Kelsey was surprised when Connor nodded. "I'll keep my distance."

"Okay, then, we're partners." She should have experienced a moment of triumph, but all Kelsey could think was that she'd just made a deal with the devil.

Certainly, when Connor smiled, he looked like sheer temptation.

"Got to hand it to you, Kelsey, you're one hell of a negotiator. Two outta three ain't bad."

It wasn't until Connor strode away that Kelsey realized he'd never agreed to her second condition.

As Kelsey stepped into the florist shop the next morning, cool, floral-scented air washed over her. She breathed deeply, enjoying the feeling of a refreshing spa treatment without the outrageous prices. She wasn't a big believer in aromatherapy, but the stress of dealing with Connor might drive her to alternative measures. Anything to stop her pulse from jumping each time she saw him—and to keep her hormones under wraps and in control for the next ten days.

Why couldn't life be easy? Why couldn't she plan an elegant, trouble-free wedding? The kind where the biggest worry was the ice sculpture melting too quickly in the summer heat. Instead, she got Connor McClane, a man guaranteed to make women melt with nothing more than a look.

"Kelsey! Thanks so much for coming!" Lisa Remming, Kelsey's friend and the owner of In Bloom, circled the checkout counter to greet her with a hug. As always, Lisa dressed in clothes inspired by her favorite flower—bird of paradise. Her long brown hair and blue eyes were complemented by a sleeveless fiery-orange blouse and swirling olive-green skirt. "I feel so bad for calling you."

"Don't be silly." Kelsey waved off her friend's apology and pulled out her checkbook from her purse. "It's no problem."

"I still can't believe I'm doing flowers for Emily Wilson's wedding! There isn't a florist around who wouldn't kill for this job."

Hiding a smile, Kelsey teased, "Wow, who knew florists were so bloodthirsty?"

Lisa made a face, then gave Kelsey another hug. "I totally have you to thank for this."

The two women had gone to high school together, and

Lisa was one of the few people in whom Kelsey confided. By the time she'd moved in with her aunt and uncle, Kelsey had gotten accustomed to blending in and going through her teen years unnoticed. Telling her fellow students she was a long-lost member of the wealthy Wilson family would have shoved her under a microscope.

The only worse fate would have been the exclusive prep school her aunt had suggested she attend.

"I really hate asking you to do this," Lisa said as she reached behind the counter for an invoice.

"A deposit is standard practice."

"I know, but— We're talking about the Wilsons. It's not like they're going to leave me holding the bill. But with the flowers for the church and the bouquets and the boutonnieres, I have to pay my suppliers and—"

"And that's why you need the money up front." Kelsey tore off a check. The amount for the deposit alone would have depleted her own meager bank account, but Aunt Charlene had given her access to the special account established for Emily's wedding.

"Thanks." Lisa breathed a sigh of relief as she noted the deposit on the invoice. "This wedding is going to mean the world to my business." She laughed as she pressed a button on the cash register and slid the check inside. "Like I need to tell *you* that, right? You'll be flooded with calls after Emily's friends see the amazing job you're doing. Have you thought anymore about getting your own place?"

Excitement pulsing through her veins, Kelsey nodded. "I've put down first and last month's rent on the space in downtown Glendale, near the antique shops."

Lisa gave a squeal. "And you didn't even say anything! When are you moving in?"

"As soon as the current renters move out. The landlord's supposed to give me a call."

"You must be so excited! I know I was when I first opened this place. Do you have all the furniture and office equipment you'll need? Have you thought about hiring a support staff and—"

"Whoa, Lisa! Don't get carried away," Kelsey said with a laugh that sounded far too shaky.

"I'm not. Don't tell me you of all people—with your day planner and your endless lists—haven't thought of these things."

In fact, she *had,* and only days ago she'd been riding high on her plans. Now, with Connor back in town, she feared she'd put the honeymoon before the wedding, and her stomach roiled at the thought of losing control. "I don't want to get too far ahead of myself."

"What are you talking about?" Lisa challenged. "Emily's wedding is only a week and half away. You aren't too far ahead. If anything, you're behind!"

"Well, thank you for giving me that combination vote of confidence and total panic attack."

"I'm sorry. But I know how much effort you've put into this, and I want to see it pay off for you."

I want Emily to be happy. What do you *want?*

With Connor's words ringing in her head, Kelsey insisted, "Emily's happiness comes first."

"Honey, Emily's happiness *always* come first," Lisa deadpanned.

"That's not fair, Lisa," Kelsey insisted quietly.

Emily and Aileen could have turned their backs when their unknown and potentially unwanted cousin showed up to live with them. Instead, they'd done everything possible to include Kelsey. It certainly wasn't their fault she'd never fit in.

"I know." Lisa's sigh expressed an unspoken apology. "But

I also know you've played second fiddle to both your cousins for as long as I've known you. I don't want you to be so focused on Emily's wedding that you lose track of your dream."

"I haven't and I won't."

Despite her determined vow, a touch of guilt squirmed through Kelsey. She'd kept silent about renting the shop for exactly the reasons Lisa mentioned. Her aunt wouldn't want her attention on anything other than the wedding. But the shop was nothing compared to Connor McClane. The man was a living, breathing distraction.

"Emily's wedding *is* my dream," Kelsey added. "A high-profile event with an extravagant budget and built-in publicity thanks to my uncle's business contacts and my aunt's country-club friends—it's guaranteed to put my business on the map."

"I agree, and I can't believe you pulled it off in only two months!"

"It *was* short notice, wasn't it?" Kelsey asked, fiddling with the zipper on her purse.

"Yes, but you did it!"

Kelsey nodded. Thanks to working almost nonstop, she'd pulled off planning the event in a fraction of the time it normally took, but Emily had insisted on a June wedding... hadn't she?

Sudden doubts buzzed through her mind like annoying insects, unrelenting and unavoidable. Had Emily pushed for the summer wedding? Or was the idea Charlene's...or Todd's? Kelsey had been so focused on getting everything done on time, she hadn't stopped to wonder about the short engagement. Until now...until Connor had stirred up the hornet's nest of doubt.

Connor hung up the phone after ordering breakfast and ran his hands over his face. He hoped the distraction of food would wipe the nightmare from his memory. It wasn't the first time disturbing images had invaded his sleep.

The beginning of the dream was always the same. Connor watched his client, Doug Mitchell, arrive at his wife's apartment through the tunnel-eye view of a telephoto lens; only when he tried to stop the man from attacking his estranged wife, did the dream shift and alter, keeping him off balance, unsure, helpless. Sometimes he froze in place, unable to move a muscle, unable to shout a warning. Other times, he ran through air thick as quicksand, each move bogged down by guilt and regret.

But no matter how the dream changed, one thing remained the same: Connor never arrived in time to stop Doug.

A sudden knock at the door jarred the memories from Connor's thoughts. Undoubtedly the Wilsons had picked the best hotel around for Emily's reception, but no one's room service was *that* fast. Besides, he had an idea who might be on the other side of the door, and it wasn't the maid with fresh towels.

Opening the door, he summoned a smile for the woman standing in the corridor. "Morning."

Emily Wilson beamed at him, looking like a Hollywood fashion plate of old in a yellow sundress layered beneath a lightweight sweater and a scarf knotted at her neck. "Connor! I'm so glad you're here. I know I should have called first, but—"

He waved off her not-quite-an-apology and held the door open. "Come on in."

As she breezed into the hotel room and set her handbag next to his laptop, Connor was glad to see the computer logo flashing across the screen. Last thing he needed was for Emily to see the dossier on her fiancé.

Emily took her time looking around the suite's miniature living area: a cluster of armchairs and end tables encircling the entertainment center. The added touches of a stone fireplace, balcony overlooking the pool and hot tub spoke of the hotel's five-star accommodations, but Connor doubted she was impressed. After all, she'd grown up surrounded by luxury and wealth.

"What are you doing here, Em?"

"I wanted to see you." She blushed as prettily now as she had at eighteen, but somehow for Connor the effect wasn't the same.

An image of Kelsey flashed in his mind, and he couldn't help making the comparison between Emily and her cousin. It was the difference between a sepia photograph—all soft, dreamy hues—and a full-color, HD image that instantly caught the eye.

As a hotheaded teen, Emily had been his unattainable fantasy. But now it was Kelsey and her down-to-earth reality who kept intruding into his thoughts.

Like yesterday evening, when he'd stood on the balcony and watched to see if the Arizona sunsets were still as amazing as he remembered. As he watched the blazing light slowly fade on the horizon, it wasn't past evenings that came to mind. Instead he thought of the way sunshine caught the fire in Kelsey's auburn curls…

"I snuck out like when we were kids."

Emily's words jarred Kelsey from his mind. He told himself the swift kick in the gut was remembered pain and not anything current or life threatening. But, dammit, he didn't need the reminder that as far as the Wilsons were concerned, he'd never be good enough. And while Kelsey might not look like her blond-haired, blue-eyed cousins, she was still a Wilson, and some things never changed.

Judging by Emily's impish grin, she'd enjoyed reliving her youthful rebellion and the walk down memory lane. Too bad the trip wasn't so pleasant for him. Feeling his smile take a sardonic twist, he asked, "Still can't risk being seen with me in public, huh, Em?"

Her eyes widened in what looked like genuine dismay. "No, Connor! It's not like that." She reached out and grasped his arm, and the frantic expression did take him back in time, filling his thoughts with memories of the girl so desperate to make everyone else happy, she'd made herself miserable.

Relenting slightly, he leaned one hip against the arm of the sofa and reminded her, "We're not kids anymore, and we're too old to be sneaking around."

"I know." Fidgeting with her engagement ring, she added, "But I wanted to see you, and I didn't want…anyone to get upset."

"You mean Todd?" Connor asked pointedly.

"You have to understand, he's very protective of me. I'm sorry the two of you didn't hit it off when we met for dinner in San Diego last month."

Connor held back a snort of derisive laughter at the irony. No, he and Todd hadn't hit it off. In fact, at the end of the night they'd nearly come to blows. Connor could admit he hadn't walked into the restaurant with a totally open mind. It was entirely possible Connor would dislike any man who met with the Wilsons' approval on principle alone. But within fifteen minutes of meeting Todd Dunworthy, Connor had stopped thinking about the past and started worrying about Emily.

In that short span of time, Dunworthy bragged about his Scottsdale loft apartment, his top-of-the-line SUV, his various summer homes in exotic ports of call, all of which would have been little more than annoying except for one thing.

He talked about Emily the same way. She was new and bright and shiny just like the fancy Lexus he drove, and Connor hadn't been able to shake the feeling that Dunworthy wouldn't have thought twice about tossing her aside for a newer model.

And the bad feeling roiling through Connor's gut like acid

ever since he'd been hired by Doug Mitchell got so much worse. Outwardly, Doug and Todd Dunworthy had as little in common as, well, as Connor and Todd did. But from the moment he met Doug, the cold look in the man's eyes and the way he spoke about his wife set Connor's teeth on edge, too reminiscent of the way his father had talked about his mother, the bitter blame he'd placed on her for dying and saddling him with an unwanted kid to raise.

But Connor had set aside his personal feelings and taken the job. *Taken the money,* his conscience accused. If only he'd listened to his gut then…

Taking a deep breath, Connor looked out the window, hoping the daylight might dispel his dark thoughts. Only, it wasn't the sunshine that broke through the shadows, but memories of the sunset, memories of Kelsey, that eased the weight on his chest.

The spark in her dark eyes, the stubborn jut of her chin, her determination to stand up to him…even if she barely stood up to the height of his shoulder. He didn't doubt for one second she'd be a formidable opponent, and he was glad to have her on his side.

Turning his focus back to Emily, he said, "I'm sorry, too, Em." And he was. He wanted her to be happy, and he was sorry Dunworthy wasn't the man she—or more important, he suspected, her parents—thought him to be.

Something in his tone must have given his suspicions away, because Emily's already perfect posture straightened to a regal, Charlene-like stature. "Todd is a wonderful man," she insisted. "I love him. I really do, and I can't wait to be his wife."

How many times had Emily repeated that statement before she started believing it was true? The words had a mantralike sound to them. Or maybe more like the punishment meted out by a second-grade teacher: *I will not chew gum in class. I will not chew gum in class.*

"I should go," she murmured.

"Emily, wait." A knock on the door broke the tension. "Look, that's room service. I ordered way too much food. Stay and have breakfast with me."

Without waiting for her response, he stepped around her and opened the door. The waiter wheeled in the cart, filling the room with the scent of bacon and eggs. He pulled the covers off the steaming plates and revealed a meal large enough for two.

"I shouldn't," she protested, eyeing the food with a look of longing. "I need to watch what I eat or I won't be able to fit into my dress."

Connor tried to smile; dieting before a big occasion was undoubtedly a prerequisite for most women, but he didn't think it was the dress Emily had in mind. He'd shared only a single meal with Dunworthy, but he could still see the smug smile on the bastard's face as he waved the waiter and the dessert tray away with a laugh. "Gotta keep my bride-to-be looking as beautiful as ever!"

"Come on," Connor cajoled. "You're not going to make me eat alone, are you?"

Sighing, she slid onto the chair and confessed, "This smells amazing."

"Dig in," he encouraged. "Nothing like carbs and cholesterol to start the day right."

The spark in her eyes reminded him of the old Emily, and she grabbed a fork with an almost defiant toss to her head. "Thank you, Connor."

"Anytime, Em," he vowed, knowing her gratitude was for much more than a simple offer to share breakfast.

He picked up his own fork, ready to dig into the eggs,

when a hint of spice seemed to sneak into his senses. Normally sides like toast or muffins were an afterthought, something to eat only if the main meal wasn't filling enough. But the powder-sprinkled muffin on the edge of his plate suddenly had his mouth watering.

He broke off an edge and popped it into his mouth. The moist confection melted on his tongue, tempting his senses with sugar, cinnamon and...*Kelsey.*

The hint of sweet and spicy had filled his head when he stood close to her, urging him to discover if the cinnamon scent was thanks to a shampoo she used on the red-gold curls she tried to tame or a lotion she smoothed over her pale skin.

If he kissed her, was that how she'd taste?

"What's Kelsey doing today?"

The question popped out before Connor ever thought to ask it, revealing a curiosity he couldn't deny yet didn't want to admit. He set the muffin aside and shoved a forkful of eggs into his mouth in case any other questions decided to circumvent his thought process.

After taking a drink of juice, Emily said, "Oh, she's likely running herself ragged with wedding preparations, making sure everything's going to go according to plan."

Her words sent suspicion slithering down his spine. At a small, low-key wedding, the bride's cousin might be the one behind the scenes, making sure everything went *according to plan.* But not at the Wilson-Dunworthy wedding, where professionals would handle those kind of details.

"What, exactly," he asked, "does Kelsey have to do with the wedding preparations?"

Emily frowned. "Didn't she tell you she's my wedding coordinator?"

"No," he said, setting his fork aside and leaning back in the chair, "no, she didn't."

"I'm lucky to have her working on the wedding. She's amazing when it comes to organization, and she's taking care of everything."

Everything, Connor thought wryly, including him.

Chapter Four

So much for unbiased. So much for impartial. So much for finding his insider in the Wilson camp, Connor thought. Kelsey was involved in this wedding right up to her gorgeous red head.

"She started her business over a year ago," Emily was saying. "My father offered to finance the company, but she wouldn't take the loan. She's always been weird about money."

Ignoring his grudging respect for Kelsey's decision and the curiosity about her *weirdness* when it came to her family's money, Connor focused on what she was getting from the Wilson family name. "So this wedding's a big deal to Kelsey, huh?"

"Oh, it's huge! She's counting on my wedding being the launching pad for Weddings Amour. The business is totally her baby, and she loves it. Says it makes her feel like a fairy god-mother, starting couples out on their own happily-ever-after."

Connor let out a snort of disbelief. He hadn't read any

fairy tales since he was six and figured it had been nearly as long since he'd believed in happily-ever-after.

"What?" Emily demanded.

"It's—nothing." He stabbed at his eggs. "The whole thing is crazy. Fairy godmothers, everlasting love, all of it—"

It was impossible. He'd seen far too many marriage vows broken from behind the telescopic lens of his camera. Those couples had likely had dream weddings, too, but the dream couldn't survive reality. And sometimes—like with Cara Mitchell—happily-ever-after turned into a living nightmare.

"Well, don't tell Kelsey her business is a joke. She takes it very seriously."

"I bet she does."

Seriously enough that Charlene Wilson had put Kelsey in charge of "attending to him." He'd overheard the comment yesterday but hadn't realized he'd be in the hands of a professional.

"Why all the questions about Kelsey?"

"Just curious." When Emily's eyes narrowed thoughtfully, he added, "I don't remember you talking about her when we were going out, that's all."

She shrugged. "I didn't know her then."

"Didn't *know* her? She's your cousin, right?"

"I, uh, I meant I didn't know her well."

"Uh-huh." Emily was a horrible liar and not much better at keeping secrets. He could have pressed. A few pointed questions, and Emily would have told him everything.

Connor refused to ask. Even as curiosity stacked one row of questions upon the next, he wouldn't ask. Not about why Emily hadn't known her own relative, not about why Kelsey had gone to public school instead of the exclusive prep schools her cousins had attended, not about why she was *weird* when it came to the family fortune.

He wasn't back in Arizona to find out about Kelsey Wilson.

Returning his focus to that goal, he asked, "What's Todd up to today? He must have a lot of free time on his hands while you and your mother and Kelsey take care of all the wedding details."

"Oh, no. He has a meeting this morning. He'll be at his office most of the day."

"Really?" Now, this could be something. Connor forced himself to take a few bites of waffle before he asked, "What kind of meeting?"

"I'm not sure." A tiny frown tugged her eyebrows. "Todd doesn't tell me much about his work." Laughter chased the frown away. "Just as well. I'd be bored silly."

"I doubt that. You're smart, Emily. Smarter than you give yourself credit for."

"Thank you, Connor," she said softly.

"How'd you two meet anyway? I don't think you've said."

"At a department store." She smiled. "We were both shopping for Christmas presents for our mothers, but he didn't have a clue. Finally he asked me for help. It was really cute."

"Hmm. Almost as cute as when we met."

"Oh, you mean in that sleazy bar where you had to fight off those bikers who were hitting on me?"

"A bar you weren't old enough to be at in the first place," Connor pointed out.

"Luckily you were there to rescue me," she said, lifting her glass in a teasing toast.

"Yeah, lucky," Connor agreed as he tapped his own glass against hers.

Emily might not know it, but he was here to save her again.

The tiny butterflies taking flight in Kelsey's stomach as she drove toward the hotel turned into radioactive monsters by the time she stepped into the lobby. She'd been crazy to make a deal with Connor McClane. Somewhere along the way she was going to lose her soul.

Although they hadn't made plans to meet this morning, the best way to keep an eye on Connor was to embrace their partnership. As she walked by the three-tiered fountain toward the elevators, the doors slid open. Kelsey gasped and ducked into an alcove—the same alcove to which Connor had pulled her aside the day before—and watched in disbelief as her cousin walked by.

What was Emily doing at Connor's hotel?

Her cousin rarely left the house before noon, and it was barely nine o'clock. What was Emily doing up so early? Or had she stayed out too late? Kelsey's stomach churned at the thought. She hated to think her cousin would be so susceptible to Connor's charms. *And what about you?* her conscience mocked. *How easily did you agree to work with Connor in this very spot?*

But that was different! That was about business and keeping an eye on Connor and keeping him away from Emily…not that Kelsey had done a bang-up job at either so far.

Emily slipped on a pair of sunglasses and smiled at a bellboy, who nearly tripped over his feet as she walked by. She didn't look as if she'd rolled out of bed with her ex-lover, but then again, Kelsey had never seen Emily look less than perfect. Ever.

Kelsey stayed hidden as her cousin sashayed across the lobby and out the automatic doors, then made a beeline for the elevator. "So much for his promises," she muttered as she jabbed the Up button.

"But why am I even surprised?"

She stomped out of the elevator on the fourth floor. Had she really believed Connor would keep his word?

Maybe she had. Which only went to prove how some

people never learned. Rapping on Connor's door hard enough to bruise her knuckles, she thought she'd be better off banging her head against the wood.

"Kelsey." Opening the door, Connor greeted her with an assessing look and not an ounce of shame. Bracing one arm on the doorjamb, he said, "I'm surprised to see you here."

"Are you?" Determined to ignore the masculine pose that could have come straight from some sexy man-of-the-month calendar, she ducked beneath his arm and made her way inside. She refused to have an argument in the hall where any guest, bellhop or room-service waiter might walk by. "If I'd shown up a few minutes earlier, it would have been a regular family reunion."

"You saw Emily?"

"So much for your promise to keep your distance!"

Connor frowned. "I said I'd stay away. I can't help it if she comes to see me."

"Right. And I'm sure she forced her way inside your hotel room. Probably tied you up and had her way with you, too."

Connor pushed away from the door and stalked toward her with that challenging expression still in his eyes. "That would really mess up your plans, wouldn't it?"

"She's engaged, Connor. Doesn't that mean anything to you?"

"Yeah. It means she's about to make a mistake."

Connor stepped closer, and the only mistake Kelsey could concentrate on was her own in thinking she could confront Connor face-to-face and not be overwhelmed by his masculine sensuality. He hadn't shaved and the morning stubble only made him that much more appealing. Worse, she could practically feel the erotic scrape of whisker-rough skin against her cheeks, her neck, her breasts—

Afraid he could read her every thought by the glow in her cheeks, Kelsey ducked her head. Her gaze landed on the nearby breakfast tray, on a white coffee cup and a pink bow-shaped smudge left by Emily's lipstick. The mark may have been left on Connor's cup, not on the man himself, but the reminder that Emily had been there first doused Kelsey like a bucket of ice water. "Emily's only mistake was inviting *you*."

"Yeah, I bet that's tough on you, isn't it? When you told me yesterday working together would be strictly business, I didn't realize that meant you were getting paid."

"So I'm coordinating Emily's wedding. Don't act all offended like it was some big secret. I thought you already knew."

"Yeah, well, I didn't. If I had—"

"You would have what?"

Scowling at her, he said, "Look, if you want to work together, I need to know you care more about your cousin than you do about your business."

If she wanted to work together! Just yesterday, she thought agreeing to work with Connor was possibly the most foolish thing she'd ever done. And now she had to fight to keep the opportunity?

Yes! a voice inside her head argued. *Because it's the only one you'll get. How else will you keep an eye on him? How else will you keep him from stopping the wedding?*

"Of course I care about Emily."

A sardonic twist of a smile lifted one corner of Connor's mouth. Darn him for making even sarcasm look sexy! "I know you care about her. The question is, do you care enough to put her first over everything else you want?"

The intensity in his eyes transformed the question from a challenge about her loyalty to Emily into something more personal. Something dark and revealing about his past. *Prove that you care…*

It was a test Emily had failed. She hadn't cared enough, or

she'd cared about her family's approval more. Was Emily the only woman who hadn't passed, Kelsey wondered, or were there other women who hadn't given Connor the proof he needed?

"You can't prove you care about someone," she stated flatly. "Not in words. Actions show how you truly feel."

Like Connor showing up for Emily's wedding…and Emily showing up at Connor's hotel room. Trying not to think what those actions meant, Kelsey continued, "I'm here. That alone should prove—"

"That you're a clever businesswoman? I already knew that."

Tightening her grip on her purse strap, Kelsey fought for control. She couldn't pretend she didn't have a lot riding on Emily's wedding.

As she racked her brain for a way to prove her loyalty, Kelsey realized nothing she said would be enough. Meeting his gaze, she stated, "I can't prove it to you, Connor. Because love and caring aren't about proof. They're about faith. So, if I'm supposed to trust your gut when you tell me Todd isn't right for Emily, you're going to have to trust me when I tell you Emily's happiness matters most."

With his gaze locked on hers, Connor stayed silent long enough for Kelsey to anticipate half a dozen responses. Would he laugh in her face? Turn away in cynical disgust?

Seconds ticked by, and she held her ground by pulling off a decent imitation of her aunt. She kept her back straight, her head held high, and still managed to look down her nose at a much taller Connor.

He ruined the hard-won effect with a single touch, tracing a finger over her cheek. The steel in her spine melted into a puddle of desire.

"Good to have you back on the team," he said softly. "We have work to do."

* * *

Connor knew he'd crossed the line when Kelsey's eyes widened to a deer-caught-in-the-headlights look. He needed to back off. If he pushed, she'd bolt. But it was the urge to ignore his own boundaries that had him pulling back even further.

If anyone could make him *want* to trust again, Kelsey might. And that sure as hell wasn't the kind of thought a man wanted to have while sober. Especially not a man like him about a woman like her.

Kelsey was a Wilson, and he'd already learned his lesson when it came to how Wilson-McClane relationships ended. He knew better than to make the same mistake twice... Didn't he? Just because he'd indulged in a minor fantasy—discovering the five freckles on Kelsey's cheek *did* combine to make a perfect star—didn't mean he was losing his grip on the situation. He had everything under control, even if that star-shaped outline made him wonder what other patterns he might find on Kelsey's body....

Far too aware of the bed only a few feet away and Kelsey's teasing scent, that alluring combination of cinnamon and spice, Connor redirected his focus. "Are you hungry? I could order more room service."

"No, thank you." Her words were too polite, bordering on stiff, and they matched her posture.

"All right," he said, thinking it just as well they get out of the hotel room before he ended up doing something as stupid as touching Kelsey...and not stopping. "But you really don't want to go on a stakeout on an empty stomach." Connor didn't know if his sudden announcement loosened anything, but Kelsey definitely looked shaken.

"Stakeout?" Echoing the word, her brown eyes widened.

"Don't worry. We'll stop for staples along the way." He grabbed her hand, pulled her from the room and out into the hall.

She protested every step of the way and all throughout the elevator ride down to the lobby. "Are you insane? I am *not* going on a stakeout."

Her voice dropped to a hiss as the elevator door opened, and she even managed a smile at the elderly couple waiting in the lobby.

"You agreed to this, remember? Equal partners?"

As he strode across the lobby, Connor realized Kelsey was practically running to keep up with his long strides, and he slowed his steps.

Jeez, it'd be faster if he picked her up and carried her. A corner of his mouth lifted at the thought of Kelsey's reaction if he tried. "You really are tiny, aren't you?"

"I— What?"

She bumped into him when Connor paused for the automatic doors to open. He had the quick impression of soft breasts against his back before Kelsey jumped away.

Tiny, he decided as he looked over his shoulder with an appreciative glance, but curved in all the right places.

Something in his expression must have given his thoughts away. Kelsey glared at him. "I am not going on a stakeout."

"How are we going to find anything out about Todd if we don't watch him?"

"I thought you'd hire someone!"

"Right. Because the Wilsons would believe whatever some guy I *paid* has to say about their golden boy."

Score one for the away team, Connor thought, when Kelsey stopped arguing. Pressing his advantage, he guided her outside. "Besides," he added, "staking people out is what I do."

"You—you're a cop?"

He couldn't blame her for the shock in her voice and gave a scoffing laugh. "No. I'm a private investigator. Turns out we're both professionals," he said. "And if it makes you feel any better, I do have a friend working another lead. But he's in St. Louis."

"What's in St. Louis?"

"A maid who used to work for the Dunworthy family. She either quit or was let go a few months ago."

"So?"

"She pretty much disappeared after that, and I want to hear what she has to say about her former employers."

Midmorning sunlight glinted off the line of luxury cars brought around by the valets: Lexus, BMW, Mercedes. He'd come a long way from his bike days. Too bad. He would have enjoyed getting Kelsey on a Harley. Once she loosened up a bit, she'd love the freedom of hugging the curves, wind whipping through her hair, speed pouring through her veins. He could almost feel her arms around his waist…

Kelsey waved toward the visitor's lot. "We can take my car."

It didn't look like loosening up would happen anytime soon. "Sorry, sweetheart, but I'll bet Dunworthy has already seen your car."

Connor signaled a valet, and within minutes a vintage black Mustang pulled up to the curb. Seeing the question in Kelsey's eyes, he explained, "It's Javy's. Something less flashy would be better for surveillance, but borrowers can't be choosers."

He tipped the valet and opened the passenger door for Kelsey. When she looked ready to argue, he said, "Todd has a big meeting at his office." He'd looked up the address after Emily left. "I'm curious to find out who it's with. How 'bout you?"

As she slid into the passenger seat, Kelsey muttered something he couldn't quite make out.

Connor figured it was just as well.

* * *

"I cannot believe I'm doing this," Kelsey muttered from her slumped-down position in the passenger seat.

"You've mentioned that," Connor replied.

They were parked in a lot across the street from Todd's office. The row of two-story suites lined a busy side street off Scottsdale Road, the black glass and concrete a sharp contrast to the gold and russet rock landscape, with its clusters of purple sage, flowering bougainvillea and cacti. Connor had circled the building when they first arrived, noting all the building's entrances and confirming Todd's car wasn't in the lot.

"What if someone sees us?"

"What are they going to see?" he retorted.

She supposed from a distance the car did blend in. Thanks to heavily tinted windows, it was unlikely anyone could see inside. Tilting the vents to try to get a bit more air to blow in her direction, Kelsey admitted, "This is a bit more boring than I expected."

"Boring is good," Connor insisted. Despite his words, he drummed his fingers against the steering wheel in an impatient rhythm, clearly ready for action.

"I'm surprised Emily didn't tell me more about your job."

"Why would she?"

"Because to anyone not sitting in this car, being a P.I. sounds exciting." When Connor stayed silent, she asked, "Do you like it?"

"Yeah. Most of the time."

The tapping on the steering wheel increased like the sudden peaks on a lie detector, and Kelsey sensed he was telling her not what he thought she wanted to hear, but what he *wanted* to believe. Something had happened to change his mind about the job she suspected he'd once loved. "It must be difficult. Seeing so much of the darker side of life."

"It can be. Sometimes human nature is dark, but at least my job is about discovering the truth."

Was it only her imagination, or had he emphasized that pronoun? Subtly saying that while he pursued truth and justice, she— "You think *my* job is about telling lies?"

"Selling lies," he clarified.

"I promise a beautiful wedding and give the bride and groom what they're looking for. That's not a lie."

"Okay," he conceded, "maybe not the beautiful wedding part, but the sentiment behind it? Happily-ever-after? Love of a lifetime? Till death do us part? Come on!"

"Not every marriage ends with the bride and groom riding off into the sunset. Real life comes with real problems, but if two people love each other, they work it out."

He snorted. "Not from my side of the video camera, they don't."

Irritation crackled inside her like radio static—annoying, incessant and almost loud enough to drown out a vague and misplaced feeling of disillusionment. All these years, she'd heard about Connor and Emily as a modern-day Romeo and Juliet, but the story of star-crossed lovers lost all meaning if one of the players didn't believe in love.

And while Kelsey's faith might have been shaken by what happened with Matt, she still longed for those happily-ever-after and love-of-a-lifetime dreams Connor cynically mocked.

"My aunt and uncle never believed you loved Emily," she said, disappointed. "Everything you've said proves them right."

"Your aunt and uncle weren't right about me—no matter what they think."

Dead certainty ricocheted in his voice, and Kelsey regretted the tack she'd taken. Too late to back down and far too curious about what made Connor tick, she pressed, "Either you believe in love or you don't. You can't have it both ways."

"I just don't want to see Emily get hurt. That's why I'm here."

She opened her mouth, ready to push further, when Connor pulled the handle on the driver's-side door. "I'll be right back."

Kelsey grabbed his arm. "Wait! Where are you going?"

"To check the rear lot. Todd might have pulled in back there while we've been watching the front." With one foot already on the asphalt and refusing to meet her gaze, Connor seemed more interested in escaping her questions.

"I'm coming with you." She scrambled to unlock the passenger door. When she sensed an oncoming protest, she said, "Partners, remember? You're the one who dragged me along. You aren't leaving me now."

"Forget it! He'll recognize you."

"Todd knows what you look like, too," she argued as she turned back toward him.

"Fine," he bit out as he dropped back into the seat, "but there's something you have to do first."

Thanks to her questions, a noticeable tension vibrated through Connor, evident in his clenched jaw and the taut muscles in the arm he'd braced against the wheel. But the tension gradually changed, not easing, but instead focusing to a fine, definitive point—one that seemed wholly centered on her.

His intense gaze traveled over her hair, her face, her mouth… The gold flecks in his green eyes glowed, and Kelsey's skin tingled as if warmed by his touch. Surely he wouldn't try to kiss her. Not here, not now! Time raced by with each rapid beat of her heart, a single question echoing in her veins.

Why *didn't* he kiss her? Right here, right now—

Her pulse pounded in her ears, drowning out the sound of passing traffic. The heat shimmering on her skin could put the mirage hovering above the asphalt to shame. Shifting his body in the driver's seat, Connor eased closer. The scent of his aftershave, a clean fragrance that called to mind ocean breezes and sun-kissed sand, drew her in. Like waves rushing to the shore, helpless to resist the undeniable pull, she reached for him....

But instead of a roll on the beach, Kelsey crashed against the shoals, her pride battered against the rocks when Connor suddenly turned away. He twisted his upper body between the seats and reached into the back. "Here, take this."

Kelsey stared dumbly at the baseball hat he held.

"See if you can cover your hair."

Her hand was still raised in an attempt to reach out and capture a passion obviously only she felt. An admission of her willingness to make a fool of herself.

Kelsey jerked the hat from Connor, eager to grab hold of anything to save face. "Do you really think this will make a difference?"

"A huge one." Almost reluctantly he added, "Your hair is unforgettable."

But he'd forget all about her and her hair once Emily was a free woman again. Unforgettable. Yeah, right.

Kelsey didn't realize she'd spoken the words until Connor murmured, "It's the kind of hair a man fantasizes about. Trust me."

But she couldn't. She'd nearly made a fool of herself seconds ago, and in case she ever forgot, she had the living, breathing epitome of Connor's perfect woman as her cousin. Kelsey couldn't compare; she never had.

Jerking back toward the door to put as much room as possible between them, she shook back her hair and pulled it away from her face with sharp, almost painful movements. Unable to hide behind her long locks, she felt exposed, vulnerable. Even more so when Connor's gaze remained locked on her features.

"How's that?" she asked, as she twisted her hair into a bun and shoved the bright red Diamondbacks cap into place. When

Connor continued to stare, Kelsey fisted her hands in her lap to keep from yanking off the ridiculous hat. Finally, she demanded, "What?"

Shaking his head, Connor seemed to snap out of his stupor. "I hadn't realized how much you look like Emily."

His words hit like a punch in the stomach. Look like Emily? Not a chance. She'd seen the disappointment in the Wilsons' faces when they first saw her. If Emily and Aileen were beautiful Barbie dolls, then Kelsey was clearly supposed to be Skipper, a younger, blonder version. But she looked *nothing* like her cousins, a point driven home at every Wilson function, with every meeting of their friends and associates. The surprise—if not flat-out disbelief—when Kelsey was introduced as one of the Wilsons.

I hope they had her DNA tested, Kelsey had heard one uninformed, high-society snob whisper. *It wouldn't surprise me if that girl ended up being a con artist out for the family fortune.*

Kelsey had struggled to hold her head high and hold back the tears when she'd wanted to lash out at the woman. She was every bit her mother's daughter, *not* her father's, and inside she was as much a Wilson as Gordon, Aileen and Emily. But outside—where it counted—she couldn't be more different.

"Give me a break!" She tried to laugh off the remark, but the fake sound stuck in her throat. "Emily and I look nothing alike! She's tall and thin and blond and—beautiful!"

Her voice broke on the last word, and Kelsey had never been so close to hitting anyone. Giving in to the impulse, she socked Connor in the shoulder. She had a quick impression of dense muscle and bone, but he caught her hand before she could fool herself into thinking she could do more damage.

"Hey!" A quick tug of her arm had her falling against him. "So are you!"

"Tall? Blond?" Kelsey shot back sarcastically.

"Beautiful!" he retorted.

"But I'm not—"

"Not Emily?" he interjected softly. He brushed an escaping strand of hair—her unforgettable hair—back from her face, and the touch she'd only imagined became reality as he traced his index finger over her eyebrow, across her cheekbone, and skimmed the corner of her mouth. Heat and hunger combined with a tenderness that snuck beneath her defenses. "There's more than one ideal for beauty, Kelsey."

Still pressed against his muscular chest, she knew Connor was the epitome of masculine beauty for her, and she had the devastating feeling that would never change, even years from now. He was the best of the best, and she was a long shot, the dark horse.

"Stop it," she whispered furiously.

"You don't have to be Emily. You can just be yourself."

The deep murmur of his voice reached inside and touched that vulnerable place, but this time instead of opening old wounds, his words offered a healing balm. And meeting his gaze, Kelsey realized he understood her vulnerability in a way no one else could because he'd felt the same way. He'd never been good enough to date the daughter of the wealthy Wilsons, and she had never felt good enough to *be* one of the wealthy Wilsons.

"Connor…" Just one word, his name spoken in a hushed whisper, broke the connection. He blinked, or maybe Kelsey did, because when she looked again, his sexy smile was back in place, all sense of vulnerability gone. "Except for right now. Right now you have to be someone Todd won't recognize."

"Right." Kelsey pulled back, and Connor let her go. She might not have a sexy smile to hide behind, but she could be businesslike and professional…or as businesslike and professional as a wedding coordinator spying on a future groom could be.

"Come on," she muttered as she tugged the brim lower. She didn't know if she'd need the hat to hide her identity from Todd, but maybe she could use it to hide her emotions from Connor. "Let's do this."

She climbed from the car and was headed straight for the building by the time Connor caught up with her. Grabbing her hand, he said, "This way."

With Connor leading the way, they walked half a block before crossing the street and doubling back behind Todd's building. But the lot was empty except for some abandoned crates and an overflowing Dumpster.

"Let's go. Todd's meeting must have been canceled," Kelsey said. She walked around to the front of the building without bothering to take the circular route that got them there, her low heels striking the steaming pavement.

Connor caught up to her as she reached the front of the building. "Look, I admit this was a dud, but—" He cut off with a curse.

Kelsey didn't have time to take a breath before he shoved her into a recessed doorway and nearly smothered her with his body. Her vehement protest came out a puny squeak.

"Don't move." The husky whisper and warm breath against her ear guaranteed she couldn't take a single step without falling flat on her face. "Todd's pulling into the parking lot."

No, no, no! This could not be happening! Swallowing against a lump of horror, Kelsey fisted her hands in his T-shirt and tugged. "Let's go," she hissed.

"Can't. He'll see us if we move. Just…relax."

Despite the advice, every muscle in his body was tense, primed and ready for action. But it was Kelsey who jumped when the car door slammed. "He'll see us."

"No, he won't. He's heading for his office."

She had to take Connor's word for it. With his body

blocking every bit of daylight, she couldn't see beyond his broad shoulders. Too bad the rest of her senses weren't so completely cut off. Instead, the scent of his sea-breeze after-shave combined with potent warm male, and the masculine heat of Connor's chest burned into her skin where he made contact with her. Kelsey locked her knees to keep from sinking right into him.

Heart pounding in her ears, she whispered, "Where is he now?"

"Unlocking the door."

She felt as much as heard his low murmur and hissed, "We should go." Right now, before the heat went straight to her head and she did something unforgivably stupid, like melt into a puddle of desire at Connor's feet.

Chapter Five

"I am not meant for a life of crime."

Seated in a restaurant not far from Dunworthy's business, Connor pressed a beer into Kelsey's hand. That she took it without complaint told him how much the incident at Todd's office had shaken her.

Their near miss had lasted only seconds. Connor had pulled Kelsey toward the car immediately after Todd entered the suite; she'd barely ducked inside the Mustang's ovenlike interior when he came back outside. Connor might have suspected the other man sensed something wrong if not for the way he sauntered out to his top-of-the-line SUV without checking his surroundings. If he had, it was a good bet he would have caught sight of Connor sliding into the driver's seat only a few yards away.

Connor had wanted to follow him, but with Kelsey along, the risk wasn't worth it. Not that it was her fault they'd nearly been spotted. No, Connor took full blame. He'd let Kelsey distract him. He could have driven her back to the hotel and her waiting car but had instead veered off to the restaurant, which had a bar. He figured she could use a drink. After standing in the doorway with the Arizona sun roasting his back, Connor could use a cold shower, but a cold beer was the next best thing.

Liar, a mocking voice jeered. The hundred-plus temperature was a killer, but it was the feeling of Kelsey's body pressed to his that heated his blood.

"Hate to tell you, but we didn't break any laws."

She took a long pull on the bottle, then set it back on the bar with an audible clunk. "We were trespassing."

Hiding his smile behind the beer bottle, he bit back a burst of laughter. "The parking lot is public property. We had every right to be there."

"Oh." Kelsey stared thoughtfully at the bottle. He couldn't tell if she was relieved or disappointed. Finally, she looked up, her expression resolute. "Okay, so maybe what we did wasn't illegal, but—but it was unethical. It isn't right to go around spying on people. Especially when they aren't doing anything wrong. And I don't have time to waste chasing Todd or any of your ghosts around town." She slid out of the booth.

Connor frowned. "Hey, this doesn't have anything to do with me."

"Bull. You're out to prove to Aunt Charlene and Uncle Gordon you're much better for Emily than their handpicked golden boy."

Connor recoiled against the padded booth. Was Kelsey right? Did coming back to Arizona have more to do with salvaging his ego than protecting Emily?

No. No way. He wasn't nearly that pathetic. Unfortunately,

Kelsey had almost reached the door by the time he came to that conclusion. "Kelsey, wait!"

"Hey!" The bartender called after him. "Those beers weren't free, you know."

Swearing, Connor dug out his wallet, threw a handful of bills on the bar, and raced after Kelsey. The sunlight threatened to sear his corneas after the dimly lit bar, and he shaded his eyes against the glare. "Kelsey!"

The rush of nearby traffic nearly drowned out his voice, but Connor doubted that was why she didn't stop. Jogging after her, he caught her as she reached the car. It took a second longer to realize he had the keys, and she couldn't go anywhere without him.

Dammit, what was it about Kelsey that made him so crazy? He hadn't felt like this since—since Emily.

You're a fool, boy. Just like your old man. His father's voice rang in his head. *The both of us always want to hold on to what we can't have.*

Thrusting the comparisons aside, he said, "Look, I know this afternoon was a bust, but this isn't about me."

"Really?" Disbelief colored her words, and Connor fought a flare of irritation mixed with admiration. Had to respect a woman who wasn't easily snowed.

Taking a deep breath, he forced the irritation aside. He couldn't risk losing Kelsey as a partner. That was the reason he didn't want her to leave. It had nothing to do with wanting to spend more time with the woman who had him so fascinated.

Yeah, right, his conscience mocked. Back at Todd's office, he'd been tempted to forget all about the other man and prove to Kelsey just how beautiful she was. But he refused to make out with a woman in a parked car. Especially *not* Javy's car, the same vintage automobile he'd borrowed to take Emily out on dates all those years ago.

He wasn't that same punk kid anymore, even if he was once again lusting after one of the wealthy Wilsons.

"Let me buy you lunch, and I'll tell you what I *do* know about Todd."

Back in the restaurant, under the bartender's watchful eye, Connor and Kelsey placed their orders. As soon as the waitress walked away, Kelsey leaned forward and prompted, "Okay, let's hear it."

"First, did Emily ever tell you how we met?"

Kelsey's gaze dropped as she fiddled with her napkin. "She might have."

"Well, just so you have the whole story, Emily went to a bar. She was underage and in over her head. Some guys started hitting on her. She tried to shrug it off, but she was afraid to tell them to go take a hike. Because that wouldn't have been *nice*. But I could see the panic in her eyes. She was waiting for someone to step in and save her."

"And so you did."

"And so I did." Leaning across the table, he covered Kelsey's hand, intent on claiming her complete attention. Only when her eyes widened perceptibly did Connor realize he'd nearly erased the two-foot distance separating them. He was close enough to count the freckles dotting her upturned nose, to catch hold of her cinnamon scent. Her startled gaze flew to meet his, and as the spark of attraction he saw in her brown eyes flared to life inside him, Connor was the one having a hard time staying focused.

"The, uh, thing is—when I look at Emily now, I see that same panic. She's in over her head, letting herself get pushed along because she's too *nice* to stand up for herself."

"So you rode back into town, ready to play the hero."

"I'm no hero," Connor stated flatly, leaning back in the booth and pulling his hands from Kelsey's. The softness of her skin threatened to slip beneath his defenses, making him weak. The passion in her eyes when she spoke about everlasting love and dreams coming true made him want to believe though he knew better.

Even if he didn't have countless professional examples of love gone wrong to draw from, he also had his parents' as proof of love's fallibility. During their short-lived marriage, his parents drifted so far apart that in the end, neither his father nor Connor had been able to pull his mother back to safety.

If only she'd listened— Helplessness roiled in his gut, but he'd learned his lesson.

It would take more than words to keep Emily safe; he had to have proof. But right now, words were all he had to convince Kelsey. The only way to do that would be to open up and be completely honest. "I didn't expect to like Todd when I met him. I walked into that restaurant in San Diego knowing he's the Wilsons' golden boy and everything I'm not."

"Now who needs the lesson about being himself?" Kelsey murmured.

"Nothing like having my own words shoved back in my face," he said with a smile, which fell away as he realized how much they did have in common, how easily Kelsey understood him. Their gazes caught and held, the spark of desire running on a supercharged emotional current.

A touch of pink—sunset pink—highlighted Kelsey's cheeks, and she dropped her gaze. "Not shoving, exactly. More like gently tossing."

The waitress arrived with their food, breaking the moment and giving Connor a chance to refocus on what he wanted to say. "This is about more than disliking Dunworthy on sight. It's about the way he treats people he thinks are beneath him."

"Like who?"

"Like the valet he was pushing around after we left the restaurant."

"What?"

"I was pulling out of the lot when I saw Todd grab the kid and shove his face an inch from the bumper to show where he'd *dented* the car." Leaning forward, Connor added, "It was a rental, Kelsey. You can't tell me he had any clue whether that scratch was there before or not. But he's the type of guy who likes to intimidate people, especially people who can't or won't fight back."

"What did you do?"

"Jumped out of my car and pulled him off."

"And Todd actually grabbed this kid in front of Emily?"

Connor snorted. "No. She'd left her sweater in the restaurant and had gone back for it. By the time she came out, Todd was wearing a crocodile grin and the valet had pocketed a tip the size of his monthly paycheck."

Something else Dunworthy had in common with the Wilsons—thinking money could make anything or anyone disappear. Not that he blamed the kid for taking the cash. How could he when he'd done the same thing ten years ago?

"You don't think Todd would hurt Emily, do you?" Kelsey asked, disbelief and worry mingling in her expression.

"I don't know," he said. "All I know is that he thinks he can do whatever he damn well wants as long as he pays for the privilege."

"Kelsey! Where have you been all day?" Emily rose from the table in the middle of the Italian restaurant. "I've been calling you since first thing this morning."

Kelsey braced herself against Emily's exuberant greeting, hesitantly patting her cousin's slender shoulder blades. First thing this morning, Emily had been with Connor. Kelsey seriously doubted she'd been on her cousin's mind. "I've, um, been busy."

"What have you been doing?" Emily demanded as Kelsey slipped into a seat next to her and across from Aileen and her husband.

"I was—" Kelsey's mind blanked as she met her cousin's curious gaze, and she couldn't think of a single excuse.

I was with Connor. We spent the day spying on your fiancé, which was possibly the craziest thing I've ever done, right up to the time I thought Connor might kiss me.

"Kelsey!"

She jumped at the sound of her aunt's voice, terrified for a split second that she'd said the unbelievable words out loud. "What?"

Charlene frowned with a question in her eyes. "You paid the florist, didn't you?"

"Yes! Yes, I did." As if the forty-minute errand explained her absence during most of the day.

"Good. I hope it wasn't a mistake going with such a small shop. As worried as that woman sounded, you'd think she was down to her last dollar."

Irritation buzzed like a rash under Kelsey's skin. "Her name is Lisa Remming, and she's an amazing florist. A deposit is standard policy. We signed a contract stating she could cancel the order if it wasn't paid on time," she added, knowing her friend would never have considered canceling such an important order.

"All right, Kelsey. You've made your point," Charlene said. Kelsey thought she might have caught a hint of respect in her aunt's expression.

But Emily's eyes widened, and she grabbed Kelsey's hand. "Lisa wouldn't do that, would she?"

"No, of course not," she reassured her cousin, feeling like

a jerk for worrying her cousin just to make a point with Charlene. "The flowers are going to be beautiful."

Emily smiled, relieved someone else had solved the problem. "Thank goodness. I can't imagine getting married without the right bouquet."

Kelsey, personally, couldn't imagine getting married without the right groom. She *wanted* to believe Todd was that man for her cousin, but ever since Connor had rolled into town, doubts had swirled through her mind like a desert dust devil.

"Emily, darling!" a masculine voice called out. Dressed in designer slacks and a slate-blue silk shirt, Todd Dunworthy approached, his perfectly groomed blond hair glinting, and his teeth flashing in a blinding smile.

Sheep's clothing, Kelsey thought suddenly. Expensive, designer-crafted sheep's clothing...if she believed Connor. But that was the question. *Did* she believe him?

"Sorry I'm late," Todd apologized without looking away from his fiancée. "My meeting ran late."

"Your meeting?" Kelsey didn't realize she'd spoken the words out loud until all eyes turned her way. Tempted to blurt out that he'd spent less than five minutes at the office, she choked back the words. She couldn't say that without revealing her own presence. And, as she'd told Connor, Todd's meeting could have changed locations. Hoping Todd would reveal that was the case, she pressed, "I mean, what meeting, Todd?"

He waved his hand carelessly, and his sleeve pulled back to show a hint of the gold watch he wore. "Just business. You wouldn't be interested," he said, flashing a wink that was more condescending than charming.

"Oh, but I am," Kelsey interjected, when Todd would have changed the subject. He shot her a look clearly meant to back her down—*to put her in her place*—but Kelsey stood her ground. She could almost feel Connor at her back, giving her the strength to do the right thing. "You'll be family soon, and I hardly know anything about what you do."

"Honestly, Kelsey, enough about work," Emily interrupted, despite the fact that Todd had remained completely—suspiciously?—silent. "We have more important things to discuss."

Ever the peacemaker, Emily turned the conversation to the wedding and her honeymoon. She smoothed over the tension like a pro until, on the outside at least, everything *looked* perfect.

But as the conversation moved on to drinks and appetizers and who wanted to try the chef's special, Kelsey couldn't help noticing how her cousin's gaze would occasionally drift off in the distance. And she wondered if maybe, just maybe, Emily was waiting for Connor—or *anyone*—to rescue her again.

Connor drummed his fingers against the steering wheel, his gaze locked on the Italian restaurant. Candlelight flickered in the antique sconces, illuminating the rustic red brick, aged pergola, and carved wooden doors.

After taking Kelsey back to the hotel and her car, Connor called Jake Cameron, eager to hear what the man had found. But the conversation hadn't gone as he'd hoped.

"I told you this would take some time," Jake had said, sounding more frustrated and less confident than during the last call.

"Yeah, I know. You also told me you had a date with Sophia Pirelli. You had to have found *something*."

Silence filled the line, and Connor might have thought the call was disconnected, except he could still sense his friend's tension coming across loud and clear. "Jake—"

"Look, I'm seeing her again. I'll call you later."

He'd hung up after that, leaving Connor to battle his own tension and frustration. Unwilling to sit in his hotel room and go over the same information on Dunworthy again, he'd headed for Todd's condo, planning to talk with some of the man's neighbors, when he spotted the familiar SUV leaving the parking garage.

As Connor followed Dunworthy from his Scottsdale loft, careful to stay two car lengths behind, he had plenty of time to make some calls, and discovered the studio-sized units cost well over two million dollars. Knowing the man would pay such an outrageous price for an exclusive address to call home, Connor should have expected what was to come.

He'd already trailed Emily's fiancé from one expensive store to another, growing more and more disgusted as Dunworthy racked up a small fortune in purchases. Wine shops, jewelers, tailors. Connor had held back far enough to keep Dunworthy from spotting him, but not so far that he couldn't see the dollar signs in the salespeople's eyes.

The afternoon had proved a dud just like the meeting that morning, and Connor wished Kelsey had come along. He missed her company—an odd admission for a man who worked alone. He missed her wry comments and witty comebacks, not to mention the tempting thought of kissing her. It was no longer a question of if, but when…

He did have one lead, thanks to a call he'd overheard Todd make on his cell phone, but he would have to wait to follow up.

He sat up straight in the driver's seat as the restaurant's carved doors opened. "'Bout time," he muttered as the elder Wilsons stepped outside along with Aileen and her husband. Todd and Emily followed, and even though Connor had his gaze locked on the other man, it didn't take much to distract him. Just Kelsey.

She stood apart from the rest of the group—not so far she couldn't hear the conversation, just far enough she couldn't be easily drawn in. He'd noticed her do that at the hotel when he'd crashed their little reception planning session. She'd trailed a step or two behind her aunt and cousin, hiding behind the copious notes she took in her day planner. Observing, but not really joining.

Just the way he did. He never would have thought his job as a private eye and Kelsey's job as a wedding coordinator would give them something else in common, but there it was. Still, the Wilsons were more than Kelsey's clients; they were her family. So what was the reason for that distance?

Now wasn't the time to worry about it. Connor jerked his gaze away from Kelsey. He didn't let his attention stray back to her, not even once, surprised by how hard that was.

Todd slapped his future father-in-law on the back, then kissed Charlene's cheek and said something to make the older woman laugh.

I'll be damned, Connor thought, his respect for Dunworthy as an adversary rising a few notches. He'd never seen the woman crack a smile, yet Todd had Emily's mother eating out of his hand.

The group, a silent film of family togetherness, said their goodbyes amid hugs and kisses, with Kelsey drifting just outside the happy circle. They broke into pairs, the elder Wilsons off to the left with Aileen and her husband, Emily and Dunworthy to his car—illegally parked, Connor noted—alongside the restaurant. Kelsey, the odd woman out, headed toward the back of the restaurant, crossing the parking lot…alone.

Todd's SUV engine roared. He should follow, Connor knew. His hand went to the ignition, but he didn't turn the key. A gut feeling, the kind Kelsey had sardonically discounted, held him in place even as Todd backed his vehicle away from the restaurant.

He had to go now if he had any hope of following. Instead, he leaned forward. Kelsey had nearly disappeared around the building. That side of the restaurant wasn't as well lit. Her hair looked brown in the meager light, the shadows dousing its fiery color. Dressed in a denim skirt and lace-trimmed green T-shirt, she looked smaller than usual…younger and more vulnerable.

Connor had already pushed the car door open before he caught sight of the dark shape of a man cutting across the parking lot and heading her way. Surprise drew Kelsey up short. Connor was still too far away to hear what she said, but he was close enough to see the guy reach out to grab her.

It was his nightmare brought to life. Close enough to see, too far away to help… For a split second, Connor froze until he realized this was no dream and the woman in danger wasn't Cara Mitchell. It was *Kelsey*.

Adrenaline pounded through his veins. A short burst of speed, the rhythmic thumping of feet against pavement, and he was there. Muscles flexing, he had the guy's arm twisted behind his back, his face shoved against the side of the restaurant.

"You okay?" he demanded of Kelsey, surprised by the breathless gasp fueling the words. His heart pounded like he'd run half a mile instead of thirty yards. Trying to outrun the past…

"Kelsey?" He could feel her behind him but didn't risk looking over his shoulder. "Are you okay?"

"Connor, what—" Too stunned by his sudden appearance to get the words out, Kelsey pressed a hand to her pounding heart, surprised the organ was still where it was supposed to be. For a second, she thought it had jumped right out of her chest.

"Did he hurt you?"

She blinked, the question not quite registering, and stared at her ex-boyfriend, who was pressed like a pancake against the restaurant's brick wall. Matt Moran had hurt her. He'd wounded her pride, trashed her self-confidence, hitting her where she was most vulnerable with the reminder she could never compare to her oh-so-beautiful cousin.

Matt made a strangled, high-pitched sound that might have been her name. "Kelsey! Tell him I wouldn't hurt you."

Connor shot her a quick glance. "You know this guy?"

The tension eased from his shoulders, but Kelsey knew he could be back in battle mode in a split second. The masculine display shouldn't have impressed her. She'd never advocated violence as a way to problem-solve. But seeing her former boyfriend pinned to a wall, well, it did her heart some good.

"Yes. You can let him go. He just wanted to talk to me."

Only, Kelsey hadn't wanted to hear anything Matt had to say. She'd already heard it all, ironically enough, from Connor.

He let go of the other man's arm and spun him around. "I take it you don't want to talk to him," Connor said. "Can't blame you there." He gave the other man a hard, intense look, then seemed to sum up Matt's entire character with a single shake of his head. Too bad Connor hadn't been around when Kelsey first met Matt.

Oh, who are you kidding? a mocking inner voice asked. She would never have noticed Matt if Connor had been around. But for all their differences, Connor and Matt had one glaring similarity.

"Kelsey, please," her ex-boyfriend practically whimpered. "You've gotta talk to Emily and tell her she can't marry that guy!"

Even without glancing in Connor's direction, she could feel his gaze. Heat rose to her face. She wanted to ignore both men at the moment, but she focused on Matt who was suddenly, oddly enough, the lesser of two humiliations.

"Emily's in love with Todd, and their wedding is going to be perfect." Determination rang in her voice, but Kelsey wondered who she was hoping to convince.

"You don't understand!" Matt took a single step in her direction, but froze when Connor uncrossed his arms. Keeping a nervous eye on the other man, Matt weakly finished, "I love her."

"Believe me. That is one thing I *do* understand."

He'd offered the same pitiful excuse as an explanation for using her, for taking advantage of her feelings, for making love to her and imagining Emily in her place.

Her ex-boyfriend had the grace to hang his head in shame but not enough sense to know when to give up. "Maybe if I could talk to her—" Matt pressed.

"Oh, for Pete's sake, get over it!"

His eyes widened in surprise, but Kelsey felt a shock when the words sank into her soul, and she realized the real object of her anger. She was tired of feeling like a fool for believing his lies. Of accepting his unacceptable behavior. Of shouldering the blame for the failure of their relationship when Matt was at fault.

"Let it go, Matt, and move on. I have."

Maybe that wasn't entirely true. As far as love was concerned, she certainly wasn't ready to take the plunge again, but might it be worthwhile to test the water?

"The lady asked you to leave." Connor crossed his arms over his broad chest, suddenly seeming to take up twice as much space and ready to literally enforce her advice for Matt to move on.

With a single, pitiful glance at Kelsey, Matt shrank back into the shadows. She didn't know if he'd heard a single word she said, but it didn't matter. *She'd* listened.

"Man, you've had your work cut out for you, haven't you?" Connor asked, once Matt had left. "How many of Emily's exes have you had to deal with?"

Emily's exes. Kelsey crossed her arms over her stomach, some of her earlier pleasure fading. The toe she'd stuck in the deep end felt chilled by frigid water. "So far, you're the only one. Matt isn't one of Emily's ex-boyfriends. He's mine."

Kelsey didn't know why she spilled that bit of information.

It wasn't as if she wanted Connor to feel sorry for her. She didn't know *what* she wanted from him.

He kicked at the asphalt and glanced in the direction the other man had disappeared. "Hell, Kelsey, you shoulda told me that before. I wouldn't have been so gentle."

The unexpected comment startled a laugh from her. It bubbled inside, shaky at first but growing stronger until she felt lighter, buoyed by the emotion and perhaps the chance to let go of the past. "How exactly do you throw a man *gently* against a wall?"

"*Gently* means he gets to slink off under his own power. *Not so gently* requires an ambulance."

"I guess Matt doesn't know how lucky he was."

"You're right, Kelsey. Something tells me he has no idea."

Certainty filled Connor's deep voice. Just listening to him made her feel free from the shame and embarrassment that had held her down for so long. Stepping closer, he crooked a finger beneath her chin. "You okay?"

She nodded, feeling his finger slide along the sensitive skin beneath her jaw. "Yes."

Concern gave way to relief and then anger. "You should have had someone walk you to your car. You have no idea what could happen—"

"Connor, I'm okay," Kelsey interrupted, worried by the tension that was evident in the set of his shoulders. A tension that seemed rooted in a different incident from a different time. "I wasn't in any danger."

Exhaling a breath, Connor seemed to release the pressure building inside and shake off whatever memories had caught him in their grasp. "You still need to be more careful."

True, Matt had startled her, coming out of the shadows the way he had, but he'd lost the power to hurt her long ago. And despite Connor's warning that she should be more careful, *he* was the most dangerous threat around. His lethal charm tore through her defenses, and a question that should have come to her much, much sooner sprang to mind. "What are *you* doing here, anyway? How did you even know we'd be having dinner tonight?"

Connor glanced at the front of the restaurant. A frown darkened his expression before he shook his head and blew out a breath. "Well, I *was* following Todd."

"What!"

"That's how I knew he was at the restaurant," he explained slowly, as if she had trouble keeping up. "So, tell me about dinner."

"Not so fast. You first."

"Okay," he said agreeably. "I haven't had dinner yet, and I'm starving!"

"I meant, tell me what you found following Todd."

"I will, but I really am starving. Come on." With a last look at the now-empty spot in front of the restaurant, he caught Kelsey's hand and said, "Let's go."

"Go where?" she demanded even as she followed alongside, far too aware of the tingle that raced up her spine as his fingers entwined with hers. The innocent touch certainly shouldn't have weakened her knees, but Kelsey could barely concentrate beyond the heat of his skin pressed to hers.

"To find someplace to eat."

Despite the extreme heat during the day, the temperature had lowered with the sunset. A gentle breeze carried the scents and sounds of nearby shops: gourmet coffee, decadent chocolate, the rise and fall of laughter and the faint strains of jazz music.

A group of girls walked toward Kelsey and Connor, heading in the other direction. Tall and beautiful, long limbs left bare by short skirts and tank tops, their not-so-subtle glances at Connor quickly turned to confusion as they shifted to Kelsey.

She didn't need a thought bubble over their heads to know what they were thinking: *What is* he *doing with* her? And after the run-in with Matt, Kelsey couldn't stop that question from digging deeper and deeper.

"Hey." Connor tugged at her hand. "You still with me?" he asked, as if he had somehow lost *her* interest.

"I'm here," she said. Now if she could only focus on *why* she was there. "Did you find anything on Todd?"

Connor took his time answering, waiting until he'd found a casual dining restaurant with outdoor seating. Cooling misters hissed overhead, the sound blending with the distant strains of an acoustic guitar being played on an outdoor stage. After giving the waiter his order, Connor leaned back in his chair and said, "If I'd found anything, you'd be the first to know. Unfortunately, all he did was shop."

"All afternoon?"

He laughed at her startled response. "I thought you'd be impressed."

"Surprised is more like it," she muttered, thinking of Todd's excuse. Still, she hesitated before confessing, "Todd was late for dinner. He said it was because of a business meeting."

"What? That five-second trip to his office this morning?" Connor scoffed.

"Maybe he didn't want to tell Emily he'd gone shopping for her."

"Except he was shopping for himself—unless Emily's taken up imported cigars."

"Um, no."

After a waiter dropped off glasses of ice water and Connor's steak sandwich, he said, "What else?"

"It was dinner, Connor, not an inquisition," she said as Connor dug in with both hands.

Truthfully, Kelsey hadn't *wanted* to find anything. She

wanted to believe Todd and Emily would have a beautiful wedding followed by a happy marriage. "It's probably nothing but—" she paused, not believing her own words "—none of Todd's family are coming to the wedding."

"Did he say why?" he asked, sliding his plate of fries her way.

Kelsey shook her head at the offer and said, "His parents already had a trip to Europe planned, and his sister is pregnant and didn't want to travel."

Connor shrugged. "So it could be nothing."

She blinked. Connor had jumped on even the slightest inconsistency in Todd's behavior. She couldn't believe he was letting this one go. "Are you serious? Can you imagine my aunt and uncle *not* showing up to Emily's wedding?"

"Not every family is like yours."

"Okay, fine. Forget the Wilsons. You might be the P.I. expert, but I'm the wedding expert, remember? And families *always* come to weddings!"

Connor's gaze cut away from her as he balled a paper napkin between his fists, and Kelsey knew. This wasn't about Todd's family or her family or families in general. It was about Connor's. A family she knew nothing about, one she couldn't recall Emily ever mentioning.

"You know, I don't think Emily's ever talked about your family."

"Why would she?"

Because, at one time or another, Emily had told Kelsey nearly everything about Connor. So much that Kelsey felt she'd known him long before she first caught sight of him at the airport. But she certainly couldn't tell Connor how she'd listened to those stories the same way a teenager might pore over celebrity magazines for the latest gossip on the current Hollywood heartthrob.

"I don't know. Maybe because if things had worked out like you'd planned, they would have been *her* family, too."

Connor gave a rough bark of laughter. "Emily had enough family to deal with without adding mine to the mix. Besides, my parents died before I met Emily."

The abrupt comment hit Kelsey in the chest, and she felt ashamed for pushing. She ached for his loss, an echo to the pain she still felt over the death of her own mother.

"Oh, Connor." Her defenses crumbled to dust, and with her heart already reaching out, her hands immediately followed. The heat of his hands—strong, rawboned, and masculine—sent an instant jolt up her arms. Her heart skipped a beat at the simple contact, but it was the emotional connection that had her pulse picking up an even greater speed. For a second, as their eyes met, Connor looked as startled as she felt.

Taking a breath deep enough to force her heart back into place, she focused on the reason she'd dared touch him in the first place. "I'm so sorry. I lost my mom when I was sixteen. Do you want—"

"It was a long time ago," he interrupted, jerking his hands out from hers in a pretense of reaching for his wallet to pull out a few bills. "I should get going. I'll walk you back to your car."

Stung by his abrupt withdrawal, Kelsey ducked her head before he could see the embarrassed color burning in her cheeks. Focusing on her purse, she searched for the keys she knew perfectly well were in the outside pocket.

"No need. I'll be fine," she insisted, and started walking. But if she thought she could out-stubborn Connor, he quickly proved her wrong.

"You will be fine," he agreed, his light touch against her lower back a complete contrast to the steely determination in his voice. "Because I'm walking you to your car."

Kelsey didn't argue, even though Matt was probably long gone. Thanks to Connor, he'd learned his lesson. Too bad she had yet to learn hers. Because no matter what Connor said about how beautiful she was, actions spoke louder than words, and all the compliments in the world couldn't erase the hurt of reaching out to Connor only to have him pull away.

Chapter Six

Early the next morning Kelsey stood outside her shop, gripping the key tightly enough to dig grooves into her palm. The unexpected phone call from her landlord couldn't have come at a better time. She still had plenty left to do for Emily's wedding, but she couldn't think of Emily without thinking of Connor. And Kelsey definitely did *not* want to think of him. Last night, she'd felt a connection—that loss and difficult childhoods gave them something in common. But Connor didn't want common.

He didn't want *her*.

With the morning sunlight glinting off the windows, she couldn't see inside, but in her mind's eye she pictured *her* shop. The subtle green and pink colors, the faded rose wallpaper, the shabby-chic-style parlor where she would meet with clients. Romantic without being overblown; classy while still being casual.

It was going to be perfect. Excitement jazzing her veins, Kelsey stuck the key in the lock, opened the door and blinked. With her dream office so firm in her thoughts she could practically smell her favorite peach potpourri, reality hit like a slap to the forehead.

No soft colors, no floral wallpaper… Shabby, yes, but chic?

"Not even close," Kelsey muttered as she flicked on the lights and stepped inside.

The landlord had shown her the space a few weeks ago, when it had been a struggling craft store. Shelves and bins had lined every wall, filled with yarn and cloth, paints and silk flowers. She'd focused on the space, knowing everything else would go when the other store closed. But she never stopped to think about the mess left behind.

Holes from the now-absent shelves marred the walls with peg-board consistency. The carpet had a two-tone hue thanks to the areas exposed to foot traffic, and the bare fluorescent bulbs overhead buzzed like bug zappers in August. No wonder the landlord had left the key hidden outside instead of meeting Kelsey.

But Kelsey hadn't spent her childhood living in sub-par apartments without learning a thing or two from her mother. "Wilson women against the world," she murmured as she pulled the phone from her purse and called the landlord.

If there was one thing Connor hated, it was being wrong. The only thing worse was being wrong and knowing he had to apologize. Meeting his own gaze in the mirror, he knew he owed Kelsey a big apology. He'd seen the hurt in her chocolate eyes at his abrupt withdrawal and he felt like a jerk. She'd reached out to him—physically and emotionally—and he'd pulled away.

He could justify his actions with the same excuse he always used when thoughts of the past intruded. That time was over and done, enough said. And yet, the sympathy and under-standing in Kelsey's expression made him *want* to talk about the past. He'd wanted to turn his wrist, take her hand into his and hold on tight. That completely foreign desire had so rattled him, that he'd locked his jaw and put an early end to the evening.

After showering and throwing on some clothes, Connor called Kelsey's cell. The phone rang four times before she answered, sounding breathless and sexy and— "Where the hell are you?" he demanded before he could keep the words from bursting out.

And what was she *doing* to give her voice that husky, bedroom quality?

"I'm…working."

She was *lying*. Before he could remind himself what Kelsey did or who she did it with was none of his business, he heard a loud clatter followed by an abbreviated scream and a thump that sent his heart racing. "Kelsey!" Silence filled the line, giving Connor plenty of time to imagine half a dozen dangerous possibilities. "Kelsey!"

"I'm here. I'm fine," she said after what sounded like a scramble for the phone. "I knocked over a ladder and a bucket of spackle went flying."

Ladder? "Spackle?"

"You know," she said, her voice sounding slightly muffled, and he imagined the phone held against her shoulder. "That compound stuff you use to patch walls."

"I know what spackle is. The big question is, why do *you* know what it is?"

"I'm just handy that way," she said a little too brightly, and Connor flashed back to the hurt in her eyes. Her answer might have been different if he hadn't pulled away the night before. "Kelsey—"

"I've found an office space to rent. That way I'll have more room to sell my lies about happily-ever-after to unsuspecting brides and grooms."

Connor flinched despite her light-hearted tone. Seemed as if he might have even more to apologize for than he'd thought. "What's the address?"

"Why?" she asked, as if she thought he planned to come by and torch the place.

"Because," he said after a deep breath and a ten count for patience, "I owe you an apology." Kelsey didn't respond, and in the silence, Connor knew she wanted more. That need rose up again, pressure building inside him as words he'd held back for years struggled to get out. "I owe you an apology," he repeated, "and an explanation."

"I'm an idiot," Kelsey muttered as she washed spackle from her hands in the tiny bathroom. She would have liked to look herself in the eye as she spoke those words, but the bathroom was missing a mirror, had no hot water, and a questionable-at-best toilet.

Why had she given Connor the address? Why had she invited him to invade her place? The dream office that filled her thoughts so strongly that morning had faded over the past several hours of hard work. The last thing she needed was Connor's presence to overwhelm what was left of her lace-and-roses dream in a deluge of cotton and denim.

Not to mention his cynicism.

Yet she'd been unable to resist the demand in his voice or his promised apology.

The ring of the bell above the front door alerted her to her first visitor and saved her from her own thoughts. "Kelsey?" a familiar female voice called out.

She banged on the faucet handle a few times to turn off the

water and hurried out, shaking her hands to get them dry. "Lisa? What are you doing here?"

Walking through the shop with a bouquet of gerbera daisies in one hand and a bottle of wine in the other, her friend cast a dubious look around. "Not quite what I expected," she said as she met Kelsey at the back of the shop.

"It needs work," Kelsey admitted. "But I called the landlord and talked him into reducing the first month's rent if I handle the repairs."

"And that's why I'm here," her friend announced as she set the wine and flowers on the ladder. "I know you too well. You're always willing to help your friends, but you never ask for help. Of course, I had no idea you'd need this much help, but it's a good thing I called Trey, too." Trey Jamison was another good friend, and she frequently hired him as a DJ for her weddings.

"You didn't have to do that," Kelsey told Lisa.

"Yes, I did because you wouldn't. I knew you'd be here all alone with no one to help you and…"

Lisa turned as the bell announced another arrival, her words trailing away. Kelsey couldn't blame her friend. She felt pretty speechless as Connor stripped off his reflective glasses and locked that green gaze on her from across the shop. "Hey."

"Hey," Kelsey responded, the word far more breathless than she wanted to admit. Her stomach did a slow roll at the sight of him. Just as she'd feared, he shrank the space until it encompassed only the two of them. Thoughts of lace and roses fell away, overwhelmed by Connor's masculine presence. Her senses took in every bit of him—the faded gray T-shirt that stretched across his chest, the jeans that clung to his muscular legs, the low murmur of his voice.

Lisa's silence didn't last nearly as long as Kelsey's. Her friend gripped her arm and whispered, "Who *is* that?"

"Connor McClane," Kelsey murmured back.

"Connor—" Lisa's eyebrows rose. "Emily's ex? What is he doing here?"

Emily's ex. Kelsey's heart cringed at the description. "Good question," she muttered as his promised apology and explanation rang in her mind.

Before she had the chance to ask, Trey pushed through the doorway. With his long hair caught back in a ponytail, and wearing an oversize T-shirt and raggedy cutoffs, he looked ready to work. But after gazing around, he said, "Way to go, Kelse!" Walking over, he spun her in an exuberant hug. "This place is great."

"You think?" she asked, with a laugh at her friend's enthusiasm.

"Well, it will be when you're done with it, right?" He glanced at Lisa and Connor for confirmation, and only then did Kelsey realize she had yet to introduce them.

"Oh, I'm sorry. Trey, Lisa, this is Connor..."

The introduction faded away as she caught sight of the scowl on Connor's face. Instinctively she stepped out of Trey's embrace, which was *crazy*. Because Trey was just a friend and crazier still because Connor could *not* be jealous.

Could he?

Still, Connor was less than friendly as he crossed the shop to greet Trey. The handshake the two men exchanged seemed more like a prelude to battle than a customary introduction. "Good to meet you," Trey said, his smile growing wide even though Kelsey thought she saw him subtly flexing his hand once Connor released it.

"Pleasure," Connor said, the word sounding anything but.

"Okay, let's put all this testosterone to use," Lisa said, bringing a heated blush to Kelsey's face. "Where do we start?"

"Yeah, give us the list," Trey said, holding out his hand.

"You guys don't have to do this. You can't give up your weekend to help me out."

"Like the time you filled in for me when I got snowed in back East and didn't have anyone to open up the flower shop?" Lisa challenged before glancing at Trey expectantly.

Immediately he picked up where she'd left off. "Or the time you shoved chicken soup and hot tea down my throat to get my voice back in time to DJ that last wedding?"

"That's different," Kelsey protested.

"Why? Why are you the only one allowed to help?" Lisa demanded. "When do we get to return the favor? And hey, we're not dummies. We all know helping you helps us."

"Yeah, as long as she doesn't forget her friends when she's off coordinating weddings for the rich and famous," Trey whispered in an aside to Lisa.

Overwhelmed by their generosity, Kelsey blinked back tears. Growing up, it had always been Kelsey and her mom— Wilson women against the world. But maybe that was only because Olivia hadn't had friends as amazing as Lisa and Trey.

"All right! All right! I give in. And I promise to remember all the little people," Kelsey laughed before grabbing the list as well as a handful of paint swatches, wallpaper samples and various store ads from her day planner.

"Trey, here are the paint colors and wallpaper. If you could pick them up from the hardware store along with a carpet steamer, that would be great. Lisa, here's a picture of the drapes I want for the front window. Could you see if they have a large area rug to match? Anything to hide this carpet."

Even as Kelsey split the shopping between her friends, she was aware of Connor's speculative gaze focused on her. What was he thinking? she wondered. That her romantic trappings were literally that—traps for couples foolish enough to believe in love?

"Got it, boss," Trey said, saluting her with the green and pink paint samples. "Want me to pick up lunch while I'm out?"

"No need. Sara's catering our workday. Her word, not mine," Lisa laughed as she grabbed Trey's arm and led him toward the door.

"Man, I wanted pizza and beer. Sara'll probably bring mini quiches and crudités." As the two of them walked outside, the laughter and casual camaraderie went with them, leaving behind a tension that for Kelsey buzzed as loudly as the fluorescent light overhead.

Ready to take the offensive, she turned to Connor. What apology did he want to give? What explanation? Her lips parted on those questions, but he beat her to the punch.

"How many of your friends are working Emily's wedding?"

Just like that, momentum changed, and Connor had her backpedaling and on the defensive. "Lisa and I went to high school together, and I've made friends with some of the other people I've worked with. But I never would have hired them if I didn't think they'd do an awesome job."

She lifted her chin, ready to battle for her friends the same way she had when she hired them for Emily's wedding. But if this was a fight, Connor didn't play fair.

Reaching up, he tucked a loose curl behind one ear. His eyes glowing with a warmth that stole the fight from her spirit and the breath from her lungs, he murmured, "It wasn't a criticism. Only an observation. Your friends obviously care a lot about you. Just like you care about them."

Intensity lit his emerald eyes, and Kelsey could almost believe he wanted her to look out for him, to care about him—but that had to be a delusion due to lack of oxygen from the breath he'd stolen with his nearness. "I do," she managed to murmur.

"So why was it so hard for you to accept their help?"

She started to deny it, but when Connor's eyebrows rose

in challenge, she knew he wouldn't believe anything but the truth. And maybe if she told him, he would understand why Emily's wedding was so important. "Fixing things is what I do. It's what I'm good at. I wasn't brought up as one of the wealthy Wilsons. I was raised by my mother. We didn't have much, but growing up I didn't know that. All I knew was that I had an amazing mother who taught me how to cook delicious meals without spending more than a few dollars and how to clip coupons to make the most of what little money we had."

A memory came to mind, and Kelsey smiled. "Our favorite day was Black Friday, but we didn't just shop for Christmas. We bargain-hunted for the whole year. My mom taught me how to look at secondhand furniture and see beyond the layers of flaking paint or rust. She showed me how to strip away the exterior to the natural beauty beneath."

Her smile faded away. "But then she died, and I came to live with my aunt and uncle. None of the things I knew how to do mattered anymore. Coupons and discount stores and second-hand furniture were as foreign to them as paying hundreds of dollars for a pair of shoes was to me. They had people to shop and clean and fix things." Kelsey gave a short, sad laugh. "The only thing broken in their house was me. I know they cared about me, but…I just didn't fit, no matter how hard I tried."

"Kelsey." The low murmur of Connor's voice mirrored the tenderness in his gaze. This time it was Kelsey's turn to pull away, to try to escape.

"That's why the wedding is so important. It's my chance—" her *only* chance, because if she screwed this up, why would the Wilsons or anyone trust her again? "—to prove that I can do this, that I'm good at *something*. So I really hope your gut's wrong, Connor, and that Todd is everything my family thinks he is. Or all this hard work is going to be for nothing."

"It won't be for nothing because you're going to be a

success with or without Emily's wedding. Maybe if you *were* more like Emily or Aileen, more used to everything going your way, you'd be more likely to give up. But a single setback won't stop you. You're stronger than that." Catching her hands and smiling at the streaks of spackle marring her skin, he said, "You aren't afraid of hard work."

Strong…unafraid… Kelsey liked the sound of that, but she wasn't feeling the least bit of either as Connor stroked his thumbs across the palm of her hands. She felt downright weak and terrified by the desire coursing through her at such a simple touch.

Her fingertips tingled, tempted to chart the planes and angles of his face, the strong column of his throat. The broad shoulders and wide chest covered by cotton as soft as Connor's body was strong. But she curled her hands into fists. She wouldn't—couldn't—reach out to him again. The embarrassment of Connor pulling away was too painfully fresh in her mind, and her heart was too vulnerable to risk rejection a second time.

In the end, she didn't have to reach out; she didn't even have to move. It was Connor who pulled her closer, Connor who lowered his head, Connor who brushed his mouth against hers. Any thought of him pulling away disappeared as he deepened the kiss. He buried one hand in her hair and wrapped the other around her waist, holding her body tight to his, as if she were the one who might back away.

But escape was the last thing Kelsey wanted.

Instead she wanted to capture this moment, bottle it up, save it for a time when memories were all she would have left of Connor. But even that proved impossible, as he slanted his mouth over hers, his lips and tongue stealing her breath, robbing her of her ability to think, and leaving her with no choice but to feel….

Her breasts against the hard wall of his chest, her heart pounding desperately enough to match the rapid beat of his, the firm press of his fingers against her hip. She splayed her fingers across his back, searching out as much contact as possible, the material thin enough, soft enough, heated enough, that she could imagine his naked skin and the play of muscles beneath her hands.

"Connor." His name escaped her on a breathless sigh as he trailed a kiss across her cheek to her jaw, his warm breath setting off a chain reaction of shivers down her spine. She swayed closer, her hips brushing against his solid thigh. The heated contact weakened her knees, and all she wanted was to sink to the floor, pull Connor down with her and feel the weight of his body on top of hers.

She might have done just that if not for the ring of the bell and an embarrassed "Oops. Pretend I was never here."

Kelsey tore away from Connor in time to see her friend Sara backing out of the door with a platter of food in her hands. She wanted to call Sara back, but it was too late, leaving Kelsey with little choice but to face Connor. With his eyes dark with passion, his chest rising and falling, it was all she could do not to dive back into his arms.

Two seconds ago an interruption was the last thing she wanted. But now with passion clearing, she realized it was exactly what she needed. Already Connor was going to her head; it wouldn't take much for him to go straight to her heart. "That, um, was Sara. I should ask her to come back inside."

Her friends were waiting, her dreams were waiting and she didn't dare push them aside. Not even for Connor. No matter how much she wanted to.

Hours later, Connor looked around Kelsey's shop, amazed by the transformation. The scent of paint filled the shop, and the soft pink and green colors highlighted the walls. The carpets had been shampooed, and the new rug and drapes stored in the back would soon complete the new look. Kelsey's self-proclaimed talent for stripping away the layers and revealing the beauty beneath was on magnificent display in all the work she'd done.

How could she possibly doubt her own worth, her own ability? Connor wondered...until he tried to imagine Emily—or heaven forbid, Charlene—dressed in a T-shirt and cutoffs, with their hair covered by a bandana, a streak of pale pink war paint on one cheek and spackle on the other. None of the other Wilson women would be caught dead looking the way Kelsey did right then. Yet seeing her eyes sparkle as she laughed with her friends, celebrated every small success and worked her *ass* off, Connor didn't think he'd ever seen a woman look as vibrant, as alive, as *sexy,* as Kelsey.

As if feeling the heat of his gaze, Kelsey glanced his way. Heat flared in her cheeks, and she ducked her head, taking a sudden interest in flipping through the phone directory, cell phone in hand as she searched for a plumber.

A phone call to her uncle, and her plumbing problems would have been solved. Hell, a single call to Gordon Wilson and *all* her problems would have been solved. Gordon could have easily set up Kelsey in a furnished, upscale Scottsdale or Paradise Valley suite instead of a work-in-progress strip mall in downtown Glendale.

He'd meant every word when he called Kelsey strong and fearless. She'd been only sixteen when she went to live with her aunt and uncle, an age when most kids would have lost themselves in a world filled with wealth and privilege. But not Kelsey. She'd stayed true to herself, to the lessons her mother had taught her. Even now, when her family's money could make her dream an instant success, Kelsey refused to take the easy way out…not like he had.

He'd had his reasons for taking the money Gordon Wilson had offered him to leave town all those years ago, reasons he believed justified his actions, but he couldn't help thinking that had Kelsey faced the same choice, she would have found another way.

She flat-out amazed him. He would have liked to ignore the emotion spilling through him, but Connor had learned his lesson when it came to ignoring feelings…even if this one wasn't hitting his gut as much as it was pulling at his heart.

"Place looks great, doesn't it?"

The sudden question jerked Connor from his thoughts, and he turned to face Lisa. Judging by the woman's sharp gaze, he doubted Kelsey's shop was on the woman's mind. "It does. You, Trey and Sara were a huge help," he added.

Kelsey's friends had thrown themselves into helping, Trey especially. But despite the close eye Connor kept on the other man, he hadn't seen any proof Trey and Kelsey were anything other than friends. And yet Trey's touchy-feely familiarity had set Connor's teeth on edge. A reaction as unfamiliar as it was uncomfortable.

He rarely felt possessive over a woman, and certainly not after a kiss or two. But then again, what a kiss! He could still taste her, could smell the cinnamon and spice he'd come to associate with Kelsey. No too-sweet floral scents for her. Nothing expensive, nothing fancy, just…Kelsey.

"You weren't too bad yourself," Lisa said with enough tongue-in-cheek attitude to make Connor wonder if she'd noticed how he strove to outlift, outwork, out*do* Trey. Turning serious, she said, "We're all glad to help Kelsey. She's the kind of friend who always takes care of everyone else. This is the first chance we've had to pay her back."

"I doubt she expects payment."

"She doesn't. It's in her nature to help." The brunette paused, and Connor sensed her debating over her next words. "I think a lot of it comes from taking care of her mom."

"Kelsey told me her mother died when she was sixteen." But despite what she'd told him, Connor knew he had only part of the story. Why had Kelsey's mother—Gordon Wilson's sister—raised Kelsey on her own? Single mom or not, she should have had the family fortune at her disposal, and yet that clearly hadn't been the case.

What had caused the rift between Kelsey's mother and her family? And what about the father Kelsey never mentioned? Connor didn't ask Lisa those questions. It was up to Kelsey to offer answers…if he asked her.

With a glance at her watch, Lisa told him she had to go, but she left with a few final words he translated into a warning. "Kelsey's a great girl. She deserves the best."

Connor waited for the woman to add that Kelsey deserved better than him, but when she merely gazed at him in expectation, he realized Lisa wasn't telling him Kelsey deserved better *than him;* she was telling him Kelsey deserved the best *from him.*

"Well, I finally found a plumber who can come this week…" Kelsey's voice trailed off as she walked from the back room, cell phone in hand.

Connor stood alone in the middle of the shop. Even with the progress they'd made, bringing her dream closer to reality, he overwhelmed the place. If anything, the shop's increasingly feminine decor only served as a larger reminder of Connor's masculinity. And after that kiss, Kelsey didn't have any doubt whatsoever about his undeniable and—she was beginning to fear—irresistible masculinity.

"Lisa had to take off," he explained.

"Oh. She was probably afraid I'd put her to work again if she didn't sneak away."

"I don't think so. Your friends will obviously do anything for you."

Uncomfortable with the praise, Kelsey countered, "Like Javy would for you."

Connor frowned. "Yeah. He thinks he owes me, but the truth is, his family bailed me out when I was a kid. Nothing I've done would be enough to repay them."

Despite the explanation he'd promised earlier, Connor's voluntary statement caught Kelsey off guard, surprising her almost as much as his kiss. She shook her head and protested, "Just because I spilled my guts doesn't mean you have to—"

"I want to," he interrupted. "I should have told you about my past last night, but I haven't told anyone since Señora Delgado pried it out of me as a kid."

"You—you didn't tell *anyone?*" Kelsey prodded.

You didn't tell Emily?

His penetrating gaze read into the heart of her question, hearing what she *hadn't* asked, and he vowed, "I didn't tell anyone."

And suddenly Kelsey wasn't sure she wanted to know. Listening to what he had to say seemed to take on a greater significance because Connor wanted to tell *her,* to confide in her, something he'd never told Emily.

Without saying another word, Connor stepped forward, his long strides erasing the distance between them. He caught her hand and led her over to the love seat her friends had surprised her with. She'd been overwhelmed by their generosity. The sofa would be the perfect place for her soon-to-be-married couples to sit side by side and decide floral arrangements, wedding invitations, dinner menus.

But as soon as Connor sank down onto the love seat, she

decided it would be the perfect place for her to curl up in his arms, the perfect place to kiss him and never stop. The masculine-feminine contrast sent a slow roll of awareness through her stomach as he settled back against the rose-covered cushions. In faded cotton and rough worn denim, he should have looked out of place; instead, his broad shoulders and wide chest looked far more comfortable and inviting than the floral chintz ever could.

Swallowing, she folded onto the couch beside him, one leg bent and angled toward Connor. He stared straight ahead, keeping his silence, and Kelsey sensed his thoughts drifting back to a past he'd purposely chosen not to face…until now.

Taking a deep breath, he said, "My father was a truck driver. Eighteen-wheeler. He worked hard, drank hard. He was…strict."

The tension in Connor's shoulders and the way his hands tightened into fists gave a clear definition of the word. Her heart ached for the boy he'd been, a boy she could picture so easily. Dark hair that was too long, a body that was too skinny, and a gaze that was too old. She could see him in her mind as if, somehow, he'd been there all along.

Crazy, she thought, but she felt she knew him so well. And now that Connor was willing to give out answers, did she dare ask more questions? Could she risk getting to know him even better?

In the end, no matter the potential danger to her heart, Kelsey had to ask. Not because she needed to hear the story… but because Connor needed to tell it. "And your mother?" she asked softly.

One by one his fingers unclenched then slowly laced together as if cradling something precious. "She was a dreamer. She was always…looking for something. Always hoping for a better life, only she never found it. I was eight when she died.

She'd been taking art lessons, or maybe it was a dance class. I can't remember."

Connor cleared his throat. "Anyway, this place wasn't in the best part of town. I begged her not to go. I knew something bad was going to happen. But she went anyway. No one knows exactly what happened," he added, the tension pulling at his shoulders revealing how much not knowing still troubled him, "but the police figured a mugging went wrong. Either my mom fought back or the guy panicked, and the gun went off."

"Oh, Connor, I'm so sorry." Just as she feared, her heart ached a little more at the telling, and she longed to reach out to him, to comfort him. But she didn't. This time it was her turn to twist her fingers together, strangling the desire to touch him.

Because—despite his kiss—she still feared her touch wasn't the one Connor wanted.

But he never told Emily about his family. He's telling you! Aching or not, her heart had the strength to argue, and Kelsey felt her resistance crumbling.

"The guy stole her purse and wallet," Connor went on as if she hadn't spoken. "It took three days before the police figured out who she was."

"Didn't your dad report her missing?"

"He was on a long-distance drive. He didn't know anything was wrong."

"But when your mother didn't come home, someone must have tried to get hold of him. The people you were staying with—" As soon as she said the words, realization flooded Kelsey and her breath caught. "You were alone, weren't you?"

"My mom thought I was old enough to take care of myself, and it should have only been for a few hours."

Hours that had stretched into days.

"Wasn't there anyone you could call? A friend of the family?"

"Probably, but hell, I was eight. My mom had told me she

was going to be right back. Calling someone would have been like admitting something was wrong, admitting she wasn't coming back. Ever."

Kelsey felt heartsick at the thought of the frightened, abandoned boy Connor had been. "You were so young. How did you get on without her?"

"My dad and I stumbled along, but he always blamed my mom for dying. If she'd been happy with her life, if she hadn't always been out looking for more and expecting something better, she'd still be alive. If she'd just *listened* to me. I could have—"

Saved her. Connor didn't say the words, but they rang in the silence and underscored everything he did. "It's not your fault, Connor," she insisted, and this time she couldn't keep from reaching out and grasping his hands as if she could somehow heal the pain and guilt with her touch. "People make their own decisions, and you aren't responsible for their choices."

"No, only for my own," he agreed darkly, but tension tightened his hands into rock-hard fists.

Her family was so wrong about Connor. He wasn't out to ruin Emily's wedding—he was trying to save her from a past he couldn't possibly change. But Kelsey still wasn't convinced Todd was the threat Connor thought him to be. After all, Connor's *gut reaction* had pinned Matt to the restaurant, mistakenly seeing her ex-boyfriend as a physical threat. Wasn't it possible Todd was as harmless as Matt, and Connor was looking through the eyes of the past and seeing a danger that wasn't there?

"I can't imagine what that must have been like to lose your mother so suddenly." *So violently.* "But don't you think maybe that's colored the way you see people?"

"People like Dunworthy?" he asked with a wry twist to his lips. He pulled his hands out from beneath hers in the pretense of shifting to face her on the love seat. "I know you think I'm wrong about him, but it's because of my past that I'm sure I'm right." As if sensing her doubt, he asked, "Haven't you ever met someone and instantly known the kind of person they are?"

Thoughts of her first impression of Connor assailed Kelsey. The bad boy. The troublemaker. The man out to ruin Emily's wedding and destroy Kelsey's chance to prove herself to her family, to make her mother proud... But he was so much more than that.

"Maybe once or twice."

"Like when you met me?"

One corner of his mouth kicked up with the teasing comment, but the smile lacked full-force charm, his heart not in it. The emotional waters had gotten too deep, and Connor was clearly pulling back to shallower depths. And Kelsey almost wished she had stayed on the surface, wished she could still see Connor the way he wanted to be seen—cocky, self-confident, unbreakable. But she felt herself going under, caught by the pull of this man who was so much more than the rebel he played.

Struggling to break free, she focused on the easy out Connor had taken and followed him to more solid ground. "I knew you were going to be trouble the moment I met you. Does that count?"

"Talk about biased," he murmured. "How many Connor McClane stories have you heard over the years?"

"More than a few."

"More than a few hundred, if your aunt and uncle had anything to say about it." The teasing tone stayed in his voice, but Kelsey could tell her family's poor opinion of him still rankled. He was clearly out to prove the Wilsons wrong, but Kelsey suspected he had as much to prove to himself. "And here I've been a perfect gentleman."

"Well, not perfect," she argued. But who wanted perfect? Perfect was for women like her cousins; Kelsey much preferred the real thing to Ken-like perfection.

"I'm crushed. Señora Delgado will be so disappointed."

"Señora Delgado?"

"Javy's mother."

"How did you and Javy meet?"

"We went to school together. Mrs. Brown's sixth-grade glass."

"And you two became fast friends?"

"Nah, we hated each other. I can't even remember why. Oh, wait, it had something to do with a girl. We thought we were pretty hot stuff on the playground. Both trying to impress Alicia Martin. Unfortunately for us, she had a thing for older men."

"Eighth grader?" Kelsey guessed, playing along to maintain the teasing mood.

"Worse. P.E. teacher. And man, the guy was old. Like twenty-five. Anyway, we bonded over a couple of cafeteria juice boxes, and I started hanging out with him at his mother's restaurant. Before long, I was washing dishes and bussing tables. If the Delgados hadn't fed me through most of junior high and high school, I don't know what I would have done. Probably would have dropped out to work full-time if Maria hadn't stopped me."

Kelsey knew the drop-out rate was horrible, especially in Arizona, but as much as she'd hated school, she never once considered not finishing. "How did she stop you?"

"By telling me I *should*," Connor said wryly. "She said anyone foolish enough to give up a free education didn't deserve one."

Smiling at the woman's use of reverse psychology, Kelsey said, "I think I'd like to meet her. Not every woman has enough influence to keep a boy in school *and* teach him to clear dishes off a table."

"You're on. Let's go to the Delgados' restaurant. Maybe Maria will be there."

Kelsey swallowed. Was Connor asking her out? On a *date?* She waited for the little voice in her head to tell her this was a bad idea, but she didn't hear it. Possibly because it was drowned out by the *big* voice screaming, "Go for it!"

She knew the voice of reason would be back, loud and clear, and ready to say "I told you so" if she let herself fall for Connor. But that worry, like the voice, seemed far off, and she couldn't resist the chance to spend more time with Connor.

"I'm a mess," she said in weak protest. "I can't go anywhere looking like this."

As Connor's gaze swept over her, Kelsey felt her face heat. She could only imagine what he saw. She had spackle under her nails, drywall dust in her hair, and more splotches of paint than freckles covering her arms. She was sweaty and disheveled, and even though Connor had worked as hard as anyone, he looked—

Gorgeous, she thought with a sigh, taking in the lock of dark hair he'd constantly pushed back from his paint-streaked forehead, the hint of five o'clock shadow shading his jaw, the damp T-shirt that molded to his shoulders and chest.

"I'll pick you up at your place in half an hour," he said as he stood and reached down to pull her to her feet.

Kelsey shook her head, ready to refuse, and yet when she opened her mouth she said, "An hour."

"Forty-five minutes."

"An hour." She laughed as she shoved him toward the door. "And not a minute sooner."

Chapter Seven

Mariachi music greeted Connor as he opened the car door. Judging by the nearly full parking lot, the restaurant was packed. The lunch hour tended to draw patrons from nearby businesses; at night, the place had more of a party atmosphere. The music would play, tables would be pushed aside to create a dance floor, and he was *definitely* looking forward to slow dancing with Kelsey.

He was looking forward to the entire evening with an anticipation that caught him off guard. After spilling his guts the way he had, escape should have been the only thing on his mind. He never talked about his past—*never*—and as little as two days ago, the thought of opening up about a time that still left him feeling lost and vulnerable would have tied his stomach into barbed-wire knots. And the thought of confiding in a Wilson!

Connor shook his head in disbelief, even as he admitted

Kelsey was no ordinary Wilson. She might not fit the Wilsons' model of perfection, but she fit his.

He rounded the car to open Kelsey's door, a split second too late, as it turned out. She already had one shapely leg extended, but he was in time to reach out a hand to help her out. Surprise lit her gaze, as if she hadn't considered his invitation to dinner a *real* date.

And despite the casual, last-minute offer, Connor realized he very much wanted this to be a real date. The kind of date where everyone in the restaurant would know Kelsey was with him. The kind where he never wanted the night to end and where, when the evening finally *did* end, a good-night kiss was not only expected, but breathlessly anticipated.

And when that time came, Connor vowed, he'd make sure there was no doubt in Kelsey's mind.

"You look amazing," he murmured, placing a hand at the small of her back.

Pleasure brightened her eyes and put color in her cheeks despite the less-than-original compliment. But hell, it was more than her looks. It was Kelsey. *She* amazed him.

"Thank you." She smoothed her hands over the embroidered skirt she wore. "I was hoping it wouldn't be too dressy."

"It's perfect." The flared skirt and off-the-shoulder blouse had a Spanish touch that emphasized her curves, and he wondered again how she could be so oblivious to how good she looked.

But that mix of confidence and insecurity was so much a part of Kelsey. He'd watched her divide the workload and make decisions without hesitation this afternoon, giving him an idea of how good a wedding coordinator she must be. Yet that confidence completely deserted her when it came to her personal life.

Living with the Wilsons had done that to her, Connor was

certain of it. They'd stripped her of her confidence, of her faith in her abilities, which they deemed worthless and beneath them.

Same way they'd declared *him* worthless and beneath them.

Connor shook off the dark thoughts as they stepped inside the restaurant. The scent of sizzling fajitas and salsa reminded him Trey hadn't been too far off about Sara's lunch. The caterer had brought delicate sandwiches and a fruit salad that looked more like a table centerpiece than something to eat.

"Man, I'm starving. I had a total slave driver nearly work me to death and only feed me bread and water."

"It was sandwiches, not just bread. And sparkling water, if that makes you feel any better." Kelsey laughed. "Besides, *you* volunteered, remember?"

"Yeah, I did." And he'd gladly do it again. Just looking into her excited brown eyes, listening to her laughter, made him feel—Connor thought for a moment, searching for the right word—happy. At peace. With nothing to prove, nothing to make up for. For the first time in his life, despite spilling the story of his sorry, less-than-sterling past, Connor felt he could be himself and that alone would be enough.

Except you didn't tell Kelsey the whole *story,* his conscience argued, dimming his contentment.

He hadn't told her about the money he'd taken, money he'd given to the Delgados to save the restaurant that pulsed with life around them. The business meant the world to Maria, especially following the dark days after her husband passed away. But Miguel's medical bills and the damage caused by an accidental grease fire had almost ruined the restaurant financially. In an effort to save it, Connor had taken the money from Gordon Wilson instead of throwing the check back in the smug SOB's face.

He knew what the older man thought. That he was nothing more than a gold-digging opportunist. But he was starting to think Kelsey might be the one Wilson, the one woman, to understand.

Was that why he'd invited her here? So she could meet Maria Delgado and see how important the woman was to him? So she could see for herself why he'd taken the money?

"Kelsey—"

"How about this? I'll pay for dinner tonight, compensation for all that slave labor?" she suggested as she stepped forward to talk to the hostess.

"Kelsey, wait." He caught her hand, wanting, *needing* to tell her the whole truth.

The seriousness in his tone made her eyes widen. "Hey, if you want to pay—"

"It's not that. I need to tell you—"

"Connor! *Mijo!*"

Hearing the familiar voice, Connor turned toward the sound with a large dose of relief and only the smallest amount of disappointment. The moment was gone, and he focused on Maria Delgado as she moved among the crowded tables toward him. She hadn't changed from the woman he remembered. Sure, she had a touch more gray in her waist-length hair and a few more wrinkles, but her dark eyes were as warm and welcoming as ever.

"*Señora!*" Connor bent to wrap his arms around the diminutive woman.

"My son told me you had come home! It is so good for you to be back!"

"It's good to see you, too." Seeing the undisguised interest in the older woman's eyes, he added, "Maria Delgado, this is Kelsey Wilson."

"Pleasure to meet you, Mrs. Delgado. Connor has told me a lot about you and how much your family means to him."

Maria beamed at him like a proud mother. "Connor, he is

family," she said to Kelsey. "And for him to bring you here, you must be very special. Never has he brought a young lady to the restaurant."

The implication that he'd brought Kelsey "home" to meet his family should have sent panic shooting like warning flares through his system, and yet seeing the two women talking and laughing together felt...*right*.

Kelsey also ignored the too-telling observation, but an adorable blush lit her cheeks as she added, "Your restaurant is amazing. I have to admit, I've never cared for Mexican food, but the quesadilla I had the other day was delicious."

"I always say, people who do not like Mexican food have not had *my* food." Maria pressed a hand against her bosom, pride shining in her dark eyes.

As Maria led them through a maze of crowded tables, Connor asked, "Where is Javy tonight?"

The *señora* waved a dismissive hand. "Ah, that boy. He is out with some girl. I tell him he needs to settle down, but does he listen? No. My son, he is too handsome for his own good. He does not have to work to get these girls' attention. Too often he chooses the easy way. He does not realize some things you must work for." She turned to Kelsey in a shared feminine confidence, a twinkle in her dark eyes. "But Connor, he is just handsome enough, no?"

"No. I mean, yes," Kelsey stuttered, flustered by the question. Connor was ready to jump in and rescue her from having to answer when she made her own save. "I think Connor is more than handsome enough," she said in a whisper plenty loud enough for him to overhear, "but he still has his work cut out for him."

Señora Delgado chortled and gave what sounded like a quick prayer beneath her breath. "Come, I will give you the best table in the house."

"I thought all the tables were the best tables," he teased with a wink at Kelsey as he placed his hand on the small of her back.

"*Sí*," the older woman agreed, "they are all the best."

Kelsey grinned, sharing his humor in the *señora's* unflappable logic.

After showing them to a secluded table in the back, Maria kissed Connor's cheek and went back to work. Kelsey's hand touched the ladder-back chair, but Connor beat her to it. As he pulled it out for her, he leaned close. Close enough to catch the cinnamon scent of her skin. Close enough to see the freckles she'd tried to hide beneath makeup. Close enough to hear her breath catch in reaction to his nearness. "You should know by now, Kelsey," he murmured, "I'm not afraid of a little hard work."

Her eyes widened, but just like she had with Señora Delgado, Kelsey found her own footing and knocked him for a loop when she said, "I'm counting on it."

Time froze as the moment held them in its grip. The restaurant, with its loud music and bright lights, faded away, leaving behind only Kelsey's gorgeous brown eyes and softly parted lips. A burst of laughter from a nearby table broke the moment, and Kelsey sank into the chair he held for her. Connor had little choice but to take his own seat and curse the table separating them.

A waiter came by with menus, but Connor could tell by the frequent glances she sent his way Kelsey's mind wasn't on dinner. Finally she set the menu aside and said, "Is it true what Señora Delgado said before? You never brought anyone here?"

He'd let her get away with the unasked question before, but not this time. "Come on, Kelsey. Are you interested in *anybody* or in Emily?"

At first she looked ready to protest, only to square her

shoulders and meet his gaze head-on. "Okay. Did you ever bring Emily here?"

"No. The Delgados are like family to me, and I wasn't sure Emily would get that." He hadn't been able to picture Emily at the rustic, homey restaurant. He still couldn't…and yet Kelsey fit in so perfectly. He'd never had a doubt about bringing *her.*

Not waiting for her to ask why—or wanting to look too closely for a reason himself—Connor pushed back from the table. Kelsey's eyes widened in surprise as he held out his hand and said, "Come on. Let's dance."

As Kelsey took Connor's hand, it occurred to her that she had no idea how to dance to the Latin-flavored beat pulsing from the speakers. But that didn't stop her from following him onto the tiny dance floor, where the music instantly switched to a ballad.

Connor's smile flashed as he pulled her into his arms. "Couldn't have planned it better myself."

"I'm not so sure you didn't."

"This wasn't me. It must be fate."

Kelsey didn't know about fate, but being held in Connor's arms certainly felt like a dream. She wasn't the only one who had dressed up for the evening. Connor had showered and shaved, brushed his dark hair back from his forehead. A touch of sexy sophistication replaced a bit of his bad-boy image thanks to the white button-down shirt and black slacks he wore instead of his usual T-shirt and jeans. No matter what Maria Delgado said about her son, it was Connor who took Kelsey's breath away. He was the most gorgeous man she'd ever met, and the sheer look of masculine appreciation in his eyes made her feel beautiful. But even as the physical connection robbed her of her breath, the emotional connection threatened to steal her heart.

Listening to him talk about his past and seeing his love for Señora Delgado revealed a different side of Connor. A fiercely loyal and caring side that would be as easy to fall for as his cocky grin and killer body.

Right, her conscience told her. *And the fact that Connor never shared that side of himself with Emily, never told her about his childhood, never brought her to the restaurant, that has* nothing *to do with it.*

Kelsey wanted to shove the goading voice aside, but it was impossible to ignore. Connor had trusted her with the heartbreak of his past and a happier part of his present, and it was almost impossible not to think of the future. Not a forever future, of course, but the immediate future—and how she'd gladly spend what time she and Connor had left in his arms.

For the first time in years, Kelsey didn't feel like she'd come in a distant second to her too-beautiful cousin, an irony her disapproving conscience couldn't overlook, as Connor was the one man in a position to best make comparisons…

"You're too quiet," Connor murmured in her ear. "It makes me nervous."

Kelsey laughed at the thought of *anything* making Connor nervous. "Don't be. I was just thinking."

"Hmm. Those might be the most nerve-racking words a man ever hears. Should I ask *what* you've been thinking?"

Not brave enough to admit the whole truth, Kelsey said, "Only that we don't have much time left."

Connor cocked an eyebrow. "Until the wedding?"

"Until you leave."

"Ready to see me go, huh?"

"Surprisingly, no," Kelsey said, although Connor didn't seem surprised by her admission.

Because it was so obvious how her heart slammed into her chest every time he came near? How her knees turned to jelly with a single look? It wasn't something she wanted to admit to herself, forget giving Connor that kind of ammunition. Because even though telling her about his past and bringing her to meet his surrogate mother might have melted the walls around her heart, nothing said Connor felt the same.

"Good," he said. "Since I'm not ready to leave."

"Because you haven't figured Todd out yet?"

Connor scoffed. "I did that a long time ago. No, it's you I'm still trying to figure out."

This time it was Kelsey's turn to laugh. "I'm no mystery. I've already spilled all my secrets."

"I think there's more to discover. But I've already figured out a few things on my own. Like how you feel in my arms…how you taste when I kiss you…how I can make you blush without even trying."

Feeling her face heat, Kelsey protested, "Like you aren't trying right now."

"Naw," he said with a grin that did more than make her face heat as he lifted a hand and traced a pattern on her cheek. "If I was really trying to make you blush, I'd tell you how much this star on your cheek turns me on—especially when I think about all the other shapes I might find…and where I might find them."

Kelsey swallowed. She'd spent her whole life hating the freckles that marked her pale skin, but in a split second, in a single sentence, Connor had made her forget every teasing comment, every self-conscious thought.

"Connor." The lone word was all she could manage, but every bit of the emotion she felt echoed in her voice.

Making a sound deep in his throat that could have been a groan, he protested, "Don't look at me like that or I'll end up doing something not meant to be done in public."

Kelsey did lower her gaze, from the hunger in his eyes and

past his too-tempting lips, to stare at his throat. Not because of what he'd said, but because she didn't have the courage to look him in the face and say what she wanted to say. "There are…more private places."

Connor's arms flexed, pulling her closer, and his voice was a deep rumble in her ear as he said, "My hotel room."

Seemingly without conscious thought, an image flashed in Kelsey's mind—Emily leaving Connor's room—and she blurted out, "My house."

Bringing their dance to a halt, Connor stepped back slightly and nudged her chin up. "Are you sure?"

Even though he was asking about so much more than a simple destination, Kelsey met his gaze and repeated, "My house."

She felt slightly guilty as Connor pulled her through the restaurant. "Shouldn't we say goodbye?"

"Maria'll understand," Connor insisted without breaking stride.

Deciding she'd rather not think about how much the woman might understand, Kelsey focused on keeping up with Connor's long strides. Her heart pounded wildly in her chest, but the crazed rhythm had less to do with how fast they were going and so much more to do with what would happen once they got back to her place. And Kelsey didn't think Connor could walk fast enough….

And he must have felt the same, she realized when they reached the car. Instead of unlocking the door, Connor turned and pulled her into his arms.

"I've wanted to do this from the moment I saw you."

The husky words would have been easier to believe had Kelsey spoken them, but coming from Connor, they sent a thrill rushing through her as enticing as his kiss. "You wanted to do this at the airport?"

"At the airport. In your car on the way from the airport. The first time we came to the restaurant." His voice dropped to a husky murmur. "My hotel room."

Kelsey shivered, her thoughts instantly turning to the king-size bed where she wouldn't have to imagine the press of Connor's body against her own. His green eyes glowed as if he'd read her thoughts and was right there…in his hotel bed…with her.

Ducking his head, he caught her lips in a kiss that picked up right where the last had left off. The hunger and intensity didn't have to build; passion and desire had shimmered between them all evening like desert heat. Kelsey sank her hands into his dark hair, her fingers sifting through the silky strands. With Connor leaning against the side of the car, Kelsey didn't have to stretch to reach his mouth; they were perfectly aligned—lips to lips, chest to chest, thigh to thigh.

Connor slid his hands down her back, his fingers claiming the soft flesh of her hips as he pulled her tighter into the vee of his body. Kelsey thought if it were possible to pass out from pure pleasure, she might sink to the ground on the spot.

Instead, she broke away from his kiss. Hiding her face against his neck, she murmured, "My house, remember?" And then she gave in to temptation and pressed her mouth to the strong column of his throat, right where his pulse pounded in time with the pulsing Latin beat coming from the restaurant.

His throat jerked as he swallowed, and he pushed away from the car door without breaking their embrace. He reached back for the door handle and fumbled for a second before he broke away with a muffled curse and twisted around to get a better grip. But instead of pulling the door open, Connor paused, hand in the air as if he'd forgotten what he was doing. Seeming to shake off the hesitation, he opened the door for her.

But in that split-second hesitation, the intensity dissipated like smoke from a doused fire. Her heart still pounded from the kiss, and her breath was far from steady, but the mood had definitely changed. He wouldn't meet her gaze, and Kelsey couldn't help wondering… "Connor, what's wrong? Did I do something—"

"No," he bit out. His fierce expression lessened when he saw her flinch, but frustration filled his movements as he ran a hand through his hair. "No, you didn't do anything wrong. It's just—this is crazy. *You* make me crazy! I haven't made out with a girl in a car since Emily, and now here I am with another Wilson—"

His words cut off abruptly, but not before the small thrill Kelsey experienced at the thought of driving Connor McClane crazy was buried by a wave of doubt and insecurity as she imagined Connor and Emily making out in a car.

And—could this really *get* any worse—not just any car. The vintage Mustang belonged to Javy, who'd undoubtedly owned it for years. Back when Connor would have borrowed the hot car to pick up Emily…

Humiliation burning in her cheeks, Kelsey wanted nothing more than to go home, but she dreaded getting in that car. It didn't matter that she and Connor had already driven all over town in it; now, all she could see was Emily in the passenger seat, wind whipping through her blond hair. Emily, searching for a favorite song on the radio. Emily, slipping into the back seat where Connor waited…

"This was a mistake."

"Kelsey—"

"Can we go?" she interrupted. Maybe if she closed her eyes, she could picture herself somewhere else.

"No."

"What?"

Connor's dark frown told her she'd definitely heard right the first time. "No. I'm not gonna let you run off."

"There's nothing else to talk about, Connor. You and Emily—"

"All right. Fine. Let's talk about how there hasn't been a 'me and Emily' for *years*. I can't change my past, and I can't change yours."

"*My* past?"

"How much of this is about me and Emily? And how much of it is about *you* and Emily? How many times have you felt you couldn't live up to your cousins? How many times have the Wilsons made you feel second best?"

How many? Kelsey couldn't count the numerous times she'd tried walking in her cousins' footsteps only to fall in disgrace again and again. "Uncle Gordon and Aunt Charlene treated me *exactly* like they treated Aileen and Emily. But that was the problem. I'm—not like those girls."

"You don't have to be, Kelsey. You're you. That's more than enough."

Honesty and desire glowed in Connor's eyes. But as much as she longed to believe him, as she slid into the passenger seat Kelsey couldn't help feeling like she was trying yet again to fill Emily's place.

Shoving the key into the ignition, Connor started the car, and they were silent throughout the ride back to Kelsey's; the rumble of the engine was the only sound. Only as they pulled into her driveway did she find the courage to ask the question shouting through her thoughts the whole time.

"Why did you stop? If it wasn't about Emily—"

Connor sighed. "We were in the middle of a public parking lot where anyone could walk by. I should have the self-control to keep my hands to myself. But being back here has me acting like a hotheaded kid again. *You* make me feel like a hotheaded kid," he practically growled, not sounding the least bit happy about the idea. "Not Emily. *You*."

"I want to believe you. But this is all happening so fast, and it isn't easy to change how I feel after a matter of days!"

"I know. But I'm gonna keep trying."

Connor walked her to the front door, where he leaned close, giving her ample time to pull away. If his earlier kiss had struck like a flash of lightning, this was like the slow promise of a sunrise. Kelsey felt the gentle rays first, the touch of warmth against her cheeks as his fingers slid into her hair. And then light blazed behind her eyelids as he kissed her.

Heat poured through her, starting where his mouth brushed against hers then spreading out to all parts of her body, all the way down to her tingling fingertips and toes. Just when he'd left her knees weak and her willpower completely shaken, he eased away, ending the kiss slowly, reluctantly. "I want to see you tomorrow."

"I can't—"

"Kelsey."

"Not because of, well, anything. I'm busy tomorrow."

"With your shop?"

Kelsey shook her head regretfully. "The shop will have to wait a few days. I'm meeting Emily for brunch, and then we're going shopping for bridesmaids' gifts. Assuming that doesn't take all day, I have to meet with a friend who's putting together an audiovisual presentation for the reception."

"What time?"

"In the afternoon."

"Dunworthy has a meeting set up for tomorrow at six. Interested in another stakeout?"

Kelsey forced herself not to look over at the Mustang. The vehicle had somehow turned into so much more than a simple car. It was a physical reminder of Connor's past with Emily. A past Kelsey wasn't sure she could ignore. "Do I even want to know how you came across the information?"

"Nothing illegal. I got it the old-fashioned way. I overheard a conversation he was having on his cell phone." Connor frowned. "Well, I guess the cell phone part isn't old-fashioned, but the eavesdropping was."

"It could be nothing. A dead end like the other day."

"Could be. Wanna find out?" His eyebrows rose in exaggerated challenge, and Kelsey couldn't say no.

"See you tomorrow."

Kelsey knew she should open the door and step inside instead of gazing after Connor like a lovesick teenager, but she couldn't tear her gaze away as he walked down her driveway to the car.

He turned back before she had the chance to duck indoors, seeming unsurprised to find her staring after him. "There's something you should know, Kelsey. I might have kissed your cousin in this car. But I never slept with her."

"In the car?"

His lips kicked up in a smile, but the look in his eyes was completely serious. "Or anywhere else."

Chapter Eight

The next afternoon, standing in her sun-filled kitchen, Kelsey poured steaming black coffee into a thermal mug. She'd tossed and turned most of the night, her sleep plagued by dreams. Even now, she was haunted by images of gliding down an endless, rose-strewn runner toward her groom—toward Connor—only to watch, helpless, as he smiled his devastating smile and walked away with Emily.

"It's just a stupid dream," she muttered, as if speaking the words aloud might give them more strength. "I'm not marrying Connor. I'm not *falling* for Connor."

So she'd had temporary a lapse of judgment, of sanity. She'd been caught in the moment—the restaurant's party atmosphere, the sexy rhythm of the music that had seeped into her soul and pulsed in her veins…

Oh, who are you kidding? an all-too-knowing voice

demanded. She hadn't been caught up in the moment; she'd been caught up in the man.

Maybe she should ask Emily how she'd dated Connor for months *without* sleeping with him. Although Emily never divulged intimate details, Kelsey assumed they had made love. Now that she'd met Connor, it seemed even harder to believe Emily—or any woman—could resist.

Knowing now that Emily *had* resisted made Kelsey wonder if her cousin's feelings for Connor were as strong as she'd once believed, or if Connor was right and Emily had only been using him. What was it he'd said—he was Emily's lone act of rebellion? But even if that were true, it didn't necessarily change his feelings. Maybe coming back wasn't about picking up where they'd left off, but about finally taking that relationship further.

Her stomach felt more than a little sick at the thought, and she thrust the glass pot back into the machine, grabbed the to-go lid and slapped it onto the mug. But her aim must have been slightly off, and the cup tipped, splashing coffee over the countertop.

Gasping, Kelsey dove for a manila envelope lying nearby, snatching it out of the way of the java flood. She clutched the package to her chest with a relieved sigh. Emily's life in pictures filled the envelope, most dating back to the days prior to digital CDs.

Kelsey shuddered at the thought of telling her aunt she'd ruined the photos of Emily's first piano recital, first ballet, first play. She had to get back in control. Her near destruction of the photographs was a small symptom of a larger problem.

She was letting Connor get under her skin.

She'd taken possession of her own shop the day before, the realization of a dream that sometimes seemed as old as she was. Her thoughts should have been consumed by plans for polishing the place until it shined, expanding her nonexistent advertising budget, hiring the support staff Lisa had mentioned.

Instead Connor filled her thoughts and her dreams, and was far too close to edging his way into her heart. Was this how her mother felt when she met her father? Kelsey wondered. Had Donnie Mardell become more important to Olivia than her own hopes and dreams? More important than her own family?

Kelsey forced herself not to panic. Surely she wouldn't make that big a mistake, not with her mother's life as an example. How many times had Olivia warned Kelsey to rely on herself and not to risk leaning on someone who would let her down in the end?

"Wilson women against the world," Kelsey murmured, the familiar motto calming her as she set the envelope safely aside and unrolled a swath of paper towels.

The sudden sound of the doorbell caught her off guard. She didn't have time for unexpected guests any more than she had time for unexpected doubts. Dropping the paper towels over the spilled coffee, she headed toward the front door as the bell pealed again. After a quick glance through the peephole, Kelsey pulled the door open.

As if her thoughts had somehow conjured him out of thin air, Connor leaned against the doorway. How was it that he looked better every time she saw him? Was it because she now knew his shoulders were as strong as they looked? How solid his chest had felt beneath her hands? How his hair had felt like warm silk against her fingers? And how his mouth had worked magic against her own?

"Hey, Kelsey," he said before striding inside.

Trailing after him as if *he* owned the place and she was the uninvited guest, she asked, "What are you doing here?"

He stopped to face her, a frown replacing his cocky smile. "I thought you were coming with me. Todd's meeting, remember?"

"That's not until six," she protested as she walked into the kitchen to the mess she'd left behind.

"What happened in here?"

As much as she would have liked to lay the blame at Connor's feet, she said, "Don't ask." She balled up the soggy paper towels, groaning at the coffee-colored stain left behind on her beige Formica, and tossed them into the trash. She grabbed the envelope of photographs and her purse and brushed by Connor on the way to the door.

"I have to meet my friend about the audio-video presentation for the reception, remember?"

Connor shrugged. "So we go there first and stake out the meeting after."

She should say no. She should keep him far, far away, and not just because of the havoc he might wreak on Emily's wedding. "I'm already running late." As a flat-out denial, the words fell short.

"So let's go."

"Okay, but—" Kelsey straightened her shoulders. "I'll drive." She should have known it wouldn't make any difference how matter-of-factly she made that statement, Connor would see through it.

Judging by the look in his dark eyes, he did see—straight through to her heart. "Sounds like I need to work even harder."

"Connor—"

"It's okay," he interrupted. He stepped closer, and Kelsey tensed, half in preparation to defend her decision and half in anticipation of his approach. But nothing could have readied her for Connor cupping the back of her neck and pulling her into a kiss.

To her dismay, it ended before it even began. A quick press of lips again her own, and then it was over. And Kelsey had to clench her hands into fists to keep from grabbing the front of Connor's T-shirt and demand that he do it again. That he do it *right*.

As he pulled away, he gazed at her flustered—heated—face and smiled. "I never could resist a challenge."

"Are you sure this is right?" Kelsey asked.

Connor's directions to Todd's meeting had brought them to a Scottsdale neighborhood that rivaled her aunt and uncle's when it came to exclusivity, opulence and sheer expense. The winding roads led them past multileveled mansions surrounded by artfully arranged desert landscapes, sparkling water fountains and wrought-iron gates.

They were practically the first words she'd spoken since they'd dropped off Emily's pictures earlier. Kelsey had been grateful to focus on the straightforward directions of right, left, north and south rather than try to traverse the dangerous path her heart was traveling down.

Catching a street sign carved into a boulder, Connor said, "Turn here. This is it."

"Nice place." Irony filled Kelsey's voice at the understated description. The two-story home had a circular entryway, decorative columns, and floor-to-ceiling windows.

When she tapped on the brake, Connor insisted, "Don't stop." With a glance out the back, he said, "Okay. We should be good here. Go ahead and turn around."

Kelsey glanced in the rearview mirror. Thanks to a neighboring oleander hedge, she could barely see the house. Hopefully Todd wouldn't notice the two of them lurking in her car a block away. After turning the car to face the house, she asked, "Now what?"

"Now we wait."

Kelsey sighed. "I don't think I have the patience for being a private eye."

Connor's lips quirked into a smile. "That's okay. I'm not planning on changing careers and becoming a wedding coordinator, either. Besides, it's almost six."

"Todd will be late," Kelsey predicted. "He's always late." Tardiness was one of her aunt's pet peeves. A sign, according to Charlene Wilson, that showed a person believed his time more important than those around him. Somehow, though, she smothered her annoyance when it came to Todd.

"So he isn't perfect after all."

"I never said he was."

Connor made a thoughtful sound but hardly embraced her words. No surprise. *She* wasn't the one Connor wanted to impress. He was determined to prove her aunt and uncle wrong about Todd. But would that really be enough to make Connor let go of the past? Would Connor ever believe he was good enough, or would it take being good enough for Emily for him to see his own worth?

She sighed and sank lower in the seat, not wanting to think too hard on the answer to that question. Seconds later a car rounded the corner, and Kelsey impulsively grabbed Connor's arm. "Look!"

Her heart skipped a beat at the feel of his warm skin and muscle beneath her palm. When he leaned closer for a better look, her pulse quickened.

A woman sat behind the wheel of the luxury car, and Kelsey wondered if Connor might get his proof. Neither of them spoke as they waited for Todd's arrival and the meeting to unfold. Ten minutes later, Todd's SUV pulled up. When he climbed from the vehicle and casually glanced in their direction, Kelsey gasped.

"Relax," Connor advised. "He can't see us."

As she focused on the scene outside, Kelsey frowned in confusion. Todd flashed a smile at the woman as he walked up the driveway, but when he reached out to shake the woman's hand, the gesture was not only platonic but professional.

Connor swore. "I don't believe it. That woman's a Realtor. There's a lockbox on the front door."

Sure enough, the brunette led Todd to the front door, where she opened the small box and pulled out a key. With a flourish she turned the handle and waved Todd inside. Since Emily hadn't mentioned a new home, Kelsey wondered if the place was a wedding gift. Despite her questionable opinion of the man, she couldn't help feeling impressed by the romantic and extravagant gesture.

"We should go."

"Just—wait," Connor ground out.

A few minutes later Todd and the Realtor exited the house. Judging by the smile on the woman's face, Kelsey assumed the meeting had gone well. She shook Todd's hand again, nodded enthusiastically over whatever he said, and waved as he drove off.

"That's that," Kelsey said as she reached for the ignition. Connor stopped her with a touch, closing his hand over hers and slipping the keys out of her grasp before she ever realized his intention. "Connor, what—"

"Come on."

Connor kept a firm grip on Kelsey's hand as they walked toward the house despite her repeated tugs and her sharply whispered protests. As long as he had the keys, she couldn't go anywhere without him. So why exactly was she trying to pull away? The better question: why was he still hanging on?

"Connor! Stop! We're going to get caught!"

"Doing what? You know, I'm really starting to wonder about this guilty conscience of yours."

"You should," she muttered, "considering I didn't *have* one until you came along."

The front door opened, and Kelsey dug in her heels deep enough to leave divots in the grass. The Realtor looked surprised, but only for a moment. Professional smile in place, she asked, "Are you two interested in the property?"

Kelsey's grip tightened on Connor's hand. A quick glance in her direction revealed a panicked look that screamed *busted*. Fortunately, he had a bit more experience when it came to covering his butt, as well as any curvaceous female backside he dragged along for the ride.

Flashing a smile, he said, "My fiancée and I were driving through the neighborhood and noticed the lockbox. We don't have an appointment, but—"

"Oh, I'd love to show you around."

The inside of the house lived up to the exterior's elegant promise. Gorgeous views, a wide-open floor plan and every upgrade imaginable—travertine floors, granite countertops, stainless-steel appliances. The decor matched the surrounding desert with golds and browns and a hint of green.

"The house is beautiful," Kelsey said, once she'd realized the Realtor wasn't going to accuse them of trespassing.

"It's only been on the market a few days," the Realtor said as she concluded the six-bedroom, four-bath, media-room tour back at the front entry. "Another couple is interested in the property for their first place."

"Right. 'Cause this is the perfect starter home," Connor muttered.

Kelsey opened her mouth, ready to insist she didn't need a mansion, only to remember she and Connor weren't engaged. They wouldn't need a starter home or any other kind.

"Out of curiosity," he said, "can you tell how much the other couple is offering?"

The woman's smile was both sympathetic and hopeful. "I don't think money was an issue, but I have several other properties I'd be more than willing to show you." She pulled a card from her pocket and held it out to Connor. "Give me a call, and I can give you a list of houses that might fit your lifestyle."

Connor managed a nod, but as they walked out of the house, he crushed her card in his hand. *"Fit my lifestyle,"* he bit out. "Not to mention my budget."

His body thrummed with frustration, and Kelsey expected him to chuck the card into the street. Finally he shoved it into his pocket and stalked toward her car.

Kelsey didn't bother to ask for her keys back when Connor automatically went to the driver's-side door. Instead, she slid into the passenger seat. Trying for a practical tone, she said, "We already knew Todd has money."

"Yeah, we did," he said with a grim twist to his lips. "I'm starting to think the guy might be perfect after all."

"No one's perfect," Kelsey insisted. "Everyone has their faults and—"

"And the Wilsons certainly saw mine."

"You were a kid," she argued. "You can't believe what happened back then has anything to do with the man you are now."

Muttering what sounded suspiciously like "Don't be so sure," he cranked the engine and peeled away from the house.

Kelsey slapped a hand down on the armrest, but her tight grip slowly loosened. Despite his obvious frustration, Connor kept the car under perfect control. Within minutes they were on the freeway, but the turn he took wouldn't lead to her house.

Streetlights flickered on as daylight faded, marking the way toward an older part of Phoenix. They passed an abandoned drive-in, a boarded-up gas station and liquor store, the only business likely to thrive in such a depressing neighborhood. She could have asked where they were going, but as they drove by houses with peeling paint and duct-taped windows, lawns choked by weeds and neglect, she already knew.

A few minutes later Connor braked to a halt, gravel crunching beneath the wheels. He didn't say anything or make a move to get out of the car. With both hands still gripping the wheel, he stared at the trailer park across the street.

Kelsey had seen plenty of mobile home communities before. Manufactured homes, they were called now. Houses laid out in neat rows, with flower beds and swimming pools like any other nice, little neighborhood.

This was not that kind of place. The dirt lot, with its haphazard trailers and junkyard of vehicles, made the use of the term *park* an irony. The murmur of the engine was the only sound until Connor gave a sudden, harsh bark of laughter. "This is it. Where I came from. Who I am."

"No, it isn't." Unlocking her seat belt, Kelsey shifted on the seat to face him. The fading sunset glowed in the distance, casting his profile in bronze. "This isn't you any more than where I grew up makes me who I am."

"You're a Wilson. You're—"

Connor cut himself off, giving Kelsey the chance to interject, "I *am* a Wilson. But I'm not Emily. I'm not Aileen. And I wasn't raised like them."

"I know. On the outside looking in," he said, as he turned to look at her. Face-to-face, Kelsey could see the gold flecks in his green eyes. "That's what I thought when I first met you. The Wilson outsider."

That insight, pointing how she'd always felt—a part of and yet apart from her family—made Kelsey feel as if Connor knew her better than anyone. His words and the tenderness in his gaze crept inside her chest and wrapped around her heart. Somehow, being on the outside didn't matter so much when he was there with her. "You were right," she said softly.

But if he could somehow see inside her, Kelsey felt she was starting to do the same and getting to know the real Connor. His coming back to Arizona had to do with more than simply disliking Todd or even with proving her family wrong. His return had to do with a guilt *inside* him. As if by stopping the wedding, he could somehow make up for a past he could not change.

"And maybe that's why I can see you so clearly. This isn't who you are, Connor," she repeated. "Maybe it's who you were, but that's all. I've seen who you are now. You're a good friend, a good man—"

A sound rose in Connor's throat, part denial, part despair, and he jerked open the car door as if desperate for escape. Kelsey winced as he slammed it behind him, but she didn't hesitate to follow. He couldn't shut her out that easily!

"Connor, wait!" She scrambled out of the car after him, trying to keep up with the long strides that carried him across the weed-and-trash-strewn lot. She gasped as her foot hit an uneven spot on the heaved asphalt. She took a tottering step, arms windmilling for balance, but gravity won the battle, and she hit the ground.

"Kelsey!" Connor swore beneath his breath. "Are you okay?"

With a close-up view of the weeds and trash littering the trailer lot, Kelsey felt a moment's relief that she hadn't landed in a black, greasy puddle inches from her face.

"I'm fine," she insisted, even as Connor leaned down to help her up. Flames of heat licked at her. Some from the heel of her hand that had scraped across the pavement, some from the blazing heat bouncing off the black surface, but mostly from the sheer embarrassment of Connor witnessing her utter clumsiness. "Really, I—" She sucked in a quick breath as he took her hand to pull her to her feet.

Beneath his tanned skin, Connor went pale. "You're hurt."

Taking a hesitant glance down, she breathed out a sigh of

relief. "It's nothing. Only a scratch." A few thin lines of blood showed through the abraded skin on her palm, but other than the slight sting, she was fine.

Running his thumb gently across the scrape as if he could heal by touch alone, Connor said, "I never should have brought you here. It's my fault."

"It was an accident that could have happened in front of my own shop! It is *not* your fault." Gentling her voice, she added, "You're not responsible for every bad thing that happens. I don't know why you feel that way, but Connor, looking for dirt on Todd won't change things. Especially when—" she took a deep breath, reluctant to say the words but knowing she had to "—when it doesn't seem like there's anything to find."

"There is," he said flatly, refusing to consider failure. "Jake's still following a lead in St. Louis, and I'm not giving up here. I know guys like Dunworthy. He can only keep up this golden boy B.S. for so long. He's gonna slip. The closer it gets to the wedding, the more pressure there's gonna be, and he'll slip. I know it—"

"In your gut," Kelsey finished with a sigh. She turned her hand within his. Even through that light touch, she could feel the tension tightening his shoulders and arms and radiating down to the fingers she linked with hers. As gently as she could, she suggested, "Maybe it's time to stop listening to your gut."

"I can't." He gritted the words out of clenched teeth.

"Why not?"

"Because the last time I didn't listen, a woman was nearly killed."

Connor reached over and cranked the car's air conditioner to full blast, even though he doubted the frigid air would help. Sweat soaked the back of his neck, but it had little to do with the outside temperature despite the hundred-plus heat. The relentless sun, which bounced off every shiny surface to pinpoint on him as if he were a bug trapped beneath a kid's magnifying glass, had nothing on Kelsey's questioning glances.

He felt as if he was burning up from the inside out...all thanks to four little words.

You're a good man.

Kelsey had looked him straight in the eye with those words, her soft voice packing the same punch as a sonic boom. He didn't deserve that kind of faith. He'd disappointed too many women in the past: his mother, Emily, Cara Mitchell...

The more Kelsey trusted in him, the more he longed to believe in that trust, the worse it would be when he finally, irrevocably, let her down.

He sucked in a lungful of air, the heat threatening to suffocate him. He needed space—space to breathe, space to run, space that wasn't filled with Kelsey's cinnamon scent, her concerned glances, her soft voice...

"Connor..."

She was going to ask him what happened with Cara. His grip tightened on the passenger armrest, inches from the door handle and escape...even if escape meant paying the price for hitting the ground running at forty miles an hour.

No, telling truth was better. More painful, maybe, but at least Kelsey would realize he wasn't the man she thought he was.

"One of the first things I learned after opening my business was that you don't turn down work. You might not like the job, you might not like the client, but if it pays the bills, you take the job."

Kelsey slowed for a red light. Freedom beckoned, but Connor kept his hand on the armrest. "I didn't like Doug Mitchell. I didn't like the job, even though catching cheating spouses has always been part of the P.I. business. My gut told me he was bad news, but I didn't listen."

Silence filled the car, and Kelsey's gaze was as tangible as the trickle of sweat running from his temple. "What happened?" she murmured.

"I did what I was paid to do. I followed Cara Mitchell. To the grocery store, the salon, the gym… It was tedious, boring," he added, reminded of the conversation they'd had waiting for Dunworthy's meeting. "And I thought maybe Doug was wrong. That he was worried about nothing and his marriage was one of the few that would make it."

His hand cramped, and try as he might, he couldn't loosen his grip. His fingers seemed to have melded into the padded vinyl. "But then, one Tuesday, Cara drove south on the freeway. And I kept thinking it was Tuesday, and Tuesday was art class. So why was she going in the wrong direction? Before long, she ended up at a motel and when this guy opened the door, I thought here we go. I was wrong, and Doug was right."

"So she was having an affair?"

"Sure seemed that way," he said with a grimace. "Meeting some guy, staying behind closed shades, and leaving an hour later with her hair mussed and her makeup smudged… What else would you think?"

"What did *you* think?"

"I—I didn't know. It was suspicious, sure. But it wasn't proof, you know? Not one hundred percent take-it-to-the-bank proof. And in my gut I didn't believe it. Maybe I'd gotten too close. It happens, P.I.s falling for their marks, but that wasn't it. I wasn't attracted to Cara Mitchell. But I guess I—*liked* her. Respected her. She smiled at kids in the store, took the time to talk to little old ladies. She told cashiers when they gave her back too much change! I just didn't believe she was having an affair. But her husband wanted an update. He was the client, and he paid to know what I'd seen."

"But…you didn't actually *see* anything."

Connor winced at her logical protest. "And that's exactly what I told Doug. Only it didn't matter. Far as he was concerned, I'd seen enough and was off the job."

If only it had ended there…

"I couldn't get over my gut feeling that I was wrong. Wrong about Cara, wrong about what I'd seen. I thought if I followed her a few more days, I'd know for sure." Kelsey hit the gas as another red light turned green, and Connor desperately wished he was still the one driving. He'd go from zero to sixty in a split second if pure speed would give him the chance to outrun his memories.

"I was across the street watching when Doug came home from work in the middle of the day. I don't know if he hoped to catch Cara in the act, or if his rage and jealousy got to be too much. I heard her scream. I rushed into the house."

"But you stopped Doug, right?"

"Not soon enough. Cara was badly beaten and nearly unconscious by the time I got into the house and pulled Doug off her."

He could still see her, bloody and bruised, lying on the floor because of him. "The guy she went to see was a counselor. He'd rented the motel room to give her a safe place to stay, but he couldn't convince her to leave Doug, even though he'd been abusing her for years. If I'd listened to my gut—"

"But you *did* listen. You listened when you knew you didn't have the whole story. Cara Mitchell would likely be dead if not for you. You saved her life, Connor."

"If I hadn't taken the job—"

"Someone else would have. Someone who wouldn't have *cared* about a gut feeling. Once the job was over, that would have been it. They wouldn't have given Cara Mitchell a second thought."

Connor opened his mouth, ready to argue, but Kelsey's words ran deeper into his soul, soothing some of his guilt. Not that he believed he was any kind of hero. But he'd witnessed Doug's determination. He wasn't the type of guy to give up easily. Had Connor turned down the job, Doug *would* have found another P.I.

"Maybe—maybe you're right."

As Kelsey stopped for another red light, she turned to meet his gaze straight on. "I know I am," she said with the same certainty as when she'd vowed he was a good man.

Would she still think so when he told her about the money her uncle had paid him to leave town? No one had ever put the kind of faith and trust in him that Kelsey did, and every ounce of self-preservation inside him resisted the thought of telling her the truth.

Even if she gave him the chance to explain, even if she understood his reasons, the truth would change things. And yet he had to tell her. If he wanted her to believe he truly was a good man, if *he* wanted to believe that, he had to tell her.

But not tonight. There'd already been enough revelations about the past. And in case finding out about the money did change things, well, Connor selfishly wanted to hold on to Kelsey's faith in him for a little while longer.

"You know, this isn't necessary." Side by side on her couch, Kelsey watched as Connor placed the last piece of tape over the bandage on her hand. As far as a protest went, her words were pretty weak. Just like the rest of her, she thought.

Connor smoothed his thumb across her palm, his gaze intent on his task. A lock of dark hair had fallen across his forehead, shadowing his eyes and adding the slightest touch of softness to the hard planes and angles of his features.

Little shocks zapped up her arm, but it had nothing to do with pain. If she hadn't been sitting next to Connor, she probably would have melted into a puddle at his feet.

"It would have been tricky to do this on your own. Besides, it was the least I could do," he said, guilt and concern filling his expression as his hand rose to brush her hair back from her cheek.

And Kelsey couldn't resist his caring side any more than she'd been able to resist the other facets of his personality: the bad boy, the loyal friend, the protective warrior. They all combined to make up the man Connor was—the man Kelsey loved.

Her every instinct shouted in denial, but it was a useless protest. She'd been falling for him since the moment they met, a slow-motion tumble that landed her in this place, in this time, in his arms…

The intimacy of the moment pulled her closer. Her job, her family, even Connor's relationship with Emily seemed like distant, insignificant concerns. His fingers tunneled into her hair. Her amazing hair, Kelsey thought, recalling the words he'd spoken outside of Todd's office. She hadn't believed him then, but she did now. On the day she confronted him in his hotel room, he'd demanded she prove her loyalty to Emily, and she'd told him actions, not words, proved how a person truly felt. And Connor was a man of action, and he proved his feelings by trusting *her*—with his past, with his close friendship with the Delgados. How could she do anything but trust him in return?

"The last thing I'd ever want to do is hurt you, Kelsey," he vowed, that sense of responsibility carving a groove between his eyebrows.

"You didn't," she promised. "You won't."

Despite her words, doubt lingered in his gaze. Leaning forward, she brushed her lips against his, actions once again backing up words. Because whether Connor knew it or not, she *was* his. Body and soul. She shifted closer but couldn't get close enough.

Her hands charted a course her body longed to make, following a path from his shoulders to his chest, where she could feel his heart pounding a wild rhythm, and to his flat stomach and muscled thighs, which tensed beneath her hands.

Connor's hands stayed buried in her hair, but like the emotional connection moments before, the physical connection was so deep that with her every touch her own body responded. She felt the brush of his fingers trailing from her collarbones down to her breasts, to her stomach, ticklish enough to tremble at the imaginary contact.

Connor ended the kiss for a much needed breath but kept his mouth pressed to her cheek, her jaw, her throat...

A shrill buzz started them both. After the first few bars, Connor recognized his phone's ring tone, but the electronic device—one he never went anywhere without—was the last thing on his mind. He nearly groaned in frustration at the very thought of ending the kiss, of pulling away from Kelsey's embrace.

Maybe his battery would die. Maybe the signal would cut out.

His wishes went unheard as the phone rang again. Desire gradually clearing from her eyes as her breathing slowed, Kelsey pushed at his shoulders, and he had no choice but to back away.

"It's not important," he vowed, hoping his words were true as he fumbled with the phone. "I'll turn it off." He actually had his thumb on the button when he saw the number glowing on the small screen, and hesitated.

Just a split second, but the slight pause didn't get by Kelsey. "Who is it?"

The husky, passion-filled sound of her voice sent another shaft of desire straight to his gut. He could still turn the phone off. Turn it off and pretend the interruption had never taken place. The lie hovered in his thoughts, but meeting her gaze, he couldn't take the easy way out. "It's Emily."

Kelsey's eyes widened, and the warmth in them chilled even as the fire in her cheeks suddenly blazed. "Well, then, you should answer it."

"Kelsey—"

"Answer the phone, Connor."

Biting back a curse, he nearly barked into the phone, "Yeah?"

"Connor…is that you?"

"It's me. What's up?" Silence followed the brusque demand, and wouldn't it figure if the damn signal cut out *now*. "Em? You still there?"

"Yes. I'm here. What are you— Never mind. You sound like you're busy."

Forcing the slang definition of *busy* from his thoughts, he cleared his throat and asked, "What's wrong?"

"Nothing, really. Can't I call without you assuming something's wrong?"

A note of desperation had entered her voice, telling Connor it was more than an assumption. "Yeah, sure you can. So, what's up?"

"I guess I wanted to talk," she offered, uncertainty filling her voice.

Connor couldn't help glancing over at Kelsey. Her face turned away from him, she was determinedly ignoring the conversation going on only a cushion away.

Hesitation cost him for the second time in a matter of minutes when Emily said, "This was a bad idea. I shouldn't have called."

"Em—" The line went silent before he could come up with even a halfhearted protest. Flipping the phone closed, he slid the tiny device back in his pocket.

"What did she say?"

"Not much."

"She didn't say why she called?"

"No." And he didn't care. At least, not nearly as much as he cared about what was going through Kelsey's mind. "Kelsey—"

"It's okay."

"Really?" Connor asked, doubt lacing the word.

But when Kelsey met his gaze, a smile teased her lips. A little shaky around the edges, but a smile just the same. And Connor felt something in his heart catch at her remarkable strength and resiliency. He knew the call had to bring up reminders of his relationship with Emily as well as Kelsey's long-ingrained feelings of inferiority.

"Really," she insisted. "Like you said, we can't change the past, and I think it's time we both moved on."

Chapter Nine

"Kelsey, this is a surprise." Emily rose from the large oak table in her parents' kitchen, where she'd been flipping through a bridal magazine, and gave her a hug.

"I had a free morning and wanted to come by and invite you to breakfast." Kelsey mentally cringed at the half-truth. She *did* have a free morning, but the invitation was an excuse to find out what that phone call to Connor meant.

Emily wrinkled her nose. "I can't. I'll never fit into my wedding dress if I stuff myself with waffles."

So Emily was still dieting. Almost every bride thought about dieting before the big day even if they didn't stick with it. Or need to lose a single pound, Kelsey thought, as Emily walked over to the pantry—slender, graceful, and gorgeous. A powder-blue silk robe wrapped her body, and her hair was pulled back in a simple ponytail.

"You can keep me company while I have some tea and toast," her cousin suggested, a hopeful note coming to her voice.

"I'd love to. It'll give us a chance to talk."

After setting a kettle on the stove, Emily popped a piece of what looked like whole-wheat cardboard into the toaster. "What did you want to talk about?" she asked, once Kelsey declined her offer of toast in favor of fresh strawberries.

About that phone call last night, Kelsey thought. *The one you placed an hour after your oh-so-perfect fiancé met a Realtor at your dream house.*

"Uh…" Unable to jump into the conversation, her mind blanked and the last thing she expected popped out of her mouth. "I saw Matt the other night."

"No!" Looking appropriately horrified and curious, Emily sank back against the tan-and-gold-flecked granite countertops. "What happened?" Before Kelsey could answer, Emily waved off the question. "No, don't start yet."

She plopped a tea bag in a mug the size of a cereal bowl, poured the hot water and dropped her hot toast—sans butter—onto a plate. Settling eagerly onto the chair next to Kelsey, she said, "Okay, tell me everything. Did he beg you to take him back? Has he come to his senses and realized that other woman can't compare to you?"

Kelsey managed a small smile, knowing Emily didn't realize the irony of her words. Kelsey had never told her cousin *she* was the woman Matt was in love with. As blind as Kelsey had been to her ex's infatuation, Emily had missed the signs, as well. Of course, she was used to attracting male attention. Matt's shy and awkward behavior had been nothing new.

"No, he didn't beg me to come back." Though some begging had been involved, she recalled with satisfaction, thinking of Matt pleading with her to call Connor off.

But it was the look in Connor's eyes when he'd touched

her cheek that stayed in her mind, replaying like the romantic comedies she enjoyed. Last night's kiss was another memory that played over and over, and unfortunately her mind didn't come with a handy remote. The images had flickered across her eyelids for hours.

She'd talked a good game last night, declaring the past over and done for both of them, but could it be that easy? Facing Emily on a day when her cousin looked gorgeous—as usual— and Kelsey felt tired and cranky and worn by comparison, could she really believe Connor was over Emily?

Waving the desert-dry toast, Emily decreed, "You're better off without Matt."

"Yeah, that's what—that's what I think, too."

"You're an amazing woman, Kelsey. You're sweet, successful. You own your own business, and you're so totally organized."

Rolling her eyes, Kelsey ignored the heat rising in her cheeks. "I don't know about amazing."

"Do you know how impressed Daddy was when you didn't take money from him to start your business?"

"I couldn't. Your parents have already done so much for me." And Kelsey had never forgotten that her father had gotten her mother pregnant—with her—in the hope of getting his hands on the Wilson fortune. She was *not* her father's daughter, and she flat-out refused to step anywhere near the tracks he'd left behind. "I couldn't take money from them. Your mother's referrals have been the real boost the business needed."

Referrals that hinged on Emily's wedding going off without a hitch.

You're going to be a success with or without Emily's wedding. Connor's words echoed in her mind. *A single setback won't stop you.*

He was right, Kelsey realized. Weddings Amour was her

calling, her dream, one she would fight for. One wedding was not going to make or break her business.

Just like her family's approval or disapproval would not make or break *her*. She was stronger than her cousin, and if Connor was right about Todd, Kelsey needed to do what she could to look out for Emily.

With the reminder in mind, Kelsey said, "Enough about me. What's Todd up to this morning? Why aren't you two lovebirds hanging out?"

"He and Daddy went golfing."

Golf. Kelsey had never understood the sport. Especially not during the summer when tee-off times were at the break of dawn. "I'm surprised you didn't go with them."

Emily, along with looking chic in linen capris and argyle print polo shirts, was an amazing golfer. She gave a soft laugh. "You know. Gentlemen only, ladies forbidden."

"Hmm." That long-ago restriction, the acronym that gave golf its name, might have something to do with Kelsey's aversion to the sport. "You probably would have beaten them. Which might be why they didn't invite you."

"Oh, I wouldn't have—" A soft blush lit Emily's cheeks, and she turned her attention to peeling the crust from her toast.

"Wouldn't what, Em? Play to win?" Between the abbreviation of her cousin's name and the challenge she'd issued, Kelsey felt like a ventriloquist's dummy with Connor pulling the strings and his words coming out of her mouth. But as worried as she might be by his influence, her cousin's possible answer worried her more.

"Come on, Kelsey," Emily said, "you know how fragile the male ego can be."

"I can understand why you wouldn't want to show Todd up, but do you really want to live your life playing second best?"

"It's only a silly game of golf, Kelsey."

"I think it's more than that."

Emily's smile faded away, and Kelsey felt like she'd caught a glimpse of the real woman lost behind the beautiful facade. "Todd is a wonderful man. I love him. Really, I do, and I can't wait until we're married."

Kelsey had heard the words before, but this was the first time she sensed a touch of desperation underscoring the refrain. "Emily—" she began, but the opening of the kitchen door interrupted what she might have said.

"Kelsey, good morning," Charlene greeted Kelsey with raised eyebrows that seemed to ask why she wasn't keeping an eye on Connor as she'd been told. "I didn't expect to see you here."

Emily flashed a smile she'd perfected years ago, during her beautiful baby and pageant days. The slight tilt of her head, the perfect curve to her lips, the flash of white teeth. The smile was camera ready, but like an image captured on photo paper, it wasn't real. The moment and whatever else they might have said was gone.

"Kelsey came by to talk about the shower tomorrow and go over a few last-minute wedding details," she filled in, but the excuse only made Charlene frown.

"What details?"

"We're, um, we're going over the items Emily will carry down the aisle. You know, the something borrowed, something blue…"

"That's already decided, remember?" Charlene filled her own teacup and set the pot back on the stove. "You'll wear my pearls as something borrowed. I wore them at my wedding, and Aileen wore them at hers. It's tradition."

"Oh, right," Emily agreed. Kelsey knew her cousin thought pearls old-fashioned. Instead of making a fuss, though, Emily bowed to her mother's wishes. An argument built inside Kelsey like the steam building in the teapot, but what good would it do to stand up for her cousin when Emily wouldn't stand up for herself? "My bouquet will be tied with a blue ribbon, and my ring is new. So that leaves something old."

"I have a lace handkerchief that belonged to your great-grandmother." Adding a tea bag to the water, Charlene said, "Kelsey, run upstairs, would you? The handkerchief is in the bottom drawer of my dresser."

Charlene turned back to the counter to add sugar to her tea, and Kelsey wondered if her aunt was sending her on the errand because she didn't want to leave Emily and Kelsey alone. Still, she agreed. "I'll go get it."

During the years Kelsey had lived with her aunt and uncle, she rarely intruded on their sanctuary. Once she stepped inside, she saw the dresser had three bottom drawers. Which one would hold the handkerchief Charlene mentioned?

Kelsey started at the nearest drawer and found a collection of family mementos. Glancing through the items, she realized these were her uncle's belongings, not her aunt's. A packet of envelopes nestled among a worn-out glove and baseball cap. She slid the drawer halfway closed before she noticed the address on the top envelope. A Nevada location that had once been her home.

Hesitating, she reached for the letters. Kelsey flipped through one after the other, noting the changing addresses and postmark dates as well as the undeniable "return to sender" printed across the fronts.

"You can open them if you want."

Kelsey jumped at the sound of her uncle's voice. Gordon stood framed by the doorway. Dressed in tan slacks and a blue polo shirt, he looked more casual than usual. The hint of sunburn above his close-cropped beard told of the morning hours spent on the golf course, and his silver-blond hair had recently lost some of its structured style. But regardless of what he wore, her uncle was a tall, handsome man whose presence demanded attention and respect.

Clutching the letters to her chest, she said, "Aunt Charlene sent me to look for Great-grandmother's handkerchief. For the wedding. You know, something old—"

Gordon waved a hand. "The middle drawer is your aunt's."

Ignoring the errand that had sent her to the room, Kelsey held out the letters. "You wrote to my mother?"

Gordon nodded. "More times than I can count. But it was all too little, too late."

Too little. Kelsey flipped through the envelopes—years' worth of envelopes, years' worth of effort—seeing nothing little about it. "I don't understand."

"Your grandfather was a hard man. He wouldn't stand for any sign of defiance, and your mother—" Gordon shook his head with a bittersweet smile. "Your mother challenged him from the day she was born. They butted heads constantly, but when she refused to stop seeing your father, that was an impasse neither of them could cross."

Kelsey's hands tightened on the letters at the mention of her father. "Maybe she should have listened."

"She made a bad choice, and at the time I thought your grandfather handled the situation very poorly. Years later I realized how desperate he must have felt to make the ultimatum he did—forcing your mother to choose between her family and your father."

And her mother chose Donnie Mardell. She'd never talked about him, and not until her illness reached a point where there was no hope did she tell Kelsey the whole story. How she had defied her father to leave home with Donnie. How her father refused to accept that decision and paid Donnie to leave town, thinking that would force Olivia to come to heel.

But that plan backfired. Donnie left town, money burning

a hole in his pocket, but Olivia hadn't returned home. Instead, she fled even farther, cutting all contact with her family…to the point where Kelsey hadn't known she *had* any family.

Regret furrowed his forehead. "I'd hoped your mother could forgive me for what she saw as my decision to side with our father." Gordon shook his head. "So stubborn, the both of them. So unwilling to bend."

Instant denial rose up inside Kelsey. "My mother was brave and strong. She took care of herself and me without help from *anyone*."

"And she raised you to do the same, didn't she?"

Kelsey opened her mouth to respond, only to be silenced by her mother's voice echoing in her mind. *You may not have been raised as one of the wealthy Wilsons, but you're better than they are. Hold your head high and prove to them what an amazing young woman I've raised.*

She'd done her best, trying to prove herself instead of simply *being* herself. All the judgments, all the expectations, had her aunt and uncle put them on Kelsey…or had Olivia with her dying words?

Lifting a hand, Gordon brushed his fingertips against the edges of the envelopes, flipping through fifteen years of un-answered pleas. "She was my only sibling. The last link to my childhood and my parents. I never stopped hoping we'd have the chance to overcome the differences of the past. But she was so determined to prove she didn't need anybody." He met Kelsey's gaze with a melancholy grin. "There's no doubt *you* are your mother's daughter."

She'd spent eight years trying to be exactly that. Struggling to prove herself by trying to follow step by humiliating step in her cousins' footprints rather than simply *telling* her aunt and uncle she wasn't cut out for ballet or dressage or the lead role in the school play. Insisting on taking summer jobs to pay for her clothes and books and CDs; refusing to accept her uncle's loan to get her business going.

How many other times had she pushed her aunt and uncle away in her desperation to live up to her mother's stubborn independence? Unlike Olivia, Kelsey hadn't been totally alone, but she *had* followed her mother's footsteps when it came to protecting her heart. She'd kept people at a distance, never letting anyone—even family—too close, so she could never be let down, never be disappointed. Even with Matt…Kelsey saw now she'd purposely picked someone she liked but could never love.

And what about Connor? Had she resisted because she was afraid of his lingering feelings for Emily…or simply because she was afraid? Was she using his past as an excuse the same way her mother had held Gordon's past decisions against him? A reason not to give him—not to give *anyone*— a second chance?

Wilson women against the world. The motto that had once been a battle cry of strength and independence now seemed a cowardly whimper. And an excuse not to trust, not to fall in love…

Swallowing the lump in her throat, she asked, "Why didn't you tell me? Why let me think you'd cut my mother out of your life like your father did?"

Sorrow for the sister he'd lost pulled at Gordon's features. "Olivia was gone, and I didn't want to make you choose between your memory of her—your *good* memories of her— and the truth I could have told you."

Kelsey wondered if she might have been better off knowing the truth, but how could she fault her uncle when he'd made such an unselfish decision? "I'm so sorry, Uncle Gordon."

"Don't be. I know how much your mother meant to you, and I'd never want to take that away. Besides, I'm proud of you, Kelsey. Of your determination and drive. I'm sure your mother would be, as well."

Kelsey tried to answer, but the words were blocked by the lump in her throat. Swallowing, she said, "Uncle Gordon—"

"Kelsey, can't you find the handkerchief?" Charlene entered the bedroom and stepped around her husband. She frowned at the drawer Kelsey had left open. Her heart skipped a beat as her aunt crossed the room. But Charlene merely pushed the drawer shut, opened the correct one and lifted the handkerchief without sparing the envelopes in Kelsey's hand a single glance.

"Here it is," she said with an exasperated sigh. "I might as well hold on to it."

Kelsey blinked, the past falling away as she refocused on the present. "Isn't Emily downstairs?"

"Todd invited her to brunch."

She'd missed her chance to talk to Emily about her feelings for Todd and about the wedding, but Kelsey couldn't think about anything but the letters in her hands.

"Speaking of brunch," Gordon said, "I'm starved. You wouldn't believe the calories I burned beating that future son-in-law of mine. Although I do think he might have let me win."

"Nonsense," Charlene said briskly. "Experience trumps youth every time."

"I, um, should go," Kelsey said, ducking past her aunt. She tried to slip her uncle the letters, but he squeezed her hands and mouthed, "Keep them."

After giving a brief nod, Kelsey jogged down the stairs with her uncle's written words in her hands and his voice in her head.

You are your mother's daughter.

Connor stepped out of the shower, dropped the damp towel onto the marble floor in a limp heap and seriously considered following suit himself. He couldn't remember the last time he'd done enough reps to leave his arms and legs flopping like fish out of water.

His cell phone beeped as he pulled on a pair of well-worn jeans. The sound immediately took him back to the evening before and the reason he'd needed the killer workout. Memories of Kelsey's kiss, the feel of her curves beneath his hands, and the untimely interruption had tortured him through the night.

Only, the sound wasn't alerting him to an incoming call, but to a new message. Seeing Jake's number on the screen, he quickly dialed his voice mail.

"Come on, Jake. Tell me Sophia Pirelli gave you something on Dunworthy," he muttered while he waited for the message to play.

"Whatever happened to Sophia in Chicago still has her feeling vulnerable," Jake's message announced without preamble. "I'm getting close, though. She—she's starting to trust me. It won't be long now."

His friend said the words with an almost grim sense of finality. Once Jake found out what had made Sophia quit her job and whether or not it had anything to do with Dunworthy, Jake would be on the next plane back to L.A.

Just as Connor would be leaving Scottsdale…leaving Kelsey…

Leaving Kelsey to pick up the pieces, he thought as he snapped the phone shut and tossed it back on the dresser. If Emily called off the wedding, would it ruin Kelsey's business? He'd told her she had the strength and determination to succeed no matter what, and while he'd meant every word, he really didn't know what the hell he was talking about, did he? Could her dreams end up buried beneath a landslide of bad publicity for a wedding gone wrong?

And what about her family? The Wilsons were counting

on Kelsey. Would she see her failure as yet another time when she hadn't lived up to expectations?

But what was he supposed to do? Connor wondered. Step back and let Emily marry a guy with a narcissistic streak running like a fault line beneath his charming, sophisticated facade? Raise a glass of champagne and hope for the best?

Cara Mitchell would likely be dead if not for you. You saved her life, Connor.

He still wasn't sure he could take credit instead of blame for what happened to Cara, but he did know he couldn't have walked away. Just like he couldn't walk away from Emily.

But maybe he needed to walk away from Kelsey…

Bad enough that he'd be leaving her to deal with the professional fallout. The last thing he wanted was to leave her personal life in shambles after an affair that wouldn't—couldn't—go anywhere. It would be best to end things now, before someone got hurt.

Are you so sure it's Kelsey *you're trying to protect?* his sarcastic inner voice questioned, mocking his noble intentions for what they were—the act of a coward.

When it came right down to it, he had his own heart to protect, too. And Kelsey—with her caring, her concern, her willingness to see the best in everyone, including him—was already way too close to working her way inside.

A quiet knock on the door broke into his thoughts. He didn't bother to check the keyhole, accustomed to being able to handle anything, only to open the door and realize he could still be caught off guard.

Kelsey stood in the hallway, a lost look on her face.

"What are you doing here?" The question bordered on rude, but as he took in the uncertainty in her wide brown eyes, the sexier-than-hell freckles on her pale face, the plump lower lip she held caught between her teeth, his earlier intentions blew up in his face.

Walk away? As he caught the cinnamon scent of her skin, he couldn't even *move*.

"I went to see Emily this morning," she said as she ducked through the doorway. "I wanted to find out why she called you last night."

Last night.

The two simple words had the power to turn back time. His flesh still burned in the aftermath of her touch. He grabbed a clean T-shirt from the dresser and jerked it over his head as if he could smother the memories. Not likely. It would take much stronger fabric than simple cotton, especially with Kelsey standing mere feet from his bed.

Pushing his damp hair back with both hands, he caught Kelsey staring at him, desire and awareness swirling in her chocolate eyes. Slowly lowering his arms, he shoved his hands into the back pockets of his jeans rather than pull her into his arms. As if sensing his thoughts, Kelsey broke eye contact, her gaze skittering away as soft color lit her cheeks.

In a voice that sounded dry as the desert, he asked, "Did you?"

Blinking like waking from a dream, Kelsey asked, "Did I what?"

"Find out why Em called?"

"No. Well, maybe. It sounds like Uncle Gordon and Todd are getting pretty close. Emily says she's happy about it, but I'm not so sure."

Connor nodded. "Makes sense. Emily's always wanted her father's approval, and she's never known how to get it."

Silence followed his statement. He wasn't sure when he lost Kelsey. Her gaze was focused on the far wall, and he doubted she was captivated by the desertscape watercolor.

"Kelsey? You okay?"

"All this time, I thought I knew, but it was a lie, and I can't ask her why."

He frowned. "Ask who what?"

Shaking her head, she came back from whatever place or time had her spellbound. "Sorry. You don't even know what I'm talking about." She clutched at the oversize purse hanging from her shoulder, the lost, almost haunted look coming back.

Concern accomplished what little else could—pushing desire to the back burner. He stepped closer and watched her throat move as she swallowed—thanks to whatever she must have seen in his eyes—but he merely took her hand and led her to the couch.

"Tell me," he urged. "Maybe I can figure it out."

"If you can, you're one up on me," she said with a sound that could have been a laugh but wasn't. Still, she took a deep breath as she sank against one of the cushions and said, "Aunt Charlene walked in when I was with Emily. We told her we'd been discussing what Emily would carry down the aisle. Something old, something new…"

Kelsey seemed to expect him to fill in the rest, so Connor ventured, "Roses are red, violets are blue?"

A slight smile tweaked her lips, and she said, "Close. Something borrowed, something blue." Her smile faded as she pulled a rubber-banded stack of envelopes out of her purse. "I went looking for something old."

"And you found those?" he asked, nodding at the bundle in her hands.

"These are letters my uncle wrote to my mother. Letters I never knew about. From an uncle I never knew existed until I was sixteen."

Slowly Kelsey filled Connor in about her wrong-side-of-the-tracks father, about the demand her grandfather had made of her mother, and the money he'd paid her father to leave.

The words were a sucker punch to Connor's soul. "Your grandfather paid your father off?"

Damned if he didn't have to give the family credit. They were consistent if not original. Clearly payoffs were standard practice when it came to getting rid of unwanted boyfriends. He still remembered the look on Gordon Wilson's face when the older man handed *him* a check to stay away from Emily.

Money he still hadn't told Kelsey about…

"He took the money and never looked back. He didn't care that my mother gave up everything for him. Didn't even care that she was pregnant with me."

An old bitterness, stale and rusty, cut into Kelsey's words, and panic started to grow inside Connor. "But if he never contacted your mother, then you don't know his reasons. You don't know why he took the money—"

Kelsey gave a scoffing laugh. "Oh, believe me. I know *why*. He took the money because he was a selfish bastard. It was all he was interested in, all he wanted, and as soon as it was his, he was gone. Nothing he could say would matter, nothing he could do would ever make up for taking the money."

She might as well be talking about him, Connor thought, guilt churning inside him. There was nothing he could do to change the past. He'd known when he took the money, Emily would never understand why he'd done it, why it was so vital that he help the Delgados. Would Kelsey really be any different?

She is *different,* his conscience argued.

And, yeah, okay, he'd taken her to meet Maria with the thought that he could somehow explain. But with her past and her father's bought-and-paid-for desertion, well, she'd it said herself, hadn't she?

Nothing he could say would matter…

"I'm sorry, Kelsey," he bit out. Sorry for reasons he couldn't even tell her.

"So am I," she said as she placed the letters on the coffee table. Taking a deep breath, she seemed to come to a decision as she turned on the couch cushion to face him. "I'm sorry my mother couldn't see another choice—to let go of the past. But I've been just as guilty."

"Kelsey—"

"It's true," she insisted. "I've always kept my aunt and uncle at a distance. You saw that. I was afraid to trust them, to count on them, in case they turned their backs on me the same way I thought they'd turned their backs on my mom."

"And Gordon never told you the whole story until now?"

Kelsey shook her head. "He said he didn't want to make me choose between my loyalty to my mom and them." She caught sight of Connor's surprised look and added, "See? He's not all bad."

Surprising her, Connor said, "Yeah, I'm starting to see that." His jaw clenched. "I mean, talk about the past repeating. He looked at me and saw a guy like your father—"

"You're nothing like him," Kelsey insisted fiercely.

"Kelsey, you don't know—"

"I do. I know you're a good man."

A pained expression crossed his face. "No."

"You are," she insisted.

She thought of the way he'd taken responsibility for the women in his life: his mother, Emily, Cara Mitchell. He'd saved the woman's life, yet he held himself accountable for putting her in a dangerous situation. Then, there was the love and gratitude he showed the Delgados. And yet none of those things compared to how he made her feel. She didn't want to be a responsibility. She certainly didn't want to be family. She wanted to be the woman Connor thought she was—strong, beautiful, sexy…

She did not want to be her mother's daughter, refusing to give or take second chances. And while Connor had never actually *told* her she was sexy, he gave her the confidence to believe she was. Taking a deep breath, the emotions that had been swirling through her calmed, settled, focused on the present, on this moment, and what she wanted. "And I might be my mother's daughter, but I don't have to live my life like she did."

The confusion clouding Connor's expression dispersed as Kelsey rose to her knees and leaned closer. Crystal-clear desire and equally obvious denial filled the void. "Kelsey, wait."

Determined to wipe that denial from his eyes, Kelsey swung her knee over Connor's thighs. He caught her around the waist, the heat in his gaze burning brighter as his fingers flexed into her hips. Instead of pulling her closer, he held her steady. "Kelsey, you don't know—"

His hesitation only pushed Kelsey forward. "I know I want you to kiss me."

One kiss was all it would take to bury her doubts in a flood of need. She should have known Connor wouldn't make it that easy on her. Or on himself. A war seemed to rage inside him, the frown between his eyebrows and the lines cutting grooves in his cheeks telling the tale of the battle.

One she thought she might win when his gaze dropped to her mouth. His voice a husky rasp, he asked, "That's all you want? A kiss?"

Almost unconsciously she licked her lips, a feminine thrill rushing through her when she saw his eyes darken with desire. "It's a good place to start, don't you think?"

And she could think of only one place she wanted to finish—in Connor's arms and in his bed, with no phone calls or memories of the past to interfere. Reaching up to trace the planes and angles of his face, from the doubt still pulling at his eyebrows to the tension locking his jaw, her cousin Aileen's words rang in her head.

Connor's the kind of man who makes a woman want to live for the moment.

Maybe that was true, but all she wanted was this man, in this moment, Kelsey insisted, ignoring the greedy voice demanding more…demanding forever.

"Now," she argued with that voice, "I just want now."

"Want what?" Connor demanded, his voice a rough scrape that sent shivers down her nerve endings.

"This," she whispered as she brushed her fingertips over his mouth. "You."

Her pulse pounded so wildly in her ears, Kelsey barely heard the words, but to Connor, her response must have been loud and clear. The one word broke through his hesitation. Leaning forward, he pulled her tighter and caught her lips in the kiss she'd waited for. Just like she'd hoped, the sheer pleasure of his mouth on hers banished all doubt, erasing any worries about anything…or anyone.

His hands still on her hips, he twisted to the side, lowering her to the couch without breaking the mind-spinning kiss. She sank into the cushions, Connor's weight pressing her deeper, but even the full-body contact wasn't enough. She ran her hands down his back, breathing in his fresh-from-the-shower scent. Breaking the kiss, she trailed her lips down the column of his throat. His skin was still slightly damp, and she sipped tiny droplets of water from his skin like a woman dying of thirst in the desert.

And maybe she was, Kelsey thought, vaguely surprised by the need and desire spurring her on. After all, it had been a *long* time…

Rising on an elbow, Connor levered away from her. For a split second, Kelsey worried that something—the hotel room, the couch, *something*—had reminded him of the past, of Emily, and that he was going to pull away and leave her wanting. But neither the past nor, heaven forbid, Emily were reflected in his eyes. Instead, Kelsey saw herself as he saw her, and for the first time in her life, she felt beautiful.

"Connor." His name broke from her in a shaky whisper. She didn't think she could speak another word if she tried, but he said everything she wanted to say…everything she wanted to hear.

"A kiss is never going to be enough. I want more. I want everything."

"Okay," she breathed.

Connor's lips quirked in a half smile. "Okay?"

Nodding fiercely, she repeated, "Okay."

Taking her at her word, as limited as it might have been, Connor reclaimed her lips in a teasing, tantalizing kiss even as his fingers toyed with the buttons on her shirt. But after his determined comment, Kelsey should have known Connor wasn't playing.

Before she was even aware of what happened, Connor's hot palm laid claim to the bare skin of her stomach, stealing her breath from the outside in as Kelsey realized he'd completely unbuttoned her shirt.

"Amazing," he murmured, his eyes taking the curves rising and falling with every rapid breath.

Glancing at the off-white, no-frills bra, she gave a short laugh. She hadn't gone to Connor's hotel with seduction in mind and it showed. "Boring," she argued.

"Are you kidding?" Tracing a path across the freckles on her chest, a focused, concentrated frown on his face, Connor vowed, "I think I just found a map to the Lost Dutchman's mine."

The silly comment startled a laugh from Kelsey, and Connor's touch veered closer to hitting a different kind of gold mine. His fingers followed the map work of freckles, and her laughter faded away. Breathless anticipation took over, and she arched into his touch.

The plain material proved no match for Connor. He reached inside to cup her breast, and her nipple instantly tightened against his palm. The sheer pleasure of his touch sent her head spinning, and each gasp for breath only pressed her flesh tighter into his hand. He kissed her again, and Kelsey welcomed the exploring quest of his tongue. Her hands searched for the hem of his shirt, seeking out hidden treasure for herself. She followed the plain of his back, the valley of his spine, the rise of his shoulder blades, but none of it was enough.

Pulling her mouth away from his, she gasped, "Connor, wait."

"What's wrong?" Despite the desire pinpointing his pupils and turning his voice to gravel, Connor followed her command. Other than the rapid rise and fall of his chest, he didn't move a muscle.

And Kelsey couldn't help smiling. "You didn't want to make out in a car, and I don't want to make love on a couch. Not when the bed is only a few feet away."

Eyes dark with desire, he accused, "I told you, you make me crazy."

"The feeling's mutual."

Connor pushed off the couch and held out a hand. She linked her fingers through his and clung tight, desperate to hold onto the moment. But unlike previous interruptions that broke the mood, the walk to the bedroom, amid heated kisses and arousing touches, heightened the intensity. Her fingers clumsy with haste, Kelsey tugged at Connor's T-shirt. She stopped kissing him only long enough to push the shirt over his head and toss it aside.

In the back of her mind, she was still slightly amazed by her own actions. For the first time, need overwhelmed nerves. She could have blamed the previous interruptions or her own personal dry spell for the undeniable hunger. But the real reason was Connor. All Connor…

He pushed her shirt from her shoulders, then stripped away her bra, and Kelsey let the garments fall, too fascinated by the sheer perfection of his broad shoulders, muscular chest and flat stomach to care about the imperfection of freckles dotting her skin. Especially not when Connor seemed so fascinated by connecting the random marks and turning them into shapes: stars, triangles, hearts…

But the arousing touch was nothing compared to the intensity of his lips as they charted that same course. The damp heat of his breath against her skin was like a promise, and when his mouth made good on that promise, Kelsey's knees went weak. Connor followed her down to the mattress and reached for the waistband of her skirt. She expected him to whisk it away as quickly as he had her shirt, but instead her skirt and panties made a slow slide down the length of her legs. Inch by inch, and by the time he slipped them off, Kelsey had never been so glad to be so short.

"Connor." His name broke from her in a plea, and his green eyes glittered as he ran his hand up the inside of her thigh.

"Definitely not boring," he murmured. He stroked her skin, and waves of pleasure washed over her. She cried out his name a second time, even as he shoved aside his jeans. The well-worn denim did not make the same slow journey as her skirt. He kicked the jeans aside in a split second, then braced his body above hers.

He claimed her mouth in a kiss, his tongue plunging deep in the same moment he buried himself between her thighs. Her back arched, her body rising to meet his, and his low groan of desire escaped their kiss. And this time it was her name that broke the silence as Connor caught her hips in his hands.

That first thrust was like the striptease with her skirt: slow, seductive, measured. But then urgency took over, reckless and wild, and Kelsey had the instant thought that this must be what it was like to ride on the back of a bike—amazed, exhilarated and desperate to hold on. But unlike on a bike, the real ride began when she lost control, careening riotously, hurtling down a path that ended in a fiery explosion as she shuddered in ecstasy a second time, bringing Connor with her.

They collapsed in a heap together, both trying to catch their breath. "Definitely not boring," Connor repeated, as he brushed the hair away from her face. The look of tenderness in his gaze brought an ache to her throat, and Kelsey was glad when Connor eased away and tucked her against his side before he saw the tears burning her eyes.

With her head on his chest, Kelsey listened to his heartbeat gradually slow. But even without the weight of his body on hers, she couldn't breathe. A relentless pressure squeezed her heart, like she'd dived too deep and realized too late how far she was in over her head.

Her first impression had been wrong. Connor wasn't the type of man who made a woman want to live for the moment. He was the type of man, the *only* man, who'd made Kelsey long for forever.

Chapter Ten

Connor woke slowly, aware of two things. First it was way too early, and second, Kelsey was no longer in bed. The low murmur of her voice pulled him the rest of the way from sleep. "Everything's all set, and I'll be there to oversee the decorations and food." A slight pause followed. "Must be a bad connection. I'm—outside. I'll run out and get the cake right before the guests arrive. Yes, I'll make sure to leave plenty of time. Can I talk to Emily for a second? Oh, right. Of course. She needs her beauty sleep. I'll see you in an hour. Okay. Forty-five minutes. Bye."

A narrow shaft of light sliced through the curtains, and in the muted glow he watched Kelsey slip on her shoes. He didn't move or make a sound, but something must have given him away. She stiffened slightly and glanced his way as she straightened. "Hey," she said softly. "I was trying not to wake you."

She pushed her hair behind her ear in a nervous gesture,

and Connor felt a flicker of annoyance. What was she going to do? Slip away while he was still sleeping? And why the hell would that bother him? It wasn't as if he hadn't done the same thing before. But that was before, and those women weren't Kelsey, and he didn't want her to go.

A knot twisted in his stomach at the thought of asking her to stay. The memory of his mother's sad smile as she walked away time and time again flashed in his mind, and the words jammed in his throat. He fisted his hands against the mattress and pushed into a sitting position with a glance at the clock. "It's not even seven."

Her gaze fell from his to land on his naked chest and then cut away to search out the purse she'd left on the couch, but not before he'd seen something in her eyes that made the knot in his stomach tighten.

"I know it's early, but Emily's shower is this morning, and I have to oversee the decorations and the food and— I'm sorry."

Connor wasn't sure why she was apologizing—for the early hour, for leaving, for Emily's shower…or for the regret he'd seen in her eyes.

He'd known Kelsey would regret sleeping with him, but he'd taken her at her word when she said she wanted him. He'd believed her because—hell, because he'd wanted to believe her. But that was last night. Now, in the full light of day, with the Charlene Wilson calling the shots, everything changed.

Or, he thought grimly, everything was the same. Only this time it was Kelsey lying to the Wilsons, sneaking behind their backs to see him. It was Kelsey who pretended her relationship with him didn't exist. Familiar ground, but it hurt a hell of a lot more the second time around. And not because she'd torn open old wounds. Emily had damaged his pride, but this—this felt like something else entirely.

Tossing aside the sheet in an obvious reminder that last

night *had* happened, Connor swung his legs over the edge of the mattress and stood. Some other time, he might have teased Kelsey about the blush blooming in her face. But not this morning. Not when the heat signaled a different kind of embarrassment. He jerked on his jeans as quickly as he'd stripped them off the night before, annoyed by his body's reaction to the mere thought.

"I'm going to talk to Emily about the wedding—"

"I don't give a damn about the wedding," he said, surprised by the truth of the words. He was still worried about Emily, but as far as proving the Wilsons wrong about Dunworthy, proving them wrong about *him,* Connor no longer cared. Only Kelsey's opinion mattered, an opinion suddenly in doubt.

"I'm sorry," she repeated, before lifting distraught eyes to his.

Yeah, he got that part. She was sorry they'd slept together.

"Last night was…"

Connor's jaw clenched, waiting for the word he *knew* was coming.

"…amazing, and I'd give anything to stay in bed with you—"

"Wait? What?"

"Last night was amazing." Color flared brighter, nearly blotting out her freckles as she ducked her head. "At least I thought it was, but I'm not—"

Swallowing a curse, Connor pulled her into his arms as realization hit him like the slap upside the head he deserved. Kelsey's reactions hadn't been fueled by regret or embarrassment but by a vulnerability that played against his own insecurities. "Last night *was* amazing."

The memory combined with Kelsey's soft curves pressed against him, her warm breath feathering across his chest, was enough to remind him just *how* amazing.

"It was," Kelsey whispered. He heard the relief in her voice, felt her smile against his skin.

"This morning could be even more amazing."

"I know." Despite the apparent agreement in her words, her smile fell away, and this time, he knew he wasn't imagining the regret in her voice. Pulling out of his arms, she said, "And that's why I have to go. Because whether you give a damn or not, Emily's wedding is a week away and then you'll be going home."

She was talking about L.A., but home didn't bring to mind images of his sterile apartment. Instead, he thought of Señora Delgado's restaurant, he thought of his friendship with Javy, and he thought of every moment he'd spent with Kelsey…and he wondered what might happen if he didn't go back to L.A.

"Kelsey—"

"So, see? I have to leave," she continued despite his interruption. "Last night was an amazing moment, but it wasn't meant to last, right?"

The hope in her eyes waited for him to contradict every word she'd said, to tell her sometimes amazing moments added up to a lifetime, but he couldn't make himself say the words.

Ducking her head, Kelsey grabbed her purse off the couch and left. And even though the sound of the closing door slammed into his chest like a blow, Connor let her go. Because when it came right down to it, he was the one too afraid to ask her to stay.

Connor didn't have a destination in mind when he climbed behind the Mustang's wheel, but he couldn't stay in the hotel room any longer. Fortunately, Javy's car seemed to have a mind of its own, and he soon turned into the Delgado parking lot.

The restaurant wouldn't open for hours yet, but Connor knew Maria would already be in the kitchen, stirring giant pots of tortilla soup and prepping food. He pulled around back, the crunch of gravel beneath the tires the only sound, a sharp contrast to the night he'd brought Kelsey here when music and laughter filled the sultry air.

A metallic glint caught his eye as he climbed from the car, and he spotted a motionless wind chime made from silverware. Despite his mood, Connor smiled as a memory came to him. Furious with Javy over some scrape he'd gotten into, Maria whacked the counter with a carved spoon. The aged wood splintered on contact, adding to his mother's anger, and she'd threatened Javy with the dire prediction that if the restaurant closed, it would be all his fault; after all, how could she cook without her favorite spoon?

The statement was a meaningless heat-of-the-moment comment that had come far too close to coming true years later. Not because of a broken spoon, but due to the expenses that followed Javy's father's illness and the fire that had nearly destroyed the kitchen.

A faint humming broke into his memories, and he found Maria standing at the counter, vegetables piled high in front of her, the quick, continuous motion of the knife a steady rhythm to the song she sang beneath her breath. The rustic Delgado family recipes went back for decades, but the remodeled kitchen was completely modern with its stainless-steel counters and appliances.

Maria's face lit as he stepped inside the kitchen. "Connor! This is a surprise."

"I wanted to apologize for taking off without saying goodbye the other night."

She waved aside his apology with a flick of her knife before starting in on a jalapeno pepper, but curiosity lit her eyes as she said, "You and your Kelsey were in a hurry, no?"

Her words wiggled like bait on a hook, but Connor didn't bite. His silence wasn't enough to make the *señora* pull in her line. Watching him from the corner of her eye, she added, "That is how it is when you are in love."

Love. The word sent a flare of panic scorching through him like the grease fire that nearly destroyed the restaurant years ago. "Kelsey and I aren't in love."

Maria glared at him like she might toss him back into the water. "I was married to my Miguel for over twenty years. I know love."

Connor knew love, too. He knew the pain of losing a mother who loved him yet left him no matter how many times he asked her to stay. He knew the heartache of losing Emily, who claimed to love him but not enough to defy her parents. And Kelsey...would loving her be any different? If he told her the truth about the money he'd taken, money he'd used to save the restaurant, would love be enough to make her understand? Would it be enough for her to stand up to the family who'd taken her in when she was sixteen and scared with nowhere else to go?

"You don't understand, Maria. Kelsey's a Wilson. She's Emily's cousin—"

"And you think Kelsey is a foolish girl like Emily? Unable to think or do for herself?"

"No, she's not like that at all. She's used to taking care of herself and the people around her." He'd seen that at her shop, in her concern for her friends. Friends who had Kelsey's complete loyalty. Friends who *deserved* that loyalty.

Connor tried to picture Lisa or Trey fitting in at a Wilson family gathering and couldn't. Just as he couldn't imagine Kelsey caring what the Wilsons thought or ever, *ever* turning her back on her friends. Kelsey might not have wanted to follow in her mother's footsteps, but the path had led Kelsey to be a strong, independent woman. A woman who knew her own mind and knew what she wanted.

Suddenly it didn't matter if the Wilsons admitted they've been wrong about Dunworthy. It didn't even matter if they admitted they'd been wrong about *him*. All he cared about now was proving Kelsey *right*. She believed in him, and last night she'd wanted *him*. Now it was up to Connor to tell her the truth about the money he'd taken from her family and convince her she wanted more than a moment, that he could give her more. It was up to him to convince her that, together, they could have forever.

Kelsey struggled through the front door of her aunt and uncle's house, a huge bouquet of pink and silver helium-filled balloons trailing behind her. The carved wooden doors swung shut, catching one of the balloons in the jamb. She jumped as the loud-as-a-gunshot *pop* guaranteed her arrival wouldn't go unannounced.

"Kelsey. I expected you half an hour ago."

Okay, so she wouldn't have snuck in unnoticed anyway. "Sorry, Aunt Charlene."

"Where have you been?"

"With Connor." The truth popped out before the words even formed in her head, and she couldn't imagine what possessed her to tell the truth.

His image flashed in her mind, and she knew exactly what possessed her. She'd seen the look in his eyes when he'd caught her on the phone with her aunt. When he caught her *lying* to her aunt. If she wasn't such a coward, she would have told the truth when it mattered.

Just like she would have stayed with Connor that morning, in his hotel room, in his bed, with the courage to believe they could turn one night into something more.

Disapproval cut into Charlene's features, and Kelsey knew her aunt didn't think Connor was good enough for a Wilson—

any Wilson—but she knew the truth. She didn't deserve Connor.

"You're wrong about him," she announced, certainty backing ever word. "Connor's a good man. He isn't here to ruin Emily's life. He's here because he's worried she's marrying a man she doesn't love to please *you*."

Her aunt didn't speak. Kelsey thought maybe her words had made a difference, at least given her aunt pause. But Charlene's gaze never wavered, and as the silence grew, Kelsey knew her aunt wasn't using the silence to consider what Kelsey said. She was using the silence to make Kelsey *reconsider* what she'd said.

But she wasn't going to back down.

It was time for both her aunt and uncle to realize Connor was a good man, not some troubled kid out to steal their daughter. And they needed to let Emily go. To let her live her own life and to stop using one youthful indiscretion to keep her in line.

"Do you really think I can't see what's going on?" her aunt questioned on a sigh. "Connor McClane is out to stop Emily's wedding, and he's using you to do it! Honestly, Kelsey, I expected you to know better."

"Connor isn't using me. He wouldn't do that. I understand why you'd have a hard time believing he cares for me after how crazy he was about Emily—"

"Oh, for goodness' sake, follow me." Without checking to see if Kelsey would obey, Charlene turned on a heel and strode down the hall into Gordon's study. Kelsey reluctantly followed. "Connor wasn't in love with Emily any more than he's…"

In love with you. Her aunt's unspoken words bounced off the darkly paneled walls, hanging in the room like the scent of Gordon's cigars.

"The only thing that man has ever worried about is

himself." Crossing the room to open a desk drawer, she pulled out a manila folder. "When your uncle kept this for proof, I always thought Emily would be the one we'd show it to."

"Proof of what?" Kelsey asked uneasily as Charlene fingered a small rectangle of paper. The letters her uncle had written her mother had been shock enough. What else did her aunt and uncle have stashed away in desks and dressers?

"Proof of the kind of man Connor McClane really is." Charlene gazed at Kelsey across the polished mahogany surface, her gaze reflecting a hint of sympathy. "He must be very convincing. Emily was sure he loved her."

Kelsey didn't have her cousin's certainty. Connor had never mentioned the word *love*. But then again, neither had she, and Kelsey could no longer deny her feelings. She was in love with Connor. For a moment, she imagined saying the words out loud and punctuating them with a bold exit. Not needing any proof of the man Connor was aside from the truth written in her heart. But she wasn't that strong.

"What is it?" she whispered.

"See for yourself." Charlene slid the paper across the table. Kelsey stepped closer. It was a check. She recognized her uncle's signature, his name and address printed on the top left, the zeros following the number in the small box off to the right. But it was the person the check had been made out to that froze her gaze. Her stomach, which had been tossing back and forth, sank.

"Why do you think Connor left all those years ago? He might not have had Emily, but believe me, he got what he wanted."

Her hand shaking, Kelsey reached out and turned the check over. Connor's name was sprawled across the endorsement line. She stared at the signature rather than meet her aunt's knowing gaze. "That was a long time ago. Connor isn't the same person anymore."

Ten thousand dollars. A lot of money, but not enough to make a dent in the family fortune. Had her father held out for more? Kelsey wondered. Even twenty-four years ago, ten thousand dollars didn't go far. Ten years ago, it wouldn't have bought a new car.

"Is that what he told you? That he's changed?" Her aunt's cultured voice didn't reflect even a hint of disparagement, but Kelsey heard it all the same.

"He was a kid back when he was seeing Emily." An orphaned kid from the wrong side of the tracks. Could she blame him for taking the money? He'd told her how he'd struggled after his mother died.

But he didn't tell you about the check, a worried voice protested. She'd told him about the money her father took to abandon her and her mother, and Connor never said a word.

"Let's look at the way he's changed. Ten years ago, he nearly ruined Emily's life by convincing her to run away from her family with him. Now he's back, and this time he's out to ruin her life by convincing her to run away from her fiancé with him."

"That's not true," Kelsey argued against the ache in her chest. "He's concerned about Emily. Just like I am. She's making a mistake by marrying Todd."

"If I were you, I wouldn't be worried about Emily *or* Todd. I'd be worried about Connor McClane."

Kelsey wasn't sure how she made it through the shower. Probably thanks to her aunt's attention to detail. By following Charlene's every instruction, Kelsey moved by rote. She arranged the flowers and decorations; she picked up the cake and double-checked the catered finger food. She walked the guests through the games—silly, irreverent, last-days-as-a-free-woman tributes—followed by opening gifts.

Even in her dazed state, Kelsey could guess what each package contained. After all, she'd helped with the bridal registry, and no one would dare step outside the approved gift list. No surprises, just as her aunt demanded.

Charlene planned for every contingency. Even Connor McClane, Kelsey thought, her heart catching as his signature seemed to flash in front of her eyes, written by an unseen hand.

"Thank you, Kelsey! It's beautiful." Emily held up a snow globe. Strains of the wedding march filled the room as sparkling "snow" fell on the bride and groom waltzing through a wedding wonderland.

Kelsey offered a weak smile. She'd bought the gift B.C.— Before Connor. She couldn't *not* give her cousin a gift, but she felt as uncertain about Emily and Todd as she now did about Connor.

Kelsey had started to believe him, to trust his gut, as he called it, but now she didn't know what to believe, and her own gut was pitifully silent. "You're welcome, Emily. I just want you to be happy."

Emily masked the flicker of doubt with a wedding-portrait smile. "I am happy, Kelsey. I'm getting married!"

A half an hour later, as the guests were leaving, Kelsey started collecting the plates and utensils, her movements automatic and unthinking. She blinked in surprise when her aunt laid a hand on her arm.

"The maid can get that, Kelsey."

"It's my job—"

"And we're your family." Her expression softened to a degree Kelsey had never witnessed. "You're a beautiful woman in your own right, Kelsey, and I'm sorry if I've made you feel less than my own daughters. But there's only one thing Connor McClane is interested in, and it's not true love."

* * *

Kelsey debated calling Connor, but the conversation wasn't one she wanted to have over the phone. Stopping by his hotel room was out of the question. She'd come alive in Connor's arms the night before, letting go of the past and all her insecurities. But seeing proof of the money he'd taken, the past was in painful jeopardy of repeating. The insecurities Connor lifted with his seductive words and intoxicating touch crashed back down, hitting harder than ever. Making her question if last night had been as amazing as she'd thought…

Kelsey hit the brakes a good twenty feet shy of her driveway. The black Mustang was parked at the sidewalk, the right front tire bumped up on the curb. Mirrored glasses shielding his eyes, Connor leaned against the hood.

Ready or not, she was going to have to confront him about the money he'd taken. It wasn't something *she* could pretend hadn't happened. Nerves jerked in her stomach, and she carefully eased her foot back on the gas, her car crawling the last block.

Connor grinned as she stepped out of the car, and aching or not, her heart still sped up as he approached. Maybe he had a reason, an explanation for taking the money.

And a reason for keeping the truth from her?

Kelsey could forgive something that happened ten years ago, but why hadn't he told her? Why did she have to face the shock of another family secret?

"Hey, I went by to see Señora Delgado. You have an open invitation, and she made me promise that next time, I'd actually let you stay and eat." Connor stuck his hands in the pockets of his jeans, a hint of uncertainty in his stride weakening her resolve as she wondered what else he'd talked to the older woman about.

"Connor—"

"She likes you," he added with a crooked smile, "but then, who wouldn't?" His smile fell away when she didn't respond, and he stripped off his glasses. Worry shone in his emerald eyes. "What's wrong?"

"Wrong?" Kelsey echoed with a broken laugh, the word far too simple to describe everything that had happened. Her decision to trust him, to *sleep* with him, to defend him to her aunt…only to find out he was just like her father.

It was a long time ago, her heart argued. *Maybe he had a good reason. Maybe—*

"Why didn't you tell me?"

"Tell you what?"

"The real reason you left all those years ago. Why didn't you tell me about the money?"

A muscle in Connor's jaw flinched as if she'd slapped him. Kelsey wasn't sure what she'd expected—excuses, denials—but she hadn't counted on the dead silence that followed her words. The sun beat down on them, magnifying the pain in her head. Cicadas in a neighbor's tree started to buzz, a low pitch that soon revved louder and louder, building like the hurt and anger inside Kelsey until she couldn't keep from lashing out.

"I *told* you about my father—about the money he took to leave my mother, and you never said a word! I trusted you, I believed in you, I—"

Love you, she thought, her heart breaking as Connor stoically withstood her verbal attack. If not for that very first flinch, she wouldn't have even known he was listening.

Surely if he had some reason, some justification for taking the money beyond pure and simple greed, he would tell her. He would say…*something, anything!* But silence—*guilty* silence—was Connor's only response.

"My aunt and uncle were right about you all along," she

whispered. Just as her grandfather had been right about her father. "They were right about everything."

At her words, Connor finally reacted. A cruel, calculating smile curved his mouth, and though Kelsey never would have thought green eyes could be cold, a chill touched her as his gaze iced over. He looked every inch the bad boy her aunt had warned her about less than two weeks ago. If only she'd listened.

"Congratulations, Kelsey. Your family must be so proud. Seems like you're a real Wilson after all."

Muttering a curse beneath his breath, Connor stalked over to the car. Despite the weight of restrained sobs pressing on her chest, Kelsey let him go. She might have lived her life under the misconception of her and her mom against the world, but Connor was just as deluded, believing it was always him against the Wilsons. This wasn't about her family; it was all on Connor and the secret he'd kept.

"Mama's right. You look like hell."

Ignoring his friend's voice, Connor didn't look away from the production of sliced limes, saltshaker and shot glass he'd filled with tequila. He'd taken over the small outdoor bar at the back of the Delgados' restaurant, where they'd installed patio seating for times when the weather was nice. In the middle of June, even at eight o'clock at night, it wasn't.

He barely noticed the oppressive heat, the way his T-shirt clung damply to his skin, or the bugs that hovered around the string of multicolored lights. After shaking out salt on the back of his hand like it was rocket science, he reached for the shot glass.

Catching Connor's wrist, Javy asked, "How many of those have you had?"

Connor glared at his friend from the corner of his eye. "Counting this one? Two."

His friend barked out a laugh that ended in a curse as he let go. "You're in worse shape than I thought. Wanna tell me what happened?"

Wincing at the strong burn of the tequila, Connor replied, "You said it yourself when I brought Kelsey here. Some people never learn."

"Sorry, man."

Javy didn't say more, and the two of them sat without speaking. Mariachi music, the din of the diners, and the occasional shout from the kitchen were the only sounds.

Finally Connor shoved the shot glass aside. "It was Emily all over again. I was stupid enough to think things would be different this time. But when push came to shove, she sided with her family."

He'd seen the disappointment in Kelsey's eyes. Forget all she'd said about how he'd changed. Forget all they'd shared. She'd been waiting all along for him to show his true colors, and she'd jumped back to her own side of the tracks the minute his character came into question.

You should have told her sooner, his conscience berated him. If she hadn't found out the truth from Charlene… But would that have made a difference? Or would Kelsey's reaction have been the same?

He should have known he and Kelsey didn't have any chance at a future. Her family's disapproval would eat like acid, weakening Kelsey's feelings until they were worn clean away. He was lucky it had happened sooner rather than later. He couldn't stand to live life with Kelsey the way he had with his mother, always knowing she had one foot out the door and it was only a matter of time before she left and didn't come back.

"Wanna tell me what happened?"

"Her aunt told her I took money to leave town, to leave Emily."

"And she believed it?" his friend demanded, slumping back against the bar stool in disbelief. "Just like that? With no proof, no—"

"The Wilsons had all the proof they needed. I took the ten thousand dollars."

Shock straightened his friend's spine. "You what? But why would you—" Realization slowly spread across his features, along with a large dose of guilt. Javy swore. "Is that where you got the money you gave my mother for the restaurant?"

"Like you said, this place means everything to Maria. I couldn't let her lose it." Eyeing his friend closely, Connor said, "You never asked where I got the money."

"No, I never did." Javy let out a deep breath, reached for the bottle of tequila and poured himself a shot. For a long moment he stared into the glass before looking Connor in the eye. "I didn't want to know."

"What? In case I'd broken the law? Done something illegal?" Connor pressed. Well, why wouldn't Javy believe that? It was just the kind of thing Connor McClane would have done.

Once.

"You think *I* didn't consider it?" Javy shot back. "It's *my* restaurant! My responsibility. My family—"

"Mine, too."

"Yeah," his friend agreed, frustration and anger draining away. "But I should have been the one to come up with a solution. And you shouldn't be the one paying for it now."

"I made my choice, and I would do the same thing again. In a heartbeat. So, tell me, you gonna drink that?" Connor asked, pointing at the shot glass sitting untouched between them.

Javy slid it across the bar without spilling a drop. "Look, man, I've been trying to pay you back for years. You've gotta let me—"

"Forget it. After all your family did for me, it was the least I could do."

"Then we'll draw something up. Make you a partner in the restaurant. And I'll talk to Kelsey."

Connor shook his head. "No."

"What do you mean 'no'?" Javy demanded. "Why don't you want to tell her the truth?"

"She knows the truth. I took the money."

"Oh, come on, Connor! That's not the whole truth, and you damn well know it! If you told her *why*, Kelsey would understand."

Yeah, maybe she would…this time. But what about the next time she had to choose between him and her family?

Chapter Eleven

It had been three days since Kelsey had seen Connor. Three heartbreaking, regret-filled, uneventful days.

At first she'd been too hurt to do more than curl up on her sofa and cry. But Kelsey never believed self-pity helped anyone, so by the second day she had thrown herself into working on her shop, finishing up the details that transformed the place from a simple suite into the office of her dreams.

She'd had photographs from previous weddings enlarged and wrapped in gilded frames: an elegant wedding cake with a single piece missing; a bridal bouquet in midair with ribbons streaming; a close-up of an unseen couple's hands, fingers entwined, showing off sparkling wedding rings.

She'd hung sheer curtains and floral drapes at the windows and found a bargain on a secondhand wicker coffee table, which displayed a crystal vase and fresh flowers from Lisa's shop. She'd brought a CD player from home to fill the air with soft, lilting music.

And if her heart broke a little more with every romantic touch she added, not once did Kelsey let that slow her down.

If she had any doubts about her hard work paying off, she'd received encouragement from an unlikely source. When Charlene called earlier, the talk had centered around the rehearsal dinner that night, but nearing the end of the conversation, Charlene had fallen silent before saying, "If I haven't told you before now, Kelsey, I appreciate all you've done for Emily's wedding. We never would have been able to pull this off so quickly if not for you."

After saying goodbye to her aunt, Kelsey hung up the phone and looked around her shop. She had everything she wanted: her shop was up and running, Emily's wedding was only days away and her hard work had gained her aunt's approval.

Congratulations, Kelsey. Your family must be so proud. Seems like you're a real Wilson after all.

Guilt wormed its way through her stomach, but Kelsey pushed it away with a burst of anger as she grabbed her purse and keys. She had no cause to feel guilty, she decided as she locked the front door behind her with a definitive twist of the key. None at all. Connor was the one who'd kept secrets, told lies of omission.

And yet maybe he had a reason. After all, hadn't he encouraged her to consider that her father might have had his reasons for taking the money? At the time, Kelsey thought Connor was talking only about her father. But could Connor have been talking about himself? Hoping that she might understand why he'd taken the ten thousand dollars? And what had she told him?

Nothing he could say would matter, nothing he could do would ever make up for taking the money.

Little wonder, then, that he hadn't bothered with explanations!

She had to talk to Connor, Kelsey decided as she climbed into her car and turned the air on full blast. If she expected him to tell her the truth, she owed it to him to listen without making judgments based on her own past.

Her phone rang, reminding Kelsey that she couldn't drop everything to go see Connor. After the rehearsal, she vowed as she pulled out her cell and flipped it open.

"Kelsey?"

Startled by the unexpected male voice, Kelsey asked, "Yes?"

"It's Javy Delgado. Connor's friend."

"Javy?" She couldn't imagine why he'd call her unless… "Is Connor okay? Has something happened?"

He paused long enough to strip a few years off Kelsey's life before he said, "Do you still care about him?"

"Of course I care about him! I—" *Love him,* Kelsey thought.

"I wasn't sure after the way you treated him."

"The way *I* treated *him?* I know you're Connor's friend, but—"

"Not as good a friend as he's been to me," he interrupted. "And that's why I called even though he asked me not to."

So Connor didn't want to talk to her. He didn't even want his friend talking to her. That didn't give her much hope. "Why wouldn't he want you to talk to me?"

"He doesn't want me to tell you the truth. He's afraid it won't matter. I hope he's wrong about that. About you. Just like you've been wrong about him." Javy sighed. "The money he took, the money your uncle paid him—Connor gave it to my family. He used it to save our restaurant."

* * *

"I have what you need."

Even though Connor had been waiting for the damn call for days, it took him a moment to recognize the voice on the other end. He pushed away from the small table in his hotel room, pent-up energy surging through his veins.

"Jake, it's about time you called. Tell me what you've got is good. I can't wait to get out of this town."

The words were the biggest lie he'd told in the past five minutes. Which was about how long it'd been since he'd last tried to convince himself Kelsey Wilson wasn't worth the effort, and he'd forget all about her the second he got back to California.

"Good? No, I wouldn't call it good," Jake ground out.

Jake sounded nothing like his normal self, and although he and Connor were close, their relationship didn't include a lot of heart-to-heart talks. Still, he had to say, "You sound like hell, man."

"Doesn't matter. I got the job done. I found what I was looking for."

A garbled voice over a loudspeaker sounded in the background. "I have to go. They're calling my flight. I'm e-mailing everything you need right now. Just do me one favor."

"What is it?"

"Use it to nail that guy."

"I will."

"Good. It's about time he gets what he deserves."

As Connor flipped the cell phone closed, his friend's voice rang in his ears. Connor supposed most people would say he was getting what he deserved, too. That Kelsey turning her back on him was just desserts for the way he had taken the money and left Emily years ago.

Except maybe Kelsey's anger wasn't about his relationship

with Emily or the past he couldn't change. Maybe it was about *their* relationship right now, and the truth he'd kept from her.

Okay, yeah, she'd told him nothing could excuse what her father had done when he'd taken money to leave her mother, but maybe if Connor had explained about the Delgados' restaurant…maybe if he'd told her about the money up front so she wouldn't have had to hear about it from *Charlene,* of all people…

Could he really blame Kelsey for reacting the way she had? Between the money her father had taken and the secrets her mother had kept, she had every right to be wary.

Sure, it would have been nice if she'd learned about the money and had still been willing to believe the best about him. But he hadn't placed all his faith in Kelsey, either. He'd been afraid to tell her about the money because he'd feared his reasons—his love and loyalty to the Delgados—wouldn't matter. He'd been holding on to his own past and his own fears that *he* wouldn't matter. He should have trusted her more than that.

His computer e-mail alert sounded, letting him know Jake's report had arrived. A few taps on the keyboard, and Connor understood his friend's anger. "Don't worry, Jake. We've nailed the guy."

After Javy's call, Kelsey longed to turn the car around to go immediately to Connor's hotel, but she couldn't skip the rehearsal, not as Emily's wedding coordinator and not as a member of the Wilson family.

When her phone rang again, her heart skipped a beat as Connor's number flashed across the screen. Still, she hesitated a split second. She wanted to be able to look into his eyes when she apologized. To see that he believed her when she told him she understood why he took the money and she wouldn't expect any less of him than the sacrifice he'd made for his friends.

But after the way she'd treated him, she offered a quick whisper of thanks that he wanted to talk to her at all. Flipping the cell open with one hand, she turned into a nearby parking lot. She immediately sucked in a quick breath, but Connor interrupted any greeting or apology she might have made. "Kelsey, it's Connor. Don't hang up."

She pressed the phone tighter to her ear as if that might somehow bring her closer to Connor. "I'm not. I won't."

"Look, I can explain about the money, I swear—"

"You don't have to—"

"But not now—"

"I talked to Javy—"

"Jake called—"

"What?"

"Jake called. He found Sophia, the Dunworthy's former maid."

Trying to switch gears while her thoughts were going one hundred miles at hour, Kelsey said, "Did he find out why she quit?"

"Turns out she was fired after Dunworthy Senior caught her and Junior together."

"Caught them?"

"From what Sophia says, he'd been hitting on her for months before she finally gave in. Only to lose her job because of it."

"But didn't you say she stopped working for the Dunworthys only a few months ago?" Kelsey asked, mentally going over the timing and coming to an unbelievable conclusion. "Todd and Emily started dating six months ago. They were *engaged* two months ago!"

"Yeah, they were. Evidently sleeping with the maid was the last straw. The way I figure it, Todd proposed to Emily as a way to try to win back his family's approval."

"I can't believe he would do that to Emily!" Anger for her

cousin's sake started to boil inside Kelsey, along with a disgust at the way Todd had smiled and charmed his way into her aunt and uncle's good graces.

"It gets worse."

"Worse! How can it possibly get any worse! Is there someone else?"

"In a way." Connor paused. "Sophia's pregnant."

"Preg— Are you sure the child is Todd's? Considering the money his family has, and after the way Sophia lost her job—"

"Jake is sure of it. He believes her, and I believe him. Judging from his family's reactions, I'd say that the Dunworthys believe it, too. The family doesn't want anything to do with Todd. That's why they aren't here for the wedding." He hesitated. "You were right, Kelsey, and I should have listened to you."

"It doesn't matter now. You did it, Connor. You found the proof you needed."

"Yeah, I've got everything I need," he agreed, his voice sounding hollow. "Look, Kelsey—"

She waited, her heart pounding for everything she wanted to hear, everything she wanted to say. But the silence stretched on, the words unspoken. Finally she said, "The wedding rehearsal is tonight. I'm already on my way to the chapel."

"I'm at the hotel now. I can be there in fifteen minutes."

"Fifteen minutes," Kelsey echoed quietly, before hanging up the phone.

She had fallen in love with the small chapel the first time she saw the cottage-style building, with its cobblestone walls and stained-glass windows. The close proximity to the hotel made it an ideal location. Right now Kelsey wished the chapel were a world away, anything to delay the inevitable end. Once Connor stopped the wedding, he'd have no reason to stick around…and if he did, Kelsey feared it wouldn't be for her.

* * *

Minutes later Kelsey stood inside the empty chapel. It was as beautiful now as when she'd first laid eyes on it. She'd immediately known the perfect arrangement of flowers and candles for alongside the carved pews. Just the right placement of the wedding party on the steps leading to the altar. Exactly where the video and photographer should stand to best capture the light streaming through the windows. She'd known all of that months before Emily had gotten engaged. When Emily had bowed so easily to her suggestions, Kelsey had set in motion the wedding of her own dreams.

She was as guilty as Charlene in pushing her own ideas on Emily. It was *her* dream location for the wedding and reception. All of *her* friends were working side by side to make the day memorable. Maybe if she hadn't been so focused on what she wanted, she would have stopped a long time ago to ask if any of it was what *Emily* wanted.

But she hadn't, and now all their dreams were going down the drain—the perfect wedding to make her business, Emily's dream of marrying the perfect man, Gordon and Charlene's perfect son-in-law. Only Connor had succeeded. He was stopping the wedding as he'd said he would.

He was a man of his word, a good man, and she should have trusted him. Kelsey knew how much it must have hurt when she turned her back on him, just as much as regret and heartache were hurting her now.

A door squeaked behind her, letting in a rush of summer air, and Kelsey took a deep breath. Turning to face her aunt and uncle, she said, "Aunt Charlene, Uncle Gordon, I need to talk to you…" Her voice trailed away when she saw Emily and Todd following a few steps behind.

The one time Kelsey had counted on them being late.

"What is it, Kelsey?" Gordon asked.

"I—" She'd hoped to have a chance to talk to her aunt and uncle alone, to prepare them for what Connor had discovered, so together they could find a way to tell Emily. "I was wondering if I could speak to the two of you in private."

She tried to make the suggestion as casually as possible, but there was nothing casual about the way Charlene's eyebrows arched toward her hairline. "What's wrong? Is it the flowers? The music?"

"Relax, Char," Gordon interjected. "Weren't you saying this morning that Kelsey has everything under control?"

Her uncle's reminder and confident smile sent a sick feeling through Kelsey's stomach. How was she supposed to tell them about Todd?

Taking note of her watching him, Todd crossed his arms over his chest, a not-so-subtle challenge in his expression. "You have something to say, Kelsey?"

She took a deep breath, but before she had chance to speak, the chapel door swung open again. She heard Connor's voice a second before he stepped through the doorway. "Actually, I'm the one with something to say."

"McClane! What are you doing here?" Gordon demanded, a lightning bolt of wrinkles cutting across his thunderous expression.

Todd draped a proprietary arm over Emily's shoulders. "I told Emily inviting him was a mistake. He's still in love with her, and he's probably here because he thinks he can stop the wedding."

"I'm not in love with Emily," Connor insisted.

I'm in love with Kelsey. His heart pounded out the words he never thought he'd say, but damned if he'd say them for the first time with the Wilsons and Todd Dunworthy as witnesses.

He felt the irresistible pull of Kelsey's gaze and he couldn't help meeting her gaze any more than he could resist the earth's gravity. *Not now. Not like this,* he mentally pleaded as he looked into her eyes, willing her to understand.

"Then maybe you'd like to explain *exactly* what is going on here?" Gordon repeated.

This was his moment, Connor thought. His chance to prove he was right and the Wilsons were wrong. Wrong about Todd. Wrong about him. But his triumph rang hollow. He didn't need the Wilsons' approval. He wasn't sure why he'd ever thought he did. All he needed was Kelsey. Her faith. Her trust. Had his past and his secret destroyed that?

"Connor?" Kelsey's voice called to him.

Dressed in a blue-green print dress that hugged her curves, her hair free to curl around her face, she looked absolutely beautiful—strong and vulnerable at the same time, and he couldn't look away.

Whatever Gordon and Charlene saw in his expression had them quickly closing ranks around Kelsey. Surrounded by her aunt and uncle, the Wilson misfit suddenly looked at home within the golden circle, and Connor was alone on the outside.

Tearing his gaze away, he focused on Gordon and pulled the information he'd printed from his back pocket. "Your golden boy has a history of using women. His blue-blood family, who mean so much to you, has completely cut him off after he got one of their maids pregnant." He slapped the pages into Gordon Wilson's reluctant outstretched hand.

Charlene gasped, color leaching from her face, but doubt pulled Gordon's silver eyebrows together.

"Todd, what is Connor talking about?" Emily asked, her eyes wide as she stared at her fiancé.

"He's lying," Todd scoffed. But instead of trying to console Emily, he looked to Gordon with a can-you-believe-the-nerve-of-this-guy expression. "You know you can't trust anything McClane says."

"But you can trust me, Uncle Gordon," Kelsey insisted as she stepped closer.

"What do you know about this?" her uncle asked, taking a look at the papers.

"I know Connor is a good man." She spoke the words to her uncle, but her gaze never broke from Connor's. "He's here because he's worried about Emily. That information is true."

"Don't listen to her," Todd issued sharply. When Gordon's steely gaze cut his way, filled with the same distrust he'd pinned on Connor's seconds earlier, he quickly backed down. Relaxing his features into a more conciliatory expression, he said, "I'm afraid Kelsey has fallen for McClane's lies, but it's all a smear campaign to stop the wedding."

"How exactly is Connor McClane behind the significant amount of money your family paid this Sophia Pirelli?"

Todd's confident look faded, clay showing through the once-golden facade, but he still didn't give up. "My family let her go, so she went after us for money, claiming the kid she's carrying is mine. The money was a way to keep her quiet."

"A simple paternity test would have done the same thing and been *much* cheaper," Connor pointed out. "The kind of money your family paid… That's not hush money. It's guilt money."

Connor watched with satisfaction as the truth spread across Dunworthy's face and disgust and disappointment over the Wilsons'. Realization hit Emily last, leaving her pale and shaken as she looked from Todd to her parents. Finally her gaze locked with Connor's, and she burst into tears before rushing into his arms.

Seated in Gordon Wilson's study a half hour later, Connor nodded when the older man held up the bottle of scotch. Gordon poured two glasses, handed one to Connor and took a swallow from his own glass before claiming his spot behind the large mahogany desk.

Connor took a sip of his own scotch while he waited for the older man to speak.

"We owe you our thanks," Gordon said after a minute of silence. "When I think of my little girl married to that liar—"

At the chapel Gordon had made it clear to Dunworthy that the engagement was over and the wedding off, and that he'd live to regret it if he ever went near Emily again. Gordon and Charlene had reluctantly agreed to Emily's request that Connor drive her home after Charlene immediately tried to take charge. Emily had surprised them all, demanding some time alone. Connor thought—hoped—that she was learning to stand up for herself.

"I'm glad I found the proof I needed. I only wish I had found it sooner."

"And I wish you had come to me with your suspicions sooner."

Connor couldn't choke back a disbelieving laugh as he set the glass of scotch aside. "I'm not sure how you think that conversation would have played out, but I don't see you taking my side over your handpicked future son-in-law."

"I did not *handpick* Todd. You make it sound like some kind of arranged marriage."

"Wasn't it?"

A flush rising in his face, Gordon struggled for a calming breath. "Look, I'm trying to say that I appreciate what you've done. I don't know how we can repay you."

Pay him...

Shoving to his feet, Connor ground out, "I don't want your money."

"I wasn't offering any," Gordon shot back. He rose to glare at Connor from across the expanse of his desk.

The silent stalemate lasted several tense seconds before Gordon sighed. The tension drained from his body, leaving his shoulders a bit stooped and signs of age lining his face. "Sit back down." He gestured to the leather chair Connor had abandoned. "I've had enough drama for one night."

Hesitating, Connor glanced at the study doorway.

"Expecting someone?"

"I thought Kelsey would be here by now."

In the aftermath of the argument with Dunworthy and Emily's collapse into tears, Connor hadn't had a chance to talk to Kelsey. He'd expected her to head back to the Wilsons' with the rest of her family, where he'd been counting on the chance to talk to her.

But maybe he'd misunderstood what she'd said during the phone call. He should have known Javy wouldn't keep his mouth shut just because he'd told him to, but the more time Connor had to think, the more worried he became. Did her absence mean that Javy's explanation hadn't made a difference? That she still couldn't forgive Connor for the money he'd taken?

Gordon sucked in a deep breath as if preparing for a painful blow and admitted, "I was wrong about Todd."

They were the words Connor had come to Arizona to hear. The perfect lead-in to tell Gordon he hadn't been wrong just about Todd Dunworthy; he'd been wrong about Connor, too. But as he'd already figured out, it no longer mattered. Only Kelsey…

When he stayed silent, the older man repeated, "I was wrong about Todd. I realize now you came back to help Emily, and you have. But you still have some work to do to convince me you're good enough for this family."

"Good enough—" Connor's words broke off when he caught sight of what almost looked like respect gleaming in the older man's blue eyes. Shaking his head and wondering how a single sip of scotch could so seriously impair his judgment, he said, "You don't have to worry about me being good enough. Emily and I are friends. That's all."

As if the night hadn't already been surreal, Gordon Wilson circled his desk to clap a hand on Connor's shoulder. "Who said anything about Emily?" At Connor's surprised glance, Gordon said, "At the chapel I saw the way you were looking at my niece. You never looked at Emily like that. So don't you think it's time for you to go find Kelsey?"

Sitting in her car outside her shop, Kelsey stared at the freshly painted window. Weddings Amour scrolled across the glass in a flowing, curlicued font. The script matched the business cards and letterhead she'd had made—by the thousands, since it was cheaper to buy in bulk.

Kelsey sighed. She should have gone with the rest of her family—and Connor—back to her aunt and uncle's house. But this was Connor's moment. His moment of triumph…of success. And her moment of failure.

Not that Kelsey had expected her cousin to go through with the wedding once she realized Connor was right about Todd. Still, she felt sick with disappointment. She'd worked so hard on the wedding. Her friends had worked so hard! Lisa and Sara… Like her, they had been counting on Emily's wedding, and Kelsey hated letting them down. She dreaded calling them with the news, but that, too, was part of her job. Along with canceling the reservation at the chapel and the hotel reception, phoning all the guests, arranging for gifts to be returned. The mental list went on and on, with Kelsey's hopes and dreams sinking deeper beneath the crushing weight.

But it had to be done, and sitting in her car wouldn't accomplish any of it. Grabbing her purse off the passenger seat, she climbed from the car. As she opened the door to her shop, she tried—and failed miserably—to forget her excitement and gratitude only days earlier as her friends had pitched in to help decorate. The smell of peach potpourri drifted toward her the moment she stepped inside, but it was the memory of Connor's aftershave that filled her senses, playing games with her mind and her heart.

No matter how many unpleasant tasks lay ahead of her, Kelsey would gladly face the professional failure head-on as long as she could turn a blind eye to the personal heartbreak tearing her up inside.

"You should be happy for him," Kelsey whispered as she sank behind her desk and grabbed the box of tissues. She'd placed it there with the idea that a bride might be overcome with emotion and shed some tears of joy. She hadn't anticipated that she'd be sitting alone in her shop, tempted to put her head down and cry.

Connor had done what he'd set out to do. He'd listened to his gut, proved her aunt and uncle wrong, saved the damsel in distress. If life were a Hollywood movie, now would be the time for him to once again ride off into the sunset…this time with Emily.

He said he didn't love her.

But his lack of feeling for Emily wasn't exactly an undying declaration of love for Kelsey. Especially now that Todd was out of the picture and Emily was back in Connor's arms.

She heard the front door swing open and fought back a groan. The sign in the front window still read Closed, but she hadn't remembered to lock the door behind her. She couldn't afford to turn away potential clients, but she'd never felt less like talking about weddings with a head-over-heels-in-love couple.

Pasting on a smile, she pushed away from her desk and walked to the front of the shop. "Can I help…" her voice trailed away as she caught sight of Connor standing in the doorway "…*you?*"

"I hope so." He wore his sunglasses, as he had the first time Kelsey saw him, but the reflective shades didn't offer the protection they once had. She knew now, behind the polished lenses, his eyes were a vivid, vibrant green. Just as she could read the uncertainty behind his cocky smile and the nerves his confident stance—his legs braced wide and arms loose at his sides—couldn't disguise.

Her heart was pounding so hard, Kelsey half expected the shop's glass windows to shake from the force of the vibrations, but only her entire body trembled in reaction. "What are you doing here? I thought you were—"

"With Emily?" he filled in, taking a step farther into the shop.

"She *is* the reason you came back. To stop her from getting married."

"To stop her from getting married to the *wrong* man," he clarified. He took another step forward, and it was all Kelsey could do to hold her ground.

"Are you—" Kelsey licked dry lips and forced the words out, even though they scraped like sandpaper against her throat. "Are you the right man?"

"I like to think so. But not for Emily."

No longer holding her ground, Kelsey was frozen in place as Connor drew closer. His movements slow and deliberate, he stripped off his sunglasses and set them on the wicker coffee table amid the bowl of potpourri and a dozen bridal magazines. Without the glasses, she could see not only his gorgeous green eyes, but the vulnerability and doubt she'd caused with her lack of faith.

"I like to think I'm the right man for you."

Kelsey opened her mouth to agree he was the *only* man for her, but her voice broke on his name and she surprised them both by bursting into tears. Panic crossed Connor's features for a split second before he pulled her into his arms. "It's okay, sweetheart."

Clinging to the warm cotton of his T-shirt and breathing in the sea-breeze scent of his aftershave, Kelsey swallowed against the tears scraping her throat. "I am so sorry, Connor. I should have given you the chance to explain why you took the money. I should have known you would have a good reason, an *honorable* reason."

"I took an easy way out. Don't make it into something it wasn't."

"You were looking out for the Delgados—for your family. I shouldn't have expected anything less."

"And your family was looking out for Emily. I get that now," he said, running a comforting hand up and down her spine. "Besides, I think Gordon and I have an understanding, even if it is going to take a while for your aunt to get used to the idea."

Lifting her head from the comfort of Connor's chest, Kelsey asked, "Wh-what idea?"

"The idea of me and you." His eyes steadily searching her face, he added, "The idea of me loving you."

They were the words Kelsey longed to hear, words she'd thought she would never hear, and she had trouble believing her ears. Surely her imagination had to be playing tricks. Maybe this was nothing but a dream and she'd wake up in her bed—alone—any minute.

"Kelsey?" Connor prompted.

"In my dreams, you're wearing a tuxedo."

Glancing down at his usual jeans and a T-shirt, he swore beneath his breath. "Leave it me to mess this up. Your aunt told me—"

"No, you didn't mess up at all!" Kelsey insisted.

Connor wasn't some fantasy groom who could spout

poetry and had a picture-perfect smile. He wasn't perfect at all. He was real. Loyal and determined, and she loved everything about him—including his bad-boy past. A past that had shaped him into the good man he was now.

"It's perfect and— You talked to my aunt?"

"To your aunt and uncle both. When I asked them for permission to marry you."

Heart pounding crazily in her chest, Kelsey saved wondering about *that* conversation for another time. For now, she could only focus on one thing. "You want to marry me?"

"I love you, Kelsey. I want to spend the rest of my life with you."

"But what about what you said? About love and marriage being nothing but a lie?" she babbled over the voice in her head all but screaming, *Say yes, you idiot!*

"Yeah, well." Looking a little sheepish, he admitted, "I let my parents' relationship color the way I looked at marriage. Of course, my job didn't paint a rosy picture, either. It's one of the things that makes you perfect for me. I'll have you to remind me that sometimes happily-ever-after does come true. That is, if you say yes."

The screaming voice in her head could no longer be silenced, and Kelsey burst out, "Yes, of course. Yes! I love you, Connor. I think I loved you from the minute my aunt showed me your picture and told me it was my job to keep an eye on you. You've been on my mind and in my heart ever since."

The slow smile he gave her was vintage Connor McClane, but the love and tenderness and emotion Kelsey tasted in his kiss…that was brand-new. She clung to his shoulders, never wanting to let him go, and knowing now that she wouldn't have to. He wasn't a man of the moment; he was the man she would love forever.

As Connor slowly eased away, his breath still warming

her lips, his fingers still buried in her hair, he asked, "About your shop... How much damage will Emily canceling the wedding cause?"

It took a second for Kelsey to focus on anything outside the joined circle of their arms. "Well, um, people will understand her calling off the wedding when they find out about Todd. I don't think they'll hold *that* against me. But the chance to show all the guests an amazing wedding and the word-of-mouth publicity the ceremony and reception would have generated, that's a lost opportunity. For me and my friends. I hate disappointing them," she said, a small touch of sadness dimming her joy.

"What if you don't have to?" Connor asked, a familiar gleam in his eyes. The same look he'd had before he suggested they pair up as a team. The kind of look that told Kelsey he was about to offer some crazy solution that just might work.

"What do you mean?"

"I love you, Kelsey. And while I've never thought about it before, I suspect long engagements aren't my style. I want to marry you, and I have it on good authority that the best wedding coordinator in town has the perfect wedding already planned."

"You mean—*Emily's* wedding?" A startled laugh burst from her lips. "You cannot be serious!"

"No?"

"No! I mean, sure, everything's all planned, but it was done for Emily."

"Was it?" he challenged with a knowing lift to his eyebrows. "Was it Emily who insisted on hiring all her friends? Emily who ran around with a hundred lists to make sure every last detail was exactly the way she wanted it?"

How could Kelsey argue when Connor was right? Along the way, the lines had blurred and Kelsey had planned the kind of wedding she'd dreamed about as a starry-eyed, hope-filled little girl, not the kind of wedding she'd dreamed about as a professional career woman.

"Hey, it's just a thought," Connor said. "For all I care, we can go to Vegas or a justice of the peace—"

"Stop!" Kelsey protested in mock horror, even as excitement bubbled inside her like champagne. "A Vegas wedding? If word got out, my career would be over for sure!"

"But what about switching places with the bride? Think your career can withstand that scandal?"

"Well, as long as it's just this once…"

Her words ended in a laugh as Connor spun her around the room. "Oh, I can guarantee we'll only need to do this once," he vowed, love and commitment shining in his eyes.

"You'd really be okay with a big—and I mean, *big*— wedding, with all the Wilson family and friends in attendance?"

Lifting a hand, he traced a pattern on her cheek—the five-point star he'd confessed drove him crazy. But there was only tenderness in his touch as he knowingly said, "They're your friends and family, too."

Kelsey smiled. "You're right. They are." And now that she no longer felt she had to live up to her mother's motto of Wilson women against the world, she knew they would only grow even closer. "And soon they'll be yours, too," she teased with a laugh when Connor groaned. "Are you ready for that and all the happily-ever-after, love-of-a-lifetime, till-death-do-us-part stuff?"

Kelsey could read the answer in Connor's eyes—the promise of a future filled with happily-ever-after.

"With you?" he vowed. "I can't wait."

* * * * *

BRIDESMAID SAYS, 'I DO!'

BARBARA HANNAY

I wish to remember those who suffered the devastation of the Queensland floods in January, 2011. Many homes and lives were lost in the very places where this story is set.

CHAPTER ONE

IT BEGAN on an everyday, average Monday morning. Zoe arrived at the office punctually at eight forty-five, clutching her takeaway coffee, a necessary comfort when facing the start of the working week. To her surprise, her best friend Bella was already at work.

Bella was usually a bit late, and as she'd just spent another weekend away visiting her father in the country Zoe had expected her to be later than ever. This Monday morning, however, Bella was not only at her desk *early*, but she had a huge grin on her face. *And* she was surrounded by a semicircle of excited workmates.

She was holding out her hand as if she was showing off a new manicure. No big surprise. Bella had a thing for manicures and she often chose very out-there nail polish with an interesting assortment of decorative additions.

But as Zoe drew closer, curious to check out her friend's latest fashion statement, she saw that Bella's nails were painted a subdued and tasteful taupe. And they were *not* the focus of everyone's attention.

The grins and squeals were for a sparkling ring.

On Bella's left hand.

Zoe's cardboard coffee cup almost slipped from her

suddenly weak grasp. She managed to catch it just in time.

She was stunned.

And a bit stung, too.

Struggling to hang on to her smile, she hastily dumped the coffee and her handbag on her desk and hurried over to Bella.

She told herself she was misreading this. Bella couldn't be engaged. Her best friend would most definitely have told her if wedding bells were in the air. Zoe knew for a fact that Bella wasn't even dating anyone at the moment. Together, they'd been commiserating about their date drought, and they'd talked about trying for a double date online.

They'd even considered going on an overseas holiday together—a reconnaissance tour, checking out guys in other countries. Deepening the gene pool, Bella had called it during one of their regular Friday nights together.

Admittedly, for the past three weekends in a row Bella had travelled to her country home on the Darling Downs, and Zoe had been beginning to wonder what the attraction was. Bella had said she was worried about her widowed father, which was totally understandable, as her dad had been in a miserable slump for the past eighteen months ever since her mum died.

Bella had also mentioned her close and supportive neighbours, the Rigbys, and their son, Kent—literally, the boy next door, whom she'd known all her life.

Was something going on with this guy? Had he given Bella this ring?

Bella hadn't breathed a *hint* about a romance with anyone, but it was abundantly clear that the sparkle on her friend's finger was most definitely a diamond. And the name on her lips was…

'Kent Rigby.'

Bella was grinning directly at Zoe now, an expectant light shining in her pretty green eyes.

'Wow!' Zoe managed, squeezing her cheek muscles to make sure she was smiling and not still looking like a stunned mullet. 'You're engaged!'

Bella dipped her head ever so slightly, as if she was trying to read Zoe's reaction, and Zoe cranked her smile another notch while she hunted for the right things to say. 'So—does this mean you and the boy next door have taken the plunge after all?'

She was trying not to sound too surprised, and she *hoped* she looked happy. She certainly didn't want the entire office to realise she was totally clueless about her best friend's romance.

Just in time, she remembered to give Bella a hug, and then she paid due homage to her ring—a solitaire diamond, very tasteful, in a platinum setting, and appropriately delicate for Bella's slim, pale hands.

'It's gorgeous,' Zoe told Bella with genuine honesty. 'It's perfect.'

'Must have cost a bomb,' commented one of the girls behind her in an awed voice.

Eric Bodwin, their boss, arrived then and an awkward hush fell over the office until someone piped up with Bella's happy news.

Eric frowned, dragging his bushy eyebrows low, as if an employee's impending marriage was a huge inconvenience. But then he managed to say 'Congratulations,' with a grunting nod in Bella's direction, before he disappeared into his private den.

He'd never been the type of boss who chatted with

his staff, so everyone was used to his gruffness. Never-theless, his dampening presence put an end to the morn-ing's excitement.

The semicircle of onlookers melted away. Only Zoe remained, her head so brimming with a thousand ques-tions she was reluctant to go back to her desk. And she couldn't help feeling a tad put out that Bella had never confided in her.

'Are you all right, Zoe?' Bella asked cautiously.

'Of course, I'm fine.' Zoe touched Bella's ring fin-ger. 'I'm stoked about this.'

'But you didn't reply to my text.'

'What text?'

'The one I sent you last night. Just before I left Willara Downs, I texted you with my good news.'

'Oh?' Zoe pulled a sheepish face. 'Sorry, Bell. I took myself to the movies last night, and I turned my phone off. Then I forgot to switch it back on.'

'Must have been a good movie,' Bella said dryly, but she was smiling again.

'It was. A lovely, mushy romance.'

Bella rolled her eyes, but they grinned at each other and Zoe was ridiculously pleased that she hadn't been left out after all.

'Meet me at The Hot Spot at lunchtime?' Bella asked next.

'Absolutely.' The busy little café on the corner was their favourite, and a meeting today was top priority.

Back at her desk, however, Zoe's spirits took another dive as she came to grips with the reality of Bella's star-tling news. She was losing her best friend. Bella would move back to the country to live with Kent Rigby and that would be the end of her close friendship—their mutual support over office grumbles, their lunchtime chats, their Friday night cocktails and joint shopping sprees.

It was definitely the end of their overseas holiday plans. And it was very puzzling that Bella had never confided in her about Kent. What did that say about their supposedly close friendship?

Glumly, Zoe retrieved her phone from her handbag and flicked it on to find two unread messages—both from Bella.

At 6.35 p.m. last night:

The most amazing thing! Kent and I are engaged. So much to tell you. B xx

And then at 9.00 p.m.:

Where r u? Gotta talk. x

Zoe winced. If she'd been available for a heart-to-heart chat last night, she'd know everything now and perhaps she'd understand how this engagement had happened so quickly.

Instead, she had to get through an entire morning's work before she received a single answer to her thousand and one questions.

'You're getting *married*?'

'Sure.' Kent pitchforked fresh hay into the horse stall, then angled a meaningful glance to his mate Steve who leaned on the rails, watching. 'Why else would I be asking you to be my best man?'

Steve's eyes widened. 'So you're dead-set serious?'

'I'm serious.' Kent grinned. 'Getting married isn't something to joke about.'

'I guess it isn't. It's just that we all thought—' Steve stopped and grimaced.

'You all thought I'd carry on playing the field for ever,' Kent supplied.

'Maybe not for ever.' Steve's grin was sly. 'But heck man, you never gave the impression you were planning to settle down just yet, even though plenty of girls have tried their hardest.'

Kent's jaw tightened as he thrust the pitchfork back into the hay bale. He'd anticipated Steve's surprise—and yeah, maybe his disbelief—but his friend's reaction still rankled. It was true that he'd dated plenty of girls without getting serious. In the past. But those days were over now. He had responsibilities to shoulder.

Steve's ruddy face twisted into a baffled smile, and he scratched at the side of his sunburned neck. 'Crikey.'

'You're supposed to say congratulations.'

'Of course, mate. Goes without saying.' Balancing a booted foot on the rail, Steve leaned into the stall, holding out his hand. His eyes blazed with goodwill. 'Congratulations, Kent. I mean it. Bella's an ace girl. She's terrific. The two of you will be a great team.'

He shook Kent's hand.

'Thanks.'

'I shouldn't have been so surprised,' Steve added, accompanying the words with a shrug. 'It makes sense. You and Bella have always been like—' He held up a hand, displaying his index finger and forefinger entwined.

Kent acknowledged this truth with a nod and a smile. He and Bella Shaw had been born six months apart to families on neighbouring properties. As infants they'd shared a playpen. As youngsters they had joint swimming and riding lessons. They'd gone to school together, travelling into Willara each day on the rattling school bus, swapping the contents of their lunch boxes and sharing the answers to their homework.

From as far back as Kent could remember, their two families had gathered on the banks of Willara Creek for regular barbecues. Their fathers had helped each other with shearing or mustering. Their mothers had swapped recipes, knitting patterns and old wives' tales.

When Kent was just six years old, Bella's dad had saved his life…

And now, with luck, Kent was returning the favour.

He felt OK about it. Honestly, he was happy with the future he and Bella had planned.

Just the same, Kent would have been relieved to get a few things off his chest to Steve. In the past few years his load had mounted steadily.

When his dad had hankered for an early retirement, Kent had taken on the bulk of the farm work. Then Bella's mother had died, and her father, the very man who'd saved his life when he was a kid, had started drinking himself to death. Desperately worried, Kent had helped out there as well, putting in long hours ploughing fields and mending neglected fences.

Bella, of course, had been distraught. She'd lost her mother and now she was likely to lose her father, and if these weren't enough troubles to bear, her family's property was rapidly going down the drain.

A host of heavy emotions was tied up in their decision to marry, but although Kent was tempted to confide in Steve he wouldn't off-load his baggage, not even to his best friend.

'I hear Bella's dad's in a bad way,' Steve said. 'He's been keeping very much to himself and he needs to slow down on his drinking.'

Kent's head shot up. Had Steve guessed things were worse than most people realised?

'Tom has the beginnings of heart failure,' he said slowly.

'That's a worry.'

'It is, but if he looks after himself, he should be OK.'

Steve nodded. 'And once you're his son-in-law, you'll be able to keep a closer eye on him.'

Clearly, Steve thought their decision was reasonable, but then his eyes flashed as he sent Kent a cheeky smirk. 'You and Bella are a sly pair though, keeping this under wraps in a gossipy town like Willara.' He snapped a piece of straw between his fingers and raised his eyebrows. 'So, when's the happy day? I suppose I'll have to wear a penguin suit.'

When Zoe burst into The Hot Spot, Bella was already there, waiting in their favourite corner booth with salad sandwiches and two chai lattes.

'That was the longest morning of my life,' Zoe moaned as she hurled herself into a seat. 'Thanks for getting lunch.'

'It was my turn.'

Reaching across the table, Zoe touched the diamond on Bella's left hand. 'This is real, isn't it? You're properly engaged. I'm not dreaming.'

'It's totally real.' Bella gave a crooked little grin. 'But I must admit I still have to pinch myself.'

'You, too?' Drawing a deep breath to calm her racing thoughts, Zoe asked carefully, 'So…you weren't expecting this engagement?'

'Not really,' Bella said, blushing. 'But it wasn't exactly a surprise either.'

Zoe blinked and gave a helpless flap of her hands.

'I'm sorry, I'm lost already. You're going to have to ex-plain this.' She took a sip of her chai latte, but she was too intent on Bella's response to register the sweet and spicy flavour she usually loved.

'There's not a lot to explain.' Bella tucked a shiny strand of smooth blond hair behind one ear. 'The thing is…even when we were kids there was a lingering sug-gestion from Kent's and my parents that we might even-tually—you know—end up together some day. They teased us when we were little, then toned it down later, but all the time we were growing up it was there in the background as a possibility.'

This was news to Zoe and she couldn't help asking, 'How come you've never mentioned it?'

Bella looked contrite. 'You must think I'm crazy, talking so much about guys without ever really men-tioning Kent.'

'You spoke about him, but you said he was just a friend.'

'He was. For ages. We were just…neighbours…and good mates…' Her shoulders lifted in a casual shrug. 'To be honest, I'd never seriously thought about mar-rying him. But then—'

Zoe leaned closer. 'Is Kent the reason you've headed for home every weekend lately?'

Pink crept into Bella's cheeks and her green eyes took on a touching mistiness as she held out her left hand and admired her ring again. 'It sort of crept up on us. Kent's been so sweet.'

'Oh-h-h…' Watching the dewy smile on Bella's lips, Zoe was overcome by the romantic possibilities of her friend's situation. Her skin turned to goose bumps and she could picture it all: a wonderful, long-term friend-ship where a couple felt really comfortable with each other, and knew each other inside out—all the good bits and the bad. Then, suddenly, they were hit by a blinding and beautiful truth.

So different from Zoe's soul-destroying experience with Rodney the Rat.

'Out of the blue you just realised you were in love and meant for each other,' she said.

Bella nodded.

'And you definitely know Kent's Mr Right?'

Another nod.

Zoe couldn't believe the way her throat was choking up. 'I thought those blinding flashes of insight only happened in movies, but look at you. This is a real life friends-to-lovers romance!' To her embarrassment, a tear spilled down her cheek.

'So you understand?' Bella's smile was a mixture of sympathy and relief.

'My head's still trying to catch up, but I guess I understand here.' Not caring how melodramatic she looked, Zoe pressed a hand over her heart. 'I'm happy for you, Bell. Truly.'

'Thanks.' In a blink, Bella was out of her chair and the girls were hugging. 'I knew you'd understand.'

'Your dad must be thrilled,' Zoe said when Bella had sat down again.

To her surprise, a flood of colour rushed into Bella's face and then she paled and looked down at the sandwich in front of her. She pulled at a piece of lettuce poking out from the bread. 'Yes, he's very happy,' she said quietly.

Puzzled, and just a little worried by the reaction, Zoe wasn't sure what to say next. Something wasn't right here.

Or was she imagining Bella's tension?

She wondered if Bella's dad had expressed mixed feelings. It would be bittersweet for Mr Shaw to watch his daughter's engagement blossom so soon after his wife's death. He'd miss having her there to share the joy with him.

Zoe thought about her own parents, settled at last, running their little music shop in Sugar Bay and raising her little brother, Toby. After Toby's unexpected arrival when Zoe was fourteen, her mum and dad had undergone a dramatic transformation. By the time she'd started work and Toby was ready for school, they'd given up their nomadic existence, travelling round the country in a second-rate rock band.

But becoming conventional parents hadn't dimmed their love for one another. They'd remained fixed in a crazy love-struck-teenager groove and, although their relationship had always left Zoe feeling on the outside, she couldn't imagine either of them having to manage alone. Not for ages, at any rate.

Poor Mr Shaw...

'Earth to Zoe. Are you there?'

Zoe blinked, and realised Bella had been talking, and by the look of frustration on her face she'd been saying something important. 'Sorry. I—ah—missed what you said.'

Bella sighed and gave a little, heaven-help-me eye roll. 'I said I was hoping you'd be my bridesmaid.'

Zap!

Zoe's heart gave a jolt, like a soldier jumping to attention. She'd been so busy getting her head around Bella's new status as fiancée, she'd given no thought to her actual wedding. But bridesmaid?

Wow!

She had a sudden vision of Bella looking lovely in

white, with a misty veil…and herself in a beautiful bridesmaid's gown…

There'd be bouquets…and handsome guys in formal suits…

She'd never been a bridesmaid.

Warmth flooded her and she felt quite dizzy with excitement. 'I'd love to be your bridesmaid. I'd be totally honoured.'

This was no exaggeration. In fact, Zoe was quite sure Bella could never guess how over-the-top excited she was about this.

She'd heard other girls groan about being bridesmaids. They seemed to look on the honour as a boring chore and they told war stories about having to wear horrible satin gowns in the worst possible colours and styles.

Talk about ungrateful! For Zoe, being a bridesmaid was a wonderful privilege. She would wear anything Bella chose—puce coloured lace or slime-toned velvet—she wouldn't care. Being Bella's bridesmaid was clear, indisputable evidence that she was someone's really close friend.

Finally.

Oh, cringe. Anyone would think she was a total loser.

Well…truth was…she'd actually felt like a loser for much of her childhood. She'd had so few chances to make close friends, because her parents had dragged her all around the country, living—honest to God—in the back of a bus. There'd never been time for her friendships to get off the ground.

Her best effort had been in the fifth grade when the band broke up for a bit and her parents had stayed in Shepparton for almost twelve months. Zoe had become really good friends with Melanie Trotter. But then the band had regrouped and her parents had moved on, and the girls' letter exchange had lasted six months before slowing to a trickle, then, inevitably, dried up.

It wasn't until Zoe started work at Bodwin & North and met Bella that she'd finally had the chance to form the kind of ongoing friendship she'd always longed for. And now, here was the proof—an invitation to be Bella's bridesmaid.

Zoe beamed at Bella. 'Will it be a country wedding?'

'Yes—on the Rigbys' property—Willara Downs.'

'Wow. That sounds utterly perfect.' Ever since her childhood, travelling through endless country towns, Zoe had known a secret yearning to drive through a farm gateway instead of whizzing past. Now, she wouldn't merely be driving through the farm gate, she'd be totally involved in the proceedings.

Wow, again. She could picture Bella's big day so easily—white-covered trestle tables on a homestead veranda. A ceremony beneath an archway of pale pink roses. Male guests with broad shoulders and suntans. Women in pearls.

'So...how many bridesmaids are you planning' She tried to sound casual, which wasn't easy when she was holding her breath. Would she be sharing this honour with six bridesmaids? Hadn't she read somewhere that a celebrity had eighteen attendants—all of them in purple silk?

'Only one,' Bella said calmly as she spooned fragrant froth from the inside of her glass. 'It won't be a big flashy wedding. Just family and close friends. I've never wanted a swarm of bridesmaids.' She smiled. 'I just want you, Zoes. You'll be perfect.'

Perfect. What a wonderful word.

'I'll do everything I can to make the day perfect for *you*,' Zoe said.

There was no question—she would try her utmost to be the *perfect* bridesmaid. She would research her duties and carry them out conscientiously. No bride had ever had a more dedicated wedding attendant. 'So, do we have a date? Is there a time line?'

'Actually, we were thinking about October twenty-first.'

'Gosh, that's only a few weeks away.'

'I know, but Kent and I didn't want to wait.'

How romantic.

Zoe supposed she'd hear the phrase *Kent and I* rather a lot in the next few weeks. She wondered, as she had many times, what it was like to be so deeply in love.

But then another thought struck. Leaning closer, she whispered, 'Bell, you're not pregnant, are you?'

'No, of course not.'

'Just checking, seeing you're in such a rush, in case my bridesmaid's duties involved knitting bootees.'

Bright red in the face, Bella slapped her wrist. 'Shut up, idiot.'

'Sorry.' Zoe smiled. 'Well, a tight deadline can focus the mind wonderfully.'

'It shouldn't be too hard to organise. Everything will happen at the homestead, so we won't need to book a church, or cars or a reception venue, and the local rector is a good friend of the Rigbys.'

'So you only have to buy a wedding dress and order a cake.'

'Yes. Too easy,' Bella said with a laugh, and then as they started on their sandwiches her face grew more serious. 'I've made an appointment with Eric Bodwin. I'll have to resign, because I'll be living at Willara, but

I was also hoping we might be able to arrange time off for you as well, so you can come out and help with all the last minute organising. I don't want to burden Kent with too much of the legwork. But I know the time off would eat into your holiday allowance—'

'That's fine,' Zoe said quickly. 'I'd love a week or so in the country.' She was feeling a bit down at the thought of Bella resigning, but then she grinned. 'As a bonus, I might have a chance to wangle a nice country romance of my own.'

Bella's eyes danced. 'Now that's a thought.'

It wasn't just an idle thought for Zoe. As a young girl, experiencing constant brief tastes of country towns before moving on, she'd developed something of a penchant for the jeans-clad sons of farmers with their muscular shoulders and rolling, loose-hipped strides.

'Mind you,' Bella said, 'I've grown away from country life since I moved to Brisbane.'

'But you're looking forward to going back and settling down as a farmer's wife, aren't you?'

Bella gave her lower lip a slightly troubled chew. 'It will certainly be an adjustment.'

'I think it sounds idyllic,' Zoe said honestly. 'But then I probably have a romanticised idea of life on a farm. I've never actually been on one.'

'Why don't you come home with me next weekend?' Bella suggested with a sudden beaming smile. 'We could go together after work on Friday. It only takes a little over an hour. You can meet Kent and I can show you where we're planning to have the wedding, and you can help me to nut out the details.'

'Wow. That sounds wonderful.'

'Actually, you know how hopeless I am at organising. I'll probably hand you pen and paper and a list of phone numbers for caterers.'

'That's OK.' No doubt it was pathetic, but Zoe loved to feel needed. 'I'd love to come. Are you sure there's room for me to stay?'

'Of course I'm sure. We won't stay with my dad. He hasn't been well and he'd get in a stew about clean sheets and things. We can stay at Willara Downs. The homestead is huge and Kent's a wonderful host. His parents live in town these days, but they'll probably come out and you can meet them, too. They'll welcome you with open arms.'

Again Zoe thought of all the times her parents had whizzed in and out of country towns when she'd longed to stay. She'd been constantly looking in from the outside, never really getting to know the locals.

Now, for a short time, for the *first* time, she would be an insider.

'I'd love that. We can take my car,' she offered, eager to help any way she could. 'It's so much easier than getting the bus.'

Already, in her head, she was compiling a list of her bridesmaid's responsibilities. Number one—she would support Bella and help her to stay calm through the next nerve-wrangling weeks. Perhaps she would also help her to address the wedding invitations, and then there would be a hen night to arrange…and a bridal shower…

It was going to be fabulous. She was determined to carry out every task to the very best of her ability. Her aim was nothing less than perfection.

CHAPTER TWO

THE next weekend, fifteen kilometres from Willara Downs, Zoe heard an unmistakable flap, flap, flap coming from her car's rear tyre. Her stomach took a dive. *Not now. Please, no!*

But it was useless to hope. She'd heard that flapping sound too many times in her childhood—her dad had always been changing flat tyres on their bus. Now she knew with sickening certainty that she had no choice but to pull over onto the grassy verge and try to remember what to do.

It wasn't fun to be alone, though, on the edge of an unknown country road at dusk on a Friday evening. Zoe wished she hadn't been so convincing when she'd assured Bella she'd be fine to drive on to Willara Downs by herself, while Bella visited her dad.

Two days ago, Bella's father had been admitted to hospital. Apparently, Kent Rigby had found Mr Shaw in a very bad state and insisted on rushing him in to Willara.

Understandably, Bella had been beside herself with anxiety and Zoe had dropped her in town.

'Kent's not answering his phone, so he's probably out on the farm, but he'll understand if you turn up alone,' Bella had assured her.

'And one of us will come back to pick you up in an hour or so,' Zoe suggested.

'Yes, that will be great.'

And so…after expressing the wish that Mr Shaw was much improved, Zoe had set off happily enough— at least she was driving her own car and she felt at ease behind the wheel. And apart from concern about Mr Shaw's illness, she was dead excited about this weekend away and getting to meet Bella's fiancé… seeing the wedding venue…being part of the planning.

The very last thing she needed was a flat tyre.

Damn.

Briefly, Zoe toyed with the idea of trying the Willara Downs number to see if Kent Rigby could help. But it was such a bad way to start the weekend, to be seen as a useless city chick who wouldn't even *try* to fix a simple problem by herself.

Resigned, she climbed out. The tyre was as flat as a burst balloon, and she went to her boot to hunt for the jack and the thingamabob that loosened the wheel nuts.

Mosquitoes buzzed as she hunted. The jack was, of course, buried under all the luggage—two overnight bags, two make-up bags, two sets of hot rollers.

'You never know, there *might* be a party,' Bella had said.

Now, with their belongings scattered haphazardly on the side of the road, Zoe squatted beside the wheel, positioned the jack and got on with turning its handle.

So far so good…except she didn't really know how high she was supposed to raise the car. And once that was done…she wasn't certain she was strong enough to loosen the wheel nuts. They looked mighty tight. And even if she did get them off, would she be able to tighten them up again?

Zoe's unhelpfully vivid imagination threw up a picture of her car driving off with the back wheel spinning free and bouncing into the bush, while she struggled with an out-of-control steering wheel.

Maybe she *should* try to ring for help.

Standing again, she reached into the car for her handbag. As usual, because she really needed it, her phone had slipped from its handy side pouch to the very bottom of her bag, so she had to feel around among movie tickets, keys, lipsticks, pens, old shopping lists, tissues...

She was still fumbling when she heard the sound of a vehicle approaching. Her spirits lifted. This *might* be nice, friendly country folk only too happy to stop and help her.

The thought was barely formed, however, before Zoe felt a shaft of hot panic. If only she hadn't watched all those horror movies. Here she was—totally alone in the silent, empty bush wondering if the driver was an axe murderer, an escaped prisoner, a rapist.

She made a final, frantic fumble in the bottom of her bag, and her fingers closed around her phone just as a white utility vehicle shot around the curve.

There was only one person in the ute and all she could see was a black silhouette, distinctly masculine. He was slowing down.

Zoe's nervous heart gave a sickening thud as his ute came to a complete stop and he leaned out, one strong, suntanned forearm resting casually on the window's rim.

In panic, she depressed the call button on her phone and glanced quickly at the screen.

No signal. She was out of the network. *Oh, terrific.* There was no hope of a rescue.

'Need a hand?' the driver called.

At least he had a friendly voice—mellow and warm with a hint of good humour.

Zoe gulped, and forced herself to look at him properly. She saw dark, neatly trimmed hair and dark eyes. Not threatening eyes, but genial, friendly, and framed by a handsome face. Nicely proportioned nose, strong jaw and a generous mouth.

Already his door was swinging open, and he stepped out.

He was wearing a crisp blue shirt with long sleeves rolled back from his wrists and pale cream moleskin trousers. His elastic sided riding boots were tan and well polished. Zoe had always fancied that look—clean cut with a hint of cowboy. Surely, an axe murderer wouldn't go to so much trouble?

'I see you've got a flat,' he said, coming towards her with the easy loose gait of a man of the land. 'That's rotten luck.'

He smiled and his eyes were deep, coffee-brown—friendly eyes, with a spark of fun, and with laughter lines fanning from the corners.

In spite of her fears, Zoe couldn't help smiling back at him. 'I've just about got the car jacked up, but I wasn't sure how far I should take it.'

'I'd say you have it just right. The perfect height.'

Perfect. It was fast becoming one of her favourite words.

Suddenly, she couldn't remember why she'd been scared of this fellow. There was something about his smile and about his face that was incredibly, importantly *right*.

In fact…Zoe felt as if a gong had been struck deep inside her, and it took a magnificent effort to force her attention away from this stranger to her problem. 'I was—um—about to tackle the wheel nuts.'

'Would you like a hand with them?' He was smiling again and her skin tingled deliciously. 'If that doesn't offend you.'

'Why would I be offended by an offer of help?' *From a gorgeous man*, she added silently.

He shrugged. 'Thought you might be like my little sister—the independent type. She hates it when guys assume she needs help when she doesn't.'

'Oh, I see.' The mention of his sister relaxed Zoe even further. Actually, she was so relaxed she was practically floating, and she offered him a radiant smile. 'I'd love to say I could manage this tyre on my own, but, to be honest, I'm really not sure I *can* manage. I was just about to phone for help.'

'No need. It won't take long.'

'That's awfully kind of you.' Holding out the wheel thingamajig, she hoped her saviour didn't get grease on his clothes.

Clearly not sharing her concern for his pristine trousers, he hunkered down beside the wheel and began working smoothly and efficiently.

Nice hands, Zoe noticed. He was nice all over, actually. Tall and muscular. Not too lean, not too beefy. She suppressed a little sigh, and told herself she was a fool to feel fluttery over the first country fellow she met. Before this wedding was over she'd meet tons of cute rural guys.

But there was something special about this man, something totally entrancing about the warmth in his brown eyes and the quirk of his smile, a subtle *something* that made her heart dance and her insides shimmy.

Strange she could feel so much when all his attention was focused on her car's rear wheel.

'Now for the spare.' Having loosened the wheel, he was standing up again, and he glanced Zoe's way.

Their gazes linked and…

He went very still. And a new kind of intensity came into his eyes. He stared at Zoe…as if he'd had a shock, a pleasant, yet deeply disturbing shock.

Trapped in his gaze, she could feel her face glowing hot as a bonfire, and she was struck by the weirdest sense that she and this helpful stranger were both experiencing the same awesome rush. Deep tremors—happy and scary at once—as if they had been connected on an invisible wavelength.

This can't be what I think it is.

Back to earth, Zoe.

She realised that the stranger was frowning now and looking upset. Or was he angry? It was hard to tell. His brow was deeply furrowed and he dropped his gaze to the ground and his throat worked as he stared at a dried mud puddle.

Zoe held her breath, unable to speak or even think, and yet incredibly aware that something beyond the ordinary had happened.

Then her rescuer blinked and shook his head, as if he was ridding himself of an unwanted thought. He cleared his throat. 'Ah—the spare tyre. I guess it's in the boot?'

Turning away from Zoe, he made his way to the back of the car, skilfully stepping between the scattered pieces of luggage.

'I'm sorry,' Zoe spluttered, struggling to shake off the unsettling spell that seemed to have gripped her. 'I should have fetched the spare tyre and had it ready for you.'

'No worries.' He spoke casually enough, but when he looked back at her he still seemed upset, as if she'd done something wrong. But then, without warning, he smiled.

His smile was warm and friendly again, and once more Zoe was electrified. Instantly. Ridiculously. She found herself conjuring a picture of him in a farmhouse kitchen, smiling that same yummy smile across the breakfast table at her, after a night of delicious love-making.

Good grief. Next minute she'd be imagining him naked.

Could he guess?

'Excuse me.'

His voice roused her. Blushing, she stepped out of his way as he carried the new wheel and hefted it into posi-tion. But, heaven help her, she was mesmerised by the strength of his shoulders and the sureness of his hands as he lined up the wheel as if it weighed no more than a cardboard button, and fitted it into place.

'You've done this before,' she said.

'So many times, I could do it in my sleep.'

Zoe wasn't sure it was wise to let her mind wander in the direction of this man's sleep. Better to keep the talk flowing.

She said, 'I've watched my dad change tyres on coun-try roads enough times. I should have picked up a few more clues.'

He looked up at her, clearly surprised. 'Which coun-try roads? You're not from around here, are you?'

'No. My parents were in a band and they toured all around the various country shows.' She hoped any re-sentiment she felt for those nomadic gypsy years hadn't crept into her voice.

'Which band?' he asked, pausing in the middle of tightening a nut.

'Lead the Way.'

'You're joking.'

Laughing, Zoe shook her head. 'No, I'm afraid I'm serious.'

'Were both your parents in Lead the Way?'

'Yep. My dad was the lead singer and my mum was on drums.'

'So you're Mick Weston's daughter?'

'His one and only.' It wasn't an admission Zoe needed to make very often. Since she'd started work in the city she'd hardly met anyone who'd heard of her parents or their band.

'Amazing.' To her surprise, he threw his head back and laughed. 'Wait till I tell my old man. He's a huge fan of Mick Weston. Never missed a Lead the Way performance in Willara.'

Fancy that. Zoe beamed at him. It was heartening to be reminded that her dad had been very popular out here.

But, heavens, now she and this stranger had something in common and she found herself liking him more than was sensible. Perhaps encouraging conversation wasn't such a bright idea.

She busied herself with securing the punctured tyre in the boot and restowing all the bits and pieces of luggage.

By the time she'd finished, her good Samaritan was removing the jack. 'That's done,' he said, straightening and dusting off his hands.

'Thank you so much. It's incredibly kind of you. I

really am very grateful.' *And just a little sad that we'll
have to say goodbye now...*

He stood with his feet apart, hands resting lightly on
his hips, watching her with an enigmatic smile. 'What
about you?' he asked. 'Do you sing or play the guitar?'

''Fraid not.' Zoe returned his smile—seemed her
face was permanently set in smile mode. 'The musical
genes totally bypassed me.'

'But you inherited your dad's talent for flat tyres on
country roads.'

'Yes...unfortunately.'

Wow. Instead of rushing off, he was making conversation with her. And Zoe loved it. She was no longer bothered that he was a stranger. She was too busy
enjoying this amazing experience—the most awesome
sensation of being swept high and pumped full of excitement, as if she were riding a magnificent, shining
wave.

Were her feet still touching the ground?

She'd never felt like this before. Not with a complete
stranger. Not with this bursting-from-a-geyser intensity.
Rodney the Rat didn't count. He'd been a work colleague and she'd known him for twelve months before
he asked her out.

Truth was—Zoe usually lacked confidence around
guys. She guessed it was part of an overall lack of confidence, a problem that stemmed from her childhood
when she'd always been the new girl in town, always
arriving late in the term when all the friendship groups
were firmly established. She'd grown up knowing she'd
never quite fitted in.

But this man's gorgeous smile made her feel fabulously confident and suddenly her biggest fear was that
he would simply drive away—out of her life.

'I'll tell my dad I met the son of one of his fans,' she told him.

'Do you have far to go?' her helper asked.

'I don't think it's much farther. I'm heading for Willara Downs.'

He stiffened. 'Willara Downs?'

'It's a property near here—a farm.'

'Yes, I know.' Now, he was frowning again. 'It's my property.'

His property?

Really?

A sudden chill swept over Zoe. He wasn't…

He couldn't be…

'You're—you're not—a Rigby, are you?'

'I certainly am.' He smiled, but it was a shade too late, and with only a fraction of its former warmth. 'The name's Kent Rigby.' His smile wavered as he asked uncertainly, 'Should I know you?'

Oh, God, he was Bella's Kent…Bella's boy next door.

Kent's been so sweet, Bella had said.

No wonder he was nice. He was the man her best friend was about to marry.

A cool breeze made icy goose bumps on Zoe's skin. The purple tinged dusk crowded in and she felt suddenly, terribly weary. And wary.

'We haven't met,' she said quietly, hoping she didn't sound as ridiculously disappointed as she felt. 'But we'll soon have a lot to do with each other. I'm Zoe. Bella's bridesmaid.'

Kent Rigby's eyes darkened and his features were momentarily distorted, as if he tried to smile but couldn't quite manage it.

But if he'd been caught out, he was very good at covering it up. 'Sorry, I should have guessed,' he said, speaking smoothly once more, with no hint of disturbance. 'But I expected you to be with Bella.'

Calmly, he held out his hand.

Unhappily, she felt the warmth and strength of his hand enclose hers in a firm clasp. 'Hello, Kent.'

'Hi, Zoe.'

'I dropped Bella off at the hospital. She tried to call you to explain that I'd be arriving on my own.'

Kent had forgotten to let go of her hand. 'I'm actually on my way back from seeing Tom myself,' he said.

'How—how is he?'

'Slightly improved, thank God.'

Suddenly he realised he was still holding her hand. Letting go, he cracked a slightly embarrassed grin, then thrust his hands into his jeans pockets. He straightened his shoulders, then looked to the sky in the east where a huge full moon was already poking its golden head above a dark, newly ploughed field. 'I guess Bella will ring when she's ready to be picked up.'

'Yes.'

'We'd better get going, then. Would you like to follow me? I'll keep you in my rear vision, so I'll know you're OK.'

'Thanks.'

As Zoe followed Kent Rigby's ute she tried to laugh at herself. What a fool she'd been, getting all hot and bothered about a stranger she'd met on a road side.

Shouldn't she have guessed that a hot-looking guy like Kent would have already been taken? Hadn't she learned anything from her experience with Rodney?

OK, so she was feeling ridiculously disappointed right now, but she'd get over it. She'd been looking forward to this weekend too much to let anything spoil it. She'd been so excited about Bella's wedding and being her bridesmaid. She'd wanted to be the *perfect* bridesmaid.

That was still her goal. Having a fan-girly moment over the bridegroom had been a minor hiccup, but she'd recover in no time.

In the fading light of dusk, which just happened to be Zoe's favourite time of day, the track she and Kent were driving along emerged out of a purple-shadowed tunnel of trees onto sweeping lawns, dusky and magical in the twilight.

Zoe saw an archway of rambler roses and a weeping willow…an elegant, Federation-style house, long and low, with lights already glowing on the veranda.

The car's wheels crunched on white gravel as she pulled up behind Kent's ute in front of smooth sandstone steps flanked by garden beds filled with agapanthus and lilies. When Kent got out, she saw him silhouetted against the backdrop of his home. Damn. It was such an attractive image—but she had to stop thinking like that.

She had no choice. This gorgeous man was Bella's future husband and there was no way she would let her silly imagination give into any more reckless fantasies.

'I'll show you to your room,' Kent said with the gracious charm of a perfect host, which showed that he at least knew exactly what *his* role was.

Zoe followed him down a hallway past an elegant lounge room with deep squishy sofas and rich Oriental rugs to a pretty bedroom that was the epitome of comfort and tasteful country-style décor.

With her things stowed, she was taken out to a wisteria-scented back veranda, and soon found herself sitting in a deep cushion-lined cane chair, sipping chilled white wine while she and Kent looked out in the fading light to the most beautiful view of fields and distant hills.

She suppressed an urge to sigh. Everything about Kent Rigby's home was as gorgeous as he was. And it was all so beautifully presented she supposed he must have a housekeeper and a gardener. Lucky Bella wouldn't be a slave to housework.

As a child, looking out of the bus window, Zoe had dreamed of living in a lovely farmhouse like the Rigbys', but she'd never been the jealous type and she wasn't about to start now.

Very soon Bella would return from the hospital and take her rightful place at Kent Rigby's side. And Zoe's silly road side mistake would be a thing of the past.

Clutching an icy glass of beer as if his life depended on it, Kent struggled to ignore the girl sitting beside him. Not an easy task when he was her host and hospitable manners had been ingrained in him from birth.

Problem was, he was badly rattled and he couldn't really understand how he'd got this way. Anyone would think he wasn't used to meeting new girls—when the truth was quite the opposite.

He could only assume the problem arose because he hadn't adjusted to his newly engaged status. No doubt that would explain the crazy chemistry that had gripped him from the moment he set eyes on Bella's bridesmaid.

Why the hell hadn't he introduced himself to Zoe Weston as soon as he stepped up to help her? If he'd known who she was, he could have avoided those telling moments—those shocking spellbinding seconds when he'd felt drawn to her, as if a bizarre spell had been cast over him.

Chances were, he'd never have noticed her inexplicable appeal, that special *something* in her eyes, and in the sheen of her hair or the tilt of her smile—a quality that rocked his easy-going nature to its very foundations.

How crazy was that? He'd exchanged nothing more than a few glances with her.

Kent knew it was nothing more than an illusion. A mistake. It was more than likely that every man experienced a similar difficulty in his pre-wedding weeks. Commitment to one girl didn't automatically stop a guy from noticing other girls. Learning to ignore their appeal was part of the adjustment to being engaged or married.

In Kent's case, his commitment was binding on all kinds of levels, and there was no going back. No regrets. He was a man of his word.

Besides, if he was rational about this, there wasn't even anything particularly special about Zoe Weston. Her brown hair and blue eyes and slim build were nice enough, but her looks were average. Surely?

The imagined attraction was merely a blip, and now he could put it behind him.

That settled, Kent took a deep, reassuring draft of beer, pleased to realise he'd been overreacting.

It wasn't as easy as Zoe had hoped to relax while sitting beside Kent on his veranda. She found herself crossing and uncrossing her legs, fiddling with the stem of her wine glass, or sneaking sideways glances at her host's stare-worthy profile. Hardly the behaviour of a perfect bridesmaid.

Desperate to stop this nonsense, she jumped to her feet and leaned on the veranda railing, looking out at the parklike sweep of gardens that stretched to a timber fence, and fields of golden crops and grazing animals.

Concentrate on the wedding—not the groom.

Casually, she asked, 'Are you planning a garden wedding, Kent?'

He looked surprised, as if the question had caught him out, but he responded readily enough. 'An outdoor ceremony would be great and the weather forecast is promising. What do you think?'

Rising from his chair, he joined her at the veranda's edge, and once again Zoe was struggling to ignore his proximity. Now there was the tantalising whiff of his cologne to deal with as well.

She concentrated on the lawns and banks of shrubbery. 'A garden wedding would be perfect. Would you hire a caterer?'

'That's one of the things we need to discuss this weekend. But Bella's a bit...distracted.'

'Yes, her dad's health is a big worry for her.'

Kent nodded, then let out a heavy sigh.

'You're worried, too,' Zoe said, seeing the sudden tension in his face.

'I have to be careful what I say around Bella, but I'm angry with her dad.' Kent sighed again. 'Don't get me wrong. Tom Shaw's a wonderful guy. In many ways he's been my hero. But his wife died eighteen months ago and he dropped his bundle. He started drinking heavily, and now he has the beginnings of heart failure.'

'From drinking?'

'From drinking and generally not looking after himself.' Kent's hand fisted against the railing. 'Bella's beside herself, of course.'

'I hadn't realised his health was so bad,' Zoe said with concern. 'Poor Bell.'

'Don't worry.' Kent spoke quietly, but with unmistakable determination. 'I'll look after her. And I'm damned if I'll let Tom kill himself.'

Wow, Zoe thought. Kent had sounded so—so *noble*; he really was Bella's knight in shining armour.

And clearly he was happy in that role. He was turning to Zoe now with a smile. 'Bella said you're going to be a great help with the wedding.'

'I—I'm certainly happy to do all I can to help.'

'She claims you're a fabulous organiser and list-maker.'

'I suppose I can be. I've never organised a wedding, but I quite like planning our office Christmas party. A smallish wedding won't be too different.' To Zoe's dismay, her cheeks had grown very hot. She shot a quick glance out to the expanse of lawn. 'I imagine you'd need to hire tables and chairs.'

'Yes, definitely.'

'And table cloths, crockery, glassware et cetera.'

'I dare say.' Kent flashed a gorgeous crooked smile. 'If you keep talking like that you'll land yourself a job, Zoe.'

And if he kept smiling at her like that she wouldn't be able to refuse.

CHAPTER THREE

It was late on Sunday night before the girls arrived back in Brisbane. As Zoe drove they discussed practical matters—the style of wedding gowns and invitations, and the things they needed to hire for the garden reception. They were both tired, however, and, to Zoe's relief, they spent much of the journey in reflective silence.

She dropped Bella off at her flat in Red Hill, declining her invitation to come in for a drink with the excuse that they both had another Monday morning to face in less than ten hours.

'Thanks for spending the weekend with me,' Bella said as she kissed Zoe's cheek. 'And thanks for offering to help Kent with organising the reception. Well, you didn't actually offer, but thanks for agreeing when I pleaded. We all know I can't organise my way out of a paper bag.'

'That's OK,' Zoe responded glibly, hoping that she sounded much calmer than she felt about ongoing communication with Bella's fiancé—even if it was only via email or telephone.

'And thanks for taking your car, Zoe. So much better than bumping along in the old bus.'

'My pleasure.' However, Zoe couldn't possibly share Bella's opinion on this matter. If she hadn't taken her car, she wouldn't have had a flat tyre and she wouldn't have had a private meeting with Kent. And her weekend would have been a darned sight easier.

'Thanks for inviting me, Bell. It was—wonderful. You're going to have the most gorgeous wedding ever.'

'I know. I'm so lucky.' Bella's green eyes took on a wistful shimmer. 'You do like Kent, don't you?'

Zoe's heart took a dive, but she forced a bright smile. 'Of course. What's not to like? He's lovely. Perfect husband material. You should have snapped him up years ago.'

Bella smiled, looking genuinely happy now, as if she'd needed this reassurance. Then she grabbed the straps of her overnight bag, slammed the door and called, 'See you in the morning.'

Zoe watched as Bella hurried up her front steps, pale hair shining in the glow cast by a streetlight, then she drove on, feeling the last of her strength ebb away.

All weekend she'd held herself together—remaining upbeat and excited for Bella's sake, while keeping a lid on her own private turmoil. Dropping any interest in Kent had proved much harder than she'd expected, and now the ordeal was over she was totally drained. She just wanted to crawl into her own little space and let go.

Finally, she reached her flat in Newmarket, let herself into the kitchen, dumped her bag in the corner.

She loved her little home. For the first time in her life she had a proper place to call home that had four walls instead of four wheels.

First she checked her goldfish—Brian, Ezekiel and Orange Juice. They'd survived beautifully without her. Then she dashed out onto her balcony to make sure her pot plants were still alive.

Zoe had always kept pot plants, even when they

were in the bus. Her mum said she'd inherited Granny Weston's green thumb, and Zoe saw it as a sign that she was meant to have her own plot of land.

One day.

Back in the kitchen, she reached for the kettle. First priority was a comforting mug of tea, accompanied by a long soak in a warm bath. She could sort out her laundry tomorrow night after work. For now, she was going to be totally self-indulgent.

Five minutes later, warm, rose-scented water enveloped her, and at last she could set her thoughts free.

Unfortunately, her thoughts zeroed straight to Kent Rigby.

She let out the loud groan she'd been holding in for two whole days, ever since the road-side revelation on Friday evening. All weekend, honest to God, she'd tried unbelievably hard to stop liking Kent.

It should have been easy. He was her best friend's fiancé, and Zoe had already dated a previously engaged man. She'd been burned. Horribly. After she'd dated Rodney for several months and helped him to get over his break-up, he'd moved in with her and she'd been deeply in love with him. Then she'd come home unexpectedly early one evening and found him in bed with Naomi, his former fiancée.

Rodney the Rat.

Never again would Zoe set herself up for that kind of heartache.

So why hadn't she found the 'off' switch for her attraction to Bella's fiancé?

It was ridiculous, as if she'd contracted a mutant strain of a virus that was resistant to all known treatments.

The truth was that deep down she was genuinely

thrilled for Bella. Willara Downs was the lifestyle her friend had been born into. Bella's parents had always lived in the district. Her father would soon be out of hospital and home on his farm, and her grandfather still lived in an aged care facility in Willara township. On top of that, the Shaw and Rigby properties were adjoining and so Bella and Kent had the whole dynasty thing happening.

Beyond all these practical considerations, Bella and Kent were so sweet together, and so very at ease. Maybe they weren't all touchy-feely, but that was to be expected when others were around. Just the same, it was clear as daylight that they belonged together.

Without question, Bella fitted in. She'd found where she belonged, while once again, as always, Zoe was the outsider.

Oh, God.

Zoe dunked her face under the water to wash away her stupid tears. She had to get a grip. Had to stop this nonsense now.

Curse that flat tyre.

This problem would never have arisen if she and Bella had driven to the homestead together. If Bella had been there, from the moment Zoe met Kent she would have known who he was, and the first thing she would have seen was Kent embracing his bride-to-be. She would have been excited for Bella, and her heart would have stayed safely immune to Kent's charms.

Instead, cruel fate had delivered her a punctured tyre and twenty minutes alone with a wonderful man who'd arrived like a gift from heaven.

She kept reliving that thrilling moment—only a few seconds admittedly—when their gazes had connected. She could have sworn something huge and earth-shattering had passed between them.

Had it all been in her stupid head?

She hated to admit that she'd deluded herself, but there was no other explanation. Thank heavens Kent hadn't noticed.

His behaviour had been beyond reproach. He'd been unfailingly polite and friendly to Zoe, and he'd been wonderful about her damaged tyre, organising a replacement to be sent out from a garage in Willara and then fitting it for her.

Appropriately, he'd devoted the bulk of his attention to Bella. There'd been no sign that he was remembering the moment when he and Zoe had looked into each other's eyes and the world had stopped.

And she was going to be just as sensible.

It was time for self-discipline and maturity. Time to get a grip on reality.

Kent-slash-man-of-her-dreams-Rigby was going to marry her best friend in less than two months and she, Zoe Weston, was going to be their happy, loyal, non-jealous, and perfect-in-every-way bridesmaid.

Kent couldn't breathe. Pinned at the bottom of a dark muddy pool, he could feel his lungs bursting, his legs thrashing. He couldn't see a thing. Couldn't hear anything either, just a dull roaring in his head.

Fear, blacker than the night, pressed down with a weighty and smothering hand.

He fought, struggling, gasping…shooting awake out of a tangle of sheets.

He dragged in air. His heart raced, but he wasn't panicking. He knew it would slow down soon. He was used to this dream. He knew its familiar pattern, even though he had no real memories of almost drowning in Willara Creek.

The dreams were based on what his family had told him—that he'd been pinned under a rock and Tom Shaw had saved him, and that little Bella had been there, white-faced and sobbing.

Don't let Kent die. Please, please don't let him die...

It was years later, in his teens, that the dreams had begun. By then it had finally sunk in that all life was tenuous and that Kent's own life had nearly ended when he was six years old.

A kid showing off. All over red rover. Then a man with good instincts diving down and dragging him free.

Tom Shaw had given Kent a second chance at life, and with that gift had come responsibility.

The dreams never let Kent forget. He owed. Big time.

To: Kent Rigby<willaraKR@hismail.com>
From: Zoe Weston<zoe.weston@flowermail.com>
Subject: Caterers etc.
Dear Kent,
Thanks for your kind hospitality on the weekend. It was great meeting you and having the chance to see where the wedding will take place.

I'm sure you'll be pleased to hear that my spare car tyre held up splendidly, so thanks for your help with that as well.

As you know, I had a good chat with your mother about the best caterers to approach for the wedding and I've rung them all and am sending you their quotes as an attachment for your perusal.

I showed the quotes to Bella, but she has enough to think about with finding her dress and worrying about her dad and she's more than happy to leave the planning details to us.

I thought the menu supplied by Greenslades sounded delicious and it also provides a range of dishes to suit most tastes, but they're a little more expensive than the others.

I'm also sending a link to a website with the table settings that Bella and I think will be perfect. If you like them, I'll go ahead and place an order.

Oh, and are you still happy to use the homestead verandas if there's a threat of rain, or would you like me to look into hiring a marquee?

If there's anything else I can do to help, please let me know.

Kind regards,

Zoe Weston

To: Zoe Weston<zoe.weston@flowermail.com>
From: Kent Rigby<willaraKR@hismail.com>
Subject: Re: Caterers etc.
Hi Zoe,

Thanks for your email with the quotes and the link. Has it occurred to you that you may have missed your calling as a wedding planner?

I agree that the Greenslades menu is a standout, so let's go with them, especially as they're based in Toowoomba and they can send out a mobile kitchen. Great find.

The table settings look terrific—I'm happy to go with whatever you girls choose.

Zoe, you might be Bella's best friend, but I think

you've just become mine, too. Such a load off my mind to have this sorted so quickly and easily.

Cheers

Kent

P.S. I was wondering—do you have a favourite colour?

To: Kent Rigby<willaraKR@hismail.com>
From: Zoe Weston<zoe.weston@flowermail.com>
Subject: Re: Caterers etc.

Dear Kent,

All the bookings are made and both Greenslades and the Perfect Day hire company will be sending you their invoices with details about deposits etc.

Ouch. I hope you don't get too much of a shock.

I'm leaving the ordering of drinks to you. Bella and I will look after the flower arrangements and decorations. So now the major details are planned, but I'd also like to have a bridal shower and a hens' party for Bella, so there's a bit more to be sorted. I guess you and your best man will be having a bucks' night?

As Bella has probably told you, she's found a dress she loves, so it looks as if everything is coming together.

I can't imagine why you want to know my favourite colour. I'm not even sure I can answer that question. It depends if you're talking about a colour to wear, or a colour to look at. It can make quite a difference, you know.

Regards,

Zoe

To: Zoe Weston<zoe.weston@flowermail.com>
From: Kent Rigby<willaraKR@hismail.com>
Subject: Re: Caterers etc.
Hi Zoe,
Once again, thanks for all your help. I can't imagine how this wedding could have happened without you.

As for the question about your favourite colour, I'm afraid I can't really explain. It's a small but pleasant task Bella has assigned to me.

That's a fascinating observation you've made about colours. For now, could you give me both your favourite colour to wear and your favourite colour to look at?
Cheers
Kent

On the following Saturday morning, Bella bought her wedding dress. Zoe had been with her when she'd first seen the dress on the previous Saturday, and they'd loved it. Twice during the week Bella had been back to the shop to look at it again, and now she'd dragged Zoe along with her to approve her final decision.

'Each time I see it, I love it more,' Bella had confided, and as Zoe watched her parade across the store's plush carpet she totally understood why. The floor-length gown was very simple, but its elegant lack of fussiness totally suited Bella's blond, country-girl beauty. Its style, with beautifully embroidered straps and Grecian draping, was perfect for an outdoor country wedding.

'Kent will adore you in this,' Zoe said as she pic-

tured Bella coming across the lawn to her waiting bridegroom. 'You'll stop him in his tracks.'

She was proud that she said this with a genuine smile,
although putting the Kent nonsense out of her thoughts
hadn't been as easy as she'd expected. Emails in which
he asked about her favourite colour hadn't helped.

She still hadn't answered that one. It was silly of her,
but it felt too...personal.

'This is definitely the dress for me,' Bella said, giving a final twirl to admire her reflection in the full-
length mirror.

She paid for her dress with her credit card, then
linked her arm through Zoe's. 'OK, it's your turn now.
We have to find something really lovely for you.'

Abruptly, in the middle of the salon, Bella stopped.
'Have I told you how incredibly grateful I am for everything you're doing to help? Kent told me how brilliant you've been.'

'I've enjoyed it,' Zoe said honestly. 'So far, it hasn't
been a huge job. Really.'

'But it's such a relief to know it's all in hand,' Bella
said. 'Since my dad got sick, I've been rather distracted.'

'That's why I was happy to help.'

'You're one in a million. You know that, don't you?'

It was hard not to bask in the warmth of Bella's smile.
Zoe found it incredibly reassuring to be appreciated, to
feel needed and important.

Businesslike once more, Bella turned to a rack of
dresses. 'I thought if we chose something that didn't
scream bridesmaid, you'd be able to wear it afterwards.
Colour-wise, I was wondering about—'

Bella paused, looking at a row of dresses, and Zoe
waited. Even though she hadn't answered Kent's question about colours, she rather liked pink. She knew lots

of girls avoided pink like the plague, but she'd always thought the colour brought out the rosy tones in her skin and went rather well with her dark hair. So, she was thinking of a pretty shade of pink when Bella said, 'Green.'

'Green?'

Bella nodded emphatically. 'I can really see you in green, Zoe. It suits you beautifully. And it's so fresh, just right for a country wedding.'

Yes, green was fresh, no doubt about that. But it was also the colour of grass and trees, and there were rather a lot of both in the country. In the outdoors, green would work like camouflage, wouldn't it?

Worse, wasn't green the colour of jealousy? *Oh, cringe.* Zoe had worked extremely hard to rid herself of any jealousy. Even so, *green* was the last colour she wanted to wear to *this* particular wedding.

Bella was frowning at her. 'Don't you like green? I thought you loved it. That long green scarf of yours looks stunning with your black winter coat.'

But I won't be wearing my black winter coat, Zoe wanted to remind her. *We're supposed to be choosing a dress for a spring garden wedding. If not something with a hint of pink, why not a pretty pale primrose?*

Not that Zoe would actually say any of this out loud, not when she was still, in spite of her minor problem re the groom, trying to be the perfect, considerate bridesmaid.

With a pang of guilt, she remembered the Monday morning, almost two weeks ago now, when Bella had asked her to be her bridesmaid. She'd been ready to wear anything then, even a black plastic garbage bag.

Somewhat ashamed, she said, 'I'm sure a pale apple green could be very nice.'

'Hmm.' Bella was looking less certain now. 'I must admit I hardly wear green myself.' Already, she was heading over to a rack of pretty pastels. 'Our high-school uniform was green, so I had an overdose of it in my teenage years.'

'Oh,' Zoe gasped and smacked the side of her fore-head. 'I'd almost forgotten until you mentioned your high school. I had a message on Facebook from one of your old school friends.'

'Really?' Bella was already at a rack, reaching for a coat hanger with a rather pretty pink dress.

'I posted a message on Facebook, you see, about how excited I was to be a bridesmaid at a country wedding near Willara. I didn't actually mention Willara Downs and I didn't give full names, but I said the bride was my best friend, Bella. I hope you don't mind, Bell.'

'No, of course I don't mind. So who was it?'

'A guy. I think he's been living somewhere overseas, but he said he used to know a girl called Bella Shaw at Willara High and he wondered if she was my friend getting married.'

Bella was suddenly very still and she shot Zoe a strangely nervous glance.

'I haven't replied to him,' Zoe said, cautiously.

'What's his name?' Bella's voice was barely above a whisper now.

'I'm trying to remember. I think it might have been David. No, that's not right. Maybe Damon? Yes, I'm pretty sure it was Damon.'

'Damon Cavello?'

'Yes, that's it. I—' Zoe stopped, shocked into silence by the sight of Bella's deathly pale face and the coat hanger slipping from her hands, landing on the bridal salon's white carpet in a sea of frothy pink chiffon.

'Bell?' With a pang of dismay, Zoe bent down to pick up the fallen gown before any of the store's assistants noticed. 'Bella?' she repeated as she slipped the gown's straps onto the hanger and returned it to its rightful place on the rack. 'What's the matter?'

Bella gave a convulsive little shudder, then the colour rushed back into her face. 'Nothing. Nothing's the matter,' she said quickly. 'I just got a surprise. It's so long since I've heard from D-Damon.'

As she stammered his name her cheeks turned deep pink.

'Who is he?' Zoe had to ask. 'A high-school sweetheart?'

With a startled laugh, Bella whipped her gaze back to the rack, and began, rather distractedly, to check out the dresses. 'God, no. We were just friends.'

'Right.' Zoe frowned as she watched Bella's hands, with their smart navy-blue nail polish and sparkling diamond engagement ring, swish along the coat hangers.

Bella turned to her, eyes extra bright. 'When did you say Damon wrote to you?'

'I found his message when I got home from work last night.'

'But you haven't written back to him?'

'Not yet. I thought I'd better check with you first. I wasn't sure he was someone you wanted to know.'

'Of course you can answer him. There's no problem. Damon's—fine.'

Bella sounded calm enough on the surface, but something wasn't right. Zoe could sense her inner tension.

'Damon was always a bit of a daredevil.' Bella spoke a little too casually, as if she needed to prove she was mega cool about this subject. 'He moved back to Brisbane in the middle of his final year, and he went on to study journalism. He's been overseas for years— as a foreign correspondent, specialising in all the worst trouble spots.'

'He sounds like an adventurer.'

Softly, Bella said, 'I hate to think of the things he must have seen.'

Zoe nodded, still puzzled by the tension Bella couldn't quite disguise. 'I think he might be heading back to Australia,' she said. 'Or he could even be on his way already. So is it OK to pass on your email address?'

'Of course.' This time Bella gave an offhand shrug, as if Zoe had been trying to make Mount Everest out of a molehill.

Lifting a very pretty coffee-and-cream floral dress from the rack, she said, 'If Damon's back in Australia, he's bound to come out to Willara. His father doesn't live there any more, but his grandmother's in the same old folks' home as my grandad, and I'm sure he'll want to visit her. They've always been close. His gran shows me all the postcards he sends her.'

'That's nice.'

Bella bit her lip and gave an uncertain smile.

'Would you invite him to the wedding?' Zoe asked.

'Heavens, no.' A strange snorting laugh broke from Bella. 'He wouldn't be interested in my marriage.' Then her eyes met Zoe's and she frowned. 'Don't look at me like that, Zoe. Damon's not the type to enjoy a romantic country wedding.'

'OK. Just asking. I thought he might have been an old friend of Kent's, that's all.'

She heard the hiss of her friend's sharply indrawn breath.

'Well, yes,' Bella admitted, almost reluctantly. 'Kent and Damon were mates at one time, so I suppose I should tell Kent.' She sighed. 'Actually, he'll probably want to include Damon.'

Then, as if deliberately changing the subject, she held out the coffee-toned dress. 'Now, why don't you try this one on? I can see you in it already.'

It was pretty obvious that Bella wanted to drop the subject. 'All right.'

In the changing cubicle, however, Zoe took one look at herself in the pretty bridesmaid's dress, and she forgot about Bella and the old school friend.

The colour was perfect—tawny flowers on a creamy white background that totally flattered her complexion. But her first thought was not to wonder how she looked.

But— *Would Kent like me in this?*

This was getting tedious.

On Tuesday evening, Zoe was in the middle of important, toenail-painting research when the phone rang. She and Bella were wearing toe peepers to the wedding, and each night, following Bella's instructions, Zoe was trying out a different colour. Serious comparisons were made the next day in their lunch hour.

This evening, when the phone rang, Zoe had toe separators in place and three nails painted with rosy minx, so she was grumbling as she screwed the lid on the bottle and hobbled over to the phone. 'Hello?'

'Hi, Zoe.'

The caller was male with a smooth as molasses country drawl that she instantly recognised. Her heart tried to leap clear out of her chest.

He said, 'Kent Rigby here.'

Why was he ringing? Several scenarios flashed before Zoe. All of them impossible. *Good grief. Calm down.* He'd be ringing about another planning detail.

But when she tried to speak, she sounded distinctly breathless.

'Zoe, are you OK?' Kent sounded genuinely concerned.

'I'm perfectly fine,' she managed to insist, although it came out in a choked whisper. 'Just a bit puffed. I had to—' *quick breath* '—come running in from outside.'

Great. Now she could add dishonesty to her list of sins. Grimacing, Zoe willed herself to calm down. Developing high blood pressure before the wedding was not on the bridesmaids' list of duties.

She took another breath, deeper and slower, aiming for a tone that was friendly, but as businesslike as possible. 'What can I do for you, Kent?'

'I wondered if you've made a decision about the hens' night. I hear you're in charge of that, too.'

'Oh, right, do you want an invitation?' she teased.

Kent chuckled at her weak joke. 'My best man, Steve, has been pressuring me about a bucks' night, and I didn't want it to clash with your arrangements.'

'Actually, I sent you an email about it earlier this evening.'

'Sorry. I haven't checked my emails. I've been out on the tractor since the early hours and I just got back. Thought I'd give you a quick call while my dinner's heating up.'

Zoe pictured Kent up before dawn, out ploughing the fields as the sun rose. Farmers worked such long hours. She wondered if Bella would be the sort of wife who took her farmer husband a Thermos of coffee and a snack. Maybe they'd share a quick cuddle behind the machinery shed?

Oh, God. Stop it!

Assuming her briskest, most businesslike voice, she said, 'We'd like to have the hens' night in Willara, on the weekend before the wedding—that's the same weekend as the bridal shower. Bella's friends from Brisbane don't mind trekking off to the wilds of the country for two weekends in a row, but I think three would be expecting too much.'

'Fair enough.'

'So the girls are planning to book into the Willara pub—that is, unless you want to have your bucks' night there.'

'No, you stay with that arrangement. We'll have the bucks' party on the same night, but we'll go over to Mullinjim. It's not far out of town.'

'Great. That sounds like a plan.' Zoe let out a nervous, huffing laugh. 'So it looks like the wedding's all coming together?'

'Like clockwork. Piece of cake, thanks to you, Zoe.'

A small silence fell and Zoe was shocked to hear her heartbeats, still galloping away like a cattle stampede. She would rather keep talking than risk Kent hearing them, so she asked the question that had been on her mind for days.

'Has Bella mentioned Damon Cavello, the old school friend who made contact?'

'No,' Kent said slowly. 'She hasn't.'

There was no mistaking the surprise in his voice. A beat later, he asked, 'So…what's the wild boy up to these days?'

Zoe could quite believe why Kent had called Damon a wild boy. She'd checked out photos of him on the internet and he had the dark, scruffy, bad-boy looks of a rock-and-roll star. It wasn't a look that appealed to her—

she'd seen enough of guys like that hanging around her parents' band while she was growing up—but she knew bad boys were considered very sexy by girls confident enough to attract them.

'Damon's on his way back to Australia,' she told Kent. 'Coming from Afghanistan, I think.'

Another small silence.

'Is he OK?' Kent asked.

'As far as I know, he's fine.'

'That's a miracle.' Kent spoke with uncharacteristic cynicism, but then he quickly corrected himself. 'Don't get me wrong. I'm relieved to hear that he's in one piece. But with Damon, there's always a risk of—' He left the sentence dangling. 'Do you know if he's likely to be around for the wedding?'

'I think there's a good chance.' Zoe hoped she wasn't breaching Bella's confidence. But then, because she was curious, she couldn't help adding, 'He sounds rather mysterious.'

'Yeah.' There was a barely concealed sigh on the other end of the phone line. 'He's always been a bit of a puzzle, but Bella knew what drove him better than any of us. What did she tell you?'

'Not much at all—just that he left Willara High in Year Twelve and ended up becoming a foreign correspondent. I got the impression he's attracted to danger.'

'No doubt about that,' he muttered.

She could hear definite tension in Kent's voice now, the same tight caution she'd sensed in Bella. What was it about this Damon guy that put everyone on high alert?

'How did Bella react to the news?' Kent asked carefully.

This last question was a curly one. Zoe sensed she was on dangerous ground, and, no matter what she thought of Kent, her loyalty lay with Bella. She certainly wouldn't tell him that Bella had been rather edgy and strange when she'd heard about Damon Cavello.

'Bella said—ah—that she'd talk to you to see if you wanted to invite him to the wedding.'

'But she didn't invite him straight out?'

'No. I'm sure she wants to talk to you first. Does Damon—um—pose a problem, Kent?'

'No, not at all. I didn't mean to give that impression.' He spoke almost too smoothly. 'Bella's right. He's just an old school friend, and it'll be great to catch up with him. Actually, I'd like his email address if that's OK. I presume Bella's already made contact with him?'

Kent sounded relaxed enough, but as they said goodnight and Zoe hung up she couldn't help wondering. And worrying.

She wished she'd left it to Bella to tell him about this Damon guy. A bridesmaid was supposed to be tactful and diplomatic. Instead, she'd opened her big mouth and she had the awful feeling she'd stirred up unnecessary trouble.

CHAPTER FOUR

GRABBING a beer from the fridge, Kent snapped the top off, then went out to the back veranda.

The night was hot and still and silent. Low clouds hid the moon and the stars, and the air was heavy and stifling, as if a thunderstorm was brewing.

Tipping back his head, he downed the icy liquid, hoping to wash away the sense of foreboding that hunkered inside him.

Foreboding wasn't an emotion Kent Rigby enjoyed, and it wasn't something that normally troubled him. Most times he was too busy working hard or playing hard. Besides, he liked to keep his life on an even keel and he left the rocking of boats to others. Like Damon Cavello.

Hell.

Kent downed another icy slug, and leaned his shoulder against a timber post, staring out into the black, fathomless night. Talk about lousy timing. Why the blue blazes had Cavello come back now, just when he and Bella had everything sorted and settled?

They hadn't heard from him in years.

Sure, they'd seen his news reports on television, delivered on battlefields while he was dodging explosions and bullets, or emerging from the rubble of an earth-quake, covered in dust and grime.

Damon had made no personal contact with either of them for years. And now Kent and Bella had planned a future together, and they were doing it for all the right reasons.

Everything was working out so well. Tom Shaw was out of hospital and if he continued to follow his doctor's instructions, he'd be OK. He was looking forward to the wedding and walking his daughter down the aisle.

The rosy future Kent had planned was falling into place.

But now this Cavello bombshell had exploded.

Why now?

Zoe sat for ages after she hung up the phone. Curled in an armchair, she almost fell into her old habit of nib-bling at her thumbnail. Actually, she did chew on the corner before she remembered that she had to keep her nails pristine for the wedding. So she chewed on the inside of her lip instead. And pondered.

The vibes for this wedding weren't as upbeat as she would have liked. There were so many undercurrents, not just her own silly crush on the groom—which she *so* hoped no one had guessed—but now, with the arrival of Damon on the scene, there were Bella's and Kent's subtle but unmistakable tensions.

Zoe wished they could all snap out of it. She wanted everything to be rosy and wonderful on planet Bella-and-Kent.

Guiltily, she felt an urge to run away for a bit, but, apart from the fact that she was needed at Willara next weekend, she didn't really have anywhere to go. It was a pity her parents didn't live closer. She would have loved to see her little brother, Toby—to go and watch him play soccer on Saturday afternoon perhaps, or to go surfing with her dad, help her mum make her habitual Friday night curry.

She wondered if Toby knew how lucky he was to live in a cosy house with parents who stayed in one place with a steady job now their dad ran a music store.

One thing was certain. If she ever found the right man, she definitely wanted to settle down and to stay in one place. She wanted her children to go to school with friends they'd known since kindergarten, and she wanted them to play sports together, to make memories together…

Just as Bella and Kent had, and as their children would, too…

Zoe sighed as jealousy coiled unpleasantly inside her. Immediately she felt ashamed of herself. It wasn't as if poor Bella enjoyed a perfect family life. She'd lost her mother. She had no brothers or sisters, and her only family consisted of her ill and grieving father, and a grandparent in an old people's home.

Was it any wonder Bella had turned to gorgeous, steady Kent Rigby and his happy, well-balanced family?

Zoe launched to her feet before she had a chance to feel the lurch of pain that followed any thoughts about Kent. Tonight she was more determined than ever to get over that nonsense. This wedding would be fantastic and she would be the best possible bridesmaid.

Her job for this weekend and over the next few weeks was clear. She had to steer Bella through any muddy waters that surfaced—including old flames—until she arrived safely beside Kent at the altar.

Yes, Zoe felt better now that plan was reaffirmed.

But as she reached for the kettle she saw her hand. Damn! She'd chewed her thumbnail to a nub.

Stripped to the waist, Kent was bending under an outside water tap, cleaning up the worst of the day's grime, when he heard the squeaky hinges of the backyard gate. He looked up, blinked water from his eyes, and saw Zoe Weston poised uncertainly just inside the gate.

She was dressed in city clothes, as if she'd come straight from the office, and her crisp white blouse and charcoal pencil skirt looked totally out of place against a backdrop of gumtrees and grazing land. Kent, however, found himself helplessly captivated.

Stunned might be a better word. He couldn't stop staring.

Zoe's office clothes emphasised her neat, slim curves, and her legs, in sheer stockings and shiny high heels, were—there was only one word—*sensational*. Her dark hair was pulled back beneath a narrow velvet band into some kind of knot, and she looked sophisticated and serious and—heaven help him—astonishingly sexy.

His reaction was as bad as last time. No, worse.

When he'd met her by the road side she'd been wearing a T-shirt and blue jeans. Ever since then he'd worked hard to stop thinking about her unique qualities—not just her sensible calm manner, but the cute tilt of her head, and the blue of her eyes, and the softness of her mouth.

Now, there was something else—something about the sight of her in her smart city clothes that grabbed him by the throat and sent a jolt arrowing south.

Hell.

Why was she here? Alone?

Where was Bella? Weren't Zoe and Bella supposed to be staying at Blue Gums this weekend with Tom Shaw? Tom was so much better now and he'd started going into Toowoomba to the AA meetings.

What had happened?

Shaking off his unwanted reaction, Kent called to her, 'Hello there.'

Zoe still hadn't moved. In fact, she seemed to be as transfixed as he was—watching him with a worried, staring gaze and with a hand pressed to the open V of her snowy-white blouse.

Hastily, Kent snapped off the water and reached for his discarded shirt, using it to dry his bare shoulders and chest as he hurried over to her.

'I wasn't expecting you,' he said, stating the obvious as he thrust his arms into the sleeves of the damp and crumpled shirt. 'Is everything OK?'

'I—' Zoe began, gulping and looking uncomfortable. 'Bella asked me to come here. We were supposed to stay at her father's place, but he's—' She grimaced, and looked embarrassed.

'Oh, no. Tom isn't drunk, is he?'

Zoe nodded. 'He's in a pretty bad way, I'm afraid.'

Kent swore and slammed a balled fist against his thigh. 'Tom was doing so well. He seemed to be on the mend.' He let out a heavy sigh. 'I'm sure Bella's upset.'

'Yes. She begged me to come over to your place, while she stayed with her dad.' Zoe's eyes were round with worry. 'I hope she's OK.'

'She won't come to any harm. Tom's never violent, and he'll certainly never hurt his daughter. Not physically.' Kent pulled the limp fronts of his shirt together, and started to fumble with the lower buttons. 'Just the same, I'll phone her straight away.'

Zoe glanced at his chest and then looked away, her colour deepening.

'Come inside,' he said, doing up another button, then nodding towards the house. 'You look like you could use a cuppa, or maybe something stronger.'

'Thanks. I'd love a cuppa.'

As they walked across the lawn to the screen door at the back of the house Kent's thoughts were for Bella and her devastation over Tom's lapse. He forced himself to ignore the slim, sophisticated woman walking beside him. He paid her no attention. He couldn't afford to think about her curve-hugging skirt and her long legs sheathed in filmy stockings, or her high city heels sinking into the grass.

Sitting at the granite island bench in the Rigbys' farmhouse kitchen, Zoe wrapped her hands around a mug of hot, sweet tea, closed her eyes and drew a deep breath.

From outside came the creamy vanilla scent of wisteria mixed with the danker scent of hay and a faint whiff of animals. But the pleasant country aromas did little to calm her. She was still shaken by the scene she'd witnessed at Blue Gums.

The sight of Bella's father, staggering and incoherent, had been beyond awful, and poor Bella had been so embarrassed and upset. She'd shooed Zoe out of there as quickly as she could.

But Zoe's arrival at Willara Downs had brought an equally disturbing close encounter with Kent's naked, *wet* torso.

OK, a man without his shirt should *not* have been a big deal. Zoe had seen plenty of bare male chests. Of course she had, but this was the first time she'd had a close encounter with Kent Rigby's smooth, bulky muscles, and tapering, hard-packed abs. Not to mention the enticing trail of dark hair heading downwards beneath his belt buckle.

It was an experience destined to rattle any girl senseless. What hope had Zoe?

For pity's sake, she'd gone into mourning over the closure of his shirt buttons…

In fact, Kent had been doing up his buttons crookedly and she'd *almost* offered to help him get them straight. How sad was that? Thank heavens she'd stopped herself just in time.

Now she cringed as she imagined the surprise and disapproval in his eyes if she'd actually reached out and touched him.

It's OK. I didn't do anything stupid. I'm calming down. I'm fine. I'm back in control.

Zoe took another sip of tea and then a bite of the scrumptious shortbread that Kent's mother had thoughtfully left in his pantry. Yes, she was definitely feeling calmer now. And sanity certainly returned as she heard the deep rumble of Kent's voice down the hall. He was talking to Bella on the telephone, and she could imagine him making sure Bella was OK and that her dad was fine, too. He would be reassuring Bella and telling her he loved her.

While their conversation continued, Zoe flicked through a country life magazine with articles about kitchen gardens and new breeds of chickens, and fabulous recipes using all kinds of cheese.

Zoe tried to imagine Bella reading one of these country magazines, and being inspired by the articles. Somehow, she couldn't quite picture her friend getting her beautifully manicured hands dirty in a veggie garden, or rolling pastry, or saving her kitchen scraps to feed to the chooks.

Bella had never actually talked about her future as a farmer's wife. In fact she seemed very much a city girl these days with a fondness for beauty salons and coffee shops rather than hay bales and farmhouse cooking. But then Bella was a bit of a dark horse. She'd never talked about her father's problems with alcohol either.

Clearly there were many strands to Bella's life, and the city office girl who loved high fashion and fancy nail polish was quite possibly a brave front. Now, more than ever, Zoe could understand why her friend had chosen a steadfast and reliable partner like Kent. A good, rock-solid husband. A loving man who knew all about her, a guy who would help to shoulder her worries about her father.

There was no doubt about it. Kent was Bella's perfect match in every way.

Right. OK.

Fortunately, Zoe locked in that thought scant seconds before she heard Kent's footsteps returning down the passage to the kitchen. She had her smile fixed in place before he entered.

Even so, she felt a zap of reaction the instant she saw him. There was something impossibly appealing about Kent Rigby, something about his tanned profile, about his dark, friendly eyes and the flash of his smile that made Zoe feel as bright and shimmering as a sunrise.

Which proved how very foolish she was. Apart from the very important fact that the man was taken—by her best friend, no less—she should have enough bad memories of Rodney the Rat to douse any sparks of unwanted libido.

'How's Bella?' she asked Kent.

'She's upset, of course, and mad as hell with her dad. He'd started going to AA and we thought he was going to be fine now.'

'Perhaps he's just had one slip and he'll be back on the wagon tomorrow.'

'Let's hope so.' Kent let out a sigh. 'Tom had problems with grog when he was young, but he was dry the whole time he and Mary were married. Since her death, he's been on a downhill slide.'

'Poor man. And poor Bella. She must feel so helpless.'

Kent nodded. 'It must have been a shock for you, too, coming across him like that.'

'Well, yes, it was, but only because it was so unexpected. And Bella was so upset.' Zoe lifted her now empty mug. 'Thanks for the tea. It was just what I needed.' She stood. 'I guess you'll want to get over to Bella's place straight away.'

'Later. Tom's asleep right now and Bella wants a bit of time to sort the place out.' Kent went to the fridge, opened it and stood staring at its contents. 'I'll fix a meal for us first.'

'For us?'

'Yep—we're on our own tonight.'

'B-but you don't have to feed me.' Zoe was stammering, rattled by the possibility of a meal alone with this man. 'I can go into town. I'll stay at the pub and grab a meal there.'

'Zoe, relax.' Shutting the fridge once more, Kent grinned at her. 'You're president and secretary of our wedding planning committee. Of course, you're very welcome here. You can stay the night, and you can have the same room as last time.'

She was about to protest again, when she realised it

might come across as rude. Kent was keeping up his reputation for country hospitality. He might be upset if she refused.

'Thanks,' she said. Then, to cover any giveaway signs of attraction, she surveyed the kitchen with her most businesslike glance. 'So what can I do to help you?'

'If we dig out the sheets now, you can make up your bed while I throw a couple of steaks in a pan.'

Already Kent was heading out of the kitchen and Zoe hurried after him. The linen cupboard was in a hallway, and he flipped the louvred doors open, releasing a faint scent of lavender.

'This is where I run into trouble.' A small smile made attractive creases around his dark eyes. 'I haven't a clue which sheets I'm supposed to give you.'

Zoe gulped. Discussing bed sheets with Kent was her wickedest fantasy rolled into her worst nightmare. 'I think I used those pink striped sheets last time.'

'Terrific.' He was already lifting them from the shelf. 'I'm sure they'll do.'

His wrists brushed against her as he handed her the sheets. It was a relief to disappear into the guest room and get busy making the bed.

Once this was done, she freshened up in the bathroom, brushed her hair and changed into shorts and a T-shirt. If only she could switch off her hormones as easily as she changed her clothes.

The scent of frying steak and onions greeted her when she came back into the kitchen. And the rather fetching sight of Kent standing at the stove, changed into a clean white, correctly buttoned shirt.

He sent her another of his flashing smiles, but then

his smile went super still, and he continued to stare at Zoe, a slight frown now warring with his grin.

'What's wrong?'

'You've let your hair down.'

Zap! A bushfire scorched her skin. She fingered her hair, dark and straight like her mum's, and now skimming her shoulders. 'I didn't know it was a crime for a girl to let her hair down on a Friday evening.'

'Course it isn't.' Kent shrugged and turned back to the steaks, flipping them over. Without looking at her, he said, 'It looks great either way. In your bridesmaid's outfit you're going to knock the local yokels for six.'

The comment warranted another very stern lecture to herself. His compliment would go to her head. It should be possible to have a normal conversation with him without overreacting to every second sentence.

Desperate to appear cool and unaffected, she said glibly, 'That's reassuring to know. I'm on the lookout for a spare farmer.'

'Are you?'

It wasn't the flippant or teasing response she'd expected from Kent. His head had jerked around and his dark eyes were surprisingly intense.

Now she was more flustered than ever. 'Of course I'm not serious,' she said tightly. 'That was my poor attempt at a joke.'

Time to put an end to this subject. She looked around her. 'What can I do to help? Why don't I make a salad to go with the steak?'

Kent's thoughts were apparently elsewhere and he took a moment to answer her.

'Sure,' he said at last, and then, after a beat, his usual

smile was back in place. 'Trust a girl to want to spoil a good steak with rabbit food.'

They ate on the back veranda, looking out at the idyllic view of the soft, velvety hills and fields as they were slowly enveloped by the shadowy night.

Zoe wondered what she and Kent would talk about now. Given her recent gaffes, she wasn't sure she could cope with a conversation about Bella and the wedding. She wanted to ask Kent about the property. That was safe, and she was genuinely curious about the crops and grazing herds. Details of farm life had always fascinated her.

But it seemed Kent had other ideas. As he speared a tomato cube and a chunk of cucumber he said, 'So, tell me about yourself, Zoe.'

'Me?'

'Why not?' His smile was relaxed and easy once more and when she hesitated, he said, 'You're Bella's best friend and your friendship's not going to come to an end when we're married. I expect you'll be an important part of our lives for a very long time.'

Would she? Zoe had been hoping that her life beyond the wedding would be Kent-free. How else could she get back to normal? How could she stand the strain of an ongoing friendship with Bella and Kent if they remained close friends way into the future? Good grief, surely she wouldn't still be a jangling wreck when she was eighty?

It was an alarming prospect. Added to that, Zoe didn't really enjoy talking about herself. As a child she'd been forever arriving at new schools and answering the same old questions over and over. 'I've already told you about my parents and how I spent most of my childhood on the road.'

'But your parents have stopped touring now, haven't they?'

She nodded, then took a sip of the chilled white wine Kent had poured for her. And as she put the glass down she found herself telling him about the music shop in Sugar Bay and her little brother, Toby. And then, because he smiled so encouragingly, she told him about Toby's soccer ambitions and his endless experiments and their family's Saturday night barbecues when her parents had jam sessions with old mates.

'Sounds like they're a lot of fun,' Kent said sincerely. 'Would you like to live at the bay?'

'I—I'm not sure.' Zoe pulled a face. 'If I'm honest I feel a bit resentful that Mum and Dad waited till Toby came along before they settled down. He's having a very different childhood from mine.'

She shrugged. 'The bay's a great place to visit, but I like Brisbane, too.' *And the country.* But she wouldn't tell Kent that. 'I have to make my own life, don't I?'

'Of course.' He was watching her carefully again. 'And the world's your oyster,' he said quietly.

'Well, yes… Actually, I'm thinking about heading overseas.'

'You'll love it,' he said, but now his smile was tinged with a bewildering hint of sadness and for the first time Zoe wondered if he felt trapped at Willara Downs.

Curiosity prompted her to say, 'I've often wondered what it's like to grow up in one place and know you'll spend your whole life there.'

'Do you think it sounds boring?'

'No, not at all. Quite the opposite, actually.'

A frown furrowed Kent's brow and his dark eyes registered something very close to dismay.

Fearing she'd said too much, Zoe took a quick sip of her wine.

But whatever had bothered Kent passed and he was soon relaxed again. 'I love living here,' he said. 'It's not just the land and the lifestyle. For me, it's the strong feeling of continuity. My family's been here from the start. My great-great-great-grandfather looked after the horses on one of the earliest explorations and he fell in love with this district and settled here more than a hundred and fifty years ago.'

'Wow.' Zoe looked out at the view that had almost disappeared. 'All that history.'

Kent nodded. 'My grandfather and my great-grandfather both went away to the wars, and while they were gone the women and children ran the farms for them.' Across the table Kent's eyes met Zoe's. 'The responsibility of continuing those traditions means a great deal to me.'

'I'm sure it does. I feel goose bumps just thinking about it.' Zoe loved the idea of such permanence and such a deeply rooted sense of belonging.

'But that doesn't mean I don't love travelling as well,' Kent added with a twinkling smile.

'Have you travelled very far?'

'When I was nineteen I had a year off—backpacking with Steve, my best man, around Europe.'

'What was your favourite place?'

'Prague,' he answered without hesitation.

'That's interesting. Most people choose Paris or London or Rome. Even Barcelona.'

'Or Venice.'

'Yes.' She smiled, pleased that Kent was relaxed

again. When he looked at her with his serious expression, the world seemed to tilt ever so slightly, but everything felt in the right balance again now. 'So what did you love about Prague?'

Kent laughed. 'If Steve was here, he'd rave about the Czech beer. But for me it was the old city at Christmas time. It was snowing and unbelievably beautiful—the buildings, the pavements, the cafés, the restaurants. Everything in Prague is so old and dripping with history. Not a plastic Christmas tree in sight.'

'That sounds lovely. I must remember to try to be in Prague at Christmas.'

'Yes, do that.' For a moment there was a flicker of something in Kent's eyes. It might have been regret, but then he cracked a grin. 'And send me a postcard.'

'I will. I promise.'

'By the way,' he said, 'you still haven't told me your favourite colour.'

'And you haven't told me why you want to know.'

'Patience, Zoe. All in good time.'

'What if said I don't have a favourite?'

He laughed. 'I'd believe you. Neither do I.'

They laughed together then, and for a heady few seconds their gazes reached across the table and locked. For Zoe, it was like the moment beside the road when her entire being had felt connected to Kent's.

Then Kent broke the spell by looking away and deliberately reaching for his beer. And Zoe thudded back to earth. To reality.

She was such an idiot.

After that, they both turned their attention to their meals, but, although Zoe's steak was tender and the salad crisp, she seemed to have lost her appetite. She took another sip of wine and vowed to keep her thoughts firmly fixed on the painful truth.

How could she be so hopeless, when poor Bella was stuck at Blue Gums, caring for her dad? It was Bella who should be here, alone with Kent, and having this nice romantic dinner.

Zoe felt a little better when she and Kent left the veranda and returned to the kitchen to rinse their cutlery and plates and stack them in the dishwasher.

'I hope Mr Shaw will be OK in the morning,' she said.

'Don't worry about Tom.' Kent gave an offhand shrug. 'I'm sure he'll be fine in the morning. He'll be full of remorse and Bella will give him an earful about following doctor's orders.'

Zoe nodded. 'There was a fellow in Lead the Way with a drinking problem. He wanted everyone to turn a blind eye.'

Kent's eyes widened with interest, then abruptly he let out a sigh. 'Got to admit, it's really hard to watch Tom sink into such a state. He used to be such a fine man. He was my hero for many years. He saved my life when I was a nipper.'

'Really?' Zoe couldn't resist asking, 'What happened?'

'I was acting the fool down at the local waterhole, dived in at the wrong spot and hit my head on a rock.' With a sheepish smile Kent leaned closer and pointed to a faint thin scar on his forehead.

Zoe caught the clean, male scent of his skin, mere inches from her. She could see the scar, but his proximity also gave her the chance for a close-up study of the rest of his face, the length of his eyelashes, the graininess of his jaw, the sexy curve of his lips.

Oh, man.

Perhaps Kent sensed her indecent interest. His expression took on a strange frowning tension, and the air around them seemed to pulse. It seemed like ages before he pulled back, and he let out a strangled laugh. 'Lucky I didn't break my flaming neck. I certainly would have drowned if Tom hadn't been there. He got me off the bottom, dragged me out and revived me.'

'Thank God he did.' Oh, heavens, that sounded far too fervent. Quickly, Zoe asked, 'Was Bella there, too?'

'Yes, she witnessed the whole thing. We've both looked on her dad as a hero ever since.'

Kent's voice was so rough and solemn as he said this that Zoe knew deep emotions were tied to the statement.

'I'm sure he'll get over this road bump,' she said gently.

She was also sure it was time for Kent to leave. Regrettably, their time together had been way too pleasant.

She made a shooing motion towards the door. 'Now, thanks for a lovely dinner, but you should get going over to Bella's.'

'Yes, I'll head off now. You know where the tea and coffee are, don't you? And the TV remote.'

'Yes, thanks. I'll be fine. Don't worry about me. I'm used to living on my own. Now, go, Kent. Get out of here.'

He went.

I'm used to living on my own...

Standing at the kitchen window, Zoe watched the twin red eyes of Kent's tail lights disappearing into the black night, and she discovered a huge difference between being alone and being consumed by horrible loneliness.

Dismayed, she went through to the lovely lounge room. Like the rest of the house it was elegant yet relaxing, with deep comfy sofas, brightly coloured throw pillows. With a feminine touch, there'd be cut-glass vases filled with flowers from the garden.

For a brief, unwise moment, she indulged a childhood fantasy and imagined being the mistress of a beautiful country homestead like this one—cutting and arranging flowers from her garden, baking hearty meals for her drop-dead gorgeous, farmer husband and their children, attending meetings of the local growers' association, waking each morning to fresh air and open spaces…

And waking to the drop-dead gorgeous, farmer husband in bed beside her.

OK. Fantasy over. Back to reality. Fast.

Zoe flicked on the TV, made herself comfortable, and settled to watch one of her favourite comedies. A good dose of on-screen hilarity would soon cure her of any lingering self-pity.

But unfortunately the usually lively script was dull and unfunny this evening, and Zoe couldn't raise a chuckle. Her thoughts kept drifting…

She was picturing Kent's arrival at Blue Gums…and Bella's happy, open-arm welcome.

Stop it. Stop it. Stop it.

The couple on the TV screen were embracing, and again Zoe thought about Kent and Bella. Right about now, Bella would probably be undoing the buttons on Kent's shirt, running her hands over his lovely, hard muscles…

Oh, good grief. Enough!

Snapping off the TV, Zoe jumped to her feet. She was *not* going to succumb to this nonsense. She needed to keep busy, to keep her mind occupied with something constructive. But what could she do in a stranger's house?

Heading for the kitchen, she prayed for an answer.

CHAPTER FIVE

KENT was in a black mood. His experience at Blue Gums this evening had been depressing to say the least. Disturbing, too, as he hadn't been able to offer Bella much comfort. She'd been distracted, not her usual self and troubled by more than her father's illness. And yet she wouldn't confide in Kent, wouldn't let him help.

After the pleasant dinner conversation he'd enjoyed with Zoe, his fiancée's reception had been like a bucket of icy water. He was sure it had been a relief for both of them when he left early.

Now, home again, he approached the kitchen and saw...

Candles.

Everywhere.

On every bench top and flat surface in the state-of-the-art kitchen his mother had so faithfully designed, small candles sat, glowing warmly. And in the middle of the dancing candlelight stood Zoe, looking lovely, yet wide-eyed and cautious, rather like a naughty angel caught playing with the devil.

'I'm going to shift all this,' she announced hurriedly as soon as she saw him. 'I was planning to tidy everything before you got back.'

Black mood gone, Kent suppressed a smile as he stepped through the doorway into his kitchen.

'I—I know I've been a little carried away,' she hastened to add. 'I wanted to see how these candles looked, but I wasn't expecting you so soon, Kent. You're early, aren't you?'

'Bella's…worn out,' he said quietly.

'Oh.' Zoe frowned. 'Well, I know you weren't expecting to come home to forty-eight candles, but they're for the wedding. What do you think?'

'They're beautiful.' He gave in to the smile tugging at his mouth. *And you're beautiful, too…*

The thought sprang unbidden, and the words trembled on his lips, but thank goodness he resisted the impulse to voice them aloud.

'I wanted to get the full impact,' Zoe was explaining earnestly. 'I thought the candles would be lovely for the wedding reception. I'd like to put them in little paper bags filled with sand and they should look lovely outside in the garden. But don't worry—they're battery powered, so they're not going to burn your house down.'

'That's a relief.' Stepping closer, Kent lifted a little candle. 'And they can't blow out either.'

'No. They're called smart candles.'

'Good name.' He smiled at her, and he couldn't help adding, 'Smart candles for a smart girl.' Too late, he realised how softly he'd spoken, almost seductively, as if a weird kind of spell had taken hold of him.

In response, Zoe's blue eyes grew wider, clearly surprised. Her lips parted in a small moue.

Kent found himself staring at her soft pink lips… gazing into her lovely, expressive blue eyes…until he was lost in those eyes…

He was in free fall…

And all he could think was how badly he wanted to kiss Zoe. Now. In the middle of his kitchen. Surrounded by the glow of her candles.

He would start by sweeping her into his arms and kissing her sweet, pouty lips, and then he would sample the pale, fine skin at the base of her throat.

But perhaps Zoe could read his mind. She dropped her gaze and a deep stain spread over her cheeks. Her hand shook as she pressed it to her forehead, pushing back a strand of hair with a small sound of dismay.

Kent blinked. What the hell had come over him? Why couldn't he shake off this strange feeling of enchantment?

Zoe was the bridesmaid, for crying out loud. He had to forget about kissing her. *Say something about the candles.*

With a supreme effort, he dragged his attention away from her. What had she said? Something about putting these candles in little bags of sand?

'Do you have the sand you need?' he asked.

Zoe shook her head. 'I—I'm really mad with myself. I meant to call in at a craft shop and I forgot.'

'A craft shop? For sand?'

'In Brisbane the craft shops sell lovely, fine white sand.'

At that, he couldn't help laughing.

'What's so funny?'

'You don't need to buy sand at a craft shop, Zoe. Willara Creek is full of it.'

She shook her head, clearly unimpressed. 'But creek sand is damp and dirty and full of little twiggy bits.'

'Not all creek sand. Why don't I take you down there tomorrow and you can see what you think?' When she hesitated, he said, 'If it's not up to scratch, no harm done.'

'Bella and your mother are both coming over tomorrow. We're going to be busy with all the preparations.'

'We'll go first thing in the morning, then. If you don't mind an early start. How about a quick trip down to the creek before breakfast?'

There was more than a slight hesitation this time, but then Zoe nodded. 'Thank you,' she said, although she didn't smile. Instead she became businesslike. 'I'll shift everything out of here now.' Already she was turning off the candles.

Sitting in bed, Zoe stared into the darkness, unable to sleep.

Hugging her knees, she rocked slightly, something she only did when she was worried.

Or puzzled.

And confused.

The foreboding she'd felt about this wedding was deepening. Something *really* wasn't right—and she was pretty sure it wasn't just her feelings about the bridegroom getting in the way.

She knew Bella wasn't happy and the unhappiness wasn't only related to her father's health problems. Now Zoe was beginning to suspect that Kent wasn't happy either.

This possibility shocked her.

How could such a gorgeous, successful man, who could no doubt have his pick of any girl in the district, allow himself to walk, with his eyes wide open, into a marriage that wasn't gloriously happy?

It was the kind of question that would keep a consci-

entious bridesmaid awake all night. Pity she'd agreed
to be up at the crack of dawn.

When Zoe woke to Kent's knock the next morning she
felt more like a sleep deprived bridesmaid than a conscientious one. The thought of leaving her nice comfy
bed to look at sand in a creek bed held no appeal.

But Kent had brought her a mug of tea and a slice of
hot toast with strawberry jam, and Zoe couldn't help
being impressed by this, so she soon found herself in
his ute, bumping down a rough dirt track to Willara
Creek.

To discover the creek was stunningly beautiful.

Majestic twisted and knotted paperbarks and tall
river gums stood guard above water that was quiet and
still and cool, and edged by boulders entwined with
grevillea roots. Wind whispered gently in the she-oaks.

Charmed, Zoe watched a flight of wild ducks take
off from the water. 'It's so beautiful and peaceful,' she
said in an awed whisper.

Kent smiled at her. 'I thought you might like it.'

As she climbed out of the ute she heard birds calling to each other as they hunted for honey in the bright
red grevillea flowers.

'And here's the sand,' she said, almost straight away
seeing a small beach of nice white quartz-like grains.

'There's even better sand over here.' Kent was pointing farther along the bank.

Sure enough, he was right. Trapped among rocks,
the sand was so white it glistened. Kneeling, Zoe
studied it more closely and saw flickers of gold—pale
golden specks, shining brightly. 'Kent, that can't be
real gold?'

'No, I'm afraid it's only fool's gold. Its technical name is pyrite. But it's pretty enough for what you want, isn't it?'

'It's perfect. Absolutely gorgeous for a wedding.'

With impressive efficiency, Kent filled a couple of good-sized buckets and stowed them in the back of his ute.

Zoe took a deep breath of the fresh morning air as she looked about her at the deep pool of cool, inviting water, the smooth boulders and magnificent trees. 'I guess we'll have to go back already, but what a pity. It's so beautiful here. It almost looks as if it's been land-scaped.'

'We don't have to rush away.' Kent left the ute and squatted on the bank, looking out across the still water. 'This place has always been special. We've always kept the cattle out of here and we pump water up to troughs for them.'

'It must be amazing to have a place like this that you actually own. You'd feel a very close affinity to it.'

To Zoe's surprise, Kent didn't respond straight away. Picking up a handful of polished river stones, he skipped them out over the water, watching them bounce. As the last stone plopped he said, without looking at her, 'This is where I nearly ended my young life.'

Oh, God.

A pang of horror arrowed through Zoe, and she had a sudden picture of a little boy with dark hair and dark eyes recklessly diving and hitting his head…

This lovely man had nearly died.

Here. In this idyllic setting.

Her throat stung and she might have cried, if Kent hadn't been watching.

He sent her a grin.

She blinked away the tears. 'So this is where Bella's dad saved you?'

He nodded. 'It was nearly a year before I got back in the water.'

'I'm not surprised.' And then, she *had* to ask, 'What was it like, Kent? Can you remember? Did you know you'd nearly died?'

As soon as the questions were out she felt embarrassed by her nosiness, but Kent, to her relief, didn't seem to mind.

'I have no recollection at all of diving in, but I have a very vivid memory of opening my eyes from a deep and terrible, dark dream where I was choking. I looked straight up into Tom Shaw's face, and beyond him I could see the vivid blue sky and the tops of the river gums.'

'Did you know what had happened?'

Kent nodded slowly. 'It's weird, but I seemed to understand that I'd been given a second chance at life.'

He'd only been six—so young to be confronted with something so profound.

'I'm surprised you're still happy to come down here,' she said.

'I love it here,' Kent replied quietly. 'This place always makes me think about survival. And fate.'

'And Tom Shaw.'

His dark eyes studied Zoe's face intently, and again she felt an unwilling connection, a silent *something* zinging between them. Quicksilver shivers turned her arms to goose bumps.

'And Tom Shaw,' Kent said quietly. 'I'll never forget that debt.'

* * *

Shortly after they got back to the homestead, Bella rang.

'How are things at your place this morning?' Kent asked her.

'Dad's fine, thank heavens. He slept in late, but he's just eaten a huge recovery breakfast. And he seems really well. No coughing or shortness of breath. And of course, he's full of remorse and promises.'

'Good. So you'll be coming over here soon?'

'Actually…' An awkward note crept into Bella's voice. 'That's what I'm ringing about. I've been thinking I really should scoot into town to see Paddy.'

'Your grandfather?' Surprise buzzed a low warning inside Kent. 'But Zoe's here. Don't you two have all kinds of jobs lined up for this weekend?'

'Well…yes…but I thought I could squeeze in a *very* quick trip to town. It's just that I haven't seen Paddy for ages and you know how dreary it can be in the old people's home.' Almost as an afterthought, Bella asked, 'Is Zoe at a loose end?'

Kent glanced through the open doorway across the veranda to the garden. His mother had driven out from town to discuss wedding plans and she and Zoe were deep in conversation. They were pacing out sections of lawn and, judging by their arm-waving movements and general nodding and jotting-down of notes, they were discussing the table and seating arrangements.

They'd started over coffee this morning, chatting about the bridal shower—something about making a wedding dress from wrapping paper. Then they'd moved on to the flowers for table centrepieces at the wedding, and the kinds of pot plants that looked best in the gazebo. Zoe had wondered if there should be little lights entwined with the greenery.

The two of them were getting on like a bushfire.

But Kent knew damn well that it should be Bella who was out there in the garden with his mother. Surely, the bride should be involved in all this planning.

Renewed uneasiness stirred in him. He did his best to suppress it. Bella had always been upfront with him. She would tell him if there was a problem.

'Zoe's certainly not at a loose end,' he told her now. 'She and my mother are pretty busy, actually. If you're not careful they'll have the whole wedding planned before you get here.'

'Wonderful,' Bella said with a laugh.

'Wonderful?' Kent tried not to sound too concerned, but he couldn't shake off the troubling sense that something was definitely off kilter. Last night when he'd gone over to the Shaws' place, Bella had been moody and despondent, but that was excusable. He'd understood how upset she was about Tom.

But this morning was different. Tom was on the mend again, and Bella seemed to be leaving all the arrangements for the wedding to Zoe. Surely she should be here?

'You know me, Kent,' Bella said smoothly. 'I've never been much of a planner. Remember how I always used to leave my assignments until the last minute.'

'Yeah, I remember. But I think *you* should remember that Zoe *is* a planner, and hosting a wedding with dozens of guests is hardly the same as a school assignment. Zoe's your only bridesmaid, for heaven's sake, and she's doing an incredible job, but you can't leave it all on her shoulders.'

'Kent, you're right. I'm sorry.' Bella's lowered voice was suddenly contrite. 'I mustn't leave everything to Zoe just because she's so capable. Look, I promise to be out there very, very soon. I'll just race into town, say a quick hello to Paddy, and I'll come straight over. I'll bring a cherry pie and some of that lovely stuffed bread from the Willara bakery for lunch.'

Still worried, Kent hung up and stood with his hand resting on the receiver. He frowned as he looked through the doorway to his mother and Zoe out in the garden.

They were examining a bed of roses now, heads together—one a shower of silver curls and the other a silky, dark brown fall. The two of them were talking animatedly and doing rather a lot of smiling and nodding.

Zoe leaned forward to smell a lush pink rose bloom, and her hair swung forward with the movement. She was wearing knee-length khaki shorts and sandals, and a soft floral top with a little frill that skimmed her collarbones—so different from yesterday afternoon's pencil-slim skirt, stockings and high heels, and yet every bit as appealing.

The women moved on, and his mother became busy with her secateurs, tidying, trimming, and apparently explaining something to Zoe. Every so often, a tinkle of feminine laughter floated over the lawn.

Watching them, Kent thought that any stranger, coming upon the idyllic scene, could be forgiven for assuming that Zoe was his mother's future daughter-in-law.

His bride.

Hell. A dangerous flame leapt in his chest. Hell no. Not Zoe. It was ridiculous. Impossible. Never going to happen.

Bella should be here. Now.

* * *

As it turned out, Zoe also made a trip into Willara that morning. Having settled on their plans for the bridal shower, she and Kent's mother needed several items from the newsagent, so Zoe volunteered to collect them.

'Perhaps Kent could go with you for company,' Stephanie Rigby suggested.

Out of the corner of her eye, Zoe saw Kent tense, and felt an answering whip-crack reaction. *No.* No way could she risk spending any more time alone with her best friend's bridegroom.

Without chancing another glance in Kent's direction, she said, 'Thanks, but I know Kent's busy, and I'll be fine on my own.'

To her relief, there was no argument.

'You never know your luck,' Stephanie said serenely. 'You might run into Bella and you could double check her preferences before you buy the ribbons and the paper daisies.'

'That's a good idea. I'll keep an eye out for her. I guess Willara's so small, it's quite possible to run into people on the main street.'

Stephanie laughed. 'It happens all the time.'

'Your best chance of catching Bella will be at the Greenacres home or the bakery,' Kent suggested in a dry, unreadable tone that made Zoe wonder if he was in a bad mood.

'OK, I'll try the home, then the bakery.'

Zoe had never visited a home for the aged. Her grandparents were still quite fit and healthy and lived in their own homes, so she was already a bit nervous when she pulled up at Greenacres on Willara's outskirts. Then she walked through sliding doors into the large, tiled foyer, and came to a frozen, heart-thudding halt.

Bella was standing on the far side of the reception

area, deep in conversation—an animated, intense conversation—with a young man.

Zoe took one at Bella's companion and immediately
recognised the wild, dark hair and strong stubbled jaw
from the photos she'd seen on the internet. Damon
Cavello.

She felt a punch of shock in the centre of her chest,
but she told herself she was overreacting. Damon was an
old friend of Bella's and Kent's from their school days—
and a chance meeting with him in an aged care home
was perfectly harmless. It wasn't as if she'd caught Bella
indulging in a sly assignation. This was no big deal.

So maybe they were leaning subtly towards each
other and gazing intently into each other's eyes. And
maybe their body language suggested a deep, mutual
interest that locked out the rest of the world…

Or maybe Zoe was totally misreading the whole situation.

Unable to contain her curiosity a moment longer, she
stepped forward. 'Bella!'

Her friend jumped and turned, and when she saw
Zoe she blushed like litmus paper.

'Zoe, f-fancy seeing you here.' Bella shot a hasty
glance to the man at her side, then back to her friend.
'Are you looking for me? Nothing's happened at home,
has it?'

'There's no problem,' Zoe reassured her. 'I came
into town to buy a few things from the newsagent, and
I ducked in here first. We knew you were here and we'd
like to have your approval on—'

Zoe hesitated, uncomfortably aware of Damon
Cavello's steely and not particularly friendly gaze.
'We wanted to check on one or two—matters—for the
wedding.'

'Oh, right.' Bella was her normal colour again, and she straightened her shoulders and lifted her chin, drawing dignity around her like armour. She smiled carefully as she turned to the man beside her. 'Damon, this is my bridesmaid, my wonderful friend, Zoe Weston.'

Despite the tension zinging in the air, Zoe was aware of a warm swelling of pride when she heard herself described in such glowing terms.

'Zoe, this is Damon Cavello, an old school friend.'

'Of course.' Zoe held out her hand and favoured him with her warmest smile. 'You contacted me on Facebook. Hi, Damon, nice to meet you.'

'How do you do, Zoe?' Damon shook her hand firmly, but his smile didn't quite reach his eyes. 'And thank you for engineering this chance to hook up with the old gang.'

He nodded towards Bella and his silver-grey eyes seemed to smoulder, but his voice was relaxed enough, so it shouldn't have been an awkward moment. Zoe, however, could feel unmistakable vibes of tension. And yikes, she could practically see the electricity sparking between this pair.

'Damon has been visiting his grandmother,' Bella said.

'And you ran into him while you were visiting your grandfather. What a lucky coincidence.'

'Yes.'

An elderly woman, shuffling past with a walking frame, beamed a radiant smile on the three of them.

'Well…as I said, I was on the way to the newsagents,' Zoe continued. 'So if you two have more catching up to do, I can wait for you there, Bella.'

'It's OK. I'll come with you now. Damon and I have said our hellos.'

Damon frowned and Zoe sent him another friendly smile. 'Will we see you at the wedding?'

'Sure.' He swallowed uncomfortably as if there was a painful constriction in his throat. 'Kent kindly emailed an invitation. Asked me to the bucks' party as well.'

'Great. We should run into you again, then, either some time next weekend, or on the big day.'

'Absolutely.'

The girls had driven into town in separate vehicles, so there was no chance for an in-depth conversation during their shopping jaunt or on their separate journeys back to Willara Downs. And for the rest of the weekend they were so busy, making decorations, or party favours, or cooking sweets and canapés to be stored or frozen that they didn't have time for an in-depth talk.

It was Sunday afternoon when they were heading back down the highway to Brisbane before they were alone and the subject of Damon could be properly aired.

Not that Bella was in a talkative mood. From the moment they left Willara, she seemed to slip lower and lower in the passenger seat, slumped in despondent silence.

'Missing Kent already?' Zoe asked tentatively.

Bella gave a guilty start and she frowned like a sleeper waking from a dream. 'Sorry...what did you say?'

'I asked if you were already missing Kent.'

'Oh...yes...of course.'

'At least you'll only have to wait two more weeks and then you can be with him all the time.'

'Yes,' Bella said softly.

Zoe had used every ounce of her inner strength to remain upbeat and supportive about Bella's good fortune, despite all the worrying niggles. Surely her friend could try a bit harder to act happy. Instead of rallying, however, Bella seemed to sink into even deeper misery.

By now, they were heading down the steep Too-woomba Range, and Zoe couldn't take her eyes off the road, but she had the horrible feeling that Bella was on the verge of crying. Then she heard a definite sob.

Casting a frantic sideways glance, Zoe saw tears streaming down her friend's face. Her heart gave a sickening lurch.

'Bell,' she cried, keeping her gaze fixed on the steep, winding road. 'What's the matter?'

'I'm OK,' Bella sobbed. 'I'm just being an idiot.'

Zoe couldn't help wondering if Damon was somehow the cause of these tears, but she had no idea how to ask such a probing question. Besides, it was her duty to keep Bella focused on Kent.

'It must be awful to have to say goodbye to Kent every weekend.'

'Oh, Zoe, don't,' Bella wailed.

Don't? Don't talk about Kent?

Thoroughly alarmed, Zoe held her tongue as she negotiated a particularly sharp hairpin bend. Out of the corner of her eye, she was aware of Bella pulling tissues from the bag at her feet and wiping her eyes and blowing her nose.

It wasn't till they reached the bottom of the range and the road levelled out once more that Zoe stole another glance Bella's way. Her friend was no longer crying, but her face was pale and blotchy and she still looked exceedingly unhappy.

'I really don't want to pry, Bell, but is there any way I can help?'

Bella released a drawn-out sigh. 'I don't think so, thanks.'

'I mean—tell me to shut up, but if you want to talk—about—*anything*—it's the bridesmaid's job to listen.'

This was greeted by a shaky little laugh. 'Oh, Zoe, you're such a sweetheart.'

A nice compliment, but not exactly true. A sweetheart did not fall for her best friend's fiancé.

A few minutes later, Zoe tried again. 'So…I suppose it's just tension. You have so much on your plate just now—worrying about your dad, and so many jobs crowding in with the wedding so close.'

Bella turned away to look out of the window at rows and rows of bright sunflowers standing with their heads high like soldiers in formation.

Clearly, she wasn't looking for a chance to talk about her problem, so Zoe drove on in silence…wondering… worrying…

Then out of the blue, as they approached Gatton, Bella sat up straighter. 'Zoe, I think I do need to talk. I can't deal with this on my own. Can we pull over?'

CHAPTER SIX

Zoe took the next ramp leading off the highway and parked beneath a jacaranda tree in an almost empty picnic area. At a distant table, a family were gathering up their tea things and packing them into a basket. The mother was calling to her little girl who was scooping up fallen jacaranda blossoms.

Suddenly needing air, Zoe lowered her window and dragged in deep breaths, catching the dank scent of newly turned earth from nearby fields and the sweeter scent of the flowering trees.

Her stomach churned uncomfortably and she unbuckled her seat belt. She was dead-set nervous now that Bella was about to confide her problem. Her friend's tears pointed to a serious dilemma, and Zoe wasn't confident she had the wisdom or the strength to advise her.

Honestly, could she trust herself to put her own silly, unwanted emotions aside?

Praying she would get this right, she said gently, 'I'm ready whenever you are, Bells.'

Bella pulled another tissue from her bag and blew her nose noisily, then, after only a moment's hesitation, she took the leap. 'There's no point in beating about the bush. I'm in a mess about this wedding.'

'Ah-h-h.'

Bella shot Zoe a sharp glance. 'So you're not surprised?'

'Not entirely. I must admit I've been waiting for you and Kent to show more—er—emotion about—well—everything. And right from the first time Damon made contact, it was pretty clear he made you edgy.'

Bella nodded. 'I know. Seeing Damon again has been a kind of wake-up call.'

'You mean you really care about him?'

'Oh, I don't really know, Zoes. He sends me kind of crazy. It's like I'm still in high school. Up and down and all over the place.'

'I'm sorry. I should never have posted that rave about your wedding on Facebook. It's my fault Damon found you.'

'Gosh, don't blame yourself. I think he heard about the wedding from other people as well.' Bella was pulling the tissue in her lap to shreds.

'Damon's not trying to stop you getting married, is he?'

Zoe had a sudden vision of Damon Cavello calling out in the middle of the wedding—at that moment when the minister asked the congregation to speak up or for ever hold their peace.

Bella shook her head, then, with another heavy sigh, she kicked off her shoes and drew her feet up onto the seat, hugging her knees. 'The thing is, when Damon rang me on Saturday morning, I had to see him. I thought if I saw him just once in the flesh—if I spoke to him, I'd get the old memories out of my system. But as soon as we met—'

Hairs stood on the back of Zoe's neck as she watched the flush spread across Bella's face. She tried to make light of it. 'So your heart took off like a racehorse? Your knees gave way?'

Bella nodded, then covered her face with her hands. 'What am I going to do?'

It was a question Zoe didn't want to answer. But poor Bella hadn't a mother to turn to and she was her best friend. Praying for wisdom, Zoe took a deep breath before she spoke. 'I—I guess it all depends on how you feel about Kent.'

At first Bella didn't answer. When she did, her voice was soft, wistful… 'That's my problem. I'm so worried that Kent and I are marrying for all the wrong reasons.'

'But he's stop-and-stare gorgeous,' Zoe suggested miserably.

Bella shot her a sharp, surprised glance.

'Just stating the obvious.' Zoe's shoulders lifted in a defensive shrug, and a dull ache curled around her heart.

'Well, I'm not going to argue with your good taste,' Bella said with a watery smile. 'But I just wish Kent and I had been in some sort of long-term relationship, or had at least been dating. The truth is, we haven't really seen very much of each other since I moved to Brisbane. We only caught up again properly when I started coming home, because Dad was so sick. We were both so worried about Dad and the farm, and Kent's gone out of his way to help.'

And he feels he owes your dad big-time for saving his life, Zoe wanted to say, but she kept the thought to herself.

Instead she said, 'I never totally understood how your engagement came about. It seemed a bit out of the blue to me. What made you say yes in the first place?'

Bella looked down at her diamond engagement ring

and her stunning, dark berry fingernails—enviably dramatic and gorgeous. 'It was a bit of an emotional whirlwind. It's not all that long since I lost my mum, and then it looked like I was losing my dad as well. The farm was going to rack and ruin. I felt like I was going under, too.'

'And yet you never mentioned anything about it to me.'

'Well…to be honest, I was a bit ashamed about my dad's drinking.'

Zoe gave a guilty sigh. If she'd been a better friend, the *right* kind of friend, Bella might have felt more comfortable about sharing her worries.

'I was coming home every weekend,' Bella went on. 'And I started seeing more and more of Kent, and he was so sweet, so supportive. He's been running our property as well as his own. And of course we have a deep bond that goes way back. Then one weekend, he just looked at me and said "Why don't we just do it? Why don't we get married?"'

Bella was smiling at the memory. 'In a flash, it all seemed to make wonderful sense. It was the perfect solution, and you should have seen the smile on Dad's face when we told him. He was *so* relieved I was being taken care of.'

To Zoe it was now blindingly obvious why Bella and Kent were marrying. Kent felt a huge debt to Tom Shaw. Bella was in danger of losing her family, her farm— losing everything, in other words. Bella and Kent had a long history, a shared background that made them suited to each other in every way. Duty and friendship had won, and Kent had saved the day.

Everything might have been fine if Damon hadn't arrived on the scene, no doubt reawakening Bella's school-girl fantasies of passion and romance...

Oh, man... Zoe's thought winged back to Friday night when Kent arrived home to find his kitchen filled with candles. Her skin flamed at the memory of the way he'd looked at her...

The flash of fire in his eyes had shocked her. Thrilled her. As had the roughness of emotion in his voice.

And next morning, there'd been another moment of connection down on the creek bank...

No, she mustn't think about that now. She mustn't let her own longings confuse Bella's situation.

In fact, Zoe knew she mustn't do or say anything to influence Bella right now. She had no similar experience to draw on, no wisdom to offer. Her role was to listen...

But surely Bella must see all the benefits of this marriage? Her life could be fabulous if she went ahead with it. Kent was perfect husband material. Gorgeous looks aside, if you factored in his easy manner, his beautiful home and garden, his prosperous farm and country lifestyle in a friendly, close-knit community, Willara Downs was like the closest thing to heaven.

Then again, Zoe knew that her nomadic childhood had given her a longing for security and a love of being settled that Bella might not share.

And yet, for Bella there was the added advantage that, with Kent as her husband, her father would almost certainly recover and grow stronger. Every day he would see his daughter happily married and living close by. It was such a strong incentive for Tom to throw off his bad habits and take care of his health.

Surely these were weighty plusses.

Bella, however, was sighing. 'I was so emotional at

the time Kent came up with the wedding proposal. But I know he only made the offer because he was worried about Dad, and he felt he owed something to my family. He's always had a highly developed sense of doing the right thing.'

'So he was being heroic instead of romantic?'

'Yes,' Bella admitted in a small voice.

A marriage of convenience. The thought suffocated Zoe.

Again, she forced her own longings aside. She had no doubt that Kent possessed the necessary strength of character to make a success of anything he set his mind to. Even if his marriage wasn't based on passion, he would be a loving and loyal husband.

'But the marriage could still work,' she said softly.

Bella turned to her, her eyes wide with dawning hope. 'That's true, Zoe. Even arranged marriages can work out happily.'

'So I've heard,' Zoe agreed, trying not to sound deeply miserable. Perhaps it was melodramatic of her, but she felt as if she were saying goodbye to her own last chance for happiness.

Bella was looking down at her sparkling engagement ring. 'So…you think I should go ahead and marry Kent?'

An agonising pain burst in Zoe's throat and she swallowed it down. She opened her mouth to speak, but changed her mind, afraid she might say something she'd regret.

Bella sat up straight. 'It *is* the right thing to do,' she said with sudden conviction. 'Kent's no fool. He wouldn't have offered to marry me if he wasn't happy about it.' She shot Zoe a pleading glance. 'Would he?'

Tension made Zoe tremble. She could feel the sharpened claws of her jealousy digging deep, but she forced a shaky smile. 'From where I'm looking, you'll have a wonderful life with Kent.'

She held her breath as Bella sat, staring through the windscreen, her eyes bright and thoughtful. Outside the car, the light was fading. A gust of wind sent jacaranda bells fluttering onto the windscreen.

'But you're the only one who can make the final decision,' Zoe said at last.

'You're right. I shouldn't be putting pressure on you like this.' Nevertheless, a smile dawned on Bella's face, as pretty as a sunrise. She took Zoe's hands and squeezed them tightly. 'I know what I must do. Damon threw me off track. He's always been dangerous like that. But Kent and I made our decision for all the right reasons and we should stick to our original instincts.'

Leaning forward, Bella kissed Zoe's cheek. 'Thank you for helping me to sort this out.'

Tears stung the backs of Zoe's eyes and she blinked madly to hold them back. 'No problem. Point thirty-nine in the bridesmaid's handbook. Lots of brides have second thoughts as the big day approaches.'

'I'm quite normal, then. That's a relief.'

Zoe tried to crack another smile, but couldn't quite manage it.

It didn't matter. Bella's arms were around her, hugging her tight. 'I'm so lucky,' she whispered. 'I have the best bridesmaid in the world.'

CHAPTER SEVEN

To KENT's relief, his bucks' night wasn't too extreme. He'd heard of bridegrooms being tied naked to a pole in the main street, or bundled into a crop-dusting plane and transported to a remote outpost.

Fortunately, his best man, Steve, wangled just the right tempo. He'd done a great job of rounding up Kent's mates and the party was a blast. Not a city-style bash with strippers and pranks—just blokes enjoying themselves in a quiet country pub. Actually, the quiet country pub was growing rowdier by the minute, but the revelry was harmless enough.

There were the usual games with drinking penalties. Right now, anyone who raised taboo topics—cricket or football, the bride or her bridesmaid, the share market or politics—had to down his drink in one go. Merriment by the bucketful.

Later they'd sleep it off in the Mullinjim pub, and there'd be a few sore heads in the morning, but at least there was still a full week before the wedding.

Of course there were all kinds of comments flying about Kent's last chance for freedom.

It was a phrase that made him distinctly uneasy—but he wasn't prepared to dwell on that. He imagined most guys felt the cold snap of an iron noose about their throats whenever they thought too hard about the doors closing behind them when they stepped up to the altar.

One week to go…

He'd be glad when the tension was behind him, when he and Bella were safely settled…

Tonight, however, he had to put up with the good-natured ribbing from his mates, had to laugh as he agreed that his days as a carefree bachelor were numbered. But he wondered what the others would think if they knew how often his thoughts trailed back to earlier this evening when he'd driven through Willara and caught a glimpse of the girls at the pub.

Already in party mode after the bridal shower, Bella's friends had all been there, in shiny strapless dresses in a rainbow of colours. Looking like gaudy beetles, they'd wolf-whistled and waved glasses of pink champagne at Kent as he drove past.

He hadn't seen Bella, but she would have been in the mob somewhere, no doubt sporting a mock bridal headdress concocted from a piece of mosquito netting and a plastic tiara.

The girl he *had* seen and noted was Zoe.

She'd been standing in a doorway, chatting with a friend, and she was wearing a dress of striking tangerine silk, an exotic colour that highlighted her dark hair and slim elegance.

For a split second as Kent flashed past her eyes had met his. Startled, she'd half raised her glass.

He'd only caught that fleeting glimpse of her in the bright dress with one shoulder bared, but the image had shot a scorching flame through him. He'd remembered her in his kitchen, surrounded by four dozen smart candles and he'd felt that same thrust of longing he'd felt then.

Now, Kent consoled himself that this was the dop-
pelgänger that haunted most men about to be married—
the alter ego taking a final backward glance at freedom
before diving into monogamy.

Get over it, man.

But even now, as he chatted and joked with his mates,
his brain flashed to the memory.

Of Zoe. Not Bella.

Damn it, if he'd seen Bella at the pub he wouldn't be
plagued by these memories now. He'd be thinking only
of Bella, not Zoe with her shiny dark hair and soft smile.
But now, instead of focusing on his bride, a treacherous
part of his brain kept pressing rewind, kept replaying
a picture of Zoe's slender curves encased in a sunburst
of silk.

Why the hell now? Why tonight?

'Kent, old mate. Need to have a word.'

The voice behind Kent brought him swinging round.

Damon Cavello, glass in hand—a double shot of neat
whisky by the look of it—greeted him with a morose
smile.

They'd talked earlier, fighting to be heard above the
hubbub, but it had been a superficial catch-up, skimming over the past decade in half a dozen carefully ed-
ited sentences. Now Damon held out his hand.

'I've overlooked congratulating the lucky bridegroom.'

'I'm sure you said something earlier.' Kent accepted
the handshake uneasily, wondering if he'd detected a
hint of stiffness in Damon's manner.

'You know you're a very lucky man,' Damon said.

'I do indeed.'

'You deserve her, of course.'

'Thank you.'

Why did he have the feeling that Bella's old flame was testing him? Rattling his antlers, so to speak.

Damon offered a mirthless grin. 'Bella's a—'

'Hold it!' Kent laughed as he raised his hand. 'There's a penalty tonight if you mention the bride's name.'

'Damn, I forgot.'

Before Kent could let him off the hook, Damon tossed down the contents of his glass.

Kent inhaled sharply, imagining the fire lacing the other man's veins.

'So, where was I?' Damon asked as he set the empty glass on the bar. 'Ah, yes.' Folding his arms across his chest, he sized Kent up with a knowing smile. 'I was agreeing that you've made an excellent choice of bride. You and your future wife will be the toast of Willara.'

Kent accepted this with a faint nod.

Damon's gaze shifted to a point in the distance beyond Kent's shoulder. His chest rose and fell as he drew in a deep breath, then exhaled slowly.

To Kent's dismay, the other man's eyes betrayed a terrible pain. 'I was a fool,' he said, his voice quiet yet rough with self loathing. 'I was the world's biggest fool to head off overseas, leaving her behind.'

A nightmare weight pressed down on Kent, crushing the air from his lungs and stilling his blood. He pulled himself together. 'That may be true, mate,' he said slowly. 'You were famous for doing crazy things back then. You were legend.'

'I was, but I regret it now.'

What was Damon implying? Was this some kind of mind-game strategy?

'Are you trying to tell me something?' Kent challenged in a deliberately exaggerated country drawl. 'Are you saying that you would have married young and settled down with a mob of kids in quiet old Willara?'

'Who knows? We can't turn back time.' Damon squared his shoulders, looked about him at the happy crowd, then whipped back to Kent. 'Promise me one thing.'

Kent eyed the other man levelly, refusing to be intimidated. 'What's that?'

Temporarily, Damon lost momentum. Dropping his gaze, he tapped a short drumbeat on the smooth timber-topped bar. When he looked up again, his grey eyes were blazing ice. 'Just make sure you don't have any doubts, my friend, not the slightest shadow.'

The words struck hammer blows, but Kent refused to flinch. 'Thanks for your advice,' he said coolly. 'It's heartening to know there's another man in town who understands how lucky I am to be marrying Bella Shaw.'

Looking Damon in the eye, Kent downed his drink.

It was well past midnight when Zoe heard the tap on her door. She hadn't been asleep, although her body was worn out from the huge effort of running both the bridal shower and then the hen night. The functions had been proclaimed a great success, but now her brain couldn't stop buzzing.

When the soft knock sounded, she slipped quickly from the bed, went to the door and opened it a crack. Bella was outside in the dark passageway, wild eyed and wrapped in a pink-and-blue kimono.

'Can I come in for a sec?' she whispered.

'Sure.' Zoe readily opened the door, but threads of fear were coiling in her chest. All night she'd been watching Bella with mounting alarm.

While the bride had laughed and chatted and joined in the silly, light-hearted party games, Zoe had been aware of the underlying pulse, a ticking time bomb of tension. Plainly, things still weren't right for Bella. The strain showed in her eyes, in her smile.

Luckily, all the other party girls had been too busy drinking and having a good time to notice. But Zoe, who'd taken her hen night responsibilities seriously, had mostly drunk tonic water.

Clear-headed, she'd noticed plenty and she'd worried plenty. Most especially, she'd worried that Bella still wasn't happy with the decision she'd reached last week.

Now, her friend collapsed into the only chair in the room. 'I've just had a text from Kent,' she said. 'He wants to see me. To talk.'

'Tonight?'

'Yes, but I said it was too late. I rang back and talked him into leaving it till first thing in the morning.'

'Do you know what he wants to talk about?'

'He wants to make sure I'm totally happy about—' Bella let out a soft groan. 'He wants to discuss the wedding.'

Zoe's heart thudded. 'I assume this isn't just a planning meeting.'

'No. I'm pretty sure he wants to double check that we're both still on the same page.'

'About getting married?'

Closing her eyes, Bella nodded.

'What are you going to tell him?'

A sob broke from Bella. 'I have to be totally honest, Zoe. I don't think I can do it.'

CHAPTER EIGHT

FOR ages after Bella went back to her room, Zoe tossed and turned, her sheets damp with sweat, her thoughts rioting. Eventually, she got up and shut the window and switched on the air conditioning, but, although the system was efficient and the room cooled quickly, she couldn't settle down.

Everything was spinning round and round in her head. Bella's distress, Kent's ultimatum, the mystery surrounding Damon—and, of course, the beautiful wedding reception she'd planned....

Time crawled. It took for ever for dawn to finally arrive as a creamy glow around the edges of the curtains. Giving up any pretence of sleep, Zoe rolled out of bed and opened the curtains to a view down Willara's main street. At this early hour the little town was empty and silent, and it looked a little faded, too, like a ghost town in an old black-and-white movie.

Was Kent already on his way?

She showered and shampooed her hair, then blow-dried it and packed her bags, shoving all the leftover party glitter, shredded cellophane, cardboard and felt pens into an outside pocket. She had no idea why she was saving this stuff, couldn't imagine ever using it again.

There'd been no special arrangements made for breakfast—all the hen-night girls wanted to sleep off the party after-effects. But Zoe's room had started to feel like a jail cell. She knew Bella wouldn't eat until after she'd spoken to Kent, so she decided to go downstairs to dine alone.

As she went past Bella's door she thought she heard the soft murmur of voices. Perhaps, even now, Bella and Kent were making a decision. Just thinking about it made Zoe's eyes and throat sting with hot tears.

The hotel's dining room was old-fashioned with dark panelled walls and vases of bright flowers on the tables. It was still very early, and the room was empty, but a girl was there, ready to take orders.

Zoe glanced at the menu. It offered a full country breakfast with bacon, scrambled eggs, mushrooms and fried tomatoes, but, while she'd been ravenous an hour ago, her anxious stomach rebelled now.

She ordered tea and toast and sat in a sunny corner near a window. She was drinking her second cup of tea and eating hot buttered toast spread with local orange marmalade when a tall, broad-shouldered figure appeared at the dining-room doorway.

Kent.

Zoe's knife clattered to her plate.

Had he already spoken to Bella? If he hadn't, what was she supposed to say?

Kent came across the room, weaving past the empty tables covered by clean white cloths. He sent her a cautious smile, but it was impossible to gauge his mood.

He didn't look utterly heartbroken, but perhaps he was very good at masking his feelings. He was definitely paler than usual and there were shadows under his eyes, as if his night had been as restless and as tormented hers.

'I was hoping I'd find you,' he said when he reached her.

'Have you seen Bella?'

'Yes. We've been talking in her room for the past hour.'

A chill skittered over Zoe's arms. She was still unsure how to handle this.

'Can I join you?' Kent asked.

Zoe nodded, and once he was seated she realised she'd been holding her breath. The tension was unbearable. What had they decided?

Kent placed his hands squarely on the table. 'I wanted you to be the first to know. Bella and I are calling off the wedding.'

Zoe's heart gave a painful thud. Even though this wasn't totally unexpected, she felt as if she'd stepped from solid ground into thin air. 'I'm so sorry.' Tears stung her eyes and her throat. 'I can't begin to imagine how you must be feeling right now, Kent.'

'It had to be done,' he said with a shaky smile.

Zoe didn't know how to respond to that. She was dazed—and shell-shocked.

No wedding.

After all the excitement and planning and busyness of the past few weeks—now, nothing. *Nada.*

'How's Bella?'

'She's worn out from over-thinking this whole deal, but she's OK, I guess, or at least she will be after a good night's sleep.'

'I should go upstairs to see her. She might want some friendly support.'

'Actually, she's not here.' Kent lifted his hands in a

don't-ask-me gesture. 'She had to rush off to Green-acres. There's been some sort of problem there.'

'No...not her grandfather?'

'I think so.'

'Oh, God. Poor Bella. As if she hasn't had enough to worry about.'

'I offered to go with her, but she said she wanted to handle it herself, which was understandable, I guess.'

'Maybe there's something I can do?' Zoe was already rising from her chair.

'I told Bella to ring if we can help.'

As Zoe sat once more she let out a sigh. Her mind flashed to her excitement when Bella first asked her to be a bridesmaid. Who would have thought it would come to this?

The waitress appeared at Kent's side. 'Would you like to order breakfast, sir?'

'Ah, no...but perhaps some tea. Zoe, shall we order a fresh pot?'

Considering the awkwardness of their situation, Zoe found his politeness and self-control impressive. As soon as the girl had left she reached across the table and squeezed Kent's hand. It was meant to be a comforting gesture, but for her the brief contact still sparked the usual silly electricity.

'Thanks for being such a good friend to Bella,' he said.

Zoe gave a rueful shake of her head. 'My big chance to be a bridesmaid. Gone down the tube.'

'You would have been perfect,' he said warmly.

'Well, for that matter, I thought you and Bella would have been the perfect couple.'

'Did you really?'

Tension shadowed his lovely dark eyes as he waited for her answer.

Zoe found herself suddenly flustered. 'You had so much in common.'

'Maybe that was the problem.'

The waitress returned with the tea and a fresh cup and saucer for Kent, so they became busy with pouring and helping themselves to milk and sugar.

When they were alone again, Kent said, 'Zoe, the decision to call the wedding off was mutual.'

She was almost giddy with relief. 'Gosh, I'm—I'm—'

'Mad with us both for messing you around?'

'No, I'm not mad. If I'm honest, Kent, I've been worried for ages. The vibes weren't right between you.'

Kent grimaced and rubbed at his jaw in a way that was intensely masculine.

'But for what it's worth,' Zoe added, 'I think your motives for proposing were honourable.'

'What do you know about my motives?'

'I don't want to say anything out of place, but I'm guessing you wanted to look after Bella, and you wanted to put Tom's mind at ease.'

Kent's mouth tilted in a lopsided smile. 'You're not just a pretty bridesmaid, are you?'

Despite everything, Zoe drank in the sight of him sitting opposite her in his moleskin trousers threaded with a crocodile leather belt.

'The truth is,' he said, after a bit, 'I had a revealing chat with Damon last night. We started off toe to toe like two duelling bucks, all bluster and bravado. But then I started really listening to the guy. He was talking about Bella, and I watched his face, his body language. I heard the depth of emotion in his voice…'

Kent paused and his impressive chest expanded as he drew a deep breath. 'I don't know if he's the right man for Bella, or if she even wants him, but last night I found myself questioning—everything. I realised that I was denying Bella—denying both of us the chance to have a marriage based on something *more* than friendship.'

He was looking directly at Zoe and she felt heat spreading over her skin. She told herself to stop it. Just because Kent was no longer marrying Bella, she couldn't start imagining he was going to dive into a new relationship. And even if he did, why would he choose her?

Suddenly, with her role as bridesmaid swept away, her old insecurities were rushing back.

She was relieved when Kent returned to practicalities.

'I've told Bella I'll take the heat as far as the wedding's concerned. I'll talk to our families and friends.'

What a task. Zoe pictured the girls upstairs. They'd be getting up soon and would have to be told the news, and there were so many others who would need to know. It was all going to be awkward and embarrassing, and Kent was shouldering the load. She felt a rush of sympathy for him, another layer to add to the emotional storm inside her.

'Perhaps I could help with ringing the caterers and the hire people?'

Kent considered this. 'I'd like to say don't worry. You've done more than enough, and I'll take care of it. But with all these other calls to make, I'd really appreciate your help, Zoe. As it is, I think I'll be spending all day on the phone.'

On cue, Kent's mobile phone rang and he quickly retrieved it from his pocket. 'It's Bella,' he said as he checked the caller ID.

Zoe watched the concern in his eyes as he listened. She tried not to eavesdrop, but she couldn't help catching his rather alarming responses.

'Do you think that's wise, Bella?… What about the police?… Yes, I've spoken to Zoe. I'm with her now. Yes, sure.'

To Zoe's surprise, he handed her the phone. 'Bella wants to speak to you.'

'What's happening?' she whispered.

He rolled his eyes. 'Big drama. Bella will explain.'

Heavens, what else could go wrong? Zoe lifted the phone. 'Hi, Bella.'

'Zoe, I'm so sorry I dashed off, but you won't believe what's happened. My grandfather and Damon's grandmother have taken off.'

'Taken off?' Zoe almost shrieked. 'You mean they've run away from Greenacres? Together?'

'Yes. They've taken Damon's grandmother's car.' Bella's sudden laugh was almost hysterical. 'It's ridiculous, I know. It might only be a prank, and they're not senile or anything, but we can't let them drive off together without knowing what they plan to do. We have a lead, so Damon and I are going after them.'

'Far out. That's—that's incredible.'

'I know. I can't believe it either. But, Zoe, I'm really, really sorry to be abandoning you. I wanted to talk to you this morning, to explain everything.'

'Don't worry about me.' Lowering her voice, she said, 'Kent's explained about the wedding.'

'Is he OK?'

Zoe sent a glance Kent's way. Catching her eye, he gave her another crooked smile and she felt a flash of useless longing. 'He seems to be bearing up.'

'Zoe, can you look after Kent? Keep an eye on him?'

'I—I—' Zoe was so thrown by the thought of ongoing contact with Kent that she wasn't quite sure what to say. And yet, she couldn't overlook the pleading in Bella's voice. 'Yes, yes, of course I will.'

'Thank you. Thanks for everything, Zoes. I'm so sorry you're not going to be my bridesmaid after all, but at least we can be thankful we chose a dress you can wear to a nice party.'

Zoe rolled her eyes. The last thing on her mind was her dress.

'I'll stay in touch,' Bella said. 'But I've got to dash now. Talk soon. Bye.'

'Bye. And, Bella—'

'Yes?'

'Be careful, won't you?'

'Um…yeah, thanks for the warning.' Bella spoke softly, as if she knew very well that the warning was mostly about Damon Cavello.

Dazed, Zoe handed the phone back to Kent. 'I'm beginning to think I must be dreaming. Runaway grandparents, for crying out loud! None of this is happening, is it?' She held out her arm. 'If someone pinched me now, I'm sure I'd wake up.'

Laughing, Kent took her arm, and his warm fingers encircled her, creating a bracelet of heat. Instead of pinching her, however, he stroked a feather-light caress on the fine, pale skin of her inner wrist.

A tremor vibrated through her, and she gasped. Had he felt it?

His dark eyes flashed a message—inchoate and thrilling—unmistakable.

Her heart thundered. *Don't be an idiot.*

He was still watching her as he released her. He smiled. 'I'm quite sure you're wide awake.'

Then, as if to correct himself, he became business-like once more. 'Now,' he said. 'It's time to get cracking. We have a wedding to cancel.'

Rusty hinges squeaked as Kent pushed open the old timber gate that led to the tangle of shrubbery and weeds surrounding the Shaw family's homestead. Even on a pleasant spring afternoon, the unkempt jungle looked depressing—a far cry from the beautiful, prize-winning garden that had been Bella's mother's pride and joy. Mary Shaw would roll in her grave if she could see this mess now.

Kent called out, partly in greeting, partly as a warning. 'Tom, are you home?'

Tom's faithful border collie appeared, eyes eager and bright and tail wagging happily. Mounting the front steps, Kent greeted him. 'Where's your boss, Skip?'

'I'm in here,' called a deep male voice. 'In the kitchen.'

Relieved, Kent made his way down the hall, but his gut clenched as he thought of the task ahead of him.

He'd already broken the news about the wedding to his parents and they'd coped surprisingly well. His mother had made a gentle complaint about all the money she'd spent on her outfit.

'Where am I going to wear a brocade two-piece in Willara?' she'd demanded, with a rueful smile, but she hadn't really looked unhappy.

His father had given his shoulder a sympathetic thump and muttered that he was proud of Kent's courage.

And Bella had spoken to Tom, of course, so Kent wasn't about to drop a bombshell.

Just the same, as he entered the big, airy kitchen at the back of the old timber Queenslander it was hard to shake off the feeling that he'd let Tom Shaw down.

Kent looked about the kitchen filled with windows and painted sunshiny yellow. It had always been his favourite room in this homestead. In his primary school days, he'd regularly dropped in here for afternoon tea.

There'd always be home-made macadamia or ginger cookies and milk, and he and Bella had eaten them at the scrubbed pine table, or sometimes they'd taken their snack outside to sit in their cubbyhouse beneath an old weeping willow.

Now, Kent found Bella's father standing at the greasy stove, thin, unshaven and pale, with heavy shadows under his eyes. At least he appeared to be sober, which was something, and he was stirring the contents of a pot with a wooden spoon.

This Tom Shaw was such a different figure from the man Kent had known and admired for most of his life. It had been a rude shock to watch this man slide downhill so quickly and completely after his wife's death. He'd hated to stand by and witness his hero's self-destruction.

So, yeah…the wedding plan had been all about propping Tom up again. Now, Kent squared his shoulders.

'Evening,' Tom greeted him morosely.

'Evening, Tom.' Kent stood with two hands resting on the back of a kitchen chair, bracing himself.

'Bella rang and she explained about the wedding.'

'Yeah.' Kent swallowed. 'I'm sorry it hasn't worked out.'

'Well...actually—' Tom smiled wryly '—I'm relieved, son.'

'Relieved?'

Tom nodded. 'I know I was excited at first. It's true I was thrilled with the notion of you taking care of my Bella and Blue Gums. I could die happy. But it wasn't long before I realised something was missing. Something really important.'

Turning the flame down beneath his cooking pot, Tom folded his arms and leaned back against a cupboard. 'I've been in love, Kent. I had a great marriage, full of spark.' He fixed Kent with knowing eyes. 'That's the thing. There has to be a spark—something beyond friendship. Something to set your soul on fire.'

Kent knew he was right. This lack of a spark was exactly what he and Bella had finally acknowledged. They were very fond of each other. They were great mates. But deep down they knew the passion they both yearned for was never going to materialise.

'I'm ashamed that you were both prepared to take that huge step for my sake,' Tom said. 'Heck, Kent, marriage is a gigantic step.' His eyes took on a little of their old fire. 'I couldn't bear to think you were tying the knot to repay me for yanking you out of the flaming creek all those years ago.'

'But I owe you my life.'

'I happened to be on the spot, and I just did what anyone would have done.' Tom shook his head. 'Thank heavens you and Bella have come to your senses.'

Kent took a moment to digest this. He had a sneaking suspicion that his parents were as relieved as Tom was, although they hadn't expressed their views quite so strongly.

'I'm glad you understand,' he said quietly. 'But while we're being honest, there's something else I need to get off my chest.'

'What's that?' The other man's eyes narrowed.

Kent's grip on the chair tightened. 'It's your turn to wake up, Tom. I know it's been hard for you these past eighteen months, but you need to accept that no one else can take responsibility for your health. I can plough your fields and mend your fences, and I can even offer to marry your daughter, but none of that will help you if you can't give up your bad habits.'

Tom dropped his gaze, jaw stubbornly jutted. 'You're dead right. In fact, I'm one step ahead of you.'

'Have you rejoined AA?'

'I have and I won't miss another meeting. That last time I put on a turn in front of Bella's friend was my wake-up call. I really let Bella down.'

Kent gripped Tom's hand. 'That's great news, mate. Well done.' Now he was grinning widely. 'Doc King gave you plenty more years if you conquered the grog and worked on your fitness.'

'Yeah, so that's the plan. I want to be around to see my grandkids.' Tom gave Kent's shoulder a hearty bang. 'And your nippers, too.'

At the end of the day Zoe stood on the back veranda at Willara Downs, looking out at what had fast become her all-time-favourite view. She'd had a huge weekend and was almost dead on her feet, and Kent had insisted that she couldn't possibly drive back to Brisbane this evening.

So while he'd gone to talk to Tom Shaw, she'd prepared dinner—lamb baked with garlic and rosemary and lemon.

For an afternoon, she'd been living her fantasy—fussing about in a farmhouse kitchen, cooking a tasty dinner for the handsome farmer who belonged there.

Which only proved how foolish she was. It was time to put this episode behind her, time to forget about Kent.

The emotional connection she felt towards him and his beautiful home was out of all proportion to her true relationship. She was nothing more than Kent's former fiancée's *almost* bridesmaid.

OK. So maybe she'd promised Bella she would 'look after' Kent, but surely the kindest thing she could do was to leave quickly and without any fuss. Later she would stay in touch via email. Emails were safe.

Even though she knew all this…for now, she was enjoying her last look at this lovely view. Beyond the fence bordering the homestead's lawns and gardens stretched fields of sun-drenched golden corn and green pastures dotted with grazing cattle. Beyond that again, distant low hills nestled in a purple haze.

For Zoe there was something magical about it, especially now when it was tinged by the bronzed-copper glow of the late afternoon.

When she was small, she used to look out of the window of her parents' bus at views like this. At this time of day she would see farmers on their tractors, turning away from the chocolate earth of their newly ploughed fields and heading for home.

As the bus trundled down the highway she would watch the lights coming on in farmhouses, spilling yellow into the purple shadowed gardens. She'd watch wisps of smoke curling from chimneys into skies streaked with pink and gold and lavender. Sometimes she caught glimpses through windows of families gathered around kitchen tables.

Most evenings, shortly after dusk, her parents would turn in at a camping ground. Zoe and her mum would need a torch to find their way to the shower block, and they'd hurry back, damp and sometimes shivering in their dressing gowns. Her parents would cook a meal on their portable gas stove, and Zoe would do her homework, or read a book, or listen to the radio.

The bus was cosy enough at night, but oh, she'd coveted those warm, sturdy farmhouses. For Zoe, the simple ripple-iron-roofed dwellings surrounded by crops and fields were more beautiful and desirable than any fairy-tale castles.

Remembering those days now, she leaned on the veranda railing, drinking in details to keep them stored in her memory. The scent of newly cut grass. The deepening shadows creeping over the fields. The soft lowing of cattle. And coming from behind her, the fragrant kitchen aromas.

'I thought I might find you out here.'

Zoe turned, deliberately slowly, and smiled as Kent came to rest his arms on the timber railing beside her.

'Now everyone who needs to know knows,' he said. 'I had to leave messages for one or two folk, but at least they've all been informed.'

'How did Tom take the news?'

'Surprisingly well.'

'Wow. You must be relieved.'

'Very.' He turned, folded his arms and regarded her with a quizzical smile. 'Dinner smells good.'

'Yes, you have impeccable timing. The roast is due out of the oven right now.'

Together they went into the kitchen and Kent opened a bottle of wine. It felt incredibly domesticated and intimate to Zoe. But then, she was in full fantasy mode, while Kent was getting over a huge ordeal.

Nevertheless, he looked very much at home, pouring wine, wielding a carving knife, slipping a light jazz CD into the player. And he was lavish with his compliments for Zoe's cooking.

'I had farm-fresh ingredients,' she said. 'How could I go wrong?'

Across the table, Kent sent her a smile. 'Pity you're heading back to Brisbane tomorrow.'

It was silly to feel flustered, but there was a glitter in his dark eyes and a husky rumble in his voice that set Zoe's pulses dancing a crazy jig.

'So what are your plans for the rest of your week off?' he asked.

'Actually, I've been thinking that I might as well go back to work.'

Kent's eyebrows shot high. 'And waste the chance to take a holiday?'

'I'm not in the mood for a holiday now, and I can save this week for later. For when I go overseas.'

'Ah, yes. Christmas in Prague. Is it all planned?'

'No. I need to start booking my flights as soon as I get back.'

Kent frowned and dropped his gaze. A muscle jumped in his jaw.

'What about your plans, Kent? I know you had time set aside for a honeymoon. Are you still going to take a break?'

He shrugged. 'Not much point really. Besides, it's

the dry season and I need to keep the feed supplements up to the cattle. There's more than enough to keep me busy around here.'

Zoe was quite certain he was making excuses, but she understood. Under the circumstances, he wouldn't enjoy a holiday on his own. For her, getting back to work was about keeping busy and stopping her mind from revisiting endless if onlys...

It would be the same for Kent, magnified one hundred times.

Zoe left Willara Downs after breakfast the next morning. For the last time, she stripped the pink-and-white sheets from the bed in the pretty guest bedroom, and looked around fondly at the space she'd foolishly begun to pretend was hers.

Now it was time for reality. Back to the city. She needed to get over her silly crush on Kent, and the only way to achieve that was to stay well away from him.

Her car was parked at the side of the house, behind a hedge of purple-flowering duranta, and Kent insisted on carrying her bags, while she carried the bridesmaid's dress.

After laying it carefully along the back seat, she stepped back and took a deep breath. Time to say goodbye. *No tears, now.*

She offered Kent her best attempt at a smile.

But to her surprise he was staring at the dress, which was now a filmy river of coffee and cream chiffon on the back seat. 'You would have looked so lovely in that,' he said in a strangely choked voice.

Zoe tried to laugh. 'It's ridiculous how badly I wanted to be a bridesmaid.' She shook her head at her own foolishness.

'You've been perfect anyhow, a perfect *almost* brides-maid.' He flashed a brief quarter-smile. 'Bella couldn't have had better support.'

'Nice of you to say so.' Zoe squeezed the words past the tightness in her throat. 'But if we talk about all that now, I'm going to make a fool of myself.'

Determined not to cry, she opened the driver's door, tossed her shoulder bag onto the passenger's seat, and slipped the key into the ignition. She was blinking madly, trying so hard to be strong.

'Zoe,' Kent said softly, and his hand closed around her arm.

She ducked her head, hoping he couldn't see her struggle.

'Zoe, look at me.'

He spoke with such convincing tenderness she couldn't bear it. She was swiping at her eyes as he turned her around.

'Hey…' With the pads of his thumbs, he dried her tears.

Electrified, she was zapped into stillness by his touch. He was so close now she could see the tiny flecks in his eyes—fine streaks of cinnamon combined with hazelnut—could see his individual eyelashes…

'There's something I need to give you,' he said and he produced from his jeans pocket a slim gold box.

'What is it?'

'Your bridesmaid's gift.'

Shocked, Zoe clapped a hand to her mouth. She shook her head.

'Come on,' he said, smiling as he pushed the box into her free hand. 'You've earned this, and I went to a lot of trouble to get the right colour.'

'Oh.' Her hands were shaking.

'Here, let me open it for you.'

She watched as Kent's big hands lifted the dainty lid to reveal a bracelet made of beautiful, translucent beads of every colour.

'They're made of hand-blown glass designed by a local artist.'

'Kent, they're gorgeous.' Each bead displayed a uniquely different rainbow of colours, but the overall effect was one of beautiful harmony. 'I love it. Thank you so much.'

Setting the box on the bonnet of her car, Kent took her wrist. Oh, the intimacy of his hands, of his warm strong fingers brushing her skin. A wave of longing and regret crashed over Zoe and she was in danger of crying again. She closed her eyes to hold the tears back. Then, to her utter surprise, she felt Kent's hands cradle her face, tilting it ever so slightly towards him.

Her eyes flashed open and for breathless seconds they stared at each other, and she saw surprise—the same surprise she was feeling—mirrored in Kent's eyes.

Surprise and disbelief…

And knowledge…

And helplessness…

And then he was kissing her.

Or Zoe was kissing him.

Or perhaps they simply flowed together, drawn by a potent, irresistible magnetism, as if by some miracle they shared the same aching need, the same unspoken longing.

Zoe's senses revelled in the scent of Kent's skin, and the dark taste of coffee on his lips, the thrilling strength of his arms wrapped around her. She was quite sure she'd never been kissed with such wanting, and she certainly knew she'd never returned a kiss with such fervour.

When they drew apart, at last and with great reluctance, they stood facing each other, panting and flushed and slightly self-conscious.

When Zoe spoke, she tried to sound a thousand times more composed than she felt. 'That was unexpected.'

'For me, too. But I'm not complaining.'

No. Zoe wasn't complaining either, but she felt compelled to offer reasons…excuses… 'It's been an emotional weekend. I—I guess I needed a hug.'

'I guess you did,' Kent agreed with a smile.

'And I—ah—should be going.' She turned back to the car again. Already the magic was fading, and the reality of their situation was rushing back. They'd both been under amazing strain and the kiss was an emotional finale to an incredibly emotional weekend.

Nothing more. Certainly nothing to weave dreams around.

What could she say now? *So long, it's been good to know you?* If she looked at Kent again, she might make a fool of herself, so she spoke without turning back to him. 'I'll let you know if I hear from Bella.'

'Thanks, and I'll pass on any news from my end.'

'Emails are probably the easiest.'

'Sure.'

Deep breath. 'Goodbye, Kent.'

'Bye.'

He took a step closer, and dropped another warm kiss on her cheek. Zoe's insides were doing cartwheels. 'See you later. Maybe,' she choked.

'Make that definitely,' Kent corrected quietly.

She didn't reply and closed the car door. He tapped

on her window with his knuckle, and they waved to each other.

Her eyes welled with tears, but she blinked them clear. *Enough of this nonsense.* They'd finished this story. This was…

The End.

She took off, watching Kent in her rear vision mirror. He stood with his feet firmly planted, his hands sunk in his pockets…watching her…and when she reached the end of the drive and was at last enveloped by the tunnel of trees, he still hadn't moved.

CHAPTER NINE

To: Zoe Weston<zoe.weston@flowermail.com>
From: Kent Rigby<willaraKR@hismail.com>
Subject: The Runaways
Hi Zoe,
I hope you had a safe trip back and that everything was fine when you got home. Just wanted to thank you once again. I don't think you truly realise how big a help you've been.

Also, I've had a text from Bella, and she and Damon are still on the trail of the grandparents. They're heading north—staying in Rockhampton tonight, I think.

Are you determined to go back to the office tomorrow?

Seems a shame you can't have a decent break.
Cheers,
Kent

To: Kent Rigby<willaraKR@hismail.com>
From: Zoe Weston<zoe.weston@flowermail.com>
Subject: The Runaways
Hi Kent,
Thanks for your email and for asking if everything

was OK, but I'm afraid I came home to a minor disaster. I asked my neighbour to take care of my goldfish while I was away and she overfed them, so my poor goldfish, Orange Juice, was floating on the top of a very murky tank. By the looks of it, Anita dumped half a tin of fish food in there.

I didn't think to warn her that you can't do that with goldfish. Thank heavens I wasn't away all week or I would have lost Brian and Ezekiel as well. As it is, they look a bit peaky.

I know you must be thinking I'm a screw loose to be so upset about a goldfish, but they're the only pets I can have in this flat, so they're important. Now, I've spent most of the evening cleaning the tank.

But, yes, to answer your question, I'll be back at the office in the morning.

Bella sent me that text, too. It's a weird situation they've found themselves in, isn't it? We can only hope it all works out happily.

Best wishes and thanks again for your hospitality,
Zoe.

To: Kent Rigby<willaraKR@hismail.com>
From: Zoe Weston<zoe.weston@flowermail.com>
Subject: Thank You

Kent, you shouldn't have. Honestly. It was so sweet of you to have a goldfish delivered to the office.

The delivery boy caused quite a stir when he appeared in the doorway with a huge grin on his face and a plastic bag with a goldfish in his hand.

As if the office gossip wasn't already flying thick

and fast this morning. Quite a few of the girls were at the hen party, so of course the whole staff wanted details.

Luckily, when the delivery came I got to the door first, so no one else saw the docket and realised it came from you. That would certainly have put the cat among the goldfish, and everyone would have been jumping to the wrong conclusions.

But I'm very grateful, Kent. According to a magazine article on feng shui, three goldfish in a tank are always better than two, so your gift has restored my chances of inner peace and prosperity.

And I'm sure you'll be pleased to know that the new fish is very pretty, with lovely white markings and delicate fins. I've decided she's a girl and I've called her Ariel.

Brian and Ezekiel are very impressed.

Thank you again, and warmest wishes,

Zoe

P.S. I'm off to book my overseas trip tomorrow—with Christmas in Prague as a must.

To: Zoe Weston<zoe.weston@flowermail.com>
From: Kent Rigby<willaraKR@hismail.com>
Subject: Re: Thank You

I'm so pleased the delivery arrived safely. Sorry that it caused a stir in the office, but at least feng shui has been restored in your household. I hope you enjoy your new fish.

No news from the northern adventurers, but I'm assuming they're still hot on the trail.

Hope the travel bookings go smoothly. I'm jealous.
Cheers
Kent

The confession of jealousy was no lie. As Kent pressed send he could think of nothing he'd like more than to take off for Europe again. With Zoe.

He imagined showing her all the places he'd discovered—taking a ride on the London Eye and drinking a pint in a quaint old English pub. Dining out in Paris, or walking through the Latin Quarter. In Spain they would visit art galleries and sample tapas bars. They'd walk Italy's magical Cinque Terre. Experience Christmas in Prague.

Together.

He'd decided that Zoe would be a perfect travel companion. She was organised and yet easy-going, adaptable and fun. Sexy.

Yeah, if he was honest, he was utterly absorbed with the idea of kissing Zoe in every location. Their farewell kiss replayed in his head on an almost continuous reel.

He tried to tell himself that he was overreacting, riding on a tidal wave of relief now that he was no longer marrying someone out of a sense of friendship and duty.

So, OK, there'd been plenty of sparks. With Zoe he'd experienced the very fireworks that had eluded him and Bella. Serious sparkage that left him hungry for more than mere kisses. But Zoe was back in Brisbane now, and soon she'd be heading overseas. A man with a grain of common sense would look elsewhere.

Problem was, this man had experienced his fill of common sense. Now he wanted nothing more than to indulge in fantasies. And he kept remembering Zoe surrounded by dozens of smart little candles, kept picturing her on the bank of Willara Creek, her face soft with emotion and empathy, wanting to understand. He saw her on the road side struggling with a flat tyre. In the pub on the hens' night, in a sexy dress, bright as a flame. He remembered drying her tears just before he kissed her. Goodbye.

Zoe knew it was silly to keep checking her private emails at work and then to rush to her laptop as soon as she got home. Silly to be disappointed when there was no new message from Kent.

She wanted to move on and to put the entire Willara experience behind her, so Kent's silence was a step in the right direction.

Now that she was home, and had a little distance, she could see how dangerous her penchant for Kent had been. After her painful, harrowing heartbreak over Rodney, she was mad to hanker for another man who'd just called off his engagement.

Even though Kent and Bella's relationship had been very different from Rodney and Naomi's, the patterns were too close for comfort.

Besides, she suspected that Kent wasn't looking to settle down. She'd heard talk at the hens' night that he used to play the field, and, of course, he'd recently pulled out of commitment to Bella. It was true; he'd been gallant to the end. Just the same, he certainly wouldn't be ready to leap into a new, serious relationship.

Once and for all she had to move on. Kent's kiss had been nothing more than a spontaneous outburst of feelings at the end of an extremely emotional weekend.

And his thoughtfulness in sending the goldfish was just another example of his general niceness.

His email silence, on the other hand, simply meant there was no news from Bella—and it was a perfect opportunity for Zoe to move forward.

His silence was a desirable result. Honestly.

Very slowly, over the next twenty-four hours, the straightforward sense of this started to sink in. Zoe focused on planning her holiday.

It was going to be quite different travelling solo instead of travelling with Bella as she'd once hoped. Quite an adventure, really.

On Friday evening when Zoe arrived home from work, she was deliberately *not* thinking about Kent Rigby. She most especially concentrated on *not* thinking about him when she heard a knock on her front door.

Having just kicked off her shoes, she answered the door in stockinged feet—a distinct disadvantage when her caller was six feet two. No doubt that was why she blurted out inhospitably, 'What are you doing here?'

Kent had the grace to look a little embarrassed. 'I had business in the city and I was passing by.'

It might have been the lamest of excuses, but Kent Rigby in the flesh could obliterate Zoe's protests and doubts with a single warm smile.

One glance into the twinkling dark depths of his eyes and all her resolutions to forget him flew out of the window.

'So,' she suggested, trying to subdue her happy grin. 'I suppose you've dropped by to see how Ariel's settling in.'

'Ariel?'

'Your thoughtful gift. My new goldfish.'

Kent laughed—a lovely, sexy masculine rumble. 'Of course. I've had sleepless nights wondering. How is she?'

Zoe stepped back to let him through her doorway, conscious of his height and size and her lack of shoes and the supreme smallness of her living room. The fish tank sat rather conspicuously at one end of the low set of shelves that also held her television set.

With a wave towards it, she said, 'Ariel's the pretty one with the dainty white fins.'

Kent sent a polite nod towards the tank. 'She's a very fine specimen.'

'As you can see, she's quite at home now.'

'She is. That's great.' But he immediately switched his attention from the fish and back to Zoe. 'I know this is a bit last minute. I would have called at the office earlier today, but you were worried about wagging tongues.'

'You could have telephoned.'

'Yes.' His smile tilted. 'But I wanted an excuse to see you.'

Not fair. Zoe's resistance was melting faster than ice cream on a summer's day. Desperate to hang on to her diminishing shreds of common sense, she said, 'I haven't heard from Bella, have you?'

'Yes, she rang this morning.'

'So they're still heading north?'

'Yes, and there's an awful lot of coastline, so heaven knows how long it will take.'

Standing in the middle of her living room, Kent was watching her, unabashedly letting his eyes rove over her work clothes, her legs…

Self-consciously, she fiddled with the bridesmaid bracelet at her wrist. Unwisely, she'd taken to wearing it constantly. She rubbed one stockinged foot against the other.

He smiled again. 'So...how are you now, Zoe?'

'I'm—I'm fine.' What else could she say? She could hardly admit to feeling up and down and all over the place after one goodbye kiss. 'More importantly, how are you?'

'I'm OK. Surprisingly OK, actually.'

Memories of their kiss hovered in the air. Recklessly, Zoe thought how easy it would be to drift towards him again, to find herself in his arms, tasting that lovely, seductive mouth.

She struggled to remember all the reasons it was wrong. *He's free to play the field now. Don't get hurt. Remember Rodney!* She found refuge in her duties as a hostess. 'Would you like to sit down, Kent? Can I get you a drink?'

Instead of answering, he asked, 'Am I interrupting your plans for Friday night?'

'I—I was planning to have a quiet night in.' She'd been looking forward to a stress-free weekend for a change.

'So I can't tempt you to a quiet dinner out?'

Oh.

Zoe's mouth worked like her goldfish's. She'd spent the past week listing all the reasons why she must stop swooning over this man. Rodney the Rat had featured high on that list. Kent's own reputation as Willara's most dedicated bachelor was another point worth re-membering. But now—*shame on her*—now that he'd asked, she couldn't think of anything she'd like more than to go out with him.

Besides, she'd promised Bella she'd keep an eye on

Kent—and going out with him tonight was simply doing Bella a favour, wasn't it?

'Dinner would be lovely,' she said, trying to strike the right note between polite and casual. 'Why don't you make yourself at home while I change into something more—?' Zoe bit off the word *comfortable*… It was such a cheesy cliché and she didn't want to give Kent a whiff of the wrong idea.

'Let me get you a drink,' she said instead. Her kitchen led off the living area and she went to the fridge and opened it. Unfortunately, she hadn't been in the mood for shopping this week, so there was half a bottle of rather old white wine, the heel of an ancient block of cheese and a handful of dried apricots.

Thinking of the bounty at Willara Downs, she felt extremely inadequate in the hostess department.

'I don't need anything now. I'm happy to wait till dinner,' Kent said, watching her from the doorway. 'And you don't need to change. If you don't mind coming as you are, I think you look great in that outfit.'

'In this?' Zoe repeated, amazed. She was still in her work clothes—a dark green skirt and a cream blouse with pintucking and neat little pearl buttons.

Kent's eyes twinkled. 'Yes, in that. You have no idea how good city clothes look after a steady diet of jeans and Akubras.'

Given her own love of all things rural, Zoe had quite a fair understanding of how the trappings of a very different world might appeal.

So, five minutes later, having once again donned her high heels and given her hair and make-up a retouch, she was in Kent's ute and heading for her favourite suburban Thai restaurant. Fleetingly, she wondered if she should be wary or on guard, but such caution seemed impossible. She was ridiculously happy.

Apart from the huge fact that she was being escorted by a gorgeous guy who caught every woman's eye, she'd always loved this particular eating place. She loved coming through the swing glass doors to be enveloped by the fragrant and exotic aromas wafting from the kitchen. And she loved the sumptuous yet relaxing ambience—rich pink walls adorned with mirrors in dark, intricately carved wooden frames, and tables covered in cloths of peacock and gold.

She enjoyed the little rituals, too, like the basket of pale pink prawn crisps that came along with their menus. This evening, sharing one of her favourite places with Kent, she was filled with bubbling excitement.

They decided to choose exotic steamed fish, and chilli and ginger paste chicken. Then their drinks arrived—a glass of chilled white wine for Zoe and an icy beer for Kent—and they nibbled the prawn crisps and sipped their drinks. And they talked.

Wow, how they talked.

To Zoe's surprise, Kent did *not* bring Bella or the wedding into their conversation. He started by asking her more about her travel plans, and he told her about the places he'd enjoyed most when he'd been overseas. They moved on to movies and discovered they both loved thrillers. They talked about books, but Kent preferred non-fiction, so there wasn't quite so much common ground there.

They might have moved on to music, but their meals arrived in traditional Thai blue-and-white bowls and they soon became busy with helping themselves to spoonfuls of fluffy jasmine rice. The delicious fish had been baked in coconut milk with slices of ginger, and the chicken had been stir-fried with masses of vegetables.

Everything was wonderfully hot and spicy and at first they were too busy enjoying themselves to talk about anything except the food, but then Kent asked, out of the blue, 'Are you very ambitious, Zoe?'

Ambitious? Thrown by the question, she stared at him. Her most recent goal had been to be a perfect bridesmaid. Apart from that, she wanted to travel, but her biggest ambition was to find the right man, to settle down and start a family, which was the last thing she'd admit to this man.

Fleetingly, she remembered her childish dream to live in a farmhouse that sat safely and squarely in the middle of green-and-gold fields. She hastily dismissed it.

'Actually, I don't think I can be very ambitious,' she said. 'I like my job and I want to be good at it, but I have no desire to smash through glass ceilings.' She pulled a face. 'Don't tell your feminist little sister.'

Kent grinned. 'Your secret's safe with me. Perhaps you're content.'

No. Content she was not, especially since she'd met Kent. Lately, restless yearning had been her constant companion.

She doubted that Kent would want to hear her true ambition—to settle down with the right man, to put down roots, raise a family.

'My parents have never been go-getters,' she told him instead. 'Lead the Way might have been a huge success, if they'd had a bit more tooth and claw.'

'And you might have been the child of celebrity rock stars.'

'Imagine.' Zoe rolled her eyes. 'Actually, I think my

parents would have hated all the celebrity fuss that goes with being famous. I can't imagine my mother being a diva, stamping her foot because the limo wasn't pink.'

She laughed at the impossibility of the picture. 'What about you, Kent? Are you ambitious?'

'I have big visions for the farm—projects like land management and tackling environmental issues. It's easier to try new methods now I'm managing Willara on my own. My dad wasn't keen to change and Tom's just as bad. They want to keep doing things the way they always have. Pair of dinosaurs, both of them.'

There was passion in his voice, which surprised Zoe. 'I must admit every time I was at Willara I was always so caught up with the wedding I didn't give much thought to the business and management of your farm. But it must be quite an enterprise. You're like a CEO of your own private company.'

'Yes, and it keeps me busy.'

'But you love it.'

'I do.'

Kent smiled that special way of his that launched Zoe into outer space. Yikes, she had to calm down. Tonight was all about friendship.

Sure, there were sizzles and sparks that zapped her whenever she looked across the table. And yes, there were dark flashes of appreciation in Kent's eyes. And, most certainly, she was aware of a deepening sense of connection when they talked.

But this wasn't a date. Kent hadn't once tried to flirt with her, or to touch her, or to offer her the over-the-top compliments that Rodney had trotted out on their first date. This evening was humming along at a nice, safe, just-friends level.

Reassured by this success, Zoe found herself asking

recklessly, 'Are there any other ambitions? Do you still plan to marry and have a family one day?'

Kent stiffened with obvious surprise.

Oh, good grief. What an idiot she was.

He concentrated on helping himself to a final spoonful of fish. 'Right now I can't imagine ever lining up for another wedding.'

'And who could blame you?' Zoe said fervently.

To her relief, her awkward question didn't ruin the night. As they left the restaurant and walked into the sensuous magic of the warm spring night the scent of frangipani and honeysuckle hung in the humid air. From a pub down the road a band was sending out a deep pulsing beat.

Kent reached for Zoe's hand, threaded his fingers through hers. 'Thanks for bringing me here. It was a fabulous meal.'

'My pleasure,' she said softly, while her skin tingled and glowed from the contact.

When they reached his car, he opened the passenger door for her, and she was about to get in when he said, 'Wait a minute.'

She turned and he gently touched her cheek. 'I just wanted to tell you—you look lovely tonight.'

Her skin flamed with pleasure. 'Thank—'

Her reply was cut off by his kiss.

Which wasn't exactly a surprise—all night she'd been teased by memories of their other kiss.

This kiss was different and yet utterly perfect. Beyond friendly—oh, heavens, yes—but not pushy. Just slow and sexy and powerful enough to make Zoe hungry for more.

She was floating as she settled into the passenger seat, and it wasn't till they pulled up outside her flat that she came to her senses. It was time for a polite, but hasty exit.

A kiss was one thing, but becoming more deeply involved with this man was way too risky. He might be the most attractive man she'd ever met, but tonight he'd admitted that his long-term goals were the polar opposite of hers. She wanted to settle down. He didn't.

It was all very black and white.

'Thanks for a lovely evening, Kent.' Already, her fingers were reaching for the door handle.

'Zoe, before I forget, I have something for you.' Reaching into the back seat, Kent picked up a brown-paper packet.

'Another gift? But you've given me a bracelet and a goldfish.' She hoped this wasn't going to be chocolates or flowers—the clichéd trappings of seduction.

'It's just a book,' he said. 'I thought it might come in handy.'

She caught the dark gleam of his eyes as he smiled at her through the darkness. A book, a nice safe book. Tilting the packet, she let it slip onto her lap. It was a hardback with a glossy cover. They weren't parked near a streetlight, but there was just enough light for her to make out the title.

'A book about Prague. Gosh, how thoughtful of you.'

Flipping it open, she saw beautiful, full-page co-loured photographs, but the dim light couldn't do them justice. It seemed rude not to invite Kent inside.

'I need to make you coffee before you tackle the long drive back,' she explained in case he got the wrong idea.

So they ended up on the sofa, poring over pictures of Prague while their mugs of coffee cooled on the low table in front of them. The pictures were gorgeous—

soaring cathedrals, fairy-tale castles, steep-roofed houses, a horse and carriage in the snow...

'It's so old world and so very civilised,' Zoe said.

'I know. I couldn't think of any place more different from Queensland.'

'I can't believe I'm going to see it all. I'm booked into a small hotel just around the corner from the Old Town Square.'

Kent was silent for a bit. Frowning, he said, 'I hope you won't be too lonely spending Christmas overseas on your own.'

Zoe wondered if he was teasing her, but he looked quite genuine, and if she was honest she *was* a little worried about being on her own. But now with Bella unavailable it was a matter of travelling solo, or not at all. She looked sideways to find Kent still watching her with a troubled expression.

'I'll be fine,' she said. 'I've been doing some research, and, from what I've read, solo travellers have a much better chance of meeting people. There's always someone to share a meal or a bus ride.'

'I dare say that's true.' Kent picked up her hand and turned it over.

At the unexpected contact, Zoe's breath hitched and her heart picked up pace. 'What are you doing?'

'I'm reading your palm,' he said calmly.

She should have resisted, should have pulled her hand away, but it was already too late. She was mesmerised by his touch, by the scent of his aftershave, by the inescapable fabulousness of having him so close beside her.

Instead of protesting, she found herself playing his game. 'And what do you see in my palm?'

His eyes sparkled. 'Travel to far away places.'

'Fancy that. How perceptive.'

'And romance.'

Her palm curled instinctively. The warmth of his hands and the mellow teasing in his voice wove silken threads of longing deep inside her.

Fighting the hot urges, she challenged him. 'I thought palm readings only told you how long you're going to live and how many children you'll have.'

Kent's eyebrows lifted. 'Is that right? I'd better take another look, then.'

OK…she really should stop this nonsense. She tried to pull her hand away, but Kent was holding her firmly.

'Yes, of course,' he said. 'I can see a very long and happy life here.' With his forefinger he traced a shiver-sweet line across the centre of her palm. 'And a whole tribe of children.'

'A tribe?' Her breathlessness was caused more by his touch than his words. 'How many children are in a tribe?'

'Oh, I'd say around ten or eleven.'

'Far out.' Zoe tried to sound appalled, but she spoiled it by laughing. 'I think you'd better give up reading palms and stick to farming.'

Sure that her face was glowing bright pink, she switched her attention back to the book, still lying in her lap. It was open at a double page, showing Prague in the soft blue light of dusk. Four beautiful, ancient bridges spanned the Vltava River, and the sky and the water and the distant hills were all the exact same shade of misty blue. Even the splashes of yellow from street-lights and windows were soft and fuzzy. So pretty.

'Willara Downs is as lovely as this at dusk,' she told Kent.

To her surprise, he closed the book and set it on the

coffee table, then he took her hands, enclosing them in both of his. 'Zoe, I have a confession to make.'

Her heart skidded as if she'd taken a curve too fast.

'Would you be shocked if I told you that I fancied you *before* Bella and I called off the wedding?'

'Yes.' Of course she was shocked. Her heart was thumping so hard, she could hardly hear her own voice.

'Believe me, I was shocked, too. But I couldn't shut off my feelings.'

'But you didn't—' She pressed a hand to her thumping heart. She was scared and excited. Confused. 'You didn't call off the wedding because of me.'

'No, I didn't.' Smiling, Kent tucked a strand of her hair behind her ear. 'You don't have to feel guilty. It was only afterwards that I allowed myself to think about what had been happening. By then, I realised that I fancied you like crazy.'

She closed her eyes, searching for the strength to resist him. Kent had fancied lots of girls. This wasn't a confession of love. But even though she knew this, his words were unfurling fiery ribbons of need inside her. His touch was clouding her thoughts.

When his thumb brushed gently over her lips, she couldn't think of anything but kissing him again, of throwing herself into his wonderful, strong arms, of climbing brazenly into his lap…the bliss of skin against skin…

'You're lovely,' he whispered.

'Kent, don't say that.' She dragged herself back from the magnetic pull of his touch. 'You mustn't. We can't.'

'Why can't we?'

Remember Rodney.

But Kent was nothing like Rodney. He wasn't up and down in his moods as Rodney had been. He'd been engaged to Bella for noble reasons and he'd been very considerate of everyone's feelings when he'd broken that commitment. He was a man who took responsibilities seriously.

Even so, by his own confession, he still wasn't the marrying and settling down type.

Maybe I can simply enjoy the moment?

In a few weeks she was going to Europe, and Kent knew that, so a liaison now could only be temporary. Temporary flings were safe. They couldn't break a girl's heart. She could look on her trip overseas as her escape route.

Besides…heaven help her, she wanted this man… wanted him to kiss her, wanted his kiss so badly she was trembling. Every nerve in her body was quivering.

Kent dipped his head till his lips were almost touching hers. She looked into his eyes and saw the dark urgency of her longing mirrored there. A soft gasp escaped her, an embarrassing, pleading sound.

His mouth brushed hers, slow but insistent. 'Tell me why this is wrong,' he murmured against her lips.

She couldn't answer. If there had ever been a reason to say no, she'd lost it. His lips caressed hers again, and the last warnings in her head crumpled like tissue paper thrown on fire. She couldn't think of anything but returning Kent's kiss. Already she was winding her arms around his neck…and she kissed him.

Kissed him and *kissed* him.

Somewhere in the midst of kissing him, she kicked off her shoes and wriggled into his lap. And this time it was he who gasped. Then his hands traced the silky shape of her legs encased in tights. He dropped a fiery line of kisses over her skin from her collarbone into the V of her blouse. Then their mouths met again, and

their kisses turned molten as they tumbled sideways—
a blissful tangle into the deep red cushions.

Out of habit, Kent woke early, but this morning, instead
of bouncing out to face a day's farm work, he lay in the
soft light watching Zoe sleep. She was on her side, facing him, her dark hair tumbling over the white pillow,
her dusky eyelashes curving against her soft cheeks, her
mouth pale and slightly open. She looked so innocent
and vulnerable now, so different from the fiery, sensuous woman who'd made love to him last night.

Last night…

When he'd knocked on Zoe's door, he hadn't known
what to expect. Hadn't dared to hope that he might end
up spending the night with her. And yet, he couldn't
deny he'd been on fire since their farewell kiss at
Willara.

Even so, last night had defied all logic. He and Zoe
had shared a mere explosion of passion and excitement,
but there'd been astonishing tenderness, too. The same
kind of emotional connection he'd felt before—over
dinner conversations or on the creek bank. An amazing sense of rightness. A certainty that some kind of
miracle had been set in motion.

Briefly, as he lay there, he wondered if such thoughts
were fanciful. But then Zoe stirred beside him, opened
her bright blue eyes and smiled, and he was flooded
with a wonderful sense of buoyancy. Perhaps his life
was taking a turn in a very good direction.

CHAPTER TEN

ZOE's new version of heaven was waking up beside Kent Rigby on a Saturday morning and knowing they had the whole, delicious weekend to spend together.

They rose late, and went out to have breakfast at a pavement café that served great coffee and luscious, tasty mushrooms on thick sourdough toast. Afterwards, they walked beneath flowering jacarandas on the banks of the Brisbane River, enjoying the sunshine, and sharing happy, goofy smiles.

In the afternoon they went to a suburban cinema to see a creepy thriller movie. Like teenagers they stole popcorn flavoured kisses in the dark, and on the way home they stopped off at a supermarket and bought ingredients for a pasta dish to make at home.

In Zoe's kitchen they sipped wine while they chopped and cooked. Every chance they had, they touched and smiled and hugged and kissed. They were, in a word, entranced.

Wrapped in a bubble of bliss, Zoe wouldn't let anything intrude. No negative thoughts, no questions, no doubts. If the slightest misgiving about history repeating itself reared its ugly head, she told herself this time was nothing like her disaster with Rodney. Rodney had moved in. Rodney had promised for ever.

With Kent, she was merely enjoying a fab weekend. At the end of two days he would go back to Willara, knowing that she was about to leave for overseas. For now she was trusting her instincts and her instincts felt *fantastic*!

Their pasta sauce was bubbling beautifully and Kent was stealing yet another kiss from Zoe when the phone rang. She grabbed the receiver and trilled 'Hello-o-o,' in a super-happy singsong.

'Zoe, how are you?'

'Bella?' Zoe shot a startled glance to Kent and watched his eyebrows hike.

Bella laughed. 'Don't sound so surprised.'

'Sorry. I wasn't expecting you, Bella, and I was—um—distracted for a moment.'

'Are you all right, Zoe?'

'Absolutely fine. Why?'

'I don't know. You sound—different somehow.'

'I don't think I'm different. More importantly, how are you?' Zoe flashed another glance Kent's way.

His eyes were more cautious now, as if he felt as awkward as she did. It would be so hard to explain this to Bella. A week ago, Zoe had been focused on being the perfect bridesmaid. Last night she'd slept with the bridegroom. Admittedly, those roles were now defunct, but how would Bella react if she knew they were together so soon?

And just like that, with Bella on the other end of the line, Zoe saw her wonderful weekend in a whole new light—as an outsider might—and her brain flung up words like *impetuous, cheeky, reckless...*

Bella said, 'I'm fine, thanks. I'm in Port Douglas with our grandparents. There's been a cyclone, would you believe? But we're all OK. Just garden damage.'

'That's really bad luck about the cyclone. How's everything…going…with…Damon?'

'OK,' Bella said in a sharp, *don't-go-there* tone. 'I was actually ringing to see if you've been in touch with Kent.'

'Oh?' Zoe was instantly nervous. She widened her eyes at Kent. Pointing to the phone, she mouthed, *'Do you want to talk to Bella?'*

Frowning, he shook his head.

She swallowed. 'Yes, I've had *some* contact with him.'

'I tried his mobile, but he's switched it off, so I rang the homestead and he wasn't there either so I rang his parents and Stephanie told me he's away for the weekend.'

'Did you want Kent for anything important?'

'Not especially. I guess I just wanted to make sure he's OK. You know the wedding would have been happening right about now.'

Oh, gosh. Zoe glanced at the clock on her kitchen wall and saw that Bella was right. At this very moment, Bella and Kent should have been exchanging their marriage vows. How on earth had it slipped her mind?

'I would have liked to make certain that Kent was OK,' Bella said.

'I'm sure he's fine. He's probably decided not to dwell on the wedding too much.'

'Yes, that would be best, wouldn't it? I hope you're right.'

On the stove the sauce began to boil and spit. Zoe gestured frantically, but Kent had moved to the window and was standing with his back to her, studiously looking out into her backyard. His shoulders were squared and his back very straight. Sure signs of tension.

Zoe tried to attract him with a stage whisper. *'Pssst, can you turn that sauce down?'*

'Do you have someone there?' Bella asked.

'Yes—just—a friend over for dinner.'

'Oh, that's nice. I won't keep you, then.' But instead of hanging up, Bella lowered her voice. 'Would this friend be male by any chance?'

Zoe made the mistake of hesitating for a shade too long.

'Zoe, it's a guy, isn't it? That's why you sounded so different—sort of bubbly and excited. Who is he? Anyone I know?'

'Bell, I'm sorry. The dinner's burning, and I've got to go. But it's been fantastic to hear from you and to know you're OK.'

'All right.' Bella laughed. 'I can take a hint. But if you hear from Kent, tell him that I rang and, apart from the weather, I'm fine.'

'I will, and I'll tell him you were thinking of him.'

Zoe hung up and rushed to rescue the sauce. Kent turned from the window, and she sank back against a cupboard, letting out a groan. 'That was awful. I felt terrible lying to her.'

'You weren't exactly lying.'

'No, but I was hiding the truth and that's just as bad.'

Zoe felt sick. Hands clenched, she paced across the kitchen. And to her horror, all the reasons she shouldn't be with Kent rushed back to taunt her. What was she doing leaping into bed with another man who'd just broken off an engagement?

Spinning around, she challenged him. 'Had you re-membered that you should have been getting married right now?'

He looked uncomfortable. 'Is that why Bella rang?'

'Yes. She was worried about you. She tried the Willara Downs number and your mobile.'

Pulling his phone from his pocket, Kent thumbed a button or two. 'It's not that I don't want to talk to her. I didn't want to embarrass you. I'll call her back now.'

'Actually…I'm not sure that's a good idea. If you call back straight away, she'll probably guess you're with me. She's already figured I have a guy here.'

Grimacing, Kent stood looking down at the phone. It looked tiny in his big brown work-roughened hand. His throat rippled as he swallowed. 'I'm sure Bella will understand if I explain.'

Zoe gave a choked laugh. 'How are you going to explain that you ended up spending the weekend with her bridesmaid? It'll sound so—' she swallowed, grasping for a word '—tacky.'

'Tacky?' Kent repeated, shocked.

'Hasty, then. Indecently so.'

In two steps, Kent was across the room and grabbing Zoe's arm. 'Is that what you think? That last night was tacky?'

'No.' Suddenly, Zoe was trembling and fighting tears. 'Oh, Kent, you have to admit it might be viewed by many as indecent haste.'

He pulled her in to him, holding her against his broad chest, kissing her hair. 'Whatever's happening between us is *good*.' Gently, he tucked her hair behind her ear and kissed her brow. 'And it's no one else's business.'

Zoe closed her eyes and let her head sink against his shoulder. She loved being with this man so much— loved the way he smelled of sunlight and clean shirts, loved the hard strength of his body, and the warm reassurance of his arms wrapped around her. Loved who he was.

But she had loved Rodney, too. She'd adored him. She could never have believed he might hurt her.

'How did we let this happen so soon?' she asked Kent.

For answer, he hugged her closer, but even as warmth and pleasure seeped through her the impact of Bella's phone call remained, lifting the lid on all the difficult questions she'd doggedly resisted for the past twenty-four hours. And one thing was certain—she couldn't find answers to these questions while she was in Kent's arms.

With enormous reluctance she pulled away, went to the window and opened it, letting in a fresh breeze as if, somehow, that might clear her thoughts.

'I never meant this to happen,' she said. 'After that kiss goodbye last weekend I decided we shouldn't get too involved. It's all too soon. Too convenient.'

She looked down at her hands—rubbed the rough edge of a thumbnail. The real issue here was that Kent didn't want to settle down. He'd said so last night. She, on the other hand, wanted nothing more than to marry and start a family—to be the bride, not the bridesmaid. And Kent was exactly the sort of man… No, he was the *only* man she wanted to settle down with.

She couldn't tell him that. There was no point. 'I can't help worrying that this weekend has been a mistake,' she said instead.

'You mean you're feeling pressured?'

'Well, yes. I tried to tell you last night that we shouldn't…' She shot him an accusing glance. 'I'm sure you remember.'

'Oh, yes, I remember.' Kent's slow smile made her wince.

No doubt he was remembering the way she'd shamelessly climbed into his lap and kissed him as if there were no tomorrow. She was so hopelessly weak around him and last night she'd foolishly given in to that weakness.

Now she was determined to be strong. 'The thing is, I've been through something like this before, Kent.'

He frowned. 'How do you mean?'

'I fell for a guy who'd recently broken off an engagement. He was a work colleague and I'd known him for about twelve months. I'd even met his fiancée, Naomi, at parties. A few months after their break-up he asked me out, and I conscientiously tried to cheer him up. All went well. He moved in with me and we lived together for another six months. Until—'

Zoe paused for dramatic emphasis.

'Until he let you down,' Kent suggested.

'Yes. I came home one Friday evening and found him in *my* bed with Naomi.'

He scowled. 'That's a low-down act.'

'That's why I call him Rodney the Rat.' Zoe closed her eyes at the memory. 'He made me feel used and stupid and conned and hurt and angry. You name it—I felt it. I was devastated.'

And now…she wouldn't run the risk of being hurt again, surely? She'd been a fool to let herself fall for Kent so quickly and easily, when she'd spent the past week telling herself that it wasn't wise.

'Zoe, I swear I would never do anything to you like that.'

'I know you wouldn't hurt me intentionally, but I can't help feeling vulnerable.' Impatiently, she swept a lock of hair from her eyes. 'Maybe I'm jumping the gun. We haven't even talked about what we want from—from this. Are we having a fling—or—or—?'

'I thought we were getting to know each other.' He came to stand beside her again, and with his hands on her shoulders he turned her to look at him, trapping her with the dark, frank depths of his eyes. 'We were honest with each other when we made love, weren't we?'

Zoe couldn't deny there'd been a special openness and sincerity about last night. But that was the problem. To her, it had felt like so much more than a temporary fling and just thinking about it brought her to the edge of tears.

She took a deep breath. If she played this the wrong way, she would lose Kent, and live to regret it deeply. But her bigger fear was that she'd keep seeing him for several more weeks and *then* the novelty would wear off for him. To spend more time with him and then lose him would be so much worse. Unbearable.

The hard truth was that every moment she spent with Kent was dangerous. She'd been falling more deeply in love with him since the moment she'd met him beside the road side. If she didn't apply the brakes now, before she was in any deeper, she could end up *very* badly hurt. Again.

It was important now to list her extremely valid concerns.

'Kent, until last weekend, you were all set to marry my best friend. You were ready to vow to love her till you were parted by death.'

A muscle jerked in his jaw. 'But you know why we called it off.'

'Yes, I do. And I can understand why you want to move on with your life. But I'm not sure it's a great idea to move straight on to the bridesmaid, as if I was there, ready and waiting—like the next cab on the rank.'

Zoe knew it was a cheap shot, and a sound like a

growl broke from him. Anger flashed in his eyes and he looked so unlike his calm, easy-going self that she almost backed down and apologised. But then where would she be? In his arms with nothing sorted? Nothing solved?

Kent's eyes narrowed. 'Are you asking me to leave?'

No, no, no. That wasn't what she wanted at all. How could she let him go? She'd been so looking forward to this evening—to their shared meal, and the long night after—and then, all of Sunday still ahead of them. And their future...

She dropped her gaze to the floor. It was too hard to think when Kent was standing right there all gorgeous and frowning in front of her.

Be strong, Zoe.

She took a deep breath before she spoke. 'Perhaps we just need space to sort things out—a sort of cooling-off period.' She hoped she didn't sound as miserable as she felt.

Kent remained very still, and his dark eyes, usually so warm and sparkling, remained severe and narrowed. 'Cooling-off period? So what's that? Forty-eight hours? Four weeks?'

I don't know! she wanted to wail.

Kent, however, had made his decision. 'It's clear I should go.' Stepping forward, he dropped a light kiss on her cheek. 'I'll be in touch, then.' And just like that, he was heading out of her kitchen.

Zoe wanted to call him back.

Don't you want dinner? It's a long drive back to Willara. She shot a desperate glance to the sauce-spattered stove. They'd cooked all this pasta.

But what about your things? she almost called out, until she remembered that Kent hadn't brought any luggage. He'd slept naked, and used her spare toothbrush—because he hadn't planned to stay…

Everything that had happened this weekend had been wonderfully spontaneous and…

And now she'd spoiled it.

Stumbling behind him through the flat, she swiped at embarrassing tears. When they reached her front door, Kent turned to her again, looking so desperately stern and handsome Zoe could barely breathe.

'I guess I need to get this straight,' he said. 'While we're cooling off, what exactly are we sorting out?'

Zoe gulped. Her mind was swirling. What could she say? Was this the time for painful honesty? What else could she offer him? 'I'm worried that I'm not the right girl for you, Kent.'

He stood, wary-eyed, waiting for her to continue.

Now that she'd started, she had no choice but to confess. 'I'm afraid I'm very keen on you, keener than you realise. And I don't think you'd want to deal with that right now.' Taking a deep breath, she rushed on. 'To be honest, I'm in love with the whole picture of you and your farm and your country lifestyle.'

Kent didn't speak. Perhaps he was stunned, or simply puzzled.

And Zoe realised, now, too late, that it had been a mistake to mention any of this, but she felt compelled to explain. 'It started when I was little, living in a bus and always looking out of the window at snug farmhouses in the middle of neat, tidy fields. I thought they looked so wonderful and I developed this fantasy of marrying a farmer one day.'

'So I'm a fantasy?' he queried, looking uncomfortable. 'Along with a country wedding?'

Oh, God. Too much information.

'I'm making a hash of this,' Zoe said. 'I didn't mean that the only reason I like you is because you're a farmer.'

'OK.' He lifted a hand as if to put a stop to the conversation. 'This is getting way too complicated.'

'I'm sorry.'

'Don't apologise, but I take your point about a cooling-off period. I guess it's a good idea.'

Thud. It was ridiculous to be disappointed as soon as he agreed to the very thing she'd asked for. Zoe's throat was suddenly a scalding knot of unshed tears.

Already he was turning to leave, but she couldn't speak, was too busy keeping her lips pressed together to hold back embarrassing sobs.

'Take care,' he said gently, before he went swiftly down her steps to his ute.

Driving west against the fierce glare of the setting sun, Kent had never felt less like cooling off.

He was fired up. Burning.

Angry with himself.

Last week he'd been a step from marrying Zoe's best friend, and a week later he'd leapt straight into her bed. What was he thinking?

Of course it was a hasty, rash and thoughtless act. If one of his mates had behaved the same way, Kent would be wondering if the guy's actions were driven by a bruised ego, or by his brains dropping below his belt!

Zoe had every right to ask questions—questions he should have asked himself.

What did he want from this relationship? Was it a casual fling? Did he expect to follow his old pattern, to date her for a month or so, and then drift away?

He certainly hadn't been thinking about the long term.

After last week's close brush with the responsibility and permanence of matrimony, he'd been set free, so to speak. He was free to embrace his old ways and his plan was to prolong his bachelorhood for as long as he could.

But did he honestly expect a conscientious girl like Zoe to treat their relationship lightly? After her past weeks of hard work and dedication, shouldn't he have known better? After she'd made love with such breathtaking spontaneity and touching emotion, shouldn't he have known their liaison was already complicated?

Hell. Zoe had told him about her rat of a boyfriend, and he'd been so self-righteous.

I would never do anything to you like that. What a fool he was.

Selfish, too. He'd wanted a little fun after the tension and drama of the past weeks, and Zoe had been available. How had she put it? The next cab at the rank.

And yet—that wasn't how he thought of her. Zoe was special, amazing in so many ways—the kind of girl he could, quite possibly, marry one day…if he'd had plans to settle down.

Maybe he shouldn't have been so surprised by her confession that she had feelings for him and wanted to marry, that she'd always wanted to be a farmer's wife, for heaven's sake.

But he hadn't seen it coming, and now, instead of relaxing after a pleasant weekend, he had a lot to think about. Too much. Not a chance of cooling off.

CHAPTER ELEVEN

IT WAS ten-thirty when the delivery boy arrived at the office doorway. At least, Zoe assumed it was the delivery boy, although all she could see of him were his jeans and his grubby green and yellow sneakers. The top half of him was entirely obscured by the biggest bunch of flowers she'd ever seen.

As the flowers appeared there was a collective gasp from every female in the office. The girl at the desk nearest to Zoe stopped a phone conversation in mid-sentence. Someone else gave an excited little squeal.

Mandy, whose desk was closest to the door, got out of her seat and practically tiptoed in awe towards the mountain of blooms.

Zoe was as curious as anyone else as she exchanged smiles with her workmates. She knew everyone was trying to guess who the lucky recipient could be. Emily had recently announced she was pregnant. Joanne was turning forty soon. Jane had acquired a new and, apparently, ultra-romantic boyfriend.

At least, Zoe knew the flowers couldn't be for her. The only person who might send them was Kent and he'd embraced her cooling-off suggestion with depressing enthusiasm. It was three weeks now since she'd seen him. Three desperately miserable weeks.

In all that time, she'd made no attempt to contact him and he'd only been in touch once to report that, despite the terrible weather in the north, Bella and Damon were apparently OK. There'd been nothing personal in his message. Not a breath of romance.

The silence had been awful. At times Zoe had felt so miserable, she'd almost weakened and begged him to forget everything she'd said.

Fortunately, she'd restrained herself. She'd done enough damage last time when she'd talked about loving him. Of course she'd frightened him off.

If she'd handled everything sensibly, they would have continued to see each other on weekends and who knew what pleasing developments might have occurred?

Now, in just a few days, she would be leaving for Europe, so there was no point in even thinking about what might have been with Kent. Instead, she was hoping and praying that the exciting new foreign sights and experiences would cheer her up, and help her to put the whole Willara experience behind her.

At any rate, she could relax right now. There was absolutely no chance these flowers were for her.

At the doorway, the floral Mount Everest was handed over to Mandy, who had to turn sideways to see where she was going as she made her way carefully back into the centre of the office.

'Help, someone!' she called. 'I'm sure there's a card pinned on here, but I can't possibly reach it.'

Zoe jumped to assist her. The bouquet was so huge, it took a few moments to locate the small white envelope, but she finally found it pinned beneath a cascade of lavender orchids.

'Here!' she cried, triumphantly waving the small white envelope above her head like a trophy.

'Who's it for?' cried several voices.

All eyes in the room were on Zoe. She saw smiles of amusement, wistful faces filled with hope, others wide eyed with genuine tension. The air was shimmering with palpable excitement.

Suddenly the centre of attention, Zoe felt her heartbeats begin a drum roll as she deliberately took her time looking at the name on the envelope. Then she dropped her gaze to the white square of paper. And her heart stopped beating altogether.

There…on the envelope in clear blue ink…

Zoe Weston.

There was a painful thump in the centre of her chest, and then her heart began to pound savagely. She hadn't expected, hadn't dreamed… The paper in her hand was shaking.

Everyone was watching her.

'Oh, gosh.'

'Who's it for?' Mandy demanded.

Almost apologetically, Zoe said, 'Me.'

At first there was silence. Then a voice cried, 'Oh, wow! Congratulations!' But for Zoe this was almost drowned out by her thundering heartbeats.

Her hands were shaking so badly, she had a hard time getting the little card out of the envelope, but finally she was able to read it.

I'd like to talk. How about you?
Kent xx

A thrill burst inside her like fizzing champagne.

'Who's it from?' called Jane.

Zoe hesitated. Many of these girls had been to

Willara Downs for the bridal shower. 'Just a guy,' she said lamely. As you did.

The response was a predictable group groan.

'If a guy sends a bouquet the size of a house he must be asking you to marry him at the very least,' someone said.

'Or perhaps he's been a very, very bad boy and he's very, very sorry,' said someone else.

Zoe shook her head, but she wasn't about to tell them: *he just wants to talk.* She was still trembling as she took the flowers from Mandy and stumbled off to hunt for a bucket to put them in.

In a back room she found a metal waste-paper bin, and she filled it with water. With the flowers taken care of, she sank back against a filing cabinet and read Kent's note again.

I'd like to talk. How about you?

Every possible emotion raged war inside her. Joy. Hope. Fear. Uncertainty.

Kent was opening a door, trying to reconnect, and she couldn't think of anything she wanted more than to see him again.

But in a few days she would be flying to the other side of the world, and she'd be away for a month. Surely her sudden impatience to see him was foolish.

Just because he's sent me a bunch of flowers?

But I love him.

Did she? Really?

She'd had enough time to think about it, to try to work out if she was actually in love with the real man and not with an embodiment of her childhood fantasy.

She found herself asking how anyone ever knew for certain that they were truly in love. In three weeks her longing to see Kent had been agonising. Was that love?

Was love ever safe and certain, or was it always a great big gamble?

She reminded herself again, as she had so often in the past three weeks, of her headlong rush into love with Rodney. She'd been so certain he was The One.

She'd been such a diligent girlfriend, so anxious to please Rodney, cooking his favourite meals, hiring his favourite DVDs. She'd been so busy showing him how devoted she was, she'd never stopped to make sure he felt the same way.

Being dumped by him had awoken every one of her insecurities. Once again she'd been an outsider, without a best mate.

Lately, she'd even wondered if she had poor judgement when it came to men. Perhaps it would be much more sensible to wait to talk to Kent after she got back from her travels. Mightn't she gain a clearer perspective with the benefit of further time and distance?

At lunchtime, Zoe divided the flowers into smaller bunches and handed them out among her surprised work colleagues.

'There's no point in taking them home to my place,' she explained over and over. 'I'm leaving for Europe on the weekend. You may as well enjoy them.'

The only flowers Zoe saved were the lavender orchids, which she took home and placed in a vase on the shelf beside the fish tank.

That was the easy part. Deciding how to deal with Kent was the difficult bit. She had to ring him to thank him, and there shouldn't be any harm in a phone call. Just the same, she had to be careful not to say too much. Now, when she was about to leave, she certainly couldn't let on how much she'd missed him.

No, she would have to be very strong and in control

of this conversation. Most definitely, she mustn't allow Kent to say or do anything to spoil her holiday plans.

The phone's shrill ring sent a jolt of adrenalin punching into Kent. He willed himself to stay calm. Almost certainly, this would be yet another phone call from a wedding guest, calling to cheer him up, or to invite him over for a meal. There'd been many such calls during the past month.

Even so, Kent knew the flowers must have arrived in Brisbane, and he was picturing Zoe as he picked up the receiver. He imagined her on her sofa in her Newmarket flat, with her long legs tucked neatly beneath her, her shiny hair a dark splash against the vivid red of her sofa's upholstery. Her eyes the blue of the morning sky...

He forced a smile into his voice as he answered. 'Hello. Willara Downs.'

'Hi, Kent, it's Zoe.'

Twin reactions—elation and alarm—tightened like lassos around his chest. It was so good to hear her voice and he couldn't believe how much he'd missed her. For these past three weeks he'd spent far too much time thinking about her, missing her smile, her touch, her company.

But he couldn't believe how worried he was, too. Worried she would read too much into this gesture. He simply needed to see her again. From their first meeting, he'd been aware of a fatal chemistry, and he'd tried his best to ignore it, but it was still tormenting him like a constant ache.

He'd given in, sent the flowers and a request to make contact, and now he forced a smile into his voice. 'Hey, Zoe, it's great to hear from you. How are you?'

'I'm fine, thanks.'

She didn't sound fine. She sounded nervous, as nervous as he was.

'Your flowers arrived,' she said. 'Thank you so much, Kent. They're beautiful. There were so many of them.'

'Not too over the top, I hope. I ordered them over the phone and just named an amount. Anyway, I'm glad you liked them.'

'All the girls in the office were jealous.' After a small pause, she asked, 'How—how are you?'

'Fighting fit.' He swallowed a sudden constriction in his throat. 'But I've missed you, Zoe.'

'Oh.'

Oh? What was that supposed to mean? He needed to know if she was pleased or disappointed. 'I was wondering if you'd had enough of this cooling-off period.'

'It hasn't been much fun,' she said softly, but then added almost straight away, 'but I still think it's a sensible idea, don't you?'

'I'm not sure it's possible to sort out a relationship in isolation. I was hoping we could talk.'

She made a noise that sounded like a sigh. A sad sigh that chilled him. 'I'm leaving for Europe on Saturday, Kent.'

'So soon? But Christmas is a month away.'

'I'm going to London and Paris first. Ten days in each city, and then on to Prague.'

A curse fell from his lips before he could bite it back. He didn't want to wait another month. He'd had enough of waiting while his thoughts went round and round the same worn track. Solitary contemplation hadn't helped.

He couldn't make decisions about their relationship in a vacuum.

He wanted action. He needed to be able to touch Zoe, to share meals and conversations, to make love to her.

If they waited another month, Zoe would have all kinds of opportunities to meet suave, silver-tongued Continental Casanovas. Hell. Had she already dismissed him?

Surely she owed him another chance? He had to see her. 'I'll come down to Brisbane.' Kent glanced at his watch. It was too late tonight. 'How about tomorrow night?'

'Sorry, Kent, my parents will be here. They're coming up to Brisbane to collect the goldfish and my pot plants.'

Curse the goldfish. Why had he ever thought it was a good idea? 'What about Friday night, then?'

There was another, longer pause. 'I—I'm not sure that's a good idea. I'll be leaving early on Saturday morning. Maybe we should let this go till I get back.'

'Sorry, Zoe. That's not an option. I have to see you. I'll come to the airport. What's your flight number?'

'Honestly, there's no need to see me off.'

'You can't keep stalling.' He was bulldozing her, but he didn't care. He'd heard a quiver in her voice that hinted at her inner battle, and in that instant he'd decided there was no way he could let her leave for the far side of the world without seeing her.

'Just tell me the flight and I'll be there.'

'OK, but I'll need to make a condition though, Kent.'

'What is it?'

'Promise you won't try to talk me out of going away.'

'Agreed,' he said, with a reluctance that disturbed him.

* * *

Zoe's boarding pass was tucked into her handbag and her suitcase was already on its way down the conveyor belt as she scanned the international terminal, searching for Kent.

Despite her best efforts to remain calm, her insides were flapping like bait in a net. She couldn't wait to see him, couldn't believe he was driving all the way from Willara Downs to Brisbane airport to spend a few short minutes with her.

How amazing was that? She'd given him a chance to cool off and it seemed that he hadn't cooled.

Of course, she hadn't cooled either. She was desperate to see him. And yet she was scared. For three and a half weeks, she'd kept her feelings for Kent carefully tied up in tight little parcels, and now, when she was about to head overseas, she wanted them to stay that way.

This trip was important to her. She was looking forward to the exciting new sights and sounds and smells of foreign places.

More importantly, she was hoping that time and distance would offer her an excellent chance to sort through her emotions and get a new perspective on her hopes and dreams. It would give Kent time, too.

Right now, however, she was scared. Scared that seeing him again would unravel her tightly bound feelings. Scared that one look into the deep brown warmth in his eyes could too easily break her resolve. How awful if her emotions spilled out all over the airport, like luggage bursting from an over-stuffed suitcase.

I can't let that happen. I have to be strong.

It would be so much easier to leave now without seeing him. All she had to do was walk through the exit doors into the secure Customs area and Kent wouldn't be able to follow her. Then she could keep herself together until she was safely out of reach. Should she leave? Now?

'Zoe.'

His voice came from behind her, spinning her around, a smile already flooding her face.

Oh, wow! He looked even more wonderful than she'd remembered. He was so tall and broad shouldered and his skin was darker, as if he'd spent a lot of time outdoors.

They stood, just staring at each other. Not touching.

'I'm late,' he said. 'The traffic was insane. I was afraid I'd miss you.'

'It won't be long before I have to go.'

'That's OK. At least I'm here now.' He smiled.

Heavens, his smile was gorgeous.

Dangerous. Zoe wanted to lean in to him, to touch him, to smell him.

Instead she searched for safe conversation. 'How's everything on the farm?'

'All running along smoothly.'

'Who's looking after the garden?'

Kent smiled again, but his eyes were watching her with hawklike attention. 'I have my work cut out running the farm, and my mother's busy planting up her new cottage garden, so, for now, the garden's looking after itself.'

'That's a shame.' There would be so many weeds, and the roses would need dead-heading. All the lilies and irises would be out now, but there'd be no one to truly appreciate them.

'I might get someone in,' he said, still watching her.

Zoe nodded and told herself to forget Willara Downs.

Kent said, 'You're going to have a fabulous trip.'

She was grateful that he wasn't going to try to stop her from leaving. She hoped he had no idea how easily he could.

His eyes searched her face, again, worried now. 'You'll be careful, won't you, Zoe?'

'Of course. Don't worry. My dad's given me all the lectures about a girl overseas on her own… I have a long list of instructions. Use a money belt. Keep enough money for the day in my pocket. Stay away from the lonely spots.'

'All very good advice.'

'And I've scanned my travel documents and emailed them to myself.'

'Great. And remember to keep in touch,' Kent added.

'That, too.' She smiled. 'I have international texting on my mobile phone.'

'And you have my number, I hope.'

'Yes. I'll text you.'

'Promise?'

The dark intensity in his eyes made her heart stumble. 'I promise, Kent.'

His shoulders visibly relaxed, and it was only then that she realised how very tense he'd been. 'Text me as often as you like, Zoe. If you're having a great time, or—or a not so great time.'

'I will.' She smiled. 'Don't look so worried.'

'I can't help it. I'm letting you go.'

She didn't know what to say. She hadn't expected him to be quite so…so protective…and she was scared she'd start to cry. 'I should head off now.'

He touched her elbow. 'You can't rush off without a decent goodbye.'

It was a warning, Zoe realised, not a request. But

Kent gave her no chance to deny him. In a heartbeat, he'd gathered her in, and he was kissing her.

Not hungrily, as she might have expected after their three-week stand-off, but with devastating tenderness. And heaven help her, she couldn't even pretend to resist. He only had to touch her and her will power evaporated like mist in sunlight.

Now, he'd barely sipped at her lower lip and, already, she was trembling.

His lips brushed her top lip. A kiss, as teasing and as light as air. Heartbreaking in its sexiness. He pressed another kiss to the corner of her mouth.

Wherever his lips touched her, Zoe melted.

Her knees threatened to give away as he took the kiss dizzyingly deeper, and she had no choice but to cling to him, grabbing handfuls of his T-shirt to steady herself. Now she was truly melting all over. Melting from head to toe. Dissolving right there. In the busy airport.

The bustling crowds and the voices over the intercom faded as Zoe became lost in the deep, dark mystery of Kent's kiss. Her impending flight no longer mattered. The whole world was happening right here. In Kent's arms.

When he released her, she wanted to cry.

Gently, he tucked a strand of her hair behind her ear, and his eyes betrayed a mix of sadness and triumph. 'So, Zoe…about this cooling-off idea.'

Right now, the cooling off was quite obviously the most ridiculous idea she'd ever had.

Then again, this kiss only proved how very badly she needed a safety net. She was so susceptible to this man. She lost her head whenever he was near. His kisses made her want to cancel her flight, tear up her ticket and toss her passport in the nearest waste bin.

Snap out of it, Zoe. For heaven's sake pull yourself together. Now.

She squared her shoulders. 'I—I don't think we should change our current status before I get back.'

Kent was smiling, damn him. 'So I guess this farewell kiss was an exception.'

Somehow, miraculously, Zoe kept her face poker straight. 'Under the circumstances, it was an excusable infringement.' With deliberate brusqueness, she checked the time on her phone. 'I'm sorry. I really must go now.'

To her surprise, Kent nodded. 'Yes, you must. I hope you have a safe journey, Zoe.'

'Thanks.'

It was happening. Kent was letting her go. Why couldn't she feel relieved?

His eyes were burning and serious. 'Remember to stay in touch. Your messages can be as cool as you like, but keep them coming.'

'All right.'

She thought he might kiss her again. And he did. He dropped one last, sweet, too-tempting and too-brief kiss on her lips, and then he stepped away from her, his throat rippling.

He lifted his hand.

Zoe's vision blurred and when she tried to walk her shoes were filled with lead.

CHAPTER TWELVE

AT FIRST, Zoe managed quite well. In London and Paris there were so many famous sights she wanted to see, so many beautiful art galleries, and amazing, historic buildings. So many wonderfully enticing shops to explore. She managed to keep busy every day and she found each new experience thrilling and exciting.

She also discovered definite advantages to solo travelling—total freedom to decide what she wanted to see and where she should stay, or when and where she should eat. And she met lots of interesting fellow travellers from all over the world.

But of course, she missed Kent and thought of him often.

Too often.

No way could she pretend she didn't miss him. He was always there, as an ache beneath her breastbone, a tightness in her throat. Her solo travels would have been a thousand times better if he'd been there to share everything with her.

Even so, she was very disciplined. She restricted her text messages to Kent, allowing only one message every second day, and she kept them brief and cheerful. No mushy stuff.

Kent's responses were disappointing—often arriving much later than Zoe would have liked, even taking the time difference into consideration. And when he replied, his tone was cool and utterly lacking in anything even slightly mushy or romantic.

Clearly, he was taking her request to extend their cooling-off period seriously, and she knew she should be grateful for that. But there was always the chance that his interest in her was fading, just as she'd always feared.

Zoe hated how sick this thought made her.

She tried to cheer herself up by conjuring memories of their farewell kiss at the airport, but what an unhelpful exercise that was. She found herself missing Kent more and more every day.

It was dark when Kent got back to the homestead. He fed his dogs on the back veranda, then went into the kitchen to heat up a can of tomato soup for himself. He knew it was lazy, but it was already after eight, and he was too weary to bother about cooking a proper meal. Since Zoe left, he'd been working long hours, seven days a week, hoping that the self-imposed labour would act as a sedative.

It hadn't worked.

Nothing in his life felt right. Each night he fell into bed exhausted, but then couldn't sleep. His solitary existence, which had never bothered him before, was now suffocating.

He couldn't stop thinking about Zoe in Europe, wishing he were there. Worse, he kept reliving all the times they'd been together. Not just the lovemaking—all the everyday moments, like the evening she was here in his kitchen, making a salad while he flipped steaks, on another afternoon, preparing a roast, or sharing a sunset.

He remembered the meals they'd enjoyed on the back veranda, the conversations. Recalled Zoe's enthusiasm for the garden, remembered the morning she'd gone down to the creek with him to collect sand—the soft empathy in her eyes when she'd asked him about the accident.

Each small recollection had become painfully sharp and clear. So important.

Now that Kent had too much time to think, he realised that he'd been so caught up with the wedding plans that he'd never really noticed how perfectly Zoe fitted into life on Willara Downs. Now, despite his best attempts to ignore such dangerous thoughts, he knew that his plans for a lengthy bachelorhood were fast losing their charm.

It was not a comforting discovery. Small wonder he couldn't sleep.

For Zoe, things went from not so great to downright dismal when she arrived in Prague.

As her plane touched down she looked out at the banks of snow lining the cleared runway, and her first, her *only* thought was—*Kent should be here.*

Riding in the taxi from the airport, she couldn't stop thinking about him. She'd brought his beautiful book with her, and now the same gorgeous pictures she knew by heart were unfolding before her. She kept thinking about the night they'd shared dinner on the back veranda at Willara Downs, when Kent had first told her about Christmas in Prague.

If only he were here.

Impulsively, she sent him a text message.

1.30p.m.: I'm in Prague!!!!!!! My first glimpse of the fairy-tale skyline. Prague castle silhouetted against a winter-white sky. It stole my breath. So pretty and timeless.

She'd only come to Prague because Kent had told her about it, and now she was here, surrounded by its ancient, wintry beauty, she wanted him to be here with her. So badly. How could she enjoy the snow, the castles and the Christmas markets without him?

Loneliness descended like the snow.

She remembered all the overtures Kent had made before she left—the enormous bunch of flowers, the offers to visit her at her flat, the trip to the airport to say goodbye. Each time he'd tried to restart their relationship she'd blocked him.

Now, she had to ask why.

Why? *Why?*

Why had she been so fixated on keeping him at bay?

She was left with unanswered puzzles. She was surprised that he still seemed keen even though she'd spilled her dreams about settling down. Not that this meant he was ready to marry her. Perhaps he'd hoped to win her around to accepting a freer relationship. To Zoe, in her present lonely circumstances, that seemed to be a reasonable compromise.

However, her fixation with Kent annoyed her. She'd come away, hoping that distance and time would clear her head and her heart. But now, here she was in Prague on the far side of the world, and she still spent her whole time thinking about one man.

She missed his smile, missed his friendly brown eyes, the warmth and power of his arms about her. Missed his smell, his voice, his kisses, his touch…

And she had to ask why she'd insisted on an extension of their cooling off.

Her initial caution, so soon after the cancelled wedding, had been sensible. But was her request to continue it really such a good idea?

Suddenly, it made no sense to ration her text messages.

She had to make contact with Kent. If he couldn't be here, she needed to share her experiences by the only means she had. Opening her phone, she began to type.

4.15 p.m.: It's already dark and it's snowing and I'm wearing a new red woollen hat I bought in Paris.

5.45 p.m.: I'm in the Old Town Square. So many sounds. Church bells, a brass band playing carols, the chiming of the famous astronomical clock.

6.01 p.m.: Now I'm walking across Charles Bridge. There's a busker playing a violin. Magic.

7.10 p.m.: Goulash for dinner with five white dumplings to mop up the yummy rich beef gravy.

7.30 p.m.: Have just had my first drink of grog—a mix of rum and tea. Miss you heaps. Xx

By the time Zoe went to bed she'd had no reply from Kent. She told herself this was to be expected given the time differences, but it didn't stop her from feeling depressed and lonely and sorry for herself.

She knew it was pitiful, but she couldn't help feeling

down. She cried herself to sleep, and she slept fitfully, waking often to check her phone for messages.

There was only one, which arrived at 3.00 a.m. From her mum.

Next morning, Kent still hadn't replied, and Zoe found reasons—he'd risen early and taken off on his tractor without checking his phone. Or perhaps his phone's battery had needed recharging. She knew there were all sorts of logical explanations.

Just the same, she waited on tenterhooks. And to cheer herself up, she kept sending messages.

8.05 a.m.: From my apartment window, I look out at steep rooftops covered in snow and I can see Prague castle.
    Don't you wish you were here?

8.35 a.m.: The cars are covered in snow. The statues have snow on their shoulders. The tree branches are sagging beneath the weight of the snow. There are children tobogganing.
    What's it like at Willara?

9.15 a.m.: I'm trying to catch falling snow in my mouth. Can you tell snow's a novelty for me?

10.00 p.m.: Kent, I've been in Prague a whole day. Where are you?

At midnight, Zoe sat on her bed, wrapped in a warm quilt, staring forlornly at her phone. She'd written another message, but she wasn't quite brave enough to press Send. Kent's silence had made her desperate, but the message was so—*revealing*—and sending it was far too risky.

Heartsick, she read it again.

11.53 p.m.: Kent, I miss you so much. This cooling off isn't working any more. When I get back home, I hope we can talk.
I love you,
Zoe xxx

She'd changed the last part of the message a dozen times, had deleted and then rewritten those three telling words— *I love you*.

She knew this wasn't what he wanted to hear. How could she make such a rash confession? In the weeks since she'd left home, he hadn't given her any fresh reason to hope.

At twenty past midnight, Zoe was still huddled on the bed, but she decided she'd been too cautious for too long. What the heck? It was time to be brave.

Taking a deep breath for courage, she pressed the send button, and then she slipped beneath the covers, and tried to sleep. Her heart was pounding.

Next morning there was still no answer from Kent, and Zoe had never in her life felt as bereft as she did now.

She stood at the window looking out at the postcard-perfect scene of Europe's fairy-tale city. Overnight it had snowed again and all the rooftops and the streets were coated with glistening white. She didn't care. She didn't want to be in Prague. It was almost Christmas and she was alone and heartbroken and on the wrong side of the world.

How could she have been such a fool? How had she ever thought she could enjoy this alone?

But even if she paid the extra money to change her flights in the middle of the festive season, she didn't want to fly back to Australia if she couldn't be sure Kent would welcome her. That would be unbearable. Better to stay here in Prague and try to make the best of a bad situation.

She should try to put Kent out of her mind.

This morning she would go to the markets and buy Christmas decorations. She would school herself to live in each moment, to enjoy the ancient cobbled streets, and the old Gothic architecture, and the brightly decorated wooden huts selling handicrafts and wooden toys. Instead of dwelling on her misery, she would think of others. She would buy presents. Lots of presents. Her little brother, Toby, would love those cheeky wooden puppets.

But as Zoe walked from stall to stall she was painfully conscious of the small solid weight of her phone in her coat pocket. All morning, even though she knew it was the middle of the night in Australia, she remained on edge, waiting for the phone to vibrate against her hip, to tell her there was an incoming call.

In the afternoon, she joined a tour of Prague Castle and St Vitus Cathedral. The buildings were beautiful, and the history was epic and fascinating. The views of the city and the elegant bridges over the Vltava River were truly picturesque. Zoe soaked up the atmosphere and told herself how lucky she was to be having such memorable experiences. She told herself this over and over.

Her phone didn't ring.

By the time she'd finished the walking tour, darkness was closing in, but she didn't want to go back to her hotel room. She stayed out in the streets where the music and pretty lights were designed to lift everyone's spirits.

The air was thick with the warm smell of cinnamon and she admired the enormous, brightly lit Christmas tree which, according to the hotel concierge, had been brought down from the Sumava Mountains.

Every ten minutes or so, desperation drove her to take her phone out just to check that she hadn't missed a call.

She hadn't.

By now, her legs were leaden and aching from walking all day in the freezing cold. Her stomach was hollow with regret and self-recrimination. Her last message had been too strong. Kent didn't know how to answer her.

Or worse…

Kent had been in an accident. He was ill.

Stop it.

She would go mad if she kept this up. She should eat. The market stalls sold all kinds of wonderful hot food—corn on the cob, crumbed mushrooms and spicy sausages. Perhaps she should buy a cup of the hot mulled wine that everyone else seemed to be enjoying so much. The wine certainly looked and smelled yummy—spicy, with floating pieces of apple and orange.

At least it would keep her warm.

Slipping her phone into her coat pocket, Zoe gave it a small pat. Silently, she said: *That's it—I'm done with you for tonight.*

The thought was barely completed before she felt, through the soft kid of her glove, a gentle vibration against her fingers.

Her heart banged hard against her ribs. And then her phone began to ring in earnest.

This wasn't a mere text message. On the tiny screen she saw a name.

Kent Rigby...

Her hand was shaking as she held the phone to her ear.

Kent said, 'Zoe—'

And at that very moment a brass band struck up a noisy rendition of 'Good King Wenceslas', drowning out Kent's voice as it blasted the carol into the frosty night air.

'Sorry,' Zoe cried to him, running across the cobblestones with the phone pressed to one ear and her hand covering the other. 'I can't hear you. Hang on, Kent. Are you still there? I'm going to have to get away from this music.'

Around a corner, in a small, narrow street, she sank against a stone wall. 'Sorry,' she puffed. 'That's a little better. Are you still there?'

'Yes, I'm here.' His voice was rippling with warmth and a hint of laughter.

'Are you OK? It seems ages since I heard from you.'

'I'm fine, Zoe. How are you?'

'I'm OK. Everything's lovely here. But it's so good to hear your voice.'

'Are you homesick?'

'I am a bit, yes.' Nervously, she chewed her lip. 'Have my text messages been getting through to you?'

'They have.' There was a tiny pause. 'Thank you.' His voice sounded deeper, rougher, thick with emotion.

Zoe held her breath, wondering if he would explain his recent silence, or if he'd comment on her last message.

At least *I love you* hadn't frightened him away.

'It's beautiful here,' she said lamely.

'Where are you exactly?'

'I'm not sure. It's a little side street off the Old Town Square. Why?'

'I was hoping you weren't too far away.'

She laughed. 'Yeah, right. Like I'm just around the corner from Willara Downs.'

'I'm not at Willara Downs.'

'Where—?' she began, then froze as she heard the triumphant notes of a brass band. The music was coming from...

Inside her phone.

Surely she was mistaken?

No, she wasn't.

'Kent?' Zoe was so tense she was sure her skin had snapped. 'Where are you?'

'Right behind you.'

Heart thumping, she spun around.

And there he was.

On the street corner in a heavy winter coat, outlined by the bright lights from the markets.

She tried to lift a shocked hand to wave, but already Kent was coming towards her, and then, as fast as her shaky legs would allow, Zoe was stumbling over the snowy cobblestones.

Into his open arms.

She buried her face in his shoulder and he held her. She was crying, laughing and snuffling with happiness.

'What are you doing here?' she asked when she got her breath back.

'Looking for you, of course.'

'Kent, that's insane.' A huge sob burst from her. 'Oh, God, I've missed you so much.'

'And I've missed you.' Kent wiped her tears with a gloved hand. 'You wrote that you missed me on your first day here, and I jumped straight on the very next plane.'

Stunned, she pulled back to look into his face. His dearly loved, beautiful face. And in that moment she understood exactly why she loved him.

It had nothing to do with his farm, or his lovely homestead. Or his country shirts and his riding boots. She loved him for something else entirely. Something warm and powerful and steadfast and strong that she found shining in his beautiful brown eyes.

'Thank you for coming,' she said softly.

'Thank you for missing me,' he answered, kissing the tip of her nose.

Arm in arm and warmed by mulled wine and hot corn cobs, they walked through the snowy night to Zoe's hotel. Kent was insanely happy. *Insanely. Over the moon.*

They collected his backpack and went up the narrow stairs. In Zoe's room, they peeled off their gloves, hung up their woollen hats and coats, and removed their heavy, damp boots.

Zoe, looking all kinds of gorgeous in a soft crimson sweater and pale blue jeans, turned to him, her eyes shining with happy expectation.

He wanted nothing more than to scoop her in to him, but he remembered, just in time, that he had something even more important planned for this moment.

He said, with a rueful smile, 'Can you hang on a tick?'

'No, Kent, I can't.' Zoe was laughing and impatient,

rising on tiptoes to nuzzle his jaw. With her lips against his skin, she growled, 'I can't wait another second.'

OK, it was a whacky plan anyway, and Kent knew he couldn't wait either. He needed this. Now. Needed Zoe wrapped in his arms, needed her sweet mouth locked with his, needed the soft silk of her skin under his palms, needed her eager and hungry and loving…

Later…

Everything else could wait till later…

'So what was it?' Zoe asked much later as she lay with her head cradled against his bare shoulder.

Kent yawned. 'What was what?'

'Earlier tonight, when we got back here to the room, you asked me to hang on. What was that about? Were you going to show me something?'

'Yeah,' he said sleepily, and then he yawned. 'But it can wait.'

Gently, she ran her fingers over his chest. 'Poor Kent. You've flown all this way and you must be so jet-lagged.'

'Mmm.'

Kent slept, and Zoe lay awake. After the strain of the past few days, she should have been exhausted, but she was too happy and excited to close her eyes.

Kent had come to her as soon as she told him she missed him. How wonderful was that?

Faint moonlight spilled from the window across their bed and she watched him sleep and thought how amazing, how unbelievably perfect he was.

Her happiness was astonishing, as if she'd been living in a grey world that was suddenly flooded with colour.

Of course, in a deep corner of her heart there was still a niggle of disquiet. When Kent had swept her into his arms he hadn't promised love or marriage. But perhaps it was time to put her dreams aside. Time to put Rodney behind her and to take another risk. Didn't loving someone always involve a risk?

Bella had taken a huge risk when she dashed off to Far North Queensland with Damon Cavello. Kent had taken another big risk by travelling over here on the strength of a text message…

Anyway, why should she worry now simply because Kent hadn't actually told her in so many words that he loved her? He'd flown all this way to be with her, and he'd made love to her with a passion that made her blood sing.

Really. On a night like this, just having him here was enough.

Kent kissed Zoe awake. 'Morning, Sleeping Beauty. I've brought you coffee.'

To her surprise it was already past ten.

'Gosh, you're the one with jet lag. I should be bringing you coffee.'

Kent smiled and sat on the edge of the bed. 'Did you know you're at your most beautiful when you've just woken up?'

'I can't be.'

'But you are. I love the sleep-tumbled look.'

For a moment she thought he was going to say he loved her—no matter how she looked.

It doesn't matter. I don't need words.

Outside, the day was sunny, crystal clear and gleaming white, but they stayed in until lunchtime, making leisurely love. When they eventually went out, they ate food from a market stall, then took a train ride to Karlstejn Castle.

The castle was stunningly beautiful, and Zoe decided that Cinderella, Snow White and Sleeping Beauty had all spent time living within those spectacular walls at the top of a snowy mountain.

From the castle ramparts, the view was truly majestic. They could see for miles, and Zoe wondered—just briefly, as she had earlier that morning—if *this* setting might prompt Kent to tell her he'd changed, that he loved her and wanted to spend the rest of his life with her…

It didn't happen.

But that was OK. Nothing could spoil her happiness as they took the train back to Prague, or as they walked to Wenceslas Square to a café that served coffee and sensational apple strudel with home-made ice cream.

'Save room for dinner,' Kent warned her. 'I'm taking you somewhere special.'

So they walked off the strudel, then went back to their hotel to change. Kent had made reservations at the most gorgeous restaurant where the food was so divine it could easily have inspired a brand-new 'Bohemian Rhapsody'.

Over dinner they talked about Prague and what they knew of Czech history, and the whole time Kent's eyes were lit by a special light that kept Zoe's heart zinging.

All right, all right…

There was no talk of love. *But who needed words?*

Back at the hotel, Zoe took a long hot bath and told herself that she had to stop waiting for Kent to say *something*.

He was a farmer, a doer, a man of action, not words.

He'd bought her a bracelet and he'd sent her goldfish and flowers and given her a book. He'd rushed to the airport to farewell her. And he'd flown all this way from Australia. Why would he do all that if he didn't really care for her?

Just the same…tonight, she would pluck up the courage to mention her last revealing text message. She needed to know how he felt about it…

After drying herself, Zoe rubbed moisturiser all over her body, then slipped into the luxuriously thick towelling robe supplied by the hotel. She opened the bathroom door…

And gasped when she saw their room…

Candles…

Candles everywhere. Candles on the coffee table, on the bookcase, on the bedside tables, on the deep stone window sills. Candles on every available surface. Dainty, *little* candles.

Candles that looked strangely familiar.

Kent was standing in the middle of the room, watching her. In the flickering light, he sent her a shy, crooked smile. 'This was supposed to happen last night.'

'Wow.' Zoe pressed a hand to the jumping pulse in her throat. 'They look so lovely.'

The candles were more than lovely. They were gorgeous. Dazzling. The room danced and glowed with romantic light, while darkness hovered outside and white snowflakes fell soundlessly against the window pane.

Kent grinned. 'You probably recognise these little guys. I have to confess I borrowed your smart candles.'

Of course. Now she knew why they were so familiar. They were the same candles she'd planned to put in sand-filled paper bags for Bella's wedding. 'You brought all of them? All this way?'

'Yes. Four dozen smart candles in my backpack.' He smiled boyishly. 'I brought them to help me.'

Help him? Why? Zoe held her breath. Her heart began to thump.

Kent stepped closer and reached for her hands. 'I wanted to tell you how special you are, Zoe, but I wasn't sure I could convince you with words alone. The candles are my back-up.' His eyes shimmered. 'They stand for everything I love about you. They're bright and—'

'Wait,' she said. 'Please, don't rush over that bit.'

'What bit?'

'The—ah—bit you just said.'

'About loving you?'

'Yes.'

Kent smiled gorgeously. 'Darling girl, that's why I'm here.' His hands framed her face. His eyes shone. 'I love you so much. So much it kills me.'

She was so happy she was going to cry. But she still mustn't get her hopes up. She had to stay sensible. 'But—but this isn't a proposal or anything, is it?'

'It certainly is.'

Her heart almost leapt clear out of her chest. 'But you—you said—'

'I know what I said about long-term commitment, but that was before.' Kent's throat rippled and his eyes shimmered. 'Everything changed when you stepped on that plane, Zoe. I watched you walking out of my life, and it was like I was drowning all over again. Every moment I'd spent with you flashed before my eyes—from the first time we met by the road side and you had the flat tyre, and all those other times at Willara, and then in Brisbane.'

He took a deep breath. 'I've been falling for you from

the start, but I was planning the wedding to Bella, and I couldn't let myself think about you.'

Lifting her hands, Kent pressed them against his chest and she felt the thud-thudding of his heartbeats. 'I've missed you so much. And I've come to my senses at last. Of course, I want what you want, Zoe. I want your help with running the farm, and I want our own little family.'

It was too, too wonderful to take in. To Zoe's dismay, fat tears rolled down her cheeks and she had to blot them on Kent's shirtfront.

When she looked up again, his dark eyes burned with an intensity that made her tremble. 'Don't ever doubt that I love you, Zoe. You're exactly like these candles. You're beautiful and smart and you set me alight.'

'And you brought all forty-eight of them all this way to prove it.' Smiling, she snuggled closer and wound her arms around his neck. 'I do love a man of action.'

'So does that mean you'll marry me?'

Would she? Would she marry the most gorgeous farmer in the world and live in his lovely farmhouse set solidly and safely amidst spreading fields?

Would she embrace her most cherished dream?

For answer Zoe kissed him. 'Yes,' she said, and she gave him another kiss. 'Yes, please, I'd love to marry you.' Then she kissed him again while forty-eight candles glowed warmly in the midwinter night.

* * * * *

THE MORNING
AFTER THE
WEDDING BEFORE

ANNE OLIVER

To Sue. You're loyal, generous, compassionate and caring, touching people's lives in the best way, and a true friend on life's amazing and unpredictable journey. Thank you for always being there! Anne

CHAPTER ONE

Emma Byrne refused to give in to the nerves zapping beneath her ribcage like hysterical wasps. She was a sophisticated city girl, she wasn't afraid of walking into a third-rate strip club. Alone.

But she paused on the footpath in King's Cross, Sydney's famous nightclub district, and racked her brain for an alternative solution as she eyed the bruiser of a bouncer propped against the tacky-looking entrance.

Six p.m. on a balmy autumn Monday evening and the Pink Mango was already open for business. Sleazy business. She gulped down the insane urge to laugh—she'd been naïve enough to think the Pink Mango was an all-night deli.

But she'd promised her sister she'd deliver the best man's suit to Jake Carmody, and she would. She could.

Pushing the big sunglasses she'd found in her glove box farther up her nose, she slung her handbag and the plastic suit bag over one stiff shoulder and marched inside. The sound system's get-your-gear-off bump and grind pounded through hidden speakers. The place smelled like beer and cheap cologne and smut. Her nostrils flared in distaste as she drew in a reluctant breath.

Her steps faltered as a zillion eyes seemed to look her way. *You're imagining it,* she told herself. *Who'd give you a second glance in a dive like this?* Especially given her knee-length buttoned-up red trench coat, knee-high boots and leather gloves, all of which she'd left on the back seat of her car since last winter. Which, when she thought about it, could very well be the reason she was garnering more than a few stares…

Better safe than sorry. Thank heavens for untidy cars and a convenient parking spot.

Ignoring the curious eyes, she turned her attention to the décor instead. The interior was even tackier than the outside. Cheap lolly pink and gold and black. The chairs and couches were covered in a dirty-looking fuchsia animal print. A revolving disco ball spewed gaudy colours over the circulating topless waitresses with smiles as fake as their boobs.

At least they *had* boobs.

Most of the early-evening punters were lounging around a raised oval stage leering over their drinks at a lone female dancer wearing nothing but a fuzzy gold string and making love to a brass pole. A hooded cobra was tattooed on one firm butt cheek.

Far out. Despite herself, Emma couldn't seem to tear her fascinated gaze away. *What men like*… She'd never have that voluptuousness, nor the chutzpah to carry it off.

Maybe that was the reason Wayne had called it quits.

Shaking off the self-doubt, she blew out a deep, slow breath and turned away from the entertainment. Just what she *didn't* need right now. A reminder of her physical inadequacies.

I don't care if you and Ryan are getting married next weekend, little sister, you owe me big-time for doing this.

'I've got an appointment to get my nails done,' Stella had told her with more than a touch of pre-wedding desperation in her voice. 'Ryan's in Melbourne for a conference till tomorrow and you don't have anything special on tonight, do you?'

Stella knew Emma had no social life whatsoever since the break-up with Wayne. Of course she'd be free. Wouldn't have mattered if she wasn't. As the maid of honour, how could she refuse the bride's request? But a strip joint had *not* been part of the deal.

A man in an open shirt with a thick gold chain over an obscene mat of greying chest hair watched her from behind a desk nearby. His flat, penetrating gaze—as if he was imagining her naked and finding her not up to par— made her stomach heave. A bead of sweat trickled down her back—it was stifling inside this coat.

But he seemed to be the obvious person to speak to, so she moved quickly. She straightened her spine and forced herself to look him in the eyes. Not easy when those eyes were staring at her chest.

But before she got a word out he twirled one fat finger and said, 'If you've come about the job, take off that coat and show us what you've got.'

The hairs on the back of her neck prickled and, appalled, she tightened her belt. 'I *beg* your pardon? I'm n—'

'You won't need a costume here, darlin',' he drawled, eyeing the garment bag over her shoulder. 'We're one down tonight so you can start on the tables. Cherry'll show you. Oi, Cherry!' His smoke-scratched voice blasted through the thick air.

Emma cringed as people looked their way, glad of her dark glasses. She summoned her frostiest tone. 'I'm here to speak to Jake Carmody.'

He shook his head. 'Won't make a scrap of difference, y'know. Seen plenty just like you pass through the door hiding behind a disguise, expecting to make a quick buck on the side.'

'*Excuse me?* Just tell me where I can find Mr Carmody so I can finish my business with him and be *out of here*.'

Those pale flat eyes checked her out some more as a woman approached toting a tray of drinks. She was wearing eighties gold hot pants and a transparent black blouse. Beneath her make-up Emma saw that she looked drawn and tired and felt a stirring of sympathy. She knew all about working jobs out of sheer necessity, and was grateful she'd never been quite so desperate.

'Lady here wants to see the boss. Know where he is?'

The boss? 'There must be some mistake…' Emma trailed off. His PA had told her she'd find him at this address, but…he was the *boss* of this dive?

The woman called Cherry gave a weary half shrug. 'In the office, last I saw.'

He jerked a thumb at a narrow staircase on the far side of the room. 'Up the stairs, first door on the right.'

'Thank you.' Lips pressed together, and aware of a few gazes following her, she made her way through the club, keeping as far away from the action as possible.

The *boss?*

Despite the heat, she shivered inside her coat. His lifestyle was none of her business, but she'd never in a million years have expected the guy she remembered to be involved in a lower-than-low strip joint. He already had a career, didn't he? A degree in business law, for goodness' sake. *Please don't let him have chucked in years of study and a respectable livelihood for this…*

Sleaze Central's business obviously paid better. Money over morals.

She knew Jake from high school. He was one of Ryan's mates, and the two guys had often turned up at home to catch up with her more sociable sister and listen to music. Emma had been either working one of her after-school jobs or experimenting with her soap-making, but there'd been a few times when Stella had persuaded her to chill out with them.

Jake the Rake, Emma had privately thought him. A chick magnet. Totally cool, ever so slightly dangerous, and way too experienced for a girl like her. Maybe that was why she'd always tried to avoid him whenever possible.

Hadn't stopped her from being a little in love with him, though. She shook it away. Obviously her young eyes had been clouded by naïveté and love was definitely not in her life plan. Not ever again.

She heard him before she reached the door. That familiar deep, somewhat lazy voice that seemed to roll over the senses like thick caramel sauce. She *was* well and truly over her youthful crush on him, wasn't she? He was on the phone, and as she paused to listen his tone changed from laid-back to harassed.

The door was open a crack and she knocked. She heard a clatter as he slammed the phone down, a short, succinct rude word and then an impatient, 'Come in.'

He didn't look up straight away, which gave her a moment to slide her sunglasses on top of her head and look him over.

Sitting at a shabby desk littered with papers, he was writing something, head bent over a file. He wore a sky-blue shirt, open at the neck, sleeves rolled up over sinewy bronzed forearms. Unlike the rest of this dive, his clothing was top of the line. Her gaze lifted to his face and her heart pattered that tiny bit faster. God's gift with a sinner's lips…

An unnerving little shiver ran through her and she jerked her eyes higher. His rich, dark hair was sticking up in short tufts here and there, as if he'd been ploughing his hands through it. Her fingers itched to smooth it down—

Good grief, she was lusting after a man who owned a seedy striptease venue—a man who not only used women but exploited them. Wanting to touch him made her as low as him and as bad as those pervs downstairs. But, despite her best efforts to ignore them, little quivers continued to reverberate up and down the length of her spine.

'Hello, Jake.' She impressed herself with her aloof greeting and only wished she felt as cool.

He glanced up. His frown was replaced by stunned surprise. As if he'd been caught in a shop window with his made-to-measure pants down. She blinked the disconcerting image away.

'Emma.' Putting his pen down slowly, he closed the file he'd been working on, took his sweet time to stand—all six-foot-plus of gorgeous male—and said, 'Long time no see.'

'Yes,' she agreed, ignoring the tantalising glimpse of masculine hair visible at the neck of his shirt, the way his broad shoulders shifted against the fabric. 'Well…we've all got busy lives.'

'Yeah, it's all go these days isn't it? Unlike high school.' He came round to the side of the desk with a smile that was like a lingering caress and did amazing tingly things to her body.

She took a step back. She needed to get out. Fast. 'I can see you're busy,' she hurried on, keeping her gaze focused on his black coffee eyes. 'I j—'

'Are you here for a job?'

What? She felt her jaw drop, and for a moment she simply stared while her brain played catch-up and heat crawled up her neck. The sod. The dirty rotten *sod.* 'I phoned your office—your *other* office—and your PA told me you were here.'

Her lip curled on the last word and she tossed the garment bag onto the desk, sending papers flying every which way. 'Your suit for the wedding. If it needs altering the tailor says he needs at least three days' notice, which is why I'm dropping it off tonight. Ryan's interstate, and Stella had an appointment, so I—'

'Emma. I was joking.'

Oh. She glimpsed the twinkle in his eye and took another step back. Twinkles were dangerous. And why wouldn't he joke? Because no way did she measure up to those voluptuous creatures downstairs. 'I don't have time to joke today. Or anything else. So...um...you've got the suit. I'll be off, then.'

He watched her a moment longer, as if saying *What's your hurry?* Beneath the harsh single fluorescent light she saw the bruised smudges and feathery lines of stress around his eyes, as if he hadn't slept in weeks.

Well, good, she thought. He deserved to be stressed for making her feel like an inadequate fool. As if her self-esteem wasn't suffering enough after Wayne ending their relationship, and in this place...

'So, it's *Gone with the Wind* for us two, eh? Hope I can do Rhett Butler justice.' He glanced at the bag, then aimed that sexy grin at her. 'And you're to be my Scarlett for the day.'

She stiffened at the darkly delicious—no, *bad* thought. But her blood pulsed a bit more heavily through her body. 'I'm not your anyone. Why they had to choose a famous couples-themed wedding's beyond me.'

He shrugged. 'They wanted something sparkling and original and wildly romantic—and why not? Might as well have some fun on the big day. Everything's downhill from there.' His long, sensuous fingers curled around the edge of the desk and he aimed that killer smile again. 'Thanks for dropping it off. Can I get you a drink before you leave?'

Good heavens. 'No. Thank you.'

Crossing his arms, Jake leaned a hip against the desk, inhaling the fresh, unfamiliar fragrance that had swirled in with her. She was an energising sight for tired eyes. What he could see of her.

Tall and slim as a blue-eyed poppy. Even angry she looked amazing, with that ice-cold sapphire gaze and that way she had of pouting her lips. All glossy and plump and...

He fought a sudden mad impulse to walk over and taste them. Probably shouldn't have made that wisecrack about a job here. But he'd not been able to resist getting a rise out of her. On the few occasions she'd been persuaded to join them she'd always been so damn serious. Obviously that hadn't changed.

The muffled thump from downstairs vibrated through the floor. He rasped his hands over his stubbled jaw. 'If I'd known you were coming I'd've arranged for you to drop the suit at my office. My *other* office.'

She drilled him some more with that icy stare. And he felt oddly bruised, as if she'd punched him in the gut with her...gloved hand.

'I have to go,' she said stiffly.

He pushed off the desk. 'I'll walk you down.'

'No. I'd really rather you didn't.'

The tone. He knew well enough not to mess with it and crossed his arms. 'Okay. Thanks again for dropping the suit by. Appreciate it.'

'Glad to hear that, because it's a one-off.'

'I'll see you tomorrow night at the wedding dinner.'

'Seven-thirty.' She hitched her bag higher. 'Don't be late.'

'Emma…' She glanced back and he thought once again of poppies. About lying in a field of them on a summer's day. With Emma. 'It's good to see you again.'

She didn't reply, but she did hesitate, staring at him with those fabulous eyes and allowing him to indulge in the cheerful poppy fantasy a few seconds longer. And he could have sworn he felt a…*zap*. Then she nodded once and her head snapped back to the doorway.

He watched her leave, admiring the way she moved, all straight and sexy and *classy*. He wondered for a moment why he'd never pursued anything with her back in the day. He'd seen her look his way more than once when she'd thought he wasn't watching.

His lingering smile dropped away. He knew why. Emma Byrne didn't know the meaning of fun, and she certainly didn't know how to chill out. She wore *serious* the way other women wore designer jeans.

Jake, on the other hand, didn't do serious. He didn't do commitment. He enjoyed women—on his terms. Women who knew the score. And when it was over it was over, no misunderstandings. No looking back. But, *hoo-yeah*… He couldn't deny this lovely, more mature, more womanly Emma turned him on. Big time.

The door closed and he listened to her footsteps fade, stretching his arms over his head, imagining her walking downstairs. In that neck-to-ankle armour—which only added to the sexual intrigue. Did she even realise that? He should have escorted her down, he thought again. But the lady, and everything about her body language, had said a very definite no.

Shaking off the lusty thoughts, he rolled down his shirt-sleeves. Damn Earl, the SOB who'd fathered him, for dying and leaving him this mess to sort out. No one knew of Jake's connection to this club, with the exception of Ry and his parents and more recently his PA.

And now Emma Byrne.

'Hell.' He checked the time, then shoved his phone in his pocket. He didn't have time for that particular complication right now—he had an important business meeting to attend. Grabbing his jacket from the back of his chair, he headed downstairs.

CHAPTER TWO

AND she'd told him not to turn up late.

'She'd better have a good excuse,' Jake muttered the following evening as he swung a left in his BMW and headed for Sydney's seaside suburb of Coogee Beach, where Emma lived with her mother and Stella. As Ryan's best man he'd had no choice but to elect himself to conduct the search party.

Or maybe she'd decided she didn't want to run into Jake Carmody again so soon.

She'd always been big on responsibility, he recalled, and tonight was her sister's night, so he figured she wouldn't opt out without a valid reason. But she hadn't answered her mobile and concern gnawed at his impatience. He tapped the steering wheel while he waited at a red light. A trio of teenagers skimpily dressed for a night on the town crossed in front of him, their feminine voices shrill and excited.

Maybe Emma wasn't the same girl these days. Maybe she had decided to swap those self-imposed obligations for some fun at last. After all, apart from those few minutes yesterday, when neither of them had actually been themselves, how long had it been since he'd seen her?

His gut tensed an instant at the memory. He knew exactly when he'd last seen her. Seven months ago at Stella and Ryan's engagement party. He knew exactly what she'd been wearing too—a long, slinky strapless thing the co-lour of moon-drenched sea at midnight.

Or some such garment. He forced his hands to loosen on the wheel. Unclenched his jaw. So what if he'd noticed every detail, down to the last shimmering toenail? A guy could look.

He'd arrived in time to see her leave hand in hand with some muscled blond surfie type. Wayne something or other, Stella had told him. Apparently Emma and Wayne were a hot item.

Maybe Surfer Boy was the reason she'd lost track of time…

Frowning at the thought, he pulled into the Byrnes' driveway overlooking the darkening ocean. The gates were open and he came to a stop beside an old red hatchback parked at the top of a flight of stone steps.

Perched halfway down the sloping family property was the old music studio, where he remembered spending af-ternoons in the latter days of high school. Early-evening shadows shrouded the brick walls but muted amber light shone through the window. Emma lived there now, he'd been informed, and she was obviously still at home. In the absence of any other car on the grounds, it seemed she was also alone.

Swinging his car door open, he pulled out his phone. 'Ry? Looks like she hasn't even left yet.' He strode to the steps, flicking impatient fingers against his thigh. 'We'll be there soon.'

Pocketing the phone, he continued down the stairs. If *he* could make it on time to this wedding dinner after the hellish day he'd had, trying to stay on top of two busi-nesses, so could Emma. She was the bridesmaid, after all.

Some sort of relaxation music drifted from the window, accompanying the muted *shoosh-boom* of the breakers on the beach. He slowed his steps, breathing in the calming fragrant salt air and honeysuckle, and ordered himself to simmer down.

The peal of the door chime accompanied by a sharp rapping on her front door jerked Emma from her work. She refocused, feeling as if she was coming out of a deep-sleep cave. She checked her watch. Blinked. *Oh, no.* She'd assured Stella she'd be right along when the family had left nearly half an hour ago.

Which officially made her the World's Worst Bridesmaid.

She stretched muscles cramped from being in one position too long and assured herself her lapse *wasn't* because her subconscious mind was telling her she didn't want to see Jake. She would *not* let him and that crazy moment yesterday when their eyes had met and the whole world seemed to fade into nothing affect her life. In any way.

Rap, rap, rap.

'Okay, okay,' she murmured. She slipped the order of tiny stacked soap flowers she'd been wrapping back into its container and called, 'Coming!'

Running her hands down the sides of her oversized lab coat, she hurried to the door, swung it open. 'I…'

The man's super-sized silhouette filled the doorway, blocking what was left of the twilight and obscuring his features, but she knew instantly who he was by the way her heart bounded up into her throat.

'Jake.' She felt breathless, as if she'd just scaled the Harbour Bridge. Ridiculous. Scowling, she flicked on the foyer light. She tried not to admire the view, she really did, but her eyes ate up his dark good-looks like a woman too long on a blond boy diet.

Tonight he wore tailored dark trousers and a chocolate-coloured shirt open at the neck. Hair the colour of aged whisky lifted ever so slightly in the salty breeze.

'So here you are.' His tone was brusque, those black-coffee eyes focused sharply on hers.

'Yes, here I am,' she said, trying to ignore the hot flush seeing him had brought on and reminding herself where she'd seen him last. The flashback to the strip club made her feel like a gauche schoolgirl and it should not. But she was the one at fault tonight—and the reason he was standing in her doorway.

She gave him a careless smile, determined not to let yesterday spoil this evening. For Stella's sake. 'And running late,' she rushed on. 'I assume that's why you're here?' *Why else?*

One eyebrow rose and she knew he wasn't impressed. 'You had some people concerned.' He said it as if he didn't count himself amongst those people—where had yesterday's twinkle gone?—while he stepped inside and scanned the dining room table covered in the hand-made goat's milk soaps she'd been working on.

'You weren't answering your phone.' His gaze swung back to hers again. 'Not handy when people are trying to contact you.'

Her smile dropped to her feet. Was that *censure* in his voice? 'This from the guy who was too busy at his *other business* to answer his own mobile yesterday?' she shot back. 'You do realise I had to pry the info as to your whereabouts from your PA?'

He nodded, his eyes not flinching from hers. 'So she told me. I apologise for the inconvenience, and for any embarrassment I caused you.'

Emma drew in a deep breath. 'Okay.' She forced her mature self to put yesterday's incident to the back of her mind for now. 'As for me, I have no legitimate excuse for forgetting the time, so it's my turn to apologise that you had to be the one to come and get me.' She tried a smile.

He nodded, his dark eyes warmed, and his whole demeanour mellowed like a languid Sunday afternoon. 'Apology accepted.' He leaned down and brushed her cheek with firm lips, and she caught a whiff of subtle yet sexy aftershave before he straightened up again.

Whoa. Yesterday's tingle was back with a vengeance, running through her entire system at double the voltage. 'So…um…I'll just go…' Feeling off-centre, she backed away, ostensibly towards the tiny area sectioned off by a curtain which she used as a bedroom, but he didn't take the hint and leave. 'Look, you go on ahead. I'll be ready in a jiff and it's only a ten-minute drive to the restaurant.'

He shrugged, stuck his hands in his trouser pockets. 'I'm here now.'

Slipping off her flats, she glanced about for her heels. But her eyes seemed drawn to him as if they were on strings. He dressed like a million bucks these days. Still, those threadbare jeans he'd worn way back when had fuelled more teenage fantasies than she cared to remember. She watched him wander towards her table of supplies. With his hands in his pockets, drawing his trousers tight across that firm, cute butt…

No. Sleazy club-owner. Dragging her eyes away, she scoured the floor for her shoes. 'There's really no need to wait…'

'I'm waiting. End of story.' She heard the crinkle of cellophane as he examined her orders. 'Your hobby's still making you some pocket money, then?'

Irritation stiffened her shoulders. She glared at him. 'It's *not* just a hobby, and it's never been about the money.' *Unlike others who shall remain Nameless.* Exhaling sharply through her nose, she swiped up a black stiletto and slipped it on. 'I have to wonder why it is that helping people with skin allergies seems to you to be a waste of time.'

'I never sa—'

'Why don't you go while I…?' *Calm down.* 'Find my other shoe.'

'So uptight.' He tsked. 'You really need to get out more, Em. Always was too much work and not enough play with you.' He scooped her shoe from beneath a chair and tossed it to her. 'Maybe the wedding'll help things along.'

She caught it one-handed, dropped it in front of her with a clatter and stepped into it, then bent to do up the straps. She'd had it with people telling her how to live her life. Get out more? She let out a huff. She had familial obligations. Had she told him what she thought of the way he was living *his* life nowadays? No.

She finished fastening her shoes and straightened, pushed at the hair that had fallen over her eyes. Forget his uninformed opinion. Forget him, period. She had her *un*-fabulous job at the insurance call centre—but it paid the bills—and she had just finished her Diploma in Natural Health. And if she chose to fill her leisure hours working on ways to help people use natural products rather than the dangerous chemicals contained in other products these days, it was nobody's business but hers.

'So how's…what was her name…? Sherry?' she asked with enough sweetness to decay several teeth as she slipped open the top button of her lab coat. 'Will she be missing you this evening?'

His brows rose. 'Who?'

'The one…' *draped all over you* '…at Stella's engagement party. Stella mentioned her name,' she hurried on, in case he thought she'd actually asked. Which she had. But he didn't need to know that.

'Ah…You mean Brandy.'

She shrugged. 'Brandy. Sherry. She looked like more of a *Candy* to me.' With her suck-my-face-off lips and over-generous cleavage. And everything else Emma was lacking. 'You didn't say hello and introduce us. Was that because she was one of your *exotic dancers?*'

'You and your date left as we arrived. Was that just a curious coincidence?'

Jake watched her cheeks flush guiltily and felt an instant stab of arousal. Hell. He kept his expression neutral, but something was happening here. And the hot little fantasy he'd had last night about what she'd been wearing beneath that red coat yesterday wasn't helping.

And now she was undoing the second button of that lab coat, revealing a pair of sexy collarbones and putting in-appropriate ideas into his head.

He ground his teeth together as images of black lace and feminine flesh flashed through his mind. 'Are you going to get ready or what?' The demand came out lower and rougher than he'd have liked. Then he held his breath as she shrugged out of the coat, tossed it over the couch.

'I'm ready already.' She flashed him a cool look. 'I use the coat to protect my clothes when I'm working.'

His gaze snagged on her outfit—a short black dress shot through with bronze, hugging her slender curves to perfection. He swallowed. The legs. How come he'd never noticed how long her legs were? How toned and tanned? He did *not* imagine how they'd feel locked around his waist.

Cool it. He deliberately relaxed tense muscles. He'd wait outside, get some air.

But before he could move she picked up an embroidered purse from the couch and walked to the front door. 'Shall we go?'

He walked ahead, opened the door. 'We'll take my car.'

'I'm taking my own car, thanks.' She locked the door behind them, then headed towards the hatchback, her heels tapping a fast rhythm on the concrete.

He pressed his remote and the locks clicked open. 'Hard to get a parking space anywhere this time of night,' he advised. 'And we—make that *you*—are running late already. Stella and Ryan are waiting.'

Swinging her door open, she glanced back at him. 'Better get a move on, then.'

He started to go after her, then changed his mind. She was in a dangerous mood, and he was just riled enough to take her on. And it might end… He didn't want to think about how it might end. Because he had a feeling that anything with Emma would need to be very slow and very, *very* thorough. If you could find your way through those thorns, that was. 'I'll see you there.'

She clicked her seat belt on, turned the ignition and revved the engine. 'Ten minutes.'

Emma's stomach jittered. Her pulse raced. Trouble. She'd seen more than enough of it in Jake's hot brown eyes. As if she was performing some sort of striptease. She'd not given it a thought when she'd peeled off her lab coat. But he had. *Sheesh.* She scoffed to herself. As if he'd give her less than average body a second look when he was surrounded by all those Brandies and Candies and brazen beauties at the Pink Mango.

Flicking a glance at her rearview mirror she caught the glare of his headlights. She deliberately slowed her speed, hoping he'd overtake, but he seemed content—or irritated enough—to cruise along behind her. She could feel his eyes boring into the back of her head.

She let out a shaky sigh and drew a deep, slow breath to steady herself. Easier to blame him than to admit to that old attraction—because no way was Jake the Rake the kind of man she wanted to get involved with on an intimate level.

She accelerated recklessly through a yellow light, Jake hot on her heels. She wasn't herself tonight. Wrong. She hadn't been herself since she'd come face to face with Jake in his dingy office yesterday.

Even as a teenager he'd always made her feel...different. Self-conscious. Tingly. Uncomfortably aware of her feminine bits.

Her fingers clenched tighter on the steering wheel. She needed to get herself under control. She didn't figure in his life at all, nor he in hers. And tonight wasn't about her or him or even *them*; it was about Stella and Ryan.

She tensed as the well-lit upscale restaurant came into view, and glanced in the mirror again just in time to see Jake's car glide into a parking space she'd been too distracted to notice right outside the restaurant.

Oh, for heaven's sake, this was ridiculous. The restaurant was on a corner and she stopped at a red light, tapping impatient fingers on the dashboard. Seriously, if it wasn't Stella's night she'd turn around and go home, pull the covers over her head and not surface till Christmas—

The thump on the car's roof nearly had her foot slipping off the brake as Jake climbed in beside her. 'Don't you know better than to leave your passenger door unlocked when you're driving alone at night?'

She hated his smug look and lazy tone and looked away quickly. 'Don't you know better than to scare a person half to death when they're behind the wheel?'

'Light's green.'

She clenched her teeth, pretending that she hadn't noticed his woodsy aftershave wafting towards her, and crossed the intersection. 'What are you doing here? There's no sense in both of us being late.' She saw a car pulling out ahead, remembered at the last second to check her rear vision and slammed on the brakes.

'We'll walk in together, *Scarlett*.'

'Don't remind me,' she muttered. She slid the car into the parking spot, yanked the key from the ignition, jumped out and locked her door before he'd even undone his seat belt.

Jake took his time getting out, watching her walk around the car's bonnet to the footpath. Not looking at him. No trace of the blue-eyed poppy tonight, he thought, locking his own door. She was as prickly as a blackberry bush.

The pedestrian light turned green. She left the kerb and he fell into step beside her. 'If we're going to pull this wedding business off, we need to be seen to be getting along.'

She jerked to a stop outside the restaurant. 'Fine.'

Catching her by her slender shoulders, he turned her to face him, noticed her stiffen at the skin-on-skin contact. 'We'll need to have a conversation about that at some point.'

'There's nothing to talk about.'

Light from the window spilled over her face. Wide eyes stared up at him, violet in the yellow glow. He slid his hands down her bare arms, felt her shiver beneath his palms and raised a brow. 'Nothing?'

'Nothing.' She rubbed her palms together, her gaze flicking away. 'It's chilly. I should've brought a jacket. I left it on the bed…'

No, he thought, she'd been distracted. Grinning, he let her go. 'Lighten up, Em, and give yourself permission to enjoy an evening out for once.'

CHAPTER THREE

WITH a light hand at her back, Jake ushered Emma into the upstairs restaurant. Exotic Eastern tapestries lined the burgundy walls. On the far side, through double glass doors was a narrow balcony crowded with palms. Dreamy Eastern music played softly in the background. The tempting aromas of Indian cuisine greeted them as they made their way towards the round family table already covered in a variety of spicy smelling dishes.

'Apologies, everyone.' Jake nodded to the happy couple. 'Glad to see you've already started.'

Emma murmured her own apologies to Stella while Ryan spooned rice into two empty bowls and passed them across the table. 'We wondered whether you two had decided to play hooky.'

'We thought about it—didn't we, Em?' Jake grinned, enjoying her appalled expression, then turned to Ryan's father.

Gil Clifton, a stocky man with wiry red hair and always a genuine smile, rose and shook hands. 'Good to see you again, Jake.'

'And you. We must get around to that tennis match.'

'Any time. Just give us a call and drop by.'

'I'll do that.'

Gil's smile faded. 'I was sorry to hear about your father. If there's anything I can do…'

The mention of the old man left nothing but a bitter taste in Jake's mouth and an emptiness in his soul that he'd come to terms with years ago. As far as he was concerned Gil and Julie Clifton were the only adult support he'd ever needed. 'Got it covered, thanks, Gil.'

He kissed Julie's cheek. 'How's the mother of the groom holding up?'

'Getting excited. And, to echo Gil's words, if you want to drop by and chat…you're always welcome.'

If Jake was ever to be lost for words now was that time. Ryan's family were the only people who knew about his dysfunctional childhood, and now the whole table knew about Earl. He forced a smile. 'Thanks.'

Emma watched Julie give Jake's arm a sympathetic squeeze. It occurred to her how little she really knew of his background beyond the fact he was Ryan's mate.

'So how's business?' Gil asked as Jake moved to the two empty chairs.

'Busy as usual. Evening, Bernice.'

'Jake.' Emma's mother acknowledged him coolly, then turned the same stony gaze on Emma. 'Thank you for collecting my unpunctual daughter.'

Emma reminded herself she was Teflon coated where her mother's barbs were concerned. The others resumed their conversations while she took the empty seat that Jake pulled out beside her mother and whispered, 'Sorry, Mum.'

'Have to admire our Emma's work ethic, though,' Jake remarked as he sat down beside her. 'It's not easy juggling two jobs.'

'Two jobs?' Bernice bit off the words. 'When one's a waste of time, I—'

'Mum.' Emma counted to ten while she reached for her

table napkin and smoothed it over her lap. 'How are you enjoying the food?'

Bernice stabbed at a cherry tomato on her plate. 'You need two *proper* jobs to be able to afford a dress like that.'

Jake smiled at Bernice on Emma's other side. 'And it's worth every cent. She looks sensational, don't you think? Wine, Em?'

'No, thank you. Driving.' She acknowledged Jake's support with a quick nod and reached for the glass of water in front of her. She took several swallows to compose herself before she said, 'I bought it at Second Hand Rose, Mum. That little recycle boutique on the esplanade.'

When her mother didn't reply, Emma turned to Jake. 'I didn't know about your father,' she murmured as other conversation flowed around the table. 'I'm sorry.'

He didn't look at her. 'Don't be.' He tossed back his drink, set his glass on the table with a firm *thunk* and turned his attention to something Ryan was saying on his other side.

Ouch. Emma reached for the nearest dish, a mixed vegetable curry, and ladled some onto her plate. He didn't want to talk about his father—fine. But there was a mountain of pain and anger there, and... She paused, spoon in midair. *And what, Emma?*

He clearly wasn't going to talk about it. He didn't *want* to talk about it—not with her at any rate—and she had no business pursuing it. It wasn't as if they were close or anything.

A moment later Jake turned to her again. 'I was abrupt. I shouldn't have been.'

An apology. Of sorts. 'It must be a tough time, no matter how you and he...' The right words eluded her so she reached for the nearest platter instead. 'Samosa?'

'Thanks.' He took one, put it on the side of his plate.

'I've been thinking about you, Emma.' He leaned ever so slightly her way, with a hint of seduction in the return of that suave tone.

She could feel the heat bleed into her cheeks. 'I don't—'

'Have you considered selling your supplies over the internet?' He broke off a piece of naan bread. 'Could be a profitable business for you. You never know—you might be able to give up your day job eventually.'

'I don't want to give up my day job.' *I'm not a risk-taker. Mum depends on me financially. I can't afford to fail.*

'I could help you with your business plan,' he continued, as if she'd never spoken. He lowered that sexy voice. 'You only have to ask.'

His silky words wrapped around her like a gloved hand and an exquisite shiver scuttled down her spine. She could imagine asking him…lots of things. She wondered if his sudden interest and diversionary tactics had anything to do with taking the focus off his own family problems. 'I don't have time to waste on the computer, and I told you already it's not about the money.' *Business plan? What business plan?*

'Lacking computer confidence isn't something to be embarrassed about.'

'I'm n—' With a roll of her eyes she decided her protest was wasted—men like Jake were always right—and topped up her curry with a broccoli floret. 'I'm flat out supplying the local stores. I don't need to be online.'

'It would make it easier. And if your products are so popular why wouldn't you want to see where they take you?'

She would—oh, she *so* would. Her little cottage business was her passion, but technology was so not her; she wouldn't know where to start with a website, and her meagre income—which went straight into the household budget—didn't allow her to gamble on such a luxury. 'As I said, there's no time.'

'Maybe you need to change your priorities. Or maybe you're afraid to take that chance?' He eyed her astutely as he broke off more bread. 'The offer's always open if you change your mind.'

Was she so easy to read? An hour or so with Jake and he saw it already. Her fear of failure. Of taking that step into the unknown. He was the last person she'd be going to for help; she felt vulnerable enough around him as it was. 'Thank you, I'll keep it in mind.'

Over the next hour the meal was punctuated with great food, toasts to the bride and groom, speeches and recollections of fond memories.

Jake watched on, feeling oddly detached from the whole family and the getting-married scenario. What motivated sane, rational people to chain themselves to another human being for the term of their natural lives? In the end someone always ended up abandoning the other, along with any kids unlucky enough to be caught up in it.

Then Emma excused herself to go to the ladies' room and Julie claimed Bernice's attention with wedding talk. He breathed a sigh of relief that for now he wasn't included in the conversation.

A moment later he saw Emma on her way back and watched, admiring her svelte figure and the way her hips undulated as she walked. Nice. Last night's fantasy flashed back and a punch of lust ricocheted through his body. She'd been fire and ice yesterday at the club, and he couldn't help wondering how it might translate to the bedroom.

He saw her come to an abrupt halt as a newly arrived couple cut across her path. His eyes narrowed. Wasn't that…? Yep. Wayne whoever-he-was. Jake watched on with interest as Wayne's dinner partner hugged his arm a moment then walked to the ladies', leaving Emma and Surfer Boy facing each other.

More like facing off, Jake thought, studying their body language. Even from a distance he could see that Emma's eyes had widened, that her face had gone pale and that Surfer Boy was trying to talk himself out of a sticky situation fast. Emma spoke through tight lips and shook her head. Then, turning abruptly, she headed straight for the balcony.

Uh-oh, he thought, *trouble in paradise?*

Emma's whole body burned with embarrassment as she hurried for the nearest sanctuary. She pushed blindly through the glass doors and took in a deep gulp of the cooler air.

He'd had the nerve to introduce the girl. *His fiancée.* Rani—a dusky beauty, heavy on the gold jewellery—had flashed a brand-new sparkle on the third finger of her left hand and said they'd been seeing each other for *over a year.*

While Emma and Wayne had been seeing each other. *Sleeping* with each other.

The bastard.

He'd broken it off with Emma only a month ago. Said it wasn't working for him. No mention then of a fiancée. Obviously this Rani girl had what it took to keep a man interested.

The worst part was that Emma had let her guard down with him. She'd done what she'd sworn she'd never do— she'd fallen for him big time.

Shielded by palm fronds, she leaned over the railing and stared at the traffic below. But she wasn't seeing it—she was too busy trying to patch up the barely healed scars and a bunch of black emotions, like her own stupid gull-ibility. She'd been used. Deceived. Lied to—

'Emma.'

She jumped at the sound of Jake's voice behind her. Embarrassment fired up again. He must have seen the exchange. No point pretending it hadn't happened. 'Hi.' She ran a palm frond through her stiff fingers. 'I was just talking to an ex.'

'A recent ex, by the look of things.' Warm hands cupped her shoulders and turned her towards him. He lifted her chin with a finger, and his eyes told her he knew a lot more than she wanted him to. 'Should I be sorry?'

She shook her head. 'I'm not very good company right now.' Shrugging off the intimacy of his touch, she looked down at the street again, at the neon signs that lit the res-taurants and cafés.

'You didn't answer the question, Em,' he said softly. 'But, if you ask me, I'd say he's not worth being sorry over.'

'Damn right, he's not. That was his *fiancée.* According to her, they've been together over a year.'

'Hmm. I see.'

'Unfortunately for me, I didn't.' She stared at the street. 'We were both busy with work and after-hours com-mitments, but we always spent Friday nights together.' Frowning, she murmured, 'I wonder how he explained that to her?'

'Friday nights?' There was a beat of silence, then he asked, 'You had, like, a regular slot for him, then?'

She watched a couple strolling arm in arm below them and felt an acute pang of loss. 'We had an understanding.'

'He *understood* that you scheduled him into your work-ing life like some sort of beauty session?'

Her skin prickled. Wayne had actually been the one doing the *scheduling,* and Emma had been so head over heels, so desperate to be with him, she'd gone along with whatever he'd asked. 'He had a busy schedule too.' Obviously. 'But Friday night was ours. And he was cheating all along.'

Why the hell was she telling Jake this? Of all people. She turned to him, dragged up a half-smile from somewhere. 'I'm fine. I was over it weeks ago.'

'That's the way.' He smiled, all easy sympathy, and gave her hand a quick pat. 'The trick is not to take these things too seriously.'

These things? Being in love was just one of *these things?* 'And you'd be the expert at that particular trick, wouldn't you?' She and Wayne had had an understanding. He'd betrayed her and *that was serious.*

To her surprise, he spoke sharply. 'Contrary to what you may think, I don't cheat.'

'Because you're not with a woman long enough.' As if *she* would know his modus operandi these days…she wasn't exactly a social butterfly. She looked up and met Jake's eyes—dark, intense, like Turkish coffee. 'Sorry.' She shrugged. 'It's just that you're here, you're male, and right now I want to punch something. Or someone.' Her gaze flicked down to the street. 'Nothing personal.'

He shoved his hands in his pockets. 'Emma, yesterday—'

'You live your way, I live mine.' She waved him off. 'We're not teenagers any more.'

But was she living her life her way? she wondered as she paced past the balcony's foliage and back. Or was she living for other people?

After her father had died, leaving them virtually penniless, Emma had spent years working menial jobs after school so that they wouldn't have to sell her maternal grandmother's home, and then had supported herself through her studies. Her mother had been diagnosed with clinical depression soon after their father's death, and Stella had taken on the role of main carer, but Emma had been the one with the ultimate financial responsibility.

She didn't mind giving up her time or her money, but her mother was recovered now and Emma's sacrifices went unacknowledged and unappreciated.

And now she'd discovered the man she'd loved had been cheating on her for God knew how long, and in Jake's opinion it was because she was so focused on her work.

But Jake knew nothing about it, and she intended for it to stay that way. It did *not* excuse Wayne. Even the fact that the girl was more exotic than she was, more voluptuous… more everything…was no excuse. She was tempted to run downstairs and tell him what she thought of him, let Rani in on his dirty little secret—except she never wanted to see him again and she'd only make herself look like a fool. 'If nothing else, I expect honesty in a relationship.'

'You call a regular Friday night bonk a *relationship?*' he said.

She met his stare with a defiant stare of her own. 'It suited us.'

'It suited *you.*'

She bit her lip to stop unwanted words from spilling out. 'I thought what we had was what he wanted too.'

'Yeah, I'm sure it was.'

His dry comment riled her further. She rubbed the chill from her arms while inside her the anger and hurt and humiliation burned bright and strong. Better him thinking she was an idiot than knowing the embarrassing truth— that she was a naïve, gullible idiot.

'Sometimes I get so damn tired of doing what everyone else wants. What other people expect…' She trailed off when she saw Wayne and Rani outside an Italian restaurant on the street below. While his *fiancée* studied the menu in the window he glanced up and met Emma's eyes.

Renewed outrage surged through the other emotions in a dark wave. She refused to step back, refused to be the one to break eye contact. How dared he? Their weekly love-in had been a lie. They'd been seeing each other for months and the whole time he'd been deceiving her.

Making a fool of her.

In an uncharacteristic move, she made a rude hand gesture…and it felt good. Especially when Wayne looked away first. She spun away towards Jake, finding an oddly reassuring comfort in his presence. 'And sometimes I just want to live my own life and to hell with everything and everyone.'

'So start now, Em,' he said, his voice gentle yet firm. 'Change your life. Do what you want for a change.'

She stared into those dark eyes holding hers. What *did* she want?

All she saw was Jake.

Every rational thought flew away. Every drop of sense drained out of her as she stepped nearer to him, her eyes only leaving his to drift to his mouth.

What I want…

Before she could warn herself that this was a Really Bad Idea, she launched forward, cupped his jaw between her hands and plastered her lips to his.

Her heart gave a single hard jolt, and a little voice whispered, *This is what I've been waiting for.* The sizzle zapped all the way to her toes and back again before frustration and fury liquefied into heat and hunger. She flung herself into the moment, indulging her senses. The warmth of his mouth against hers was a counterfoil for his cool, refreshing scent—like moss on a pristine forest floor.

Caught off guard, Jake rocked back on his heels before

steadying himself, and her, his hands finding purchase on the smooth slope of her hips as he kissed her back.

Emma. Her taste—new and unforgettably sweet. The fragrance of soap and shampoo and woman all wrapped up in the texture of skin-warmed silk beneath his fingers.

She was a rising tornado of emotion and needs, and it whipped around the edges of his own darker desires. The word *complication* lurked somewhere at the back of his mind. He shrugged it away and instead, sliding his palms around to her back, hauled her closer and settled in to savour more of the exquisite sensations battering him.

'Ohh…' The sound was exhaled on a strangled gasp as firm hands pushed at his chest. She jerked out of his hold, eyes wide. 'I didn't… That was…'

'Nice,' he finished for her. His hormone-ravished body protested the gross understatement even as he knew she was just using him to get back at the drivelling idiot probably still watching the performance from the other side of the street.

As quickly as it had blown in the whirlwind subsided leaving only a tantalising whisper as she stared up at him, rolled her lips between her teeth and said, 'I don't know why I…did that.'

'You were upset. I was here.' Enjoying the way her eyes reflected her conflict, he couldn't help but grin. 'Have to tell you it wins hands down over the punch you threatened to dole out earlier.'

'I…need to see if Mum's ready to go home.'

'Emma.' He lifted a hand, dropped it when she edged farther away. 'Don't beat yourself up. It was just a kiss. And I'm sure Wayne got the message.'

She flinched as if he'd hit her. '*He* wasn't the… He wasn't look— I was… Oh, forget it.'

And in the light filtering through from the restaurant

he glimpsed twin spots of colour flag her cheeks before
she whirled around and made a dash to the door.

Shoving his hands into his pockets, he leaned a hip
against the railing while he waited for his body's horny
reaction to subside. *You kiss me like that, honey, I ain't
gonna forget.*

It was too bad she'd come to her senses so quickly. He
didn't mind being used when it came in the form of a beautiful woman in distress—particularly when the woman
had seemed oblivious that she *had,* in fact, used him. He
looked down at the street. No sign of the scumbag.

He could still smell Emma; the fresh, untainted fragrance lingered in the air, on his clothes. The flavour of
that one luscious kiss still danced on his tastebuds. The
surprise of it—of *her*—like the first green sprout emerging from the carnage of a bushfire, still vibrated along his
bones. She'd reacted without thinking for a hot and heavy
moment there, and he'd enjoyed every second.

So had she.

And he wasn't going to let her forget either. Her weekly
love-in arrangement proved she did casual. And she expected honesty from her lover. They had something in
common on both counts.

He watched her walk towards a group who were preparing to leave and smiled to himself. The upcoming wedding weekend was looking better and better.

Emma gulped in a calming breath, drew herself tall, and
walked unsteadily towards her table, trying not to remember she'd just kissed Jake Carmody senseless. Correction:
she was the one who was senseless. The dinner left-overs
had been cleared away. Only a rumpled and food stained
red tablecloth remained. And a few curious faces were
aimed her way.

'Emma...' Stella trailed off, her gaze sliding over Emma's shoulder.

The back of Emma's neck warmed. Her cheeks scorched. 'Um...sorry.' Was it possible to speak more than one word at a time? She waved a hand in front of her face. 'Needed some air.'

'We were starting to wonder whether you two had slipped away without—'

'Jake and I were just catching up.' She collected her purse. 'Mum, are you ready to leave? I've got some work to do before I go to bed.' She didn't wait for an answer, moving around the table saying her goodnights.

'Can I get a lift with you?' Stella reached for her own bag. 'Ryan's taking his parents home, and I want a couple of early nights this week.'

'Sure.' Emma steered clear of Jake, muttering a quick goodnight without looking at him, and from a safe distance on the other side of the table, then headed for the stairs.

'You okay, Em?' Stella asked beside her as they drove home. 'You're awfully quiet.'

'Wayne came into the restaurant while we were there,' she said, her voice tightening. 'With his fiancée.'

'Oh. Oh, Em. I'm sorry. You guys split up—what?— only a month ago?'

'What did you expect?' her mother piped up from the back seat. 'If you mixed with the right people like your sister, instead of hiding away in that studio night after night, y—'

'I'm not hiding.' Emma sighed inwardly. Stella had nursed their mother, then fallen in love with a wealthy man; in Bernice Byrne's eyes her younger daughter could do no wrong. 'I enjoy what I do, Mum.'

'Like you enjoyed cleaning other people's toilets and

stocking supermarket shelves after school too, I remember. Just another excuse not to meet people.'

Emma pressed her lips together to stop the angry words from rushing out. *Yeah, Mum? Where would we be if I hadn't? In a rented bedsit on the wrong side of town. Not in Gran's home, that's for sure.*

'Mum, that's not fair.' Stella spoke sharply.

'It's not, Stella. But then, life's not always fair—right, Mum?' Emma glanced at her mother in the rearview mirror. 'And sometimes it makes us hurt and lash out and say things we shouldn't. So I forgive you. You're not sorry about Wayne, Stella, and neither am I. And I don't want to talk about it. *Him.*'

'No, you'd rather kiss that good-for-nothing Jake Carmody behind the palms like some floozie,' her mother muttered.

Emma jolted, her whole body burning with the memory. And her mother, of all people, had obviously seen the entire catastrophe. Something close to rebellion simmered inside her and made her say, 'Jake's hardly a good-for-nothing, Mum—he has a well-established practice in business law.' She couldn't help feeling a sense of indignation on his behalf.

The strip club aside, she knew enough about Jake to know he'd worked hard all those years ago, taking jobs where he could get them to pay his way through uni.

Whereas Ryan came from old money. He'd graduated in the sciences and held a PhD in Microbiology—all expenses paid by Daddy. Then he'd volunteered his skills in Africa for a couple of years before hooking up again with Stella.

From the corner of her eye she saw Stella shift in her seat and turn to look at her. Suddenly uncomfortable, Emma lifted a shoulder. 'What?'

'Jake *kissed* you?' she said slowly. 'Like a proper kiss?'

'Not exactly.' Emma couldn't resist a quick glance at her mum in the mirror again. 'Mum got it right. It was more like…I kissed him.' As she relived that moment something like exhilaration shot through her bloodstream. 'What about it?'

'Ooh, that's so…hmm… You and Jake?'

Emma heard the smile in her sister's voice, could almost hear her mind ticking over.

'Wouldn't it be cool if—?'

'*Not* me and Jake. You know him. Every red-blooded female in Sydney knows him. Didn't mean anything.'

'But—'

'No buts.'

'Okay. *But*… The wedding will give you two time to catch up. You liked him well enough when we were younger, I remember.'

'Yeah—in a galaxy far, far away.'

'Not that far, Em. He lives in Bondi now. Only an hour's stroll along the coast…if you feel inclined.'

'I don't. I won't.'

But she couldn't blot him from her mind when she crawled into bed that night. She *had* been looking forward to seeing Jake again, even if it was only to assure herself she was well and truly over him.

But she didn't want to catch up with a seedy strip club owner who used women for his own purposes—both for his personal satisfaction and his burgeoning bank account.

But, oh, that moment of insanity…his lips on hers, his hands tugging her against the heat of his hard, muscled body…

And it *was* insanity. She stared up at the music room's low stained ceiling and tried not to hear the thick elevated thud of her heartbeat in her ears. She could have kept it simple. A friendly few days in the company of a good-looking guy. But she'd kissed him like one of his Brandies or Candies…and she'd changed everything.

CHAPTER FOUR

STIFLING a yawn, Emma glanced at her watch and wondered if Stella's hen's party would ever end. Twelve-thirty. The male stripper had done his thing and left to raucous feminine laughter and a wildly improper proposition or two over half an hour ago. The girls were now sitting around Emma's table drinking what remained of a bottle of vodka.

Emma had sat on one glass of wine the entire evening. She needed a clear head. She still had half a dozen orders to fill when the others left.

Emma glanced at the bleary-eyed girls in various stages of intoxication as Joni poured the remains of the vodka into her glass and laid the bottle on its side on the table. 'Don't any of you girls have to work in the morning?' she asked.

'It's Friday tomorrow,' Joni said, spinning the bottle lazily between two fingers. 'Nothing gets done on a Friday anyway.'

'Well, I don't want to be a party pooper but I've got work to finish tonight.'

Karina pointed at her. 'You need to get a life, Emma Dilemma.' She downed her drink, slapped her glass on the table and slurred, 'Seriously. Your hormones must be shrivelling up with neglect. When was the last time you got laid?'

'Kar, give it a rest.' Stella shot Emma a concerned look. 'She broke up with her boyfriend a few weeks ago.'

Karina squinted at Emma through glazed green eyes. 'You had a *boyfriend?*'

Emma could see it in Karina's eyes—*How did you find the time?*—and her whole body tightened. 'He wasn't a boyfriend as such…' She picked up her glass, touched the rim against her lips. 'He was convenient. More like a bed buddy.' Even if Wayne *had* seen their relationship that way, in Emma's book bed buddies didn't cheat. When the gaggle of giggles subsided she angled her glass in Karina's direction. 'You'd be familiar with the concept of bed buddies.'

'Totally.' Karina grinned. 'Way to go, Em,' she enthused, then raised a hand. 'Okay, enough of the true confessions. We're hungry, aren't we, girls? And since you're the only sober one here, Emma Dilemma, how about being a good little bridesmaid and fetching us a burger from that shop down the road?'

'And fries,' Joni added, stuffing another chocolate in her mouth.

'I'll go to the drive-through. It's closer.'

Karina shook her head. 'Nuh-uh. We want real hamburgers with proper meat—not that cardboard stuff.'

'Yeah,' Joni agreed. 'With lashings of bacon.'

Stella leaned to the side and massaged Emma's neck a moment. 'Come on, Em. I *looove* you, sis,' she cajoled in a boozy voice, then pulled her purse from her bag. 'My treat.'

Emma pushed up. Anything for peace. 'Okay. Providing you take your orders and eat them somewhere else. I've got to work.'

'You're a good sport, Em.' Karina stood, slung an arm around Emma's neck. She patted Emma's backside, then grinned hugely. 'Off you go, now.'

* * *

'Told you they'd still be awake,' Ryan said as the limo pulled into the Byrnes' driveway.

They'd dropped off the rest of the guys from the bucks' night, but Ry had got it into his head to kiss Stella goodnight before going home, and Jake—well, he was along for the ride. It was his responsibility to ensure nothing happened to Ryan before the big day. It had nothing to do with Emma living here too.

'Not sure they'll appreciate us gatecrashing their evening.' With a few beers under his belt, Jake stretched his long legs out in front of him. He'd assured Stella he'd look out for Ryan, and he'd done a pretty good job. He glanced at the slightly worse-for-wear groom-to-be. Mostly. Then he looked down to the well-lit studio. 'What do you suppose the girls get up to on a hens' night?'

'We're about to find out.' Ryan was already fumbling with the door.

'Steady, mate. I promised Stella I'd get you home in one piece.'

'Whoa…' Ryan murmured as the limo's lights swept an arc across the driveway, whitewashing the unexpected view of a female figure half-in, half-out of a car. 'Nice arse.'

Jake blinked at the flash of leggings-clad backside poking out of the open door, then took his time to admire the slender thighs and shapely calves rising from a pair of silver stilettos. A spark of interest danced along his veins. 'Careful,' he murmured with a grin. 'You're practically a married man.'

'Doesn't mean I'm dead.'

But Jake's attention had focused on what looked like a neon sticker in the shape of a hand on the girl's backside. 'What *is* that?' He squinted. The words *Pat Me* glittered in gold. 'Don't mind if I do,' he murmured, still grinning. His grin faded. 'Isn't that Emma's car?'

'Reckon you're right.' Both men looked at each other. *'Emma?'*

They turned back to see her unfurling from the car's depths. Dropping a loose soda can into the carton on her hip, she righted herself only to freeze in the headlights like a stunned, lanky-legged gazelle.

Incredulous, Jake felt his whole body tense as he took in the view. *Hot.* Over the leggings she wore a slinky white sleeveless top with a scooped neckline, blanched in the glare and highlighting enough curves to start her own Grand Prix.

'Eyes off, buddy.' He cleared his suddenly dry throat. 'She's about to become your sister-in-law.'

But Jake wasn't honour-bound by any such restriction. Eyes still feasting on the mouthwatering sight, he unfolded himself and climbed out, leaning an elbow on the open door. Cool air hit him. He could smell burgers.

'Emma. Wow.'

He gave himself a mental kick up the backside. *Well said.* Spoken like a freaking teenager. Where the hell were his sophisticated, urbane conversational skills? But his brain didn't seem to be functioning because all his blood had drained below his belt.

She seemed to come out of her daze, eyes widening as they met his. 'You're not supposed to be here,' she said, tight-lipped, as she turned and headed for the door at a rate of knots.

'Careful…' he called. Too late—he was already moving forward as he saw her stiletto bend and her ankle crumple. He heard her swear before she landed on that watch-worthy rear end in front of him, the carton she'd been carrying landing beside her.

Ryan rescued the carton with a muffled, 'I'll get Stella,' and made his escape as Jake squatted beside her. 'Emma?' He reached for her elbows. 'Are you okay?'

Emma groaned, but not nearly as much from the pain shooting up her calf as from her spectacular fall from grace in front of *this* man. She felt Jake's hands on her, his warm breath washing over her face, and closed her eyes. 'Just let me die now.'

She heard that rich caramel chuckle of his. He had both her shoes off before she could stop him. Gentle fingers probed her ankle, and a voice laced with calm concern and a hint of amusement said, 'So this is what you girls get up to on hen nights. Ry and I were wondering.'

She started to shuffle away from him but felt her leggings snag on the rough cement. She heard a strange sound, like Velcro parting, and stopped abruptly. 'I'm okay,' she said, gritting her teeth. Or she would be if she didn't die of embarrassment first. 'Now go away.'

He moved around behind her, slid his hands beneath her arms and hauled her upright so that his body was in intimate contact with her back. His big, hot *masculine* body. Her practically naked back. And nothing but thin torn jersey between her bare bottom and his...pelvis. Liquid heat spurted into her cheeks, along her limbs and everywhere their bodies touched.

'I told you I'm fine.' She tried to shrug away from the intimate contact but he didn't budge.

'Test your weight on it,' he ordered.

Her ankle tweaked when she set it on the ground but she stifled a wince and said, 'See? Fine.'

'Yeah, I can see.'

Ryan and the girls spilled out of the studio just as Jake swept her up into his arms. In an automatic reaction she clutched at his shoulders, and for an instant of lunacy she wallowed in the strength and heat surrounding her.

Being held against Jake's chest and carried inside was like being lifted into the clouds. She gazed up at his square shadow-stubbled chin. And just above that were…those lips.

Instant tension gripped her insides and refused to let go. Had she so quickly forgotten she'd kissed those lips? And *how?* That she'd flung herself at this man in an instant of heightened emotion was going to have to live with the reminder for the rest of her life? Or until after the wedding at least.

'It's going to be okay, Stella, don't worry,' she told her sister as Jake set her on the saggy old couch. Right now she was more concerned with that ripping sound she'd heard. 'Pass me that sarong on the armchair, will you?'

'Are you chilled?' Stella said, her voice anxious. 'Do you want a blanket or something?'

'No—and stop hovering.'

Stella pulled the sarong off the chair. 'I'm not hovering.'

'Are too.' She grabbed the proffered garment. 'Thank you.'

'Um… Before I go, I should tell you that Karina…um…' She exchanged a look with Jake, who shook his head.

Emma darted a glance between the two of them. 'What?'

Stella let out a strangled sound behind her hand. 'Never mind.'

Squatting in front of Emma, Jake prodded her ankle and began issuing orders. 'Get rid of the girls, Stella. And then you might like to kiss your fiancé goodnight and send him on his way.'

Hearing their cue to leave in that no-nonsense masculine tone, the girls scuttled out with muffled giggles.

Panic rose up Emma's throat. 'No, stay, Stell. Let Jake go.' She glared at him, winding the sarong about her torso as high as possible under her arms. 'I bet he has a million things to do.'

He met Emma's eyes full-on for a few seconds, then studied her foot again. 'Some ice would be good here, Stella, before you go.'

Seconds later Stella produced a pack of frozen peas from Emma's fridge, handed it to Jake. 'I feel responsible…'

'Don't,' Emma said, tight-lipped. 'If these guys hadn't turned up everything would've been all right.'

'So this guy'll take care of it.' Easing the improvised cold pack around Emma's ankle, Jake waved her sister off. 'You have guests to see off and a fiancé to farewell. You've called the girls a taxi, right?'

Stella nodded.

'Okay, go to bed.'

'If you're sure…' Stella's eyes flicked between the two of them.

Emma couldn't decide whether there was a glint of something playful in her sister's baby blue eyes, but her voice was concerned enough when she said, 'Phone up to the house if you need anything, Em.'

Then she disappeared outside with the rest of the gang, leaving Emma alone with Jake. The voices faded and the bustling atmosphere disappeared, leaving a tension-fraught anticipation in the gaping stillness. So still that Emma could hear the nearby surf pounding the beach. The sound of her heart beating at a million miles an hour. Jake had to be able to hear it as well. Fantastic. She groaned inwardly. 'But you have to go too,' she told him. 'The limo…'

'I can call him back. He's booked and paid for till 3:00 a.m.' His voice lowered a notch. 'Unless you want me to stay longer?'

His head was bent over her foot so she couldn't see his eyes. Just the top of his glossy dark head and those impressive shoulders making the fabric of his sexy black shirt strain at the seams. Before she could tell him no, not on his life, he straightened.

'It doesn't seem to be swollen. You sure that's the only casualty?'

'Yes.' In his line of work he might see more than his fair quota of bare backsides, but he wasn't going to see hers. She squeezed her still smarting butt and trembling thighs tighter together. 'I can take care of myself.'

'It's not your cute *derrière* I'm interested in right now, Emma,' he said, and she wondered if she'd voiced her thoughts. *And what did he mean 'right now'?*

Her cheeks flamed and she pushed the frozen pack of peas away. 'I can walk.' Holding the edges of the sarong together, she rose, ignoring the glint of pain in her ankle, and took three tentative steps. 'See? Now I want to go to bed. I appreciate your concern, but I'd like it if you'd leave.'

He ignored her. 'You should rest it. You need to be fit for Saturday.' He picked her up again and moved swiftly across the room and past the privacy curtain. He set her on her bed, laid the peas against her ankle again, then placed his hands on either side of her lower legs. Looked into her eyes. 'And, remember, as best man I've got the first dance with you.'

He'd come to her rescue and allowed her to keep her dignity. And now he sounded so genuinely caring that a wry half-smile tugged at her mouth.

'With you to remind me I'm not likely to forget.' She had to admit it felt good to be pampered for once in her life,

to have someone care enough to look out for her and not
even remotely laugh at her embarrassment. She relaxed a
little. 'Thank you. I feel like a kid again. All I need is the
warm milk and honey.'

'Warm milk and honey?'

'Mum's panacea for everything. Rather, it used to be.'
Twenty years ago.

Jake knew Emma had always been a keep-to-yourself
kind of girl, whereas outgoing, fun-loving Stella had made
friends easily. He knew, too, how Emma had changed when
her father had died.

Leaning in, he watched her gorgeous eyes widen,
smelled her soft feminine scent. 'No milk and honey,
but this—' he touched his lips chastely to her forehead
'—might help.'

He heard the barely-there hitch in her breath and
drew back. His gaze dropped to her mouth and lingered.
Unglossed but luscious. So tempting to lean down and…
He felt his blood pressure spike. His good deed damn well
wasn't helping *him*.

Don't. Her lips moved but no sound came out.

'Why not?' he murmured. 'You kissed me the other
night and I can't return the favour?'

'That was…different.' Her voice was breathless and
he got the impression she'd have pressed her rigid spine
through the wall if she could.

'Yeah,' he said, recalling the firestorm which had en-
gulfed them both for one unguarded moment. 'It was.'

'It was impulsive and selfish and I used you.'

Straightening up, he looked at her eyes, almost violet
in the dim light from the single naked globe above the
bed. 'I didn't mind. And, if we're being honest here, you
didn't mind either.' He saw colour bleed into her cheeks

and patted her leg. 'Take it from me, Surfer Boy wasn't right for you.'

'And you'd know that how...?' She stared at him out of soulful eyes. 'I sure as heck don't know Jake Carmody. You work in the sex industry.' Her voice rose with disapproval. 'You *own* that...that place. So you... It follows naturally that you're not ashamed to use and exploit women—often women with no other choices—to make money. And it's just *wrong*,' she went on. 'Does—?'

'I didn't buy the strip club. I inherited the place when Earl died.'

She frowned. 'Earl? Who's Earl?'

'My father.'

'Oh...' A slow exhalation of breath accompanied the word. She curled her fingers beneath her chin. 'So...your dad owned it.'

'Not "dad." That word implies some sort of familial bond and there wasn't any.' He refused to allow regret to intrude on his life. He didn't need family. He didn't need anyone. 'And before you say I should shut it down and walk away and there'd be one less sleazy club in King's Cross I have the staff to consider. I've found a potential buyer but we're negotiating; I want to ensure a fair deal for everyone.'

'Oh. Yes. Of course. I...' She trailed off, and maybe her eyes softened, but he couldn't be sure because for once in his life he wasn't really seeing the woman in front of him.

He scratched the niggling sensation at the back of his neck that he'd learned long ago to recognise as insecurity. He hadn't felt it in years. He made his own rules, controlled his circumstances, his life. Himself. Always.

Not this time.

He clenched his jaw against the feeling that the rules

had suddenly changed and his life was veering off course. And he might have left then but for Emma's soft voice.

'Your mother...is she...?'

'She lives in South America. She doesn't keep in touch.' After nearly two decades, her abandonment still had the power to slice at his heart. He'd always made a point of not getting personally involved in other people's lives because it would involve opening up his own.

'Do you have any siblings to help? Extended family?'

'No.'

'That must be tough for you, handling everything on your own.'

He shrugged dismissively. 'I'm a tough guy.' It was baggage he'd left behind years ago and he wasn't going there. Not for anyone.

She nodded slowly and smoothed the sarong over her legs. 'Look, I'm sorry if I sounded over the top, it's just that I have very firm thoughts about men who use women for their own purposes.'

He knew she was thinking of Surfer Boy. 'Acknowledged and understood.'

'Still, I am sorry about your dad...I can see it hurt you. If you wa—'

'Okay. Let's leave it at that.'

'So...um... How did it go with the guys' night?' She didn't seem in such a hurry to kick him out now, and he didn't know whether that was a good thing or not.

'Ry may need me to remind him tomorrow that he had a good time.'

'Did it include a visit to King's Cross by any chance?'

'Every bucks' night worth its mettle has to include a stop somewhere in King's Cross.' Unfortunately. He must be the only straight guy in Sydney who didn't find striptease a turn-on.

'Well, we girls enjoyed our own private stripper right here.' With a theatrical flick of her hair she drew her knees up to her chest, tucking the edges of the sarong beneath her feet.

'And how did that go?'

'Man, he was *hot*.' The instant the words were out her hands rushed to her cheeks. 'I've never seen a guy strip... well, not that way.' She sucked in her lips. Her cheeks were pink beneath her hands.

'Am I detecting a double standard here?' He couldn't resist teasing her. 'Okay for the girls to look but not the guys?'

'Oops!' Her pearl-tipped nails moved to her lips. 'Can I say I didn't look?'

'Afraid not.' He leaned closer. 'I have to tell you, you looked hot too, last night, in that sexy little number.'

Her smile, when it appeared, was a delight to behold. 'It *was* fun dressing up and feeling attractive for a change.'

'You should try it more often.'

'Try what?' Her smile disappeared. Her hands fell away from her face. A shadow flickered in her eyes—a blue moon sinking into an inky sea—as she crossed her arms and hugged her shoulders. 'Looking attractive? Gee, thanks heaps.'

'Fun, Emma. Just try having some fun.' He was barely aware that his hands had somehow moved towards her thighs, so close he could feel the heat from her body, and barely caught himself in time.

He jerked back and away. Pushed to his feet. If he stayed he was just un-sober enough to show her something about having fun...and he didn't want to think about the consequences if he did.

Not tonight.

'Since you don't seem to need me for anything, I'm

going to see if I can catch up with Ry after all. I haven't heard the limo leave yet.' He didn't know what demon prompted him to add, 'The night's still young. Might as well enjoy my evening off...'

He winked—he *never* winked—leaving Emma staring wide-eyed at him as he lifted a hand, then turned and walked away. ''Night.'

He let himself out and headed towards the limo at the top of the drive. He needed the brisk evening air to cool his groin. So much for keeping his past where it belonged. He'd moved on, made something of himself. Until Earl had died and all the old bad had rushed back.

He didn't need Emma messing with his head, trying to make everything all right. Maybe he should just keep things as they were. Acquaintances. Casual friends.

He came to an abrupt halt. Except...now he'd tasted her on his lips, enjoyed the slippery slide of her lithe womanly body against his. Seen and felt her respond as a woman did to a man she fancied...

Friends, *hell*. It was too late for that.

CHAPTER FIVE

'DID you ever see such a view?' Emma leaned over the balcony outside the room she was sharing with Stella for the night. 'You sure know how to pick a wedding venue. It's like some god has spread a knobbly green carpet over the Grand Canyon, then sprayed it with a fine indigo mist.'

'It helps that one of Ryan's uncles owns the place,' her sister said cheerily behind her.

Nestled on the edge of the escarpment at Echo Point, in the famous Blue Mountains west of Sydney, the exclusive boutique hotel was pure luxury. The majestic view of Jamieson Valley stretched out below them, equally breathtaking. As evening approached, soft golden light coloured the sky. Inky pools were swallowing up the valley floor, and the sun's last rays hammered the streaks of exposed rock with vermilion, carving deep purple shadows between.

Stella joined Emma at the balcony's wooden rail. 'The guys won't be seeing anything like this where they are.'

'No,' Emma murmured, drawing her tracksuit jacket closer as the air chilled. The guys and Ryan's parents were spending the night at a cosy little bed and breakfast in Katoomba, a two-minute drive away. 'But I'm sure they'll find something to entertain them.' Her tone was more caustic than she'd intended.

She was still brooding over the way Jake had swaggered out of the studio last night. She couldn't stop wondering what he'd got up to afterwards. Her fingers tightened on the cool wood. He'd *winked* at her. She knew exactly what he'd got up to.

And why on earth was she tying herself up in knots over it? It was precisely the kind of behaviour that reminded her that he had been, and obviously still was, a chick magnet. And why he was such a knee-buckling, sigh-worthy *experienced* kisser...

'So, Stella.' Forcing him from her thoughts, she linked arms with her sister and guided her back to the little glass table. 'Ryan can't wait for tomorrow. He's going to make a wonderful husband, and you're going to have lots of babies and live happily ever after, the way you always dreamed.'

She picked up their Cosmopolitan cocktails and offered a toast. 'To your last night as a single woman.'

As she sipped, Emma's gaze drifted inside, through the floor-to ceiling glass doors, to the two four-poster double beds with their embroidered snowy white covers and mountains of soft lace pillows.

Ryan's parents had footed the bill for the entire wedding and the wedding party's accommodation here tomorrow night. Ryan was their only child, and for them this extravagance was a drop in the ocean.

'You're marrying money, Stell. We might have been rich too if Dad hadn't made those bad investments just before he died.'

Stella nodded. 'Yeah, Mum never got over losing her inheritance that way.'

'She never got over *Dad*.' Even now their mother was in her own beautifully appointed room down the hall, alone. 'She let him destroy her,' Emma went on. 'Even beyond the grave she's still letting him colour her life grey.'

Emma reminded herself that she wanted no part of that pain. Wayne had temporarily clouded her vision with his good looks and smooth-talking charm, but now she saw everything through the crystal-clear lens of experience. No man would ever have that power over her again.

Stella set her glass down and touched Emma's hand. 'You've kept us together all these years with a roof over our heads and I want to thank you—'

'It was my responsibility as the elder sister to keep us safely off the streets.' She shook her head. 'You looked out for Mum—I had it easy compared to you. But I wanted a career too. All you ever wanted was to find the right man and get married.'

'Yeah.' Stella sighed. Then she smiled, her face aglow with a bride's radiance. 'But now I'm marrying Ryan I'll be in a position to help out. I've already decided—'

'Stella—'

'He and I have discussed it.'

'For Mum, then. Not for me.'

Stella met her eyes. 'You don't want to give away a bit of that independence and find someone to love and share your life with some day?'

'Love? No.' Because Stella's question had unsettled her, she cupped her suddenly cold hands beneath her armpits. 'I prefer lust. Less complicated.'

'You're hurting after what happened with Wayne,' her sister said gently, 'and that's okay because—'

'I told you last night. It was lust, not love.'

'Bed buddies?' Stella murmured, then shook her head. 'I don't believe you for one minute, Em. And I don't care what you say. You *do* want love somewhere down the track when you're over the love rat. I remember when we were kids and used to talk about the men we were going to marry. Your man had to own a house by the sea, he had to love animals, 'cos Mum refused to let us have pets and he had to own a cupcake shop.'

Emma smiled at her childish fantasies. 'What about your ivory castle?'

'We're staying in one in France.' Stella hugged her drink close to her chest. 'Not ivory, but a real medieval castle with its own resident ghost.'

Emma heard the signal for an incoming text and dug her phone out of her pocket to read the screen.

'How's the view where U R? J'

She frowned as a butterfly did a single loop in her stomach. She texted back: *'Glorious.'*

Setting the phone on the table, she reached for her drink and considered switching the thing off. She needed a clear head for tomorrow, and interacting with Jake beforehand— in any way, shape or form—wouldn't do her any favours.

A moment later another text appeared. *'Did U bring work?'*

She sipped her drink and looked at her phone a moment before answering: *'Yes.'*

Seemed he wasn't put off by her one-word texts, because the next one appeared a moment later.

'Not allowed. This weekend is about having fun.'

Fun and Jake…? A shiver tingled down her spine. He was a man who definitely knew how to have fun. She texted back: *'Is she a blonde?'*

'I have a certain brunette in mind. Meet me downstairs 4 a drink.'

The shiver spread to her limbs. *'Spending evening with sister. Remember her? 2moro's bride.'* She switched her phone off, shoved it back in her pocket.

'Who are you texting?'

'Jake.' She threw Stella an accusatory glance.

'Anything wrong?'

'He asked me to meet him for a drink.' She felt Stella's gaze and looked away, out over the darkening valley and the gold-rimmed purple clouds in the distance.

'Something you're not telling me, here?' Stella asked behind her.

'No.' She had the niggling feeling she was being set up by her sister.

'Jake likes women, but he's a good guy. Nothing like the love rat. He's not into commitment right now and, as you've clearly pointed out, neither are you…so are you going?'

'Of course not.' She turned around and met her sister's scrutiny full-on. Stella had a half-smile on her lips, as if she didn't quite believe her. Emma glared back. 'This is our last night together—you and me.' And she wanted to place some orders and research some alternative suppliers on her laptop at some stage.

'Well, I'm going to have a long soak in that to-die-for spa tub.' Stella rose, collected their glasses and walked towards the door. 'I won't miss you for an hour or so if you want to change your mind.'

'Nope.' Emma followed her in. 'I've got my music to keep me company.' So much for placing orders. Right now she couldn't remember a single item she needed, and music seemed a more soothing option.

The hotel's phone rang as Emma closed the balcony's glass doors and Stella stretched out on her bed to pick up. 'This is the bride's room,' she announced, with a bounce in her voice. 'You're speaking to the bride, who's just about to enjoy her own candlelit spa bath.' She grinned over at Emma, then rolled onto her back, listening to whoever was on the other end of the phone. 'Uh-huh. In the lobby. Ten minutes. Okay.'

Emma's pulse blipped. She sat on her own bed and un-ravelled her earphones. 'No.'

'But it's Ryan.' She hugged the phone to her chest. 'The guys had Chinese take-out and he has a fortune cookie for me—isn't that sweet of him?'

'It's not sweet, Stell, it's subterfuge.' Emma lay back and closed her eyes. 'Jake put him up to this, and I'll bet you your fortune cookie that it's Jake, not Ryan, down there.'

'Please, Em. You have to go to make sure. I can't see him now before the ceremony. It's bad luck.'

'And Ryan would *know* that.'

'*Pleeease?*'

'Fine,' she huffed, and sat up, clipping her iPod to her jacket.

'She said fine,' Stella told her caller, and hung up then grinned. 'Thanks, bridesmaid.'

Emma grabbed an elastic band from the nightstand and dragged her hair back into a tight ponytail. 'Only for you, and only because it's your wedding day tomorrow. Then I'm going for a run.'

'Take your time,' she heard Stella call as Emma let her-self out of the room and headed for the stairs.

Jake disconnected with a satisfied grin. 'You don't need me for a while, do you, Ry? She said yes.'

Ryan was stretched out on the couch, checking out their honeymoon destination on his tablet PC but he glanced up as Jake pulled on a clean T-shirt. 'You're a sneaky devil.'

'Make that *smart* and sneaky.' He stuffed his wallet in his jeans. 'And your fiancée's as much to blame as me.'

'Then she's a sneaky devil too.' He tapped the screen. 'I don't know why I'm marrying her.'

Jake grinned and waggled his brows. 'Having second thoughts? It's not too late to back out, you know.'

'Ah, but the reception's paid for. Why waste good grog?'

'There's that.' His humour fading, Jake sat down on the end of the couch and studied his best mate. 'Seriously, Ry. Why the big commitment?'

Ry looked up, and Jake saw the furrows of concentration in his mate's brow smooth out and the corners of his mouth tip up. 'When you meet the woman you want to spend the rest of your life with you'll know why.'

'But *married?*' Jake mentally shuddered at the word. 'Why would you want to spend your life with one woman? Man wasn't meant to be monogamous.'

'Says who?'

'I read it in an article. Somewhere. A reputed scientific journal, if I remember right.'

'Okay, well, *this* man's monogamous.' Ry resumed tapping his screen.

'Maybe *now,*' Jake said. 'I remember when you and those twins—'

'Past history. I was at uni and Stell and I weren't seeing each other then.'

'But how do you *know* she's the one?'

Ry's finger paused. 'When I saw my children in her eyes I knew.'

Jake stared at the guy he'd thought he knew. 'Crikey, mate—break out the violins.'

Ry squinted at something on the screen, slid a finger over its surface. 'Just because you're not into the matrimonial thing doesn't mean others aren't.'

'Fair dinkum—*your children in her eyes?*'

Ry looked up, a lopsided grin on his face. 'Yeah. We want kids. A whole bunch of 'em.' His expression sobered. 'I guess the bottom line is I love Stella. For better or worse. I don't want to imagine my life without her.'

Jake didn't want to imagine a life without women either. But *one* woman for ever? Absolutely for worse. But a curious sensation gripped his chest, as if somehow Ryan had betrayed their friendship and left him standing on the outside looking in.

'So, are you going to tell me why you're playing sneaky devil?' Ry asked, his eyes focused on the screen once more.

Jake rose to hunt up the keycard for the room. 'Because the girl needs a kick up that seriously sexy backside—'

'Which I didn't notice, remember?'

'Yeah, I remember.' Something that might feel like possessiveness—if he were the type—clawed at the back of his neck. He didn't care for the sensation and rubbed it away, swiping the keycard from the bottom of his bed. 'She needs to come out of that shell she's been living in for the past however many years. There's more to life than work.'

Ry looked up, expression thoughtful. 'And you're going to be the one to show her? Careful. That's Emma you're talking about—she's not just any woman. And she's my future sister-in-law.'

'I'm aware of that,' he muttered, fighting the scowl that came from out of nowhere to lurk just beneath the surface of his skin. He planted a grin on his face and grabbed his jacket. 'Trust me.'

The moment the door shut behind him his smile dropped away, his own words echoing in his ears. Problem was, could he trust *himself*? But from the moment Emma Byrne had walked into the club in that sexy red coat, those blue eyes smoking and sparking with every challenge known to man, he'd not been able to think past getting her naked. He'd never intended acting on it—he liked his women without prickles, after all—but then there'd been that kiss at the restaurant... Sparks that hot demanded at least some sort of exploration.

He decided to walk the short distance to sample autumn's crisp mountain air. Cold. Bracing. Invigorating. Mind-numbing. Just what he needed. His breath puffed in front of him as he strode along Katoomba Street towards the girls' hotel.

After tomorrow it would never be the same between him and Ry again. He passed a warmly lit café, packed with Friday-evening diners, and hunched deeper into the warmth of his jacket. It reminded him that back in that room with Ry he'd felt…shut out. As if Ry was about to join a club Jake wasn't eligible for. Would never be eligible for.

Clenching his teeth against the chill, he crunched through a pile of autumn leaves, sending them scattering and twirling along the pavement in noisy abandon. He didn't want to join the matrimonial club.

Shut out.

His mother had shut him out of her life too. 'You look just like your father,' she'd accused her five-year-old son. Jake was reminded of that every time he looked in a mirror. She'd left her cheating husband and young look-alike child for a new life and a new marriage. Rejected him— her own flesh and blood.

And, yeah, he might be his father's spitting image— but had he inherited Earl's genes? He'd learned a lot about women in his formative years. After all, how many kids got to grow up in the back room of a strip club? With the smell of cheap perfume and sex in their cramped living arrangements. Falling asleep to carnal sounds through his tiny bedroom's paper-thin walls.

As a teenager blocking out those same sounds while trying to finish homework, because he'd known that to escape the place, to take control of his life and become a better man than his father, he needed to study.

Jake knew how to have a good time. A good time involved no strings, no stress. No emotion. Was he like his father in more ways than looks? He clenched his jaw as he turned a corner and the hotel came into view. *Shoot me now.*

He picked up his pace. Earl had used women, whereas Jake respected his partners. The women he associated with were professional career types more often than not—unlike Earl's. They were confident, intelligent and attractive, and they understood where he was coming from. He made it clear up front that he wasn't into any long-term commitment deals and they didn't expect more than he wanted to give.

It was honest, at least.

Emma was braced to see Jake, not Ryan, waiting in the lobby. So she took the three flights of stairs rather than the elevator. Deliberately slowly. Admiring the delicate crystal lighting along the hallway, the local landscape paintings on the walls as she reached the top of the ground floor. The thick black carpet emblazoned with the hotel's gold crest.

But seeing Jake standing at the base of the sweeping staircase as she descended, one bronzed hand on the newel post, dark hair gleaming beneath the magnificent black chandelier, with his jacket slung over his shoulder like some sort of designer-jeans-clad Rhett Butler...

Her hand was gliding along the silky wooden banister or her legs might have given out. She might even have sighed like Scarlett; she couldn't be sure. She was too busy shoring up her defences against those dark eyes and the heart-winning smile. Because she knew in that instant that this man could be the one with the power to undo her.

Slowing halfway down, she leaned a hip against the staircase, sucked in a badly needed breath. *Stay cool,* she told herself. *Cool and aloof and annoyed.* He thought he'd tricked her into coming but she knew better. Didn't she? She frowned to herself. She was here, after all.

Because Stella had asked her.

Right. Straightening, she resumed her descent, concentrating on not tripping over her feet, her eyes drawn to him no matter how hard she tried to look away. That sinner's smile and those darker-than-sin eyes…

'Are you feeling all right?' he asked when she reached the bottom step.

She looked at him warily. 'Why wouldn't I?'

'You looked as if you were swaying there for a second or two. I thought you were going to swoon, and then I'd have been forced to play the hero again.'

'I did not sway. Or swoon. And you are *not* my hero. I'm guessing there are no fortune cookies either.'

He grinned. 'You're guessing wrong.' He took her elbow, led her across the glittering marbled foyer. At intervals floor-to-ceiling glass columns illuminated from within threw up a clear white light. He stopped by a little coffee table with two cosy leather armchairs. 'Sit.'

She did, gratefully, sinking into the soft black leather.

He pulled two scraps of paper from his jeans pocket, checked them both, then placed one on her lap.

'This isn't a fortune cookie.'

'I have to admit Ry and I ate them. But we saved you girls the messages.'

She unrolled the little square. '"A caress is better than a career."' Where the heck had he found *that* little gem? 'Says who? *And* it would depend on who's doing the caressing.'

But her traitorous thoughts could imagine Jake's warm, wicked hands wandering over her bare skin… Lost in the fantasy for a pulse-pounding moment, she stared unsee-ingly at the paper in front of her. *For heaven's sake.*

She forced her head up, regarded him with serene in-difference. 'This isn't from a fortune cookie. You made these yourselves.'

He spread his hands on his thighs, all innocence. 'Why would I do that?'

'To get me downstairs, perhaps?'

His smile came out like sunshine on a cold day. 'You have to admit it's inventive.'

'Deceptive, more like.'

'Hey, Ry has to take some of the credit.'

She felt the smile twitch at the corner of her mouth. 'What does Stella's say?'

'"Two souls, one heart." Appropriately romantic, Ry thought.'

And Cool Hand Jake didn't, obviously. 'She'll prob-ably sleep with it under her pillow tonight.' Desperate to distance herself from his enticing woodsy scent and the thought of those coolly efficient hands on her heated body, she pulled her earphones out of her tracksuit pocket. 'Okay, now that's out of the way I'm off for a run.'

'Not so fast.' He reached over, circling her forearm in a loose grip. 'You're going to say you've got soap orders to type up or some such rubbish when you get back. Right?'

Right. If she could only remember what... The heat of his hand seemed to be blocking her ability to process simple thought. 'I—'

'To avoid me.'

She swallowed down a gasp. He was flying too close to the truth, and it threw her for a loop. 'Why would you matter th—?'

'You know it. I know it.' Cutting her off, he leaned forward, his hold tightening a fraction, his eyes boring into hers. 'Admit it.'

'Why?' Little spots of heat were breaking out all over her body.

'I matter to you.' He smiled—grinned, actually—teeth gleaming white in the light. 'How much do I matter, Emma?'

She pushed a hand over the crown of her head, her mind a jumble. 'Stop it. You're confusing me. This is the last evening I'll see my sister before she gets married. I...I'm going to spend the evening with her—a maid of honour thing.'

'Of course. And you can. In a little while.' His thumb abraded the inside of her wrist, sending tiny tingles scuttling up her arm. 'She won't mind,' he continued in that same liquid caramel tone. 'In fact I'm betting she's enjoying her soak in the spa right now.'

'It *was* you on the phone.'

'Guilty.' He grinned again, totally unrepentant. As if he pulled that kind of stunt all the time to bend women to his will. 'She's confiscated your laptop, by the way.'

'*What?*'

'Your sister agrees with me that you need time out from work.'

She gaped at him, incredulous. 'You two discussed my *needs?*' The image popped into her mind before she could call it back, along with the overly explicit, overly stressed word, and the whole calamity hung thick in the air like a sultry evening.

His eyes turned a warmer shade of dark. 'Not all of them. But we'll get to that. Stella wants you to enjoy her wedding, not be distracted by orders and schedules. She's concerned about you. And frankly—'

'What do you mean, "we'll get to that"? Get to what?'

Her voice rose on a crescendo. A couple of heads turned their way.

'This isn't the place,' he murmured, his voice all the quieter for her raised one.

Changing his grip, he pulled her up before she could mutter any sound of protest. He was so close she could feel the heat emanating from his body, could smell expensive leather jacket and freshly showered male skin.

'The place?' she echoed. 'Place for what?'

He entwined his fingers with hers. 'Why don't we take a walk and find out?'

CHAPTER SIX

EMMA blinked up at him through her eyelashes. It took her a scattered moment to realise she was still holding her earphones in her free hand and that her other hand was captured by the biggest, warmest hand it had ever come into contact with. She told herself she didn't want to be holding his hand…but who was she kidding but herself?

'Run,' she managed, pulling out of his grasp. 'I was going for a *run*.' And if she was sensible she'd keep running all the way back to Sydney.

'I'll join you.'

She glanced at his leather jacket and casual shoes, deliberately bypassing the interesting bits in between. 'You're hardly dressed for it.'

'I'll try to keep up.' *His* gaze cruised down her body like a slow boat on a meandering river, all the way to her well-worn sneakers. 'What about your ankle?'

'It's fine.' He'd be offering to carry her next, so she conceded defeat. 'Okay, we'll walk.' Stuffing her earphones back in her pocket, she accompanied him outside and onto the street.

The air had a cold bite and an invigorating eucalypt scent that called to her senses, and she breathed deep.

'I saw a little café on the way here,' he suggested.

'I didn't come to the mountains to be shut in a stuffy café with a bunch of city slickers up for the weekend.'

'Of which we're two,' he pointed out.

'I want to see the Three Sisters by night and sample some mountain air. Come on, it's a ten-minute walk to Echo Point.'

He took her hand again. 'What are we waiting for?'

They followed the hotel wall that enclosed the beautiful garden where tomorrow's ceremony would take place until it gave way to bushland fenced off from the road. Beyond, the ground fell away more than two hundred metres to the valley floor. Neither talked, but a feeling of camaraderie settled between them. Both were absorbed in the mutual appreciation of their surroundings.

The minute the famous Three Sisters rock formation came into view Emma came to an awed stop. 'Wow.' She hung back from the main vantage point where a few tourists were milling about, unwilling to share the moment with strangers.

Floodlit, the Sisters gleamed a rich gold against the black velvet backdrop, surrounding trees catching the light and providing a lacy emerald frame. The never-ending sky blazed with stars.

She sighed, drinking in the sight. 'Aren't you glad we didn't go for coffee?'

'That first glimpse always packs a punch, that's for sure.'

His voice rumbled through her body and she realised he'd let go of her hand while she'd been taking in the view and was now standing behind her, his chin on top of her head.

'Did you know the Aboriginal Dreaming story tells us there were three brothers who fell in love with three sisters from another tribe and were forbidden to marry?' She hugged her elbows, and it seemed natural to lean back into Jake's warmth.

In response, a pair of rock-solid arms slid around to the front of her waist. 'Go on. I'm sure there's more.'

'A battle ensued, and when the men tried to capture them, a tribal elder turned the maidens into stone to protect them.'

'And right there,' he drawled lazily, 'you're viewing a lesson to be heeded about the dangers of love and marriage.'

She turned within the circle of his arms. 'The sad thing is the sisters had no say in any of it.'

'But you do,' he murmured against her brow. And bent his head.

Warm breath caressed her skin and her heart began to pound in earnest. He was going to kiss her... And she wasn't in a fit state to be running anywhere.

Her legs trembled and her mind turned to mush as anticipation spun through her and she looked up. His face was so close she could feel the warmth of his skin, could see its evening shadow of stubble. He had the longest, darkest eyelashes she'd ever seen on a man. And his eyes... had she ever seen such eyes? As bottomless as the yawning chasm they'd come to view.

Then a half-moon slid from behind a cloud, bathing his perfect features in silver, as if the gods had hammered him so.

'You can tell me no.' He loosened his hold around her waist slightly. 'Right here in front of the Sisters you can exercise your free will as a modern woman. Push me away if you want. Or you can accept what we've been tiptoeing around for the past few days and kiss me.'

'Tiptoeing?' she whispered. 'I haven't—'

'And it's time it stopped.'

'Kiss you…?' Her words floated into the air on a little white puff as she looked up into his eyes. Dark and deep and direct. Had he mentioned free will? Her will had suddenly gone AWOL; she'd felt it drift out of her and hang somewhere over Jamieson Valley with the evening mist.

His gaze dropped to her mouth. Strong fingers curled around her biceps. 'And this time I'm warning you I'm not letting you go until I'm good and ready.'

The way he said it, all male attitude and arrogance, sent a shiver of excitement along her nerve-endings. Emma heard a whisper of sound issue from her throat an instant before his lips touched hers.

Then she was lost. In his taste: rich and velvety, like the world's finest chocolate. His cool mossy scent mingled with leather. The warmth of his body as he shifted her against him for a closer fit.

She should have stopped it right there, told him no—he'd given her the option. But her response was torn from her like autumn's last leaf in a storm-ravaged forest. Irrational. Irresistible. Irrevocable.

Voices ebbed and flowed in the distance but she barely heard them above the pounding of her pulse, her murmur of approval as she melted against him like butter on a barbecue grill. Her arms slid around his waist to burrow under his jacket, where he was warm and solid through the T-shirt's soft jersey.

Jake felt her resistance soften, her luscious lips grow pliant as she opened for him, giving him full access, and he plunged right in. Dark, decadent delight. Moans and murmurs. Her tongue tangled with his, velvet on satin, and her taste was as sweet as spun sugar.

Dragging her against him, he moved closer, his fingertips tracking down her spine, over the flare of her backside, where he pressed her closer so he could feel her heat.

So she could feel his rapidly growing erection butting against her.

He felt the change instantly—subtle, but sure. A tensing of muscles. A change in her stance. She didn't move away and her lips were still locked with his, but…

Breaking the kiss with a good deal of reluctance, he leaned back to look at her. They were the same age—both twenty-seven—but she looked impossibly young with her hair scraped back from her face, her eyes huge dark pools in the moonlight, her mouth plundered.

He stroked a finger over the groove that had formed between her brows. 'You're thinking too hard.'

'One of us should.' She didn't look away. Nor did the frown smooth out.

'Okay. Talk to me.'

She took a step back. 'This…thing between us is getting way too complicated.'

'Seems pretty straightforward to me. So I'm proposing a deal,' he went on before she could argue, resting his hands on her shoulders. 'This weekend neither of us talks about work.' He touched his forehead to hers. 'We don't *think* about work. We're both between partners, so we'll enjoy the wedding and each other's company…and whatever happens *happens*. No complications. One weekend, Emma.'

'One weekend.' She leaned away, her eyes clouded with conflicting emotions. 'And then what?'

'Put next week out of your mind, it's too far away.'

Come Monday they'd go their separate ways. Back to real life and working ridiculous hours. Emma and the Blue Mountains would be nothing but a warm and pretty memory.

'Think about this instead,' he said, sliding his hands down her upper arms. 'Neither of us wants to be tied down, and we both work our backsides off. We deserve some playtime.'

'Playtime?' She stared up at him, her eyes the colour of the mist-swirled mountains behind her. 'No deal. Not with you.'

'Why not? Afraid you might enjoy yourself?'

She rolled her lips together, as if to stop whatever she'd been about to say, then said, 'I just don't want to play with you, that's all.' She turned and began walking back the way they'd come.

'Liar.' Grabbing her arm, he walked around her, blocking her path until they stood face to face. 'Tell me you didn't enjoy that kiss just now.'

She studied him a moment. 'I didn't enjoy that kiss just now.'

He laughed. 'You started it. That night at the restaurant. You blew me away with your enthusiasm and got me seriously thinking about you. And me. I haven't stopped thinking about you and me—together—since.'

'I told you, that kiss was an overreaction to a particular circumstance,' she said primly. 'And what are we—kids? *"You started it",'* she muttered with a roll of her eyes, but he thought he saw a hint of humour there too.

She looked so delightful he couldn't resist—he planted a firm smacking kiss on those pouted lips then grinned. 'I'd better get you back. Stella'll be starting to think I've kidnapped you.'

Grabbing her hand, he tugged her alongside him along the path towards the hotel. The weekend had barely begun, plenty of time to convince her to change her mind.

'So. Seen any good movies lately?'

She kept up a brisk pace beside him. 'No.'

'Me neither. Stella mentioned you swim every morning, come rain or shine. Is that true?'

'Yes.'

'So...if I were to change my early-morning jog—'

'One weekend.' She jerked to a sudden halt and looked up at him. 'And whatever happens happens?'

A strand of hair had come loose and blew across her eyes. He smoothed it back, tucked it behind her ear. 'We'll take things as they come. It'll be good, I promise.'

Oh, yes, she knew. Emma stared into those beguiling eyes. 'I bet you say that to all the girls.' She couldn't believe she was having this conversation with Jake Carmody.

She resumed walking, hoping she was headed in the right direction. Everything seemed surreal. The moonlight distorting their combined shadows on the path in front of them. The sharp eucalypt fragrance of the bushland. The way her body was responding to his proximity even now.

His seductive charm really knew no bounds. No wonder women swooned and fell at his feet. She firmed her jaw. Not *this* woman. Still, she didn't have to swoon, exactly...

He was suggesting what amounted to nothing more than a weekend of sex and sin. Heat shimmied down her spine. A weekend on Pleasure Island. She had no doubt Jake could deliver, and couldn't deny the idea called to her on more than one level. But was she game enough? Why not? It wasn't a lifetime commitment, for heaven's sake.

Since her father's death eleven years ago she'd worked her butt off to make things better for them all. Jake had made it clear to her that it was past time she took something for herself. One weekend to be free and irresponsible. And this weekend, with Stella leaving home and the love rat a disappearing blot on her horizon, was it perhaps a good time to start?

They reached the hotel and she hesitated on the shallow steps out front. Her cheeks felt hot and super sensitive, as if a feather might flay away the skin.

She turned to say goodnight and met his gaze. The heat from that kiss still shimmered in his eyes, and it took all her will-power to keep from flinging herself at him and kissing him again.

Deliberately she stepped back, aware she hadn't given him an answer and just as aware they both already knew what her answer would be. She turned towards the building.

A liveried porter swept the wide glass door open with a welcoming smile and warm air swirled out. 'Good evening, madam.'

'Good evening.' She smiled back, wondering if her cheeks and lips were as pink and chapped as they felt. From the safety of distance, she turned to Jake once more. 'Till tomorrow, then.'

'Get a good night's sleep.'

His smile was pure sin. *You'll need it*—no mistaking that message in those hot dark eyes, and her heart turned a high somersault. It continued its gymnastics all the way up the three flights of stairs.

Stella was bundled in a fluffy white hotel robe on the couch, watching a TV cook-off, when she entered.

'Traitor.' But there was no sting in the word as Emma pulled out the fortune cookie note and dropped it on Stella's lap. 'For you.' Because her legs were still wobbly, she flopped down on the couch beside her.

'"Two hearts, one soul." Ooh, I've gone all gooey inside.' Smiling broadly, Stella tucked her legs up beneath her. 'What does yours say?'

She shook her head, that overly warm sensation prickling her skin. 'Never mind.'

Stella stuck out her hand, palm up. 'Come on—give.'

'Oh, for heaven's sake.' Emma dug into her pocket again, then glued her attention to the TV screen, but she wasn't seeing it. 'It's not romantic, like yours. And that's okay because I'm not a romantic like you.' She pressed a fist to her lips to stem the flow.

'"A caress is better than a career." Of course it's romantic, silly. It's telling you to take time out and enjoy… To… *Em*.'

'Where's my computer, by the way? Jake said…never mind.' Emma could feel Stella's gaze on her and jerked herself off the couch without waiting for an answer. 'I'm going to take a bath.'

'Oh. My. Lord.'

'What?' She was in the process of ripping off her tracksuit jacket but stopped at her sister's tone. 'What's wrong?'

Stella was staring at her. And pointing. 'What have you done with my sister?'

'What are you talking about?' She shrugged her shoulders. Ran a hand around her neck. 'What's he done?'

'Ha!' Stella jabbed her finger in the air again. 'I should be asking what *Jake's* done with my sister.'

'No. It's nothing. Don't you say one word to Jake or I'll—'

'*Not* nothing.' Stella craned forward, studying Emma as if she was counting her eyelashes. 'My big sister with fresh whisker burn around her mouth. And stars in her eyes. She's never had stars in her eyes. *Never.*'

'Don't be ridiculous.' Panicked, Emma swiped at her mouth, then sucked in her lips and backed away. Tugged her T-shirt over her head and threw it on her bed. 'Do you know how cold it is outside? The air… A hot bath…'

'Emma Dilemma.' Stella grinned. 'You've just had it on with best man Jake.'

'*No.* It's such a cliché to get it on with the best man. I kissed him, that's all. No. He kissed me. We kissed each other. He started it. No biggie, okay?'

Stella shook her head. 'My sister never gets flustered when she talks about a guy. *Never.*'

Emma fumbled through her suitcase. 'He's not a guy, he's Jake. And I'm not flustered. It's nothing.'

'It's something.'

She yanked her pyjamas from her overnighter and blew out a breath then turned to Stella who was watching her with her chin on the back of the sofa. 'Okay, it's something. But it's just a weekend something. Or not. I haven't decided yet.'

Stella smiled. 'You know you'll have this room all to yourself tomorrow night…?'

'Not another word.' Emma flung up a hand. 'You breathe so much as a syllable of this conversation to Jake or anyone else and I'll sabotage your wedding night.'

And, swiping up her cosmetics bag, she fled to the bathroom.

CHAPTER SEVEN

THE wedding day dawned bright and clear. And cold. Clad in her complimentary terrycloth robe, Emma took her early-morning coffee onto the balcony to admire the cotton balls of cloud that hid the valley floor. From her vantage point she could see the garden below, where even now staff were setting out chairs, toting flower arrangements, twining white ribbon and fairy lights through the trees.

A few moments later Stella stumbled out, hair wild, eyes sparkling. 'Good morning.' She leaned a shoulder against Emma's. 'It's just perfect. Isn't it perfect? Not a cloud in the sky. By afternoon it'll be warm and still sunny. Hopefully… Can you believe I'm getting married in a few hours' time?'

Emma dropped a kiss on her sister's cheek on her way back inside. 'And there's a lot to get through before that happens.' She checked her watch. 'Breakfast is due up in ten minutes. The hairdresser will be here in half an hour.'

With less than an hour to go, the bride's dressing room on the first floor was pandemonium. Underwear, costumes, flowers. A blur of fragrance and colour. Sunshine streamed through the window. Champagne and orange juice in tall flutes sat untouched on a sideboard, along with a plate of finger food.

Stella was with Beth, the wedding planner, and her two assistants—one aiming a video camera and catching the memories. The excitement, the laughter, the nerves.

In one of the full-length mirrors Emma caught a glimpse of her reflection in a strapless bustier. Crimson, with black ribbon laces at the front, it looked like something Scarlett O'Hara would have approved of. She yanked the ribbon tight between her breasts and tied it in a double knot, staring closer.

Wow. She actually had breasts today. Enhanced by the bustier's support, they spilled over the top like something out of a men's magazine. The garment pulled in her waist and flared over her hips, leaving a strip of bare belly and the tiny triangle of matching panties tantalisingly visible. A pair of sheer black stockings came to mid thigh, held up by long black suspenders.

For an instant she almost saw Jake's reflection standing behind her, his eyes smouldering as he leaned over her to dip a finger between—

The tap on her shoulder had her spinning in a panicked one-eighty. 'What?' Her breath whooshed out and her heart skipped a beat. 'Stella. Sorry. I was—'

'A million miles away.'

Not as far as that. 'I'm here. Right here.' She gave a bright smile, then forgot about her erotic meanderings as she gazed at the bride. 'Oh, my! Gorgeous.'

Stella's figure-hugging floor-length Guinevere gown was bottle-green crushed velvet. A dull gold panel insert in the bodice gleamed with tiny emerald beads, replicated on the wide belt cinching in her waist. Full-length sleeves flared wide at the wrist and fell in long soft folds. Her coronet of fresh freesias, tiny roses and featherlike greenery complemented her rich auburn hair.

'You look stunning, Stell. Radiant and stunning. I can't wait to see Lancelot's face when he gets a load of you.'

'Neither can I.' She looked down at Emma, waved a hand. 'Um…are you planning on wearing something over that? I'm sure the guys won't mind, but this is my day and I know it's selfish but I want all the attention.'

'Getting there…' With the help of Annie, one of the assistants, Emma stepped into a voluminous skirt and shimmied into the bodice. 'I told you, Stella. You should have been Scarlett, not me.'

'And I told you already, Scarlett's the brunette. She's playful and coquettish and I really, really wanted you to be that woman today. Whereas Guinevere was pale and intense and totally and unconditionally in love with Lancelot.'

'Well, you'll have that attention,' Emma said, admiring her sister. 'Ryan, not to mention the rest of the male population, won't be able to take his eyes off you.'

Annie slipped buttons into the tiny loops at the back of Emma's dress, then handed her black lace gloves and a parasol.

'Don't forget the bridal bouquet.' Emma passed Stella a simple posy of flowers to match those in her hair. She paused with her sister at the top of the wide sweeping staircase. 'We're a clash of eras, aren't we?'

'We are. But it's going to be fun. For both of us.' Stella squeezed Emma's hand. 'Thank you for helping to make it a perfect day.'

'It's not over, it's just beginning.'

The harp's crystal clear rendition of 'Greensleeves' floated on the air as they arrived at the garden's designated bride spot. At a signal from Beth, the music segued beautifully into Bach's 'Jesu, Joy of Man's Desiring.'

'You're up,' Beth murmured to Emma. 'And don't forget to *smile.*'

She'd taken but a few steps along the petal-strewn manicured lawn when she saw Jake and Ryan up ahead. She forgot about smiling. The garden might look like a fairytale. The costumed guests might look magnificent or they might be naked for all Emma knew, because her peripheral vision had disappeared.

Rhett Butler had never looked so devastating. Black suit, dove-grey waistcoat and dark mottled cravat beneath a snowy starched shirt. His eyes met hers and he smiled. A slow, sexy, come-away-with-me smile.

'*Hi,*' he mouthed.

'*Hi,*' she mouthed back, and, *Oh, help.* Her knees went weak but she seemed to be moving forward. What was wrong with her? No man had ever captivated her this way.

Deliberately freeing her gaze, she aimed her smile at Ryan instead, looking regal in a black tunic and cowled top over silver-grey leggings and black knee-high boots. The Clifton family crest was emblazoned on his tunic— she could make out a lion and a medieval helmet in the black-and-gold embroidery.

Not that he was looking at her; his eyes were for his bride, a few steps behind. As they should be. Emma wondered for a quickened heartbeat how it would feel to have someone look at her that way, with shiny unconditional love. She rejected the thought even as it formed and concentrated on keeping her smile in place, her steps smooth and measured.

Jake's eyes feasted on Emma. The deep colour complemented her lightly tanned complexion. A wide-brimmed hat shaded her face, and he couldn't quite read her eyes, so he contented himself with admiring the seductive cleavage and the way the crimson fabric hugged every delectable curve as she moved closer.

His fingers flexed in anticipation of becoming more intimately acquainted with those curves. How long would it take him to get her out of that dress? To lay her down on the grass right here in the sunshine and plunge into her while the birds sang and the cool wind blew up from the valley....

Then she moved out of his line of sight to take her place beside the bride. Probably just as well, because any longer and it might become obvious to all where his thoughts were.

He turned his attention to Ry and Stella, and watched the couple blindly promise to handcuff themselves to each other till death did them part. A life sentence, no parole. His collar itched on Ry's behalf, and he shifted his shoulders against the tight sensation inside his shirt.

They looked happy enough. But it never lasted. There were exceptions, of course. Ry's parents—Henry VIII with a fake red beard and Anne Boleyn—were holding hands, eyes moist.

He glanced at the girls' mother in her white Grecian goddess robe, looking, as always, eternally constipated. Her marriage disaster had turned her into a bitter and twisted woman. Nevertheless, she was still beautiful. He imagined Emma would look as beautiful in thirty years' time.

But he didn't want to contemplate Emma's lovely face marred with that same perpetually pinched expression, those sparkling sapphire eyes clouded with sadness.

Who in their right mind would take the marriage risk? Only those temporarily blinded by that eternal mystery they called love. Not him, thank God.

Formal photographs followed in the gardens, then on

to the decking overlooking the mountains as the sun low-ered, turning the sky golden and the valley purple.

Emma couldn't fault Jake's behaviour. He was the per-fect gentleman. The perfect Rhett. He only touched her when the photographer required him to do so. During the five-course meal he was seated next to Ryan at the top table, so conversation between them was limited, but there was a heated glance or two when the bridal couple's heads didn't block the view.

After the speeches guests chatted over music provided by a three-piece orchestra as the desserts began coming out of the kitchen. Anne Boleyn, aka the mother of the groom, made her way to the top table.

'Beautiful ceremony, my darlings. It must be your turn next, Emma.'

'Oh, I don't think so.' Emma smiled back, then lifted her champagne glass and swallowed more than she should considering her duties. 'It's not for me.'

'Ah, you just have to find the right man.'

Smile still in place, Emma set her empty glass on the table with a thunk. 'And isn't that the killer?'

'And Jake?' Ryan's mother smiled in his direction. 'When's some clever woman going to snap you up and make an honest man out of you?'

'Alas for me, fair lady.' He put his hand on his heart. 'You're already taken.'

Laughter from the bridal couple. 'You never know, Em,' Stella murmured into her ear as her new mother-in-law walked back to her chair. 'He could be closer than you think.'

'What I'm thinking is it's about time you two cut that white skyscraper.'

The guests applauded as Stella and Ryan laughed into each other's eyes and fed each other cake. Weddings,

Emma thought. They always whipped up those romantic, dreamy, nostalgic emotions. It was hard not to be caught up in the euphoria.

She deliberately veered from those too-pretty thoughts and watched Karina knock back one glass of champagne after another. Emma pursed her lips, remembering the *Pat Me* sticker she'd discovered stuck to her backside after the hens' night. She narrowed her gaze as Karina plastered herself all over one of Ryan's cousins up against a wall. Weddings also came with too much booze and indiscriminate physical contact.

But when Ryan and Stella took to the floor for the bridal waltz to the seductive beat of 'Dance Me to the End of Love', she knew her own moment of up close was imminent and her legs started to tremble.

Jake rose and held out his hand, his eyes as beguiling as the song. 'I think it's our turn.' Emma caught the undertone in his voice and her whole body thrummed with its underlying message that went way beyond the dance floor and upstairs to that big soft bed.

When he grasped her fingers to lead her into the dance space there was something…different about the contact. And in the centre of the room, when he slid his hand to her back, firm and warm and possessive, she felt as if the floor tilted beneath her feet.

They'd never danced together, and his proximity released a stream of endorphins, stimulating her senses. The throb of the music echoed through her body. His cool green aftershave filled her nostrils. The sensuous brush of his thighs against hers beneath the heavy swish of her full skirt had her breath catching in her throat.

'Sorry,' she muttered, missing a step and trying to create some space between them—she needed it to breathe, and to say, 'I'm not a very good dancer.'

'Lucky for you I am.'

She flicked him a look. 'Lucky for you I'm feeling congenial enough to let you get away with that.'

Was there *anything* in the seductive sciences he wasn't accomplished at? She sincerely doubted it as his palm rubbed a lazy circle over her back, creating a deliciously warm friction and at the same time drawing her closer and causing her to misstep—again.

'Is it the dance, or is something else distracting you, Em?'

How typically arrogant male. But she smiled into his laughing eyes. 'Do men always have sex on their minds?'

His answering grin was unrepentant. 'Pretty much.' He dipped close and lowered his voice. 'It's on your mind too.'

She dragged in a breath that smelled of fine fresh cotton and hot man and tried not to notice. 'I'm finding it hard to concentrate on the steps, that's all.'

As Ryan swept his bride past them Emma saw Stella's eyes twinkling at her and looked away quickly. Apart from the bride and groom and Ryan's parents they were the only couple on the floor. 'People are watching us.'

'And why wouldn't they? You look amazing.' The hand holding hers tightened, and his thumb whisked over hers as he leaned in so that his cheek touched her hair. So that his chest shifted against her breasts. 'You feel amazing,' he murmured into her ear. 'Forget the audience. Listen to the music.'

Forget the music. Listen to the Voice. Her head drifted towards his shoulder, the better to hear it. When other couples joined them on the dance floor he swept her towards the window with its panoramic views. Not that she was interested in any view right now except the one in front of her.

He crooned the song's lyrics about wanting to see her beauty when everyone had gone close against her ear. She nearly melted on the spot. 'You think I've changed my mind?'

'Honey, I don't even need to ask.' His hand tightened around hers and then she realised that couples were swirling around them and they were standing still. And close. That the fingers of her free hand had somehow ended up clinging to the back of his neck. That the song had changed to something more upbeat.

How long had they been standing there? How long had she been showing him exactly how she felt? That those options she'd thought she had were down to one? Somehow she managed to yank herself into the present and remember her bridesmaid duties.

She let her hand slide down the smooth fabric of his jacket, slipped the other one from his grasp. 'I need to go.'

'Are you sure?' He lifted the heavy mass of hair from her shoulder with the back of his fingers and stroked the side of her neck, then linked his arms loosely around her waist, trapping her against him. 'Because I'm kind of enjoying where we are right now.'

She felt a series of little taps track up her spine.

'How many buttons would you say this dress has?' He slipped the top one from its tiny loop. Then another.

Her breath caught and her blood fizzed through her veins like hot champagne. 'What do you think you're doing?'

He swirled a finger beneath the fabric. 'Your skin feels like warm satin. How many buttons?' he asked again.

'Twenty two.'

He muttered a soft short word under his breath.

'Is that a problem?'

His eyes burned into hers. 'I've never encountered a

problem with female clothing I couldn't solve one way or another.' And with a slow sexy grin he released her. 'Okay, you're free. For now.'

For now? But she couldn't deny the thrill of knowing he wanted her. That he was already figuring a way to get her out of her dress. That the women casting admiring glances his way were not even on his radar tonight—Emma Byrne was.

His proprietorial hand at her back manoeuvred her through the dancers as she made her way towards the bridal table. A middle aged Fred and Wilma Flintstone twirled by, a gay couple dressed as King Arthur and Merlin, a Beauty and a Beast.

'Who's the Roman warrior chatting up Bernice?'

Emma followed Jake's gaze to a nearby table and snorted a half laugh. 'He won't get far with Mum.' But to her surprise her mother smiled at something the middle-aged guy said. Then laughed. 'Amazing.' Emma smiled too. 'Maybe I should invite him around some time as a distraction when I'm fed up with her.'

'Hang on—that's Ryan's Uncle Stan from Melbourne. Divorced last year and looking good. Go, Stan.'

Emma took that moment to break away. 'I have something I need to take care of.'

Leaving the sounds of laughter and music behind, she made her way to the honeymoon suite in another wing of the hotel with a basket of rose petals. A glance at her watch told her she had half an hour before the happy couple were due to leave the party and celebrate the end of their special day.

More than enough time to catch her breath and take a moment. Letting herself in with the keycard she'd been given at Reception, Emma flicked on the light. A soft glow filled the room, glinting on the massive brass bed and lending a rich luxury to the sumptuous gold and burgundy furnishings. She leaned a shoulder against the door, drawing in air. She really needed to increase her daily workout.

Rubbish. Emma knew her lack of fitness wasn't the reason her lungs felt as if they'd shrunk two sizes. She could try telling herself her underwear was laced too tightly. The ballroom had been badly ventilated. She'd had too much of the fizzy stuff.

But there was only one reason, and thank God he was downstairs—

'Need a hand?'

That familiar seductive drawl coated the back of her neck like hot honey, causing her to jolt and drop her little basket. She drew in a ragged breath. His question, which wasn't a question at all, could only mean one thing, and it wasn't an offer to help sprinkle her rose petals over the quilt.

'Jake…' The word turned into a moan as a warm mouth bit lightly into the sensitive spot where shoulder met neck. She simply didn't have the strength or the will to pull away. 'What are you doing here?'

He soothed the tender spot with his tongue and her toes curled up. 'What do you think I'm doing here?' In one fluid move he spun her around. The door swung shut behind them and he rolled her against the wall, his hands hard and hot and heavy on her shoulders.

He didn't give her time to answer or to think. One instant she was staring into a pair of heavy-lidded dark eyes, the next her mouth was being plundered by the wickedest pair of lips this side of the Yellow Brick Road.

He lifted his mouth a fraction and his breath whispered against her lips. 'Is that clear enough?'

Perfectly. And just clear enough to have her remember where they were and what she'd come here to do. 'Are you out of your mind?' She pushed at his chest. Uselessly. 'Housekeeping could show up here any minute.'

'Then we've got a minute.' He grinned, dark eyes glinting. 'Better make the most of it.'

Excitement whipped through her as his hands rushed down, his thumbs whisking over taut nipples, the heat of his palms searing her skin through the satin as he moulded them around her waist and over her belly with murmurs of appreciation.

There was nothing of the suave, sophisticated gentleman from this afternoon except perhaps the scent of his aftershave. This man was the wickedly handsome rogue bent on seduction that she'd always known him to be. Nothing for her to do but to look into those eyes and oh-so-willingly acquiesce.

He gathered handfuls of her voluminous skirt in his fists at either side of her, creating a cool draught around her knees as he ruched the fabric higher. 'Do you want to tell me to stop?' he murmured, leaning down to sip at her collarbone.

Only to stop wasting time. A moan escaped as the tips of his fingers grazed the tops of her stockings, then came into smooth contact with naked flesh. He slid one sensuous finger beneath a suspender and up, to track along the edge of her panties.

He grinned again as he tossed her skirt up over her breasts. 'How many layers have you got on under here?'

'I don't remember…' Moisture pooled between her legs, dampening her silk knickers, and she didn't know how much longer she could remain upright.

He watched her eyes while his finger cruised closer, curling inward, between her thighs, along the lacy edge of her knickers, almost but never quite touching where she wanted him to touch her most. And the spark she saw in his gaze ignited a burn that wasn't about to be extinguished any time soon.

'Jake…Housekeeping—'

'Tell me what you like. What you want.'

The husky demand turned her mind to mush, and she arched wantonly against his hand. Forget Housekeeping. 'Anything. Everything.' Clutching her skirt, she let her spinning head fall back against the door. 'And quickly.'

He stepped between her legs, the sides of his shoes pushing her feet wider. One sharp tug. Two. The sound of fabric ripping. And she felt her knickers being whisked away from her body by impatient hands.

She trembled. She sighed. She hissed out a breath between her teeth. 'Hurry.'

'No.' His thumb found her throbbing centre. 'A job worth doing…'

'Ah, *yesss*…' A slow, sensuous glide over her swollen flesh—one touch—and the burn became a raging inferno. *So* worth doing…

How could one finger cause such utter devastation? Her eyes slid closed. Golden orbs pulsed across her vision. She felt as if she was standing on the rim of a volcano, yet she was the one about to erupt.

He touched her a second time, and she flew over the edge and into the hot and airless vortex, her inner muscles clamping around him.

She flattened her palms against the wall for balance, her breathing fast and harsh. She felt him step away on a draught of air, and opened her eyes in time to see him grin with promises yet to be fulfilled as he slipped out through the door.

CHAPTER EIGHT

Oh...My. God. Emma sucked in a much needed calming breath. If she'd had the luxury of time she'd have slid down the wall and possibly passed out for the rest of the night.

He'd touched her twice. *Twice.* That was all it had taken to bring her to the most intense orgasm of her life. And then he'd nicked off like some pirate in the night, stealing her breath and her composure and leaving her with the possibility of facing Housekeeping alone.

Out. She realised she was still clutching her skirt up to her chest and pushed it down quickly, her cheeks flaming, at the same time thanking her lucky stars that no one had turned up yet.

A hank of hair fell over one side of her face. She pushed it behind her ear. Panicked all over again, she scanned the floor for her knickers. No sign of them. Picking up her forgotten basket, she stumbled to the bed and dumped the petals in the centre, arranging them in a hasty circle. She placed the two heart-shaped soaps she'd made with Ryan's and Stella's names in gold leaf in the centre, then made her way quickly downstairs, where the couple were preparing to farewell the guests.

She didn't see Jake amongst the crowd until he appeared in the doorway ten minutes later. Their gazes clashed hotly across the room. He was the only one who knew she was naked beneath her gown and her cheeks flamed anew. She prayed he'd stay away from her for the next little while, because they both had their respective duties before the social part of the evening was over.

Neatly sidestepping as Stella threw her bouquet in Emma's direction—she wasn't falling for that old trick—she saw Jake follow the bridal couple out.

She moved among the guests, catching up with friends and relatives. She was on tenterhooks, expecting Jake to tap her on the shoulder at any moment, and she didn't know how she was going to hide the guilty pleasure from her expression.

The band was still playing and guests lingered, enjoying the music. Some danced; others gravitated towards the bar next to the lobby. A while later, when Jake still hadn't shown his face, the glow cooled, to be replaced by an anxious fluttering in the pit of her stomach. Was he coming back? Was he expecting *her* to look for *him* after his impromptu seduction?

She didn't know what game they were playing—had no idea of the rules. *Damn him.* Collecting her hat and parasol from behind the concierge's desk, she made her way towards the bar.

Jake waved Ry and Stella off and headed straight for Reception. Business taken care of there, he stopped to collect a couple of sightseeing brochures on his way to the lobby bar.

He found a comfortable armchair in the corner, from where he could see the ballroom, and signalled the waiter. He knew Emma was still in there. He'd give her some space but if she didn't materialise in ten minutes he was damn well going in there and hauling her out.

Folding the brochures, he slid them into his jacket

pocket. His fingers collided with silk. Emma's panties. He remembered her surprise, the passion in those deep blue eyes, when he'd stripped them off. The way her lips had parted on a moan of pleasure when he'd first touched that intimate flesh.

His body tightened all over again. The next time Emma writhed and moaned against him... He smiled to himself in anticipation. He had definite plans for the way their evening was going to go.

Han Solo and Princess Leia exited, with a lone cowboy in tow. No sign of Emma. He exhaled sharply through his nostrils and rechecked his watch. Was she saying a personal goodnight to everyone in the bloody ballroom?

His order arrived with a paper napkin and a bowl of peanuts. He set the unopened bottle of champagne and two glasses on the floor beside his chair and reached for his beer.

'Good evening, Rhett.'

Jake took a second or two to catch on that the sultry come-hither voice was directed at him. He glanced up to see a well-endowed woman in her mid-thirties or thereabouts, in an embroidered medieval get-up, holding a cocktail glass brimming with blue liquid and a cherry on a stick.

He lifted his glass and drained half of it down then set it back on the table. 'Hi.'

She took his half-smile as an invitation and spread herself out on the chair opposite him, placing her glass up close to his. She lifted the little stick to her mouth.

'So.' He kept his eyes off the cleavage obviously on offer and leaned back, crossed his legs. 'Who are you tonight?'

Slipping the cherry between her glossed lips, she tossed her mane of auburn hair over her shoulder and aimed a killer smile at him. 'The Lady of Shalott.'

He took his time to say, 'No Mr Shalott?'

She giggled. The sound grated the way feet scrabbling down a rubbled cliff face to certain death grated. Clearly she thought he was interested in her as the night's entertainment. And at some other time he might have been interested. Or not.

'There *was* no Mr Shalott. It's a poem,' she informed him, in case he didn't know.

'Yes, Tennyson. Tragic circumstances. The girl loved Lancelot but he really wasn't that into her, was he?'

She leaned forward on the edge of her chair. 'But he didn't *know* her. If he'd taken the time, things might've turned out different.'

'But not necessarily for the better. Lancelot had his eye on someone else. The lady would've been disappointed.' A thought occurred to him and he tried to recall if he knew her. 'You and Ry weren't…?' He jiggled a hand in front of them.

She grinned. 'No. I had no idea the groom was going to be Lancelot. I'm Ryan's cousin. Kylie. From Adelaide.'

'Ah…yes. Cousin Kylie from Adelaide.'

He'd heard about Wily Kylie—two husbands down, on the prowl for her third. He suddenly needed a drink, and lifted his beer.

Following suit, Kylie raised her glass and tapped it to his. Her eyes drifted to his mouth. 'To a good night.'

Not if I hang around here it won't be. Like an addict, he suddenly craved the woman he'd partnered all day, not this silicone bimbo looking for rich husband number three. *Emma.* A woman with a real body and a smile that could quite possibly melt his heart if he wasn't careful.

'And a good night to you too.' He drained the glass and set it down on the napkin, then picked up his bottle and glasses, rose and executed a bow. 'Welcome to Sydney, Lady Kylie, enjoy your stay.'

He didn't wait for a reply, simply turned on his heel and headed towards the ballroom to find Emma.

Emma's hands shook so much she could barely swipe the keycard through its slot. On the third try she managed to let herself in and lean back against the door. She felt physically ill—as if the five-tiered wedding cake had lodged in her stomach.

One hand clenched on her parasol, she rubbed her free hand over her heart and up her throat. Jake hadn't come near her since their upstairs 'encounter'. For want of a better word. Never mind that she'd stupidly tried to avoid him; that was totally beside the point.

Flinging her hat into the air, she watched it sail across the room. She'd been hanging around in the ballroom, expecting him to come and find her. But he hadn't. When it came to guys like him she really was *so* naïve.

Then *she'd* found *him*. In the lobby bar…with a woman who *looked* like a woman, not some under-developed teenager.

The soft knock at the door behind her had her whirling around. Heart pounding in her throat, she yanked the door open.

Jake leaned on the doorjamb, his jacket slung over one shoulder, shirtsleeves rolled back. His hair was a little mussed, his cravat was gone, and the top button of his shirt was undone, leaving his throat tantalisingly exposed. He dangled a bottle of champagne and two glasses in his free hand.

His eyes met hers. They burned with such hot, unsatisfied hunger her throat closed over and she couldn't raise so much as a whisper. All she could think was he'd come for her. *Her.*

He lifted the bottle. 'You going to let me in? Or do you want the entire floor to know the best man's planning a hot night with the bridesmaid?' He grinned as he slid sideways and passed her, brushing his liquor-tinged lips over hers on his way. 'I hope you hadn't planned on starting without me.'

She took a moment to catch his meaning, then a wild fire swept up her neck and into her cheeks. All she managed was a gurgling sound at the back of her throat.

She closed the door and leaned back against it, heart pounding as she watched him toss his jacket over the couch, watched the way his muscles bunched beneath his shirt. His hair held the gleam of burnished gold threads amongst the brown.

He glanced back at her as he walked to a little round table topped with a crystal vase of fresh blooms. 'You weren't running out on me, were you?'

'You…you were otherwise occupied.' She found her voice.

He frowned. 'I was *waiting* for you.'

'I didn't know.' The door felt hard, the row of buttons digging into her spine.

He set the bottle and glasses down, brows raised, eyes dark as midnight. 'You *didn't know?* Jeez, woman.'

'I thought maybe you'd…' *found someone more desirable, more attractive* '…changed your mind.'

'What? This weekend's about you and me, remember?'

Her chin lifted. 'I never agreed.' Exactly.

'You…' He shook his head, eyes changing, finally comprehending. 'Come on, Emma, do you really think I'd go for that type downstairs?'

'I…hoped not.' She swallowed, relief softening her

limbs, and allowed herself a smile. 'Because then I'd have to hit you with my parasol.'

He grinned back at her, eyes wicked. 'Maybe I'll let you. Later.'

'Um…' Was she really up for an experienced man like Jake?

He popped the cork off the champagne bottle. 'Tonight's been a foregone conclusion all along, and we both know it.'

Yes. And for this moment, for what was left of the week-end, or for however long this spark burned, she knew without a doubt she wanted to make love with Jake more than her next breath.

He set the bottle down. 'Come here and kiss me.'

She needed no second bidding. Crossing the few steps between them, she flattened herself against his chest, her arms circling his neck, fingers diving into his hair as she fused her mouth to his.

Heat met heat. Not sweet and tender—not even close. Not with Jake. Nor did she want it so. This melding of selves and mashing of lips was a dark, dangerous mix of pent-up passion and long-held desires. Exactly what she wanted.

Hard hands dragged her closer, then zigged down her spine to press her bottom against him so that she could feel the steel ridge of his erection. Persuasive pressure. Promised delights.

He lifted his lips to murmur, 'Emma, Emma, you've been driving me crazy all evening. All week.'

His admission thrilled her to her toes. 'Same goes…' Dazed and dizzy, she arched her hips against his hardness and clung to him, welcoming the scrape of evening beard as he worked his lips and teeth up her throat, down the side of her neck, over her décolletage.

Impatient hands skimmed over her breasts, kneading and squeezing, deft fingers finding her aching nipples through the satin and rolling them into hardened peaks.

The delicate fragrance of the valley's sweet-scented wattle and eucalypt from the arrangement on the table mingled with the hot scent of aroused man as he laved the swell of her breasts above the neckline of her dress, then bent his head lower to nip and suck at her nipples through the fabric.

He made a sound of frustration, lifted his head and leaned back slightly to look at her. Light from the chandelier wall bracket glinted in his eyes, but the heat, the purpose she saw there, burned with its own fire.

'How many buttons did you say?'

Oh. 'Buttons...' She raised her arms to help but he didn't give her time. In a frenzy of movement, he fisted his hands in the fabric at her shoulders and yanked. She felt the satin give way down her back as buttons popped and pinged. 'Uh...'

'I know a dressmaker...'

Of course he did.

Dropping to his knees, he pushed the ruined garment and accompanying petticoats to her feet. She stepped out of the mound of puddled satin, kicked it away, leaving her wearing nothing but her laced bustier and stockings.

'You're gorgeous,' he murmured, voice husky. A corner of his mouth kicked up in a wry smile. 'And armour-plated yet again.'

Goosebumps of heat followed his gaze as it swept up her corset-trapped body to meet her eyes. 'Not quite. You do have my panties...don't you?' she finished on a slightly panicked note.

'They're mine now.' He looked down at the feminine

secrets exposed below the suspenders, then back, his eyes burning. 'I want to see all of you.'

He knelt in front of her, took off her shoes then unhitched her stockings, warm hands gliding them down her legs, breath hot on her naked skin. She lifted each foot so he could slide them off and toss them away.

Hands shaking, she started to fumble for the laces. Her breasts weren't... 'I'm not—'

Laying a finger on her lips, he shook his head.

Taking her hands in his, he spread them wide so that their bodies bumped in all the right places, then, fingers entwined, brought them in close and began to waltz. Tiny steps, his thighs pressing against hers. He swayed her towards the massive four-poster bed. She could almost hear the dusky beat of Stella's chosen song that they'd danced to earlier.

She felt the corner of the bed against her thighs as he backed her up against the bedpost. Watching her, he turned her hands palm up, kissed the inside of each wrist, where her pulse beat a rock concert's applause, then curled each finger around the smooth wooden bedpost above her head.

'And don't let go,' he ordered, squeezing them for good measure, fingers trailing down her raised arms, leaving little shivers sparkling in their wake.

The erotic pose triggered within her an avalanche of wild needs and urgent demands. Her breasts thrust upwards, straining at the bustier's confines, nipples tight to the point of pain and on fire for his touch.

'Jake...' She sighed. Wanting it all. Wanting it now.

His eyes swept over her and his smooth seduction vanished in the blink of an eye.

His fingers scrambled for the laces. When she loosened her hold on the post in a frantic effort to hasten the process he grabbed her wrists, pinning her in place, a firestorm in his dark gaze. *'Stay.'*

A thrill spiralled through her body, clenching low in her belly as he renewed his task. His hands weren't steady, she noticed, and his breathing was ragged. He swore, then a hand dived into his trouser pocket and reappeared with a miniature Swiss Army knife. A handful of condoms spilled onto the floor.

She glanced down at them, then met his eyes. 'Boy Scout?'

'Just prepared,' he muttered thickly.

His eyes darkened. She knew his intent, and her pulse kicked into a wild erratic rhythm. No trace of the suave urban sophisticate—just prime, primitive male. She loved that he'd lost control with *her*—plain and ordinary Emma Byrne.

He flicked the tiny blade open and nicked the first ribbon. The second. Her breath sucked in. So did her stomach. His knuckles grazed a nipple as he worked his way down. The erotic response echoed in her womb, drawing it tight at the same time softening and moistening the internal muscles, slackening her inner thighs.

'Jake…'

Snick, snick, snick. 'I'll buy you another one.'

'Doesn't…matter…it's…only ribbon.'

The undergarment fell apart and slid to the floor and her breasts spilled free. And suddenly it didn't matter that she didn't have the breasts she'd like to have, because he was looking at them with awe and appreciation.

'Gorgeous,' he whispered. 'Absolutely perfect.'

Dropping the knife, he filled his hands with her, thumbs whisking over the tight buds, rolling and pinching them between his fingers until she thought she'd pass out with the pleasure. Wayne had never, *never* worshipped her body the way Jake was doing.

She writhed against the post, tilting her hips and arching her back. Closer…she had to get closer… She needed more. Him inside her. *Now.*

A groan rumbled up his throat and she heard the sharp rasp of his zipper. Without taking his eyes off hers, he somehow produced a condom that hadn't fallen from his pocket and ripped the foil packet open with his teeth.

Her breath stalled in her throat as he quickly sheathed himself. 'Hurry.' Anticipation and that aching, devastating need had reached flashpoint.

Hard wide palms clamped onto her hips, a sensuous vice, holding her in place. With unerring precision he plunged deep and hard and true. A torpedo finding its target. Invading her, stretching her, filling her.

Where he belonged.

Somewhere in a dark corner of her pleasure-fogged mind she fought that concept even as she embraced it. Then all thought melted into oblivion as she gave herself wholly over to layer after layer of sensation.

His hard thighs abraded hers through the rough weave of his trousers while he hammered into her. The sound of his laboured breaths, shockingly harsh in the room's stillness, and her own rapid sighs of response.

The golden light pulsing behind her eyes as she felt her climax building, building… Her legs threatening to give way, she clung tighter to the satin-smooth pole behind her, then Jake's hands were covering hers, holding her upright. From heads to toes their bodies collided, naked skin to fully clothed.

She was slick, hot and unbearably erotic, and Jake couldn't remember the last time he'd been so turned on. She bucked against him, all wild, wanton woman, meeting his thrusts with an eagerness and energy that rivalled his own.

He hadn't expected Emma to be so utterly responsive, and the pleasure of it, of *her,* slapped through him, sharp and viciously arousing. Clenching her hands between his own he drove into her, the urge to plunder and possess riding roughshod over anything sane and rational.

He'd not known it could be like this. That need for a woman—for one woman—could be so desperate, so powerful, so consuming. Some kind of madness had seized him.

She came in a rush, all but sobbing his name, her internal muscles clamping around him, silky walls of heat that triggered his own climax.

Their joined hands slid down the sweat-slicked post and he released her, and they flopped onto the bottom of the bed together in a tangle of sated limbs, their ragged breaths filling the air.

'Come here,' he murmured when he felt able enough to move again, shifting up the bed and dragging her with him. He hauled her on top and she lay spread-eagled over his body like one of those ragdoll cats. Against his thundering heart, he felt hers pounding in unison.

'Do you realise this is the first time we've actually been horizontal together?' she said drowsily.

'Mmm,' he answered, almost as lazily. Her body fitted seamlessly against his, curves to angles, womanly soft where he was hard, as if she'd been made exclusively for him. She made him feel like the king of the universe. Already he was becoming aroused again, his body stirring as she arched a bare foot over his calf.

'Hey, you gonna get naked with me or what?' Her voice was slurred with fatigue.

He tilted her face so he could look at her, skin peach-perfect and sheened with a translucent film of moisture, eyes still glazed with residual passion.

Emma.

An unfamiliar feeling stole through him. One he wasn't sure how to deal with. He eased her off to one side. Her hair was in disarray; he smoothed it away from her face and kissed her damp brow. 'Give me a minute.'

In the bathroom he dealt with the condom, then splashed cold water on his face. He'd just had wild sex with Emma. *Emma.* Looking away from the frown he glimpsed in his reflection, he swiped a towel and dried his face.

When he came back she'd burrowed beneath the quilt and was fast asleep, dead centre in the middle of the bed, one arm flung across a pillow, long dark lashes resting on cheeks the colour of dawn.

She looked tiny, all alone in that master bed. As if the snowy mountain of quilt might swallow her up.

Vulnerable.

That odd feeling intensified. He watched the slow rise and fall of the quilt as she breathed. He'd not anticipated this…this surge of emotion. What had he done?

He should go back to his own room, he thought, even as he stripped off his shirt, tossed it over the chair. Collect a few essentials. She might need some space. Hell, *he* needed some space.

But he toed his shoes off, shoved down his trousers and jocks and stepped out of them. Retrieved the condoms from the floor, dropped them on the nightstand, then slipped into bed beside her.

She snuggled against him with a sleep murmur. Her warmth seeped into his bones, her exotic fragrance…fresh and floral and exclusively hers, surrounded him. He'd never forget that exotic fragrance. And when this attraction had run its course…

He closed his eyes.

Tomorrow. He'd think about that tomorrow.

CHAPTER NINE

THE sound of a man's steady breathing woke Emma. A hard-muscled, hairy thigh was draped over one leg, its weight effectively pinning the lower half of her body in place. A warm hand curved around her left breast.

Jake.

Her heart leapt and her body burned as images of last night with the man of her dreams flooded back. She knew it was morning because a dull apricot light shimmered behind her eyelids, but she didn't open her eyes. She lay still, not wanting him to wake yet, because she wanted to replay every glorious, mind-blowing minute. Her skin felt as if it had been rubbed all over with a stiff towel.

He'd made love to her again while the soft darkness cocooned them in its blanket of intimacy. Horizontally this time. And slowly, skilfully. Sinfully. The way only a man with Jake's experience could.

And again and again. Always different, always amazing.

Her eyes blinked open and she turned her head on the pillow to study him. As innocent as a baby but she knew better. Those perfectly sculpted lips, so relaxed in sleep, could wreak absolute havoc. Everywhere. A quicksilver shiver ran through her.

His hair was sticking up and it was an odd feeling knowing she'd had something to do with it. She smiled to herself. She itched to run her fingers through its silky softness again. Couldn't wait to feel the weight of his body on hers, to feel him come inside her again. Now. Tonight. Next week.

But reality intruded like a thief, stealing away the lovely feeling and her smile faded. This weekend was all he'd offered. All they'd agreed on. Just for fun.

And that was all she wanted too, right?

So make the most of it, she told herself, determined to ignore the feeling tugging at her and pleading for more. *Live in the moment.* They still had a late checkout and the rest of the day to spend together however they chose. A lot of fun could be packed into those few hours.

Easing her leg from beneath his, she slid a hand down between smooth sheets and hard-muscled belly… She found him semi-erect and wrapped her fingers around him. His eyes snapped open and that innocence disappeared in an instant, replaced with hot, not-quite-sleepy desire as he hardened beneath her palm.

'Good morning,' she murmured, and slid her hand down his satin-steel length and up again. 'Sorry to wake you… Actually, I'm not sorry.' She squeezed gently. 'I've got big plans for the day.'

He stuck one hand behind his head and watched her. A smile teased the corners of his mouth. 'Have you, now?'

'Mmm.' Positioning her top half over his chest, she rubbed against him once, twice, enjoying the rasp of masculine hair against her nipples, before reaching down to cup the heavy masculinity between his thighs. *Very big plans.* Resting her chin on his breastbone, she looked into his eyes. 'What about you? Any ideas?'

'I'm up for anything.' His smile was wicked and wide awake, like the rest of him.

She pushed the quilt down and took her time to admire the magnificent view of tanned skin over hard-packed muscle...and the proud, arrogant jut of his masculinity. 'I noticed.' Before he could flip her on her back and have her at his mercy again, she took charge and straddled him, reaching for a condom. 'Let's start the day on a high.'

A short while later, snuggled against him, she stretched lazily. Sunday mornings didn't get any better than this.

'Speaking of high,' Jake said, running his fingertips up and down her arm. 'What else are you up for today, Emma?'

A sneaky premonition snaked down her spine. 'Depends.'

'I'm thinking there's a playground of world-famous tourist attractions within walking distance that we should make the most of.'

She knew, and her stomach was already doing somersaults. Did she want to be suspended two hundred and seventy metres above the forest floor on a wire cable? Or be slung down the side of a cliff on the steepest funicular railway in the world?

Her whole body recoiled. She wasn't a fan of heights and she didn't care who knew it. 'Or we could explore the local galleries, or take a drive to Leura and have lunch in one of the cafés before we head home,' she suggested hopefully.

He grinned and shook his head. 'Come on, Em, where's your sense of adventure?'

'I lost it somewhere. Really,' she insisted, when his grin remained. If anything it broadened. 'I think maybe I used it all up in this room,' she finished. She stared at him, her whole body blushing at everything they'd gotten up to last night. Suddenly feeling way too naked, she sat up, pulling the sheet over her breasts. 'Is this...*us*...weird?'

His grin faded, and for a long moment he didn't answer while they watched each other. In the stretched silence she heard a service trolley lumber past the room, the clatter of dishes. Had she ever seen his eyes so dark? Something behind that gaze had her heart stumbling around inside her chest… It was supposed to be just physical. *A weekend on Pleasure Island, remember?*

'You're thinking too hard again.' Jake reached out, smoothed her hair behind her ear. 'I rebooked my room. I want another night with you. What do you say?'

Yes, please?

One more night. Her pulse was on a fast track up the side of that mountain. Free and irresponsible was calling her, and she wasn't ready to go back to her boring job and busy *unsociable* life just yet.

'It'll mean a very early start tomorrow if we're going to make it to the city in time.'

'I've decided to take tomorrow off. You?'

'Monday's busy. I've got—'

'Stay with me. Call in sick.'

'I can't just take a day off.'

His brows rose. 'Why the hell not? Your sister just got married. Your boss'll understand.' His voice turned low and smooth and seductive. 'If you want, I can convince him you need the day to recover.'

She frowned. How she chose to use her recreational time was one thing, her job was quite another. An income was a necessity. A one-night stand, even a two-night stand, was a luxury.

And didn't every woman deserve a little luxury now and again?

Still… 'I haven't interfered in your working life, Jake. Please respect mine. And, just so you know, my boss is a woman, and it happens she's a real soft touch when it comes to love and romance.' She leant over and soothed his lips with hers. 'I'll organise it myself.' And deal with the repercussions later.

'Good decision.' She felt his fingers on the back of her head, holding her still while he turned her smooch into a meltingly irresistible kiss.

'Are *you?*' he murmured against her lips a moment later.

'Am I what?'

'A soft touch when it comes to love and romance. You feel soft enough...' He drifted a finger over her cheek, a bare shoulder.

She drew back, shrugged off the words and the associated emotions she didn't want or need. Jake and love and romance were mutually exclusive. In that they were equally matched. But she couldn't quite look him in the eye, and drew circles on the crisp pillow-case with a fingertip. 'I don't want the complication of either in my life.'

'You're a career girl.'

'At least you can count on your career.' Unlike counting on a man.

'Okay, career girl. We'll both play hooky tomorrow and then take a leisurely drive back to town.' He sat up, swung his legs over the side of the bed and reached for his trousers on the floor. 'I need to go back to my room, take a shower and change. Meet me downstairs for breakfast in half an hour and we'll discuss our plans.'

'Okay.' She watched him pull last night's clothes over his magnificent taut backside. The way the muscles in his shoulders bunched as he shrugged into his shirt. Biting back a sigh, she rose and picked up the terrycloth robe she'd worn the night before, which still lay on a nearby chair. She tied the sash and followed him to the door.

'See you in a little while,' he said, bending to kiss her

before opening the door. Then Emma saw his shoulders tense as he came to an abrupt halt.

'Jake.'

She heard her mother's chipped ice voice and Emma's skin flushed to the roots of her tousled bedroom hair. Shrinking into her robe, she hugged the lapels up to her chin with both hands.

'Good morning, Bernice.' Jake's back was towards Emma, and if he was surprised or embarrassed his voice gave no sign. 'Em's about to take a shower,' she heard him say as he sauntered out, his jacket and waistcoat slung over a shoulder. 'You just caught her in time.'

Emma sucked in a fortifying breath. 'Mum.' She moved forward and pulled the door wider while she imagined slamming it shut. 'Jake was…just leaving.' Obviously. And he seemed to have taken her thought-processing skills with him.

Her mother stalked in, missing none of last night's carnage strewn across the floor. 'I came to tell you I'm driving back with Ryan's Uncle Stan.'

Was that a flicker of *excitement* in her mother's eyes? But when Emma blinked it had vanished. 'That's…great, Mum…' She trailed off. What to say?

'I wanted to make sure you'd arranged a lift, but I assume now that you're driving back with Jake.'

Emma heard the underlying criticism loud and clear. 'Thanks, but actually I'm staying on another night.' Defiance streamed through her veins. 'Make that *we're* staying another night.'

Her mother had been staring at the rumpled bed but she swung to face her. 'What about work tomorrow morning?'

'I'm taking the day off.'

'Have you no sense of responsibility, girl? And with

a man like Jake.' She exhaled her disapproval audibly through pinched nostrils.

'I never take time off. As for Jake, I like him, Mum. And so does Stella.' She hugged her arms to ward off the chill in her mother's eyes. 'He's an interesting, honest, hard-working man. I make my own decisions about the men I choose to see. And my own mistakes.'

'So you already think he's a mistake, then?'

Maybe it *was* a mistake, but she'd never know if she didn't take the risk. Jake had liberated something inside her last night and she wanted explore it, even if it was only for what was left of the weekend. 'I want a chance to find out.'

'Very well, then,' her mother replied, tight-lipped. The stony expression remained as she moved to the door. 'I'll see you at home.'

'Right. Drive safely.' Emma maintained an outward calm until the door closed with chilling formality, then swung around to lean back against it and slap her palms on the smooth wood. And a big goodbye to allowing her mother to put a blot on the morning.

It was only a little risk, she told herself, gathering her discarded garments and all the loose buttons she could locate. She tossed them into her suitcase, took out her casual clothes. A relaxing day playing tourist in the Blue Mountains was just what she needed.

And tonight… Her newly energised body tightened at the thought. It was going to be fun. Just fun.

CHAPTER TEN

AFTER waving the newly married couple off on their honeymoon, Jake convinced Emma to walk to Echo Point again later that morning. The air was cold but the sun was out for now, turning the Three Sisters a stark orange against the blue-tinged foliage. A bank of clouds was building; it would rain before nightfall.

'So Stan's driving your mum home,' Jake said as they gazed over the valley. Bernice finding him in Emma's room had been an unexpected and awkward moment. 'Did she give you a hard time?' Neither of them had spoken of the episode over breakfast, but it needed to be said.

'No more than usual.' Emma spoke casually, but he saw her posture dip as she leaned on the railing as if it might prop her up. 'I hope Stan can put her in a better mood.'

'If anyone can cheer Bernice up, Stan's your man.'

Hanging on to the rail with both hands, she leaned back at a crazy angle and looked at the sky. 'You know what? I don't want to think about her *or* work today.'

'Good girl.' He covered her hands with his. 'Today's for us.'

'Sounds perfect.' Turning to him, she tipped her face up to his, last night's sparkle still dancing in her eyes. She wore a faded tracksuit, scuffed sneakers and her hair was tied back into a loose coil which hung between her shoulderblades. Without make-up, her face glowed with good health except for some luscious-looking peach-coloured lipgloss.

She looked…radiant. Last night's gymnastics had done her a world of good. 'Let's go.' Keeping her hand clasped firmly in his, he headed towards a walking trail which pointed to Katoomba Falls.

Seeing the spectacular World Heritage sights with Emma, he discovered their mutual enjoyment of exploring nature on foot. She shared his interest in the environment and the native flora and fauna they came across. Ancient ferns, rainbow lorikeets. They even glimpsed an echidna fossicking in the bushland nearby.

He persuaded her to cross the valley on the Skyway with the promise of lunch at the revolving restaurant at the other end. She buried her face against his chest as they swung out into space so high that the shadow of their cabin was the size of a newborn's thumbnail on the Jurassic forest below.

Jake couldn't remember a day he'd enjoyed more in a long time. Simple things like sharing a can of soda while they sat on a rock with the breeze at their backs and listened to the crystal sounds of the nearby Katoomba waterfall.

He was as interested in Emma's mind and her opinions as he was in her body. Connecting with her, seeing that rare smile and finding out what they had in common, was as much a part of the day as the hot, lingering looks they exchanged, knowing the evening ahead promised to be as special as the last.

By mid-afternoon it was becoming increasingly difficult to keep his hands off her, so they cut the sightseeing short and made a fast trip back to the hotel and his suite.

Later, surrounded by white candles in the gleaming

black spa of the stunning black bathroom, with its wide
uninterrupted view, they sipped bubbly and watched the
constantly changing panorama. A curtain of rain filled the
valley floor, a blur of dull gold with the setting sun behind
as the shower moved through in brilliant contrast to the
encroaching stormy black sky.

But the best view was right in front of him.

Emma's hair was catching the sun's last feeble rays, and
the soft glow of candlelight shone on her cheeks as daylight faded.

She was facing him across a mountain of bubbles, and
in those sapphire eyes, with their stars and luminosity, he
could see a load had been lifted. She'd let herself go for
once in her life and had a good time.

How long would it take for the pressures of real life to
tarnish that glow and eclipse the sparkle? After tomorrow's
short return journey to the urban rat race it was back to
business for them both.

Which made it all the more important not to waste a
single second of what was left of tonight.

He took her glass, set both flutes on the side of the spa,
then slid forward, knees bent, so that his legs came around
hers and her belly came into contact with his. Put his hands
on her shoulders so he could look right into those eyes.
'You're a pleasure to be with, Emma Byrne.'

Emma stared into his warm brown eyes. She was going
to pay for that pleasure sooner or later. This weekend had
been one amazing adventure after another, one she'd remember for ever.

'Hey, that's supposed to make you smile, not frown.'

'I'm not fr—'

'You are. You get that little line between your eyebrows…' He smoothed it away with a fingertip. 'Okay, I've
got something guaranteed to make you smile.' His deep

voice rumbled between them and he pressed closer, his burgeoning hardness hot and impatient against her belly.

'Mmm...'

'See? Smiling already.' He nipped his way up the side of her neck to the sensitive spot beneath her ear. 'How am I doing?' Tugged her earlobe between his lips, making her tingle.

'Pretty well.' His hands were a slippery delight on her shoulders.

'Only pretty well?'

She closed her eyes the better to savour it. Him. 'You can do better.'

A slow hand cruised down to her left breast to toy with her nipple. 'How about this?' He moved his mouth over hers and murmured, 'Is this good?'

'Mmm. Good.' *Very good.* She sighed and her lips opened under his probing tongue. It wasn't only his fabulously sexy body and his skill as a lover, it was their easy rapport, their shared interests.

Or was it something deeper?

Before she could ponder or react to that significant and scary thought he surged forward, his hands on either side of her face, his dark eyes holding hers. Slowly, slowly, he pushed that glorious hardness inside her. Slow and slippery and...oh, he was persuasive. Addictive.

'Tell me it's the best you ever had,' he demanded against her lips, withdrawing inch by excruciatingly exquisite inch, leaving her breathless and arching her hips in anticipation.

'Ha!' she managed. 'Isn't that what you guys all want to know?'

'Tell me you want more.' He leaned back just enough for her to see the wicked glint in his eyes and withdrew.

'Yes,' she moaned. 'More.' And moaned again as he pushed inside her, faster now, on a wild ride to paradise.

'Come with me.' His words sounded harsh and ragged against her ear as he came deep inside her.

'Coming,' she gasped as she rode over the edge of the velvet chasm with him.

Jake had chosen the room for its awesome view and the gas fire. The flames that licked over attractive smooth river stones provided warmth and intimacy. They sat in matching hotel robes on the rug in the flickering glow and shared the cold lobster and mango salad Room Service had delivered earlier.

He watched Emma slip a slice of mango between her lips. Tousled damp hair framed her face. Her eyes reflected the fire's orange glow, turning them violet and mysterious.

He wanted to know more of her secrets. More about the product line she'd developed and why she was so passionate about it that she'd spend so much of her free time immersed in it and yet not pursue its potential further.

Was it a front to hide behind? Was she lonely or a natural loner? Was she a risk-taker or not?

She was different to the women he usually got involved with. *So* different from the synthetic types to be found in King's Cross. Emma was sparkly and refreshing, a glint of dew on spring grass on a sunny morning. Her body was slender, firm, natural. Curves in all the right places and they were all real.

'Taste.' She swirled a sliver of lobster into the buttery sauce and held it to his lips. 'It's divine.'

He opened his mouth and let her feed him. Chewed a moment, savouring the flavour, the slight pressure of her finger against his lips.

The room's muted glow cast intimate shadows. 'Nothing beats romance, huh?'

She wiped her fingers on her napkin, her movements a

little jerky. Her eyes were still on his but rather than the dreamy violet from moments ago they were quicksilver-black. 'I don't do romance.'

The flat comment surprised him. 'No?' He waved an all-encompassing hand around the room—the flickering firelight on the walls, its warmth against his skin. 'What do you call this? The candlelit spa we just enjoyed?'

'Ambience.'

'So define romance.'

'Hearts and flowers and pretty words.' Silver sliced through her gaze, a knife's glint against ebony. 'I don't need them and I don't want them.'

'Why not?' He saw the pain in her eyes before she looked away. 'Surfer Boy wasn't the romantic type?'

She shrugged. 'That's just it. He was. Something special every Friday night and a dozen red roses every Wednesday, with a pretty note to say he was thinking of me...'

Her story didn't make sense to Jake. 'You weren't being totally honest with me about him the night of the dinner, were you?'

'Just because I don't want rom—'

'It's in your eyes. That's why you're not looking at me.'

'I'm...' Her shoulders drooped. 'Okay. I didn't slot him into my schedule. He slotted me into his. And I let him. Because, you see, I was stupidly in love with him.'

Jake reached out, trailed a finger down her cheek. 'He's even more of an idiot than I thought,' he murmured.

She shook her head. 'Romance is a lie to cover a lie.'

'It doesn't have to be, Emma.'

'No romance, okay? No lies.'

'Okay...' He pressed her down and rolled her onto her back on the rug, unknotting her belt and spreading her robe wide. 'Does that mean I can't tell you you're the sexiest woman I've ever made love to by firelight?'

She reached for his robe, pushing it away, fingers stretching and flexing over his shoulders, her eyes duelling with his, a smile on her lips and that little dimple in her cheek winking as he lowered himself on top of her. 'I'm okay with that.'

They had a late checkout on Monday morning so they spent it in bed and then enjoyed a quick lunch in a charming little rustic café before returning to Sydney. Emma had phoned in sick to work—something she'd never done before.

On the trip back she was almost tempted to open her laptop which Jake had returned to her, and catch up on the orders she'd neglected. But she knew she'd not be able to concentrate. Her mind was chock-full of distracting thoughts. So she watched the scenery flash by, and with it the slow return from fairytales and magical rides—of any kind—to civilisation and real life.

Real life. Depressing thought. Closing her eyes, she feigned sleep as they reached outer suburbia and let her mind drift back over the past two days.

She heard Jake speak on his mobile with his PA about some problem with a client that couldn't wait, enjoying the deep, authoritative timbre in his voice, remembering how it sounded when he came deep inside her.

Emma's phone signalled an incoming text. She considered ignoring it, but her responsible self wouldn't allow her to. She opened it and stared at the message. 'I don't believe it,' she murmured.

Jake glanced her way. 'Something wrong?'

'Mum's gone to Melbourne. With Stan.'

'Good for her.' Jake's voice was laced with a smile.

Emma texted back a reply before slipping her phone back into her bag. 'She's never done anything so impulsive in her life.'

'Then it's time she did.' With his eyes on the road, Jake put a hand on her thigh. 'Stan's a good guy. She'll be fine.'

'Of course she will.' She hoped. Because she wasn't looking forward to the fall-out if things went wrong.

'Your mum's a hard woman, Em,' he said, moments later. 'I know she was ill for a long time...'

'Clinical depression.' Emma hugged her arms, remembering the stress she and Stella had endured as a result. 'She's recovered now, but the after-effects linger on.' *And on.*

'Your dad's death caused it?'

She shook her head. 'She was depressed long before that. Dad didn't love her and there were other women.'

'Why didn't she just kick him out or walk away?'

'Because he had absolute control of her money. Remember, her generation isn't ours. And maybe she *wanted* to play the martyr.' The angst spilled out and it felt good. Really good. As if she was sweeping it out of her life. 'Just before Dad died he invested what was left of her inheritance and lost the lot.'

She heard Jake exhale loudly. 'That's tough, Emma. That's why you were always working?'

'I couldn't let the house be sold. It would've finished Mum off. Stella, being the nurturing soul she is, took on the role of carer.'

'So, forgive me if this offends you, why the hell does Bernice treat you the way she does? And why do you let her?'

A question Emma had asked herself often enough. 'Mum never appreciated the financial side of what I was doing—she just didn't see it. And Stella's been there for her in a more physical and emotional way.'

'So you erected a barrier to protect yourself from the rejection.'

'I guess I did. She doesn't get to me any more.'

He glanced at her. 'I disagree, Emma. It's still there.'

She shrugged—maybe he was right—and watched the glimpses of the ocean through the windscreen as they neared Coogee. 'She allowed my father to ruin her life. It spilled over to her daughters.'

And it reminded Emma why she wouldn't allow herself to think of what she and Jake had as anything more than a sexy encounter. She'd enjoyed it for what it was. But never again would she rely on anyone for her own happiness.

It felt odd, pulling up in her driveway in the middle of a work-day afternoon. She felt as if she'd lived a lifetime since she'd been home.

Jake switched off the engine, and the sudden silence in the car's confines seemed to shout. She busied herself searching her bag for her keys then realised she was already holding them.

She felt his gaze as he said, 'I guess you'll want to jump straight on your laptop and check out those orders that have piled up in your absence.'

His tone suggested that even if *she* wasn't down from the clouds and quite ready to settle to work just yet he was. He was probably used to switching from pleasure to business without a blink.

She fought down an absurd disappointment and turned with a smile fixed on her face. 'It doesn't go away, does it? Even when we do.'

He smiled back. 'Okay, then.' He pushed open the door and walked around to the boot to take out her belongings.

She took a careful, calming breath before climbing out and following him to the front door. She unlocked it and he ushered her past him and inside.

'Where do you want your gear?' he said behind her.

'Here's fine.' She gestured beside her and turned to him,

suddenly feeling like a stranger in her own surroundings. Everything felt different and she didn't know what to say. How ridiculous. She was experiencing morning-after awkwardness *now?*

He set the suitcase down and placed the garment bag on top, then straightened.

'Thanks.'

'No worries.'

She didn't know what to do with her hands and clasped them in front of her. How did you say goodbye to a man you'd just spent the past couple of nights having the best sex of your life with?

You said it casually, as if it happens all the time. 'Thanks for a great weekend.'

'My pleasure.' A flicker of heat darkened his gaze.

Mine too.

'I'll let you get to it, then.'

No *We'll have to do it again sometime.* 'Yes. Better get started. So…I'll see you…around.' God, did she sound needy? Clingy? Desperate?

He nodded, those dark eyes fixed on hers but giving nothing away. 'I'll give you a call some time.'

'Right.' Tomorrow? Next week? Next year?

He bent to kiss her. Just a brief brush of those expert lips over hers. Then he must have changed his mind because his arms slid around her waist and pulled her close. Her mouth opened beneath his and she let him in, tasting him as his tongue slid over hers. Her heart thudded against her chest and she clung to his shirt a moment before he lifted his head.

His eyes had changed, she noticed, like hot treacle. But she instinctively knew he wasn't going to act on it, so stepped back first. *At least maintain a little dignity.* 'Bye, then.'

'Catch you later.'

As he turned to leave his mobile buzzed and he yanked it out of his jacket pocket. 'Carmody.' He paused on Emma's doorstep, not looking at her while he listened to the caller. He didn't look back, walking into the sunshine, his attention already focused elsewhere.

Emma closed the door and listened to the purr of his car's engine as he drove off. She rubbed a hand over the familiar ache in her chest. It couldn't be love. Not again. She wouldn't let it be.

CHAPTER ELEVEN

EMMA found it tough going over the next couple of days at work—unable to concentrate, thinking of Jake, remembering their time together, wishing she could see him again even if it was just to remind herself that he was a one-weekend wonder. But she didn't hear from him.

Get over it. They'd had a fling. One wild, sexy weekend of pleasure. He'd never promised more. He'd been totally upfront with her. At least he'd been honest, and after Wayne that counted for a lot.

She felt different, though. Being with Jake had given her a new-found confidence in herself. As a woman, as a lover, as a person. She wanted to take on the world. She wanted to get serious about her business.

She wanted to see him so she could tell him that.

Meanwhile she filled her orders and surfed the internet for new soap-making recipes and considered how she might extend her client base.

On Thursday evening, humming along with her favourite jazz CD, she collected the ingredients together for honey soap. She melted glycerin bars and honey, poured it into a shallow pan, then melted the goat's milk, adding it to the mix. She'd just set it aside to cool when she heard the doorbell chime and went to answer it.

Jake.

He was leaning on her doorframe, reminding her of the last time she'd seen him standing there, and her heart tripped and she was breathless all over again. A burst of happiness sang through her veins as she met his warm brown eyes. Tonight he wore a luxurious-looking cream jumper over black trousers.

Her smile was spontaneous. 'Hi.'

'I was on my way out and passing this way…' The timbre of his deep, familiar voice turned her insides as hot and syrupy as the mix on her kitchen bench. 'Have I caught you at a bad time?'

'No…no.' She forced the surprise and excitement from her voice. *Act natural. He's on his way out, after all.* 'Come on in. I'm just finishing some soaps.' She turned, casting a deliberately casual glance over her shoulder as she moved to the kitchen. 'What brings you by?' When he didn't answer, she stopped at the kitchen table and turned. He almost crashed into her.

'You,' he said, his eyes melting into hers.

The heat from his body seemed to shimmer right through her. He smelled of warm wool and apple and cinnamon pie.

'More specifically, your soaps.' He rubbed his knuckles together audibly. 'It's my PA's birthday next week. I'd like to buy some for her.'

'Uh-huh. Well…' She swished her own hands down her coat. Her palms were sweating. 'I've got some pretty flower-shaped ones with a "Happy Birthday" imprint somewhere. I'll—'

'No birthday imprint.' He caught her arm as she started to move away.

'Oh. Okay…' She blinked once.

'She doesn't want anyone to know.' He lifted a shoulder. 'She's shy about birthdays.' Jake lowered his voice, curling his fingers around the lab coat's thick fabric. He felt Emma's gentle warmth beneath, the smooth muscle over bone against his palm, before letting his arm drop to his side. 'I thought I'd take some extras into the office at the same time. Let some of the staff try them out.'

'Really?' Surprise and humour glinted in her eyes and her lips curved and he knew she was wise to his game.

'Really.' He smiled back. 'What can you recommend?'

She moved to the plastic containers stacked along the wall. 'They're all made with goat's milk for sensitive skin, but I have a range of fragrances. How about amber, which has a sweet woody note suitable for both sexes? Or vanilla? Or, for something extra special…' She pulled out a container, carried it to the table. 'I've got some gorgeous little cupcake shapes in different fragrances—vanilla, blueberry, cinnamon, coconut. They're my favourite stock and very popular. I can pack them in a little basket for you if you want.'

He grinned. 'Do you wash with them or eat them?'

She opened the box, closed her eyes briefly and inhaled the fragrance, her ecstatic expression reminding him of when she'd come apart in his arms. She lifted out a pretty pink sample that matched the colour in her cheeks. 'I love cupcakes to death, but I wouldn't recommend eating these.'

Amazing, this transformation from the solemn girl who'd greeted him at her door only last week. The obvious joy she got from her creative work. The sparkle it put in her eyes and the glow it brought to her cheeks. And she was right; this was no mere hobby. Little wonder she'd been insulted he'd called it such. She had something unique here, a marketable product.

He leaned a hip against the table. 'Have you given any more thought to expanding this business online? Because

I see a different woman standing here tonight. One who might be willing to take that chance now.'

'Maybe I *am* a different woman.' He noticed her eyes had turned a darker hue as she looked at him. 'You've had something to do with that. And I *am* thinking about it.' She picked up a green cake, held it to his nose. 'What do you smell?'

'Fresh mown grass?'

'It gives a bathroom a pleasant scent.' She set it down. 'So many fragrances. I love them all.'

'Which one do you use?' He leaned in to catch more of that scent he'd missed over the past few days, heard her tiny intake of breath.

'Tahitian Fantasy.' Her breath hitched again. 'Why are you really here, Jake?'

Her husky voice vibrated against his lips as he set them on her smooth neck. 'Nothing like a little Tahitian Fantasy. Because I wanted to see you again. Are you okay with that?' His hands drifted to her waist, lips tracing a line over the fragrant flesh beneath her ear.

'Ah…yes…'

'Good, because I can't seem to stay away.' He nipped at her earlobe. 'What's in it?'

'The tiare flower. Tahitian gardenia.' She arched her neck. 'It has healing properties.'

'I've got this itch…'

'Where?' she murmured.

'Everywhere,' he murmured back, moving nearer, pressing open-mouthed kisses up her neck, over her jaw. 'I itch every damn where.'

'That sounds serious.' She stepped back to see his eyes, her own dancing as she slid his sleeve up to his elbow, fingers lightly massaging his forearm. 'Do you exfoliate?'

He had to lean forward so he could drop a lingering kiss on her lips. 'Only when I'm with you.'

Her blue eyes twinkled up at him. 'Ha-ha.' She picked up a dark-coloured soap that looked like congealed breakfast cereal. 'Honey and oatmeal,' she said, and gave his chest a light prod with one finger. 'Sit down…if you've got a moment?'

'For you, yes.' He yanked out a chair and watched her fill a shallow bowl with warm water.

The last time he'd been in her place she'd been uptight and defensive and prickly. Tonight she was the relaxed woman he'd enjoyed the weekend with.

Was it only four nights ago? It felt like four weeks. He'd spent those nights in a kind of limbo, caught between wanting to call and ask if he could come over and reminding himself they'd agreed on a weekend and the weekend was finished.

Had she spent the last few nights thinking of how good they'd been together? In bed and out of it? She was fresh, honest and fun to be with. He regretted putting a time limit on their affair.

'It's almost as good as sex.' Her words had him sitting up straighter as she carried the bowl to the table, set it in front of him along with a handtowel.

'What is?'

'Push up your sleeves and put your hands in the bowl.' She moistened the soap in the water and worked it between her palms till it glistened, then slid it over and around his hand in a slow, slippery massage. 'Good?'

He watched, fascinated, her small fingers with their short neat nails gliding over his, between his. He looked up, met her eyes. 'Very good. Exceptionally good. But… Do I need to work on my bedroom technique?'

The twinkle in her eyes sharpened. Her lips stretched

into a full-on smile. 'Okay, that was my selling point before the weekend. Damn—now I'll have to think of something else.'

'We could always test the theory again, just to be sure…'

'There's nothing wrong with your technique, Jake.' She twined her fingers against his. Silky heat on silky heat.

'Nor yours.' He reciprocated, pressing his thumb into her palm and drawing lazy circles, watching her cheeks pinken, her eyes turn to liquid pools of blue desire.

His own vision was growing hazy as they continued to watch each other while they made out with their joined hands. 'Do you give all your clients the personal treatment?'

She leaned in so that her lips were a whisper away from his. 'Only the ones who knock on my door.'

'I've been thinking,' he murmured back, 'there's no reason why we can't continue seeing each other, is there?'

Her whole body stilled. 'What are you saying?'

He soothed his lips over hers just once. 'I like being with you. Don't look too far ahead. Let's just enjoy the ride. What do you say?'

'Uh-huh…'

He lifted her damp fingers to his mouth, kissed them and released her. 'In the meantime, I've got an appointment in King's Cross. If tonight goes as planned, tomorrow the Pink Mango could be looking at a new owner.'

She continued to stare at him, unblinking, gaze unfocused. 'Uh-huh.'

But she didn't seem to hear him. 'Don't congratulate me yet,' he said anyway. He wiped his hands on her little towel, then pushed up. 'Talk to you tomorrow evening.'

'Uh-huh.'

He folded the towel, set it on the table. 'I'll let myself out.'

He smiled to himself when he heard her call, 'Yes!' as clear as crystal as he walked to the door.

For Emma, the following work day dragged. Unlike what was happening with Jake, which seemed to be taking off at warp speed. She couldn't focus on anything except their unexpected sexy interlude last night.

He liked being with her. He wanted to be with her some more. It brought a smile to her lips every time she remembered. So often that her co-workers cast more than a few Emma-had-got-lucky glances her way over the course of the day.

She left the call centre five minutes before closing time; something she'd never done before. She tapped along with the beat of the latest pop song on the radio as she drove home, looking forward to Jake's call.

It was nearly six o'clock when he rang. Emma picked the phone up on its first ring.

'It's done,' he said without preamble. 'The Pink Mango's history.'

She almost heard the drum-roll of satisfaction in his voice and smiled. 'Hooray for you.'

'Can you clear your evening schedule and come out to celebrate with me?'

Her smile broadened. 'Consider it cleared.'

'I'll pick you up in thirty minutes?'

'*Thirty* minutes?'

'You'll look gorgeous whatever you're wearing,' he said, obviously familiar with the female ritual, 'and I've got somewhere casual in mind.'

Thirty-five minutes later, after three changes of clothes, she'd decided on her best jeans and an ivory jumper with a bright turquoise-and-orange scarf when he arrived.

Seeing him was like cresting the top of a rollercoaster

wave, all excitement and anticipation. He wore black jeans and a black T-shirt beneath an often washed black, white and navy flannel shirt, open down the front. Definitely casual.

'Hi.' She sounded as breathless as she felt.

'Hi.' With one arm still propped against the doorframe he tugged on her scarf, pulled her towards him and kissed her.

He tasted *sooo* good, and she felt herself rushing down the other side of that slippery breaker. Then he straightened, and with a wickedly hot twinkle in his eyes, said, 'If we don't get moving we might never get there.'

'Wait up. You forgot something last night.' She picked up a little cellophane-wrapped basket from the shelf by the door and held it out with a grin. 'Tell your PA happy birthday from me.'

He nodded, eyes twinkling. 'How much do I owe you?'

'Nothing. Free sample.'

'Are you sure?'

'Positive. Promotion's good for business.'

'Okay, but don't forget to write it off as an expense.'

Moments later they were cruising along a well-lit Bondi street bustling with Friday-night shoppers. But Jake bypassed the usual restaurants and turned into a suburban street.

She looked out at the luxury homes, roofs glinting in the streetlights. 'Where are we going?'

He pulled up in front of a buttercream wall. Beyond, Emma could see an expansive red-tiled roof. 'Welcome to Jake's Place. Home of great food and magnificent views.' He pressed a remote and the gates swung open revealing a large two-storey house.

'Wow.' She took in the view as the car came to a stop under an open carport. A long curve of beach, dark now but for a couple of lights blinking near the horizon. 'It's magnificent, Jake. You've achieved so much in such a short time.' The location alone had to be worth a fortune.

He swiped the keys from the ignition, his gaze on the black waves laced with a fine line of white in the distance. 'The bank still has a share, but we're getting there.'

Reaching across the console between them, he cupped the back of her neck with one hand, unclipped her seat belt with the other, his gaze hot with smouldering promise. And before she could blink he meshed his lips with hers.

He'd had no intention of jumping her until he'd fed her, but when Jake looked into those sapphire eyes which had kept him from the precious little sleep he'd managed over the past few nights, every thought flew out of his mind bar one. Having Emma.

'Have you missed me?' he murmured against her lips. When had he ever asked that question? he wondered vaguely, and was stupidly happy when he felt her lips curve against his mouth.

'Yes.' She sucked in a breath.

His impatient fingers found the hem of her jumper and rushed beneath to feel the firm, warm flesh of her torso, the ridges along her ribcage, and higher to the curve under her breasts. Her nipples tightened as he swirled his fingers over the crests. Beneath his hands he felt the same urgency that whipped through his own body as she strained against his palm.

'Emma...' The breathless sound registered somewhere as his own voice. 'Missed you too.' Flicking the clasp, he loosened her bra, shoved it up and out of the way so he could feast on the sweet taste of an engorged nipple. He slid his palm between her thighs, cupped her hard through the hot denim, felt her shudder and arch in response, heard her muffled sigh as she forked her fingers through his hair and pulled it tight against his scalp.

He heard a rushing noise in his ears; it might have been the sea, or her ragged breath, or the fizz of his own blood. All he knew was if he didn't get out now he'd have her here, in the car, before sanity could prevail.

Swearing and fumbling with the latch, he pushed the passenger door open. Somehow they were both out of the car and stumbling together towards the house.

His keys... In the car—somewhere. The hell with them. He had her up against the wall, mouths fused, teeth clashing, his raging erection pressing into the soft give of her belly before either of them knew what had happened.

Did she have any idea how much power she wielded over him? He never lost it like this. Her pupils were dark and dilated when he lifted his head to watch her while he snapped open the top button of her jeans.

She returned the favour, hard little knuckles against his belly as she loosened the stud.

There was a harsh zipping sound as they freed each other. And then he was lifting her against the wall and pushing into her familiar sultry heat, his tongue mimicking the action as it dived inside her mouth to drown in her taste.

Fast, furious, frantic. No time to think. Just blind, burning lust, passion and pleasure. She seemed to struggle for air, and he lifted his lips, as breathless as she, and watched her, head thrown back, neck pale and slender in the cool wash of light angling in from the street.

Then his mouth was there, on that galloping pulse, her smooth fragrant skin. Exquisite taste. Pure sensuality.

But the need she conjured in him as he rode the wave to completion, this desperation, as if she was tearing something from deep within him, was beyond his experience.

Moments later, his body still humming, he lowered her to her feet, rested his brow against hers. 'What is it with you? I can't seem to get enough—'

Protection. He froze. He'd not given it a thought. Not given Emma's welfare or safety a thought. What kind of man did that make him? He lifted her chin with a finger and stared into her eyes. 'We just had unprotected sex, Emma.'

'We didn't use a condom, no.' She didn't look fazed or alarmed. Her eyes were clear and calm, like the sea on a summer day.

'I...if anything happens...'

'It won't. I'm still on the pill.'

He relaxed a little. 'You didn't tell me.'

'You didn't ask.' She lifted a shoulder, then wiggled back into her jeans. 'And I wasn't as sure about you then...'

He caught her drift. 'I'm healthy, Emma.'

If they'd been in full light he'd have sworn her eyes darkened, and she rolled her lips together in that way she had before saying, 'I wanted *you* inside me, not a piece of rubber.'

Her words hit hard, right where his heart suddenly pounded like a hammer on steel. His fingers tightened as he adjusted his own clothing. 'I should've been more careful. I always use condoms.' Just not this time.

'I take care of my own protection,' she said.

Emma didn't want to talk about it. Not another word. *Oh, no.* Her heart suddenly cramped, twisted as she realised the full import of what she'd just admitted. She'd wanted that closer connection with him. Craved it like an addict. *Dangerous.* Had she made the right decision to continue seeing Jake after all?

She rubbed a hand over her chest. 'It's cold out here,' she said, hugging her arms. 'Can we go inside?'

He mumbled something about keys and walked to the car, fishing around in the luxury interior a moment before coming back, keys in hand. 'Come on—you can take a look around while I cook.'

She used the time alone to refocus her thoughts while she explored Jake's domain. The décor was essentially masculine but comfortable. Lots of glass, dark furniture with splashes of colour—maroon, grey, red. The wood-panelled kitchen was surprisingly clean and tidy, putting hers to shame. But then, he had enough cupboard space and mod cons for the both of them. An office with two computers and three monitors, and a fortune in the latest technology in the living room.

The upstairs bedrooms were mostly empty except for Jake's. A massive king-size bed dominated the room with its tan and navy quilt and minimal furniture. She backed away from the reminder that other women had no doubt enjoyed themselves there and hurried downstairs.

He'd slapped a couple of thick steaks on the grill and was slicing an avocado when she returned to the kitchen, but he waved away her offer of help so she wandered to the living room. Windchimes filled the balcony beyond the floor-to-ceiling windows, the sound tinkling and clacking in the gentle breeze. Solar-powered balls of crackled glass slowly spun multi-coloured lights over the deck.

He appeared moments later with the aromatic steaks, a bowl of healthy-looking salad and a loaf of crusty bread.

They ate while a blues CD poured music out of the speakers with only the solar-powered balls for lighting— 'ambience', he was quick to point out—and washed it down with a nice cabernet sauvignon while they watched a passenger ship track north, myriad tiny lights blazing.

He topped up her glass. 'What's the latest on your mum?'

'She's still in Melbourne. Staying in Stan's house, of all places. *And* she's still deciding when she'll come home.'

'Having a new man in her life's obviously done her good.' He grinned. 'Maybe she'll be a little more mellow on her return.'

'Maybe.' It helped that Jake understood, and Emma was glad she'd opened up on that topic; it felt good to share.

He rose, collected their plates. 'Why don't you go make yourself comfortable on the couch and I'll make coffee? What's your preference?'

'Cappuccino, please. With extra chocolate?'

While he attended to the coffee machine she walked out onto the deck to feel the salt breeze and hear the sound of the sea. She told herself that she was right where she wanted to be. With a guy whose company she enjoyed. She refused to let herself think beyond the ride he'd promised.

When she walked inside he'd brought the coffee and a bowl of dark chocolates and she snuggled against him on the couch. She listened to his heart beating strong and solid against her ear, the fresh fragrance of sun-dried clothes and his clean scent in her nostrils. He turned on the TV. Some old adventure movie was playing. She tuned out, closed her eyes, and moments later felt herself drifting…

'You're tired,' he murmured. 'Stay the night.'

The spell she was falling under shattered like glass. She kept her eyes closed but her mind was instantly alert. Unlike their fantasy weekend in paradise, this was the real world. And in the real world she was…falling in love with this man.

Even as the words formed in her mind she was shoving them away, squeezing them out of her heart. She refused, *refused* to fall in love again. She'd been there, done that, and had the scars to prove it. Her mother had fallen for a man who'd not loved her and it had brought nothing but pain and misery to herself, her husband and her daughters—even long after he'd died.

'You're thinking too hard again.' He curled a hand around her head and stroked her hair. 'You won't need pyjamas, and I've got a spare toothbrush.'

Oh, yes, she'd bet he did.

'So…spend the night with me?'

She opened her eyes, looked into his and felt her heart tumble further. 'I can't,' she all but whispered.

A puzzled crease formed between his brows. 'I'll drive you back in plenty of time in the morning. I can even wait while you get your swimsuit and drop you off at the beach if you want.'

'We'll see each other, Jake, but I won't be staying nights.'

A beat of silence. 'I'm not Wayne, Emma,' he said quietly.

'I know. I just need my space for a bit. This is all happening too fast.' She couldn't help it. She reached up, touched his clean-shaven jaw. 'Okay?'

'Okay. I won't pressure you. It's too soon. I get that. But if you change your mind…'

She nodded, feeling the strength drain out of her. 'Thanks. But you're right. I'm tired and, if it's okay with you, I'd like to go home now.'

He exhaled a slow, deep breath, then pushed off the couch. 'I'll get my keys.'

When a woman didn't want to spend the night with him, he… He what? Jake frowned at his darkened ceiling later that night. He couldn't remember the last time.

He swung out of bed, dragged on old shorts, T-shirt and sneakers, then headed downstairs and out into the salty night air. The chill spattered his skin with goosebumps as he made his way along a couple of streets to the beach. Black waves surged and thumped on the sand as he jogged off the road and onto the esplanade.

She had good reasons, he reminded himself, and it wasn't personal—the scumbag surfer had done a real number on her.

He'd respect her space, give her time. That fragile heart of hers was still healing, and no way was he going to be responsible for further damage. Meanwhile they could continue to enjoy what they *did* have, keeping it casual.

A car skidded to a stop a short distance away, drawing his attention. The back door swung open, something flopped onto the road and the vehicle sped off. What the...? Switching direction to the way he'd come, he increased his pace.

The small bundle of dirty fur moved, and two frightened eyes looked up at his. Jake's heart melted. 'Hey, fella. Steady.' He looked the dog over, murmuring soothing noises. No ID. Beneath the matted white fur he was skin and bone, and alive with fleas. Abandoned in the middle of the night. Poor little scrap.

'Come on, Scratch. We'll find you some place safe.' Sliding a finger beneath the grimy collar, he picked the little guy up and set off for home. In a different life he'd have kept him, but he had no choice but to hand him to the nearest animal shelter first thing.

With Scratch contained in the laundry, with a bowl of water, a left-over sausage and an old cushion to sleep on, Jake's thoughts turned to Emma again as he climbed the stairs to snatch a couple of hours of sleep.

She was sexy, had a sense of humour, and was good company in and out of bed. If she wouldn't stay the night he'd accept that. Because she was Emma. She wasn't only a lover, she was a friend. There was something so easy about being with her, and she brought more to his life on so many levels than any woman ever had.

Careful, mate. He was starting to sound like Ry. *Hell.* He flopped backwards onto his bed. That was one very dangerous thought.

CHAPTER TWELVE

THE sea was as calm as glass on Sunday morning, but the air chilled Emma's body as she waded in for her morning workout. The sun had lifted out of the ocean, spreading crimson and gold across the sky.

Sliding beneath the surface, she kept close to the shoreline between the red and yellow safety flags, swimming hard until her limbs warmed and softened. She trod water, watching the sun glimmer on the surface, and waved to a regular fellow swimmer before heading back the other way.

Jake had come by yesterday evening, late and tired. Working his day job and dealing with the sale of the club would take a toll on anyone. She'd made popcorn on one occasion and they'd made love—on every occasion. On the couch. In her tiny shower stall. In her too-small bed. But he hadn't stayed. She'd been unable to sleep for the rest of the night, knowing there was a big warm man in a big warm bed a few kilometres away who'd have been happy to share.

She headed for her towel farther up the beach. Sunday mornings brought out tourists and locals alike. Walking up the shallow steps towards the lawns bordering the esplanade, she watched a group of families set up for a picnic breakfast.

Only now, with Jake in her life, was she realising how isolated she'd let herself become over the years. She needed to make an effort to go out and socialise more.

She wrung out her hair, tied it into a high ponytail, then changed into her track suit in the change rooms, dumping her swimsuit and towel into her hold-all.

On such a beautiful day she didn't want to go home and deal with business, shut away from people and life. She'd splash out on a take-away hot chocolate on the way home. She might even add a cake to her order and sit at an outdoor table on Coogee Beach Road and people-watch awhile.

A big guy with a black-and-white dog on a leash was approaching when she reached the traffic lights. He waved and she pushed up her sunglasses. Jake? With a dog?

She waved back, and suddenly that sunshine seemed a whole lot warmer. The whole world seemed that much brighter. He was looking at her as if he wanted to eat her while he waited for the lights to change.

He crossed the road and kissed her right there on the footpath. 'Hello, gorgeous girl,' he said when he let her up for air. 'Mmm—salt.'

She licked his familiar taste from her lips. 'I wonder why.' He was a beautiful sight, even in a ratty T-shirt smudged with what looked suspiciously like doggy paw prints. She bent to pat the gorgeous black-and-white pooch of indeterminate pedigree at his feet. 'I didn't know you had a dog.'

'He's not mine, unfortunately. I walk him for an elderly neighbour who can't get out much these days. Say hello to Seeker.' He patted the dog's head. 'Shake hands, boy.'

At Jake's command, Seeker sat down and lifted a paw, big puppy eyes looking up at her and a doggy smile as wide as the beach. 'Oh, aren't you *gorgeous?*' She squatted down to ruffle his well maintained fur and was rewarded with a sloppy kiss. 'I always, always wanted a dog, but Mum said no.' *And hadn't she decided her perfect man in her perfect world would love animals?*

'I still do, but these days with my lifestyle it wouldn't be fair, so I get my animal fix with Seeker, here. Some people don't deserve pets.' He frowned. 'I had to turn an abandoned dog in to a shelter yesterday.'

'That's so sad—not to mention criminal. If you can't give a pet the time and love it deserves, don't have one. I'm going for hot chocolate. Would you like to join me? We can get take-away and walk if you like.'

His grin was one-hundred-percent contagious. 'I would. I didn't stop for breakfast. Had to give Seeker his doggy bath.'

'You groom him too?'

'It's part of the fun. He's all mine every Sunday morning unless I'm out of town. There's a dog-friendly park a ten-minute walk away. I can let Seeker off the leash. I've got his *B-A*-double-*L*.'

She laughed. 'He's gorgeous *and* smart.'

Like you, Jake thought, watching her bury her face in fur.

'So how come I've never seen you down here before?' she said, straightening.

'I don't usually come this far. I was on my way to see you, as a matter of fact. Good timing—I was hoping to catch you on your way home from the beach. If not I was going to hunt you down at your place and interrupt you.'

'Oh? Why?'

Because I can't get you out of my mind. I want to be with you all the damn time. 'Can't a guy see his favourite girl?'

She blushed, and her smile was the best thing he'd seen

all morning. 'I thought you said you were going in to the club today.'

'I am. Later.' He'd delayed his meeting with the buyer by a couple of hours—something he'd never have done for any other woman. He slung an arm around her shoulders with an unnerving feeling that with Emma he was swimming in uncharted waters. 'But here you are, so let's get that breakfast you promised and take it to the park.'

'*I* promised?' She smiled up at him, the light in her eyes reflecting the sun's sparkle off the sea. 'I never promised breakfast.'

'Okay, you buy the hot chocolate; I'll spring for the rest.'

They took their purchases to the park: two hot chocolates and a couple of cupcakes drizzled with icing. They shared half a soggy bacon and egg burger with wilting lettuce and mayonnaise, and let Seeker snaffle the other half.

After a vigorous game of chase-the-ball, which Emma threw herself into with enthusiasm, Jake suggested they walk back to his place, return Seeker on the way, and he'd drive her home on his way to the club.

They headed towards Bondi. Emma jogged a few steps ahead with Seeker, chasing a white butterfly, her slim figure as watch-worthy as any catwalk model, her ponytail bouncing and swinging in time with her steps.

They'd been lovers just over a week. With a little of the edge gone after those first frenzied encounters he'd expected the attraction to fade somewhat, as it invariably did. It hadn't. They'd had fun this morning. She'd not fussed over her sea-damp hair and lack of make-up like other women he dated would. Her tracksuit was smeared with paw-prints and covered in fur.

He'd never in a million years considered asking a

woman to come out and play ball with a dog in a park on a Sunday morning. With Emma it came naturally.

'Hope you weren't worried,' he said when they reached Mrs G's front door.

'Of course not, Jake.' The white-haired lady turned her smile on Emma. 'And you found your friend.'

'Mrs G, I'd like you to meet Emma. Emma, this is Grace Goodman—everyone calls her Mrs G.'

'Pleased to meet you, Emma. Jake was hoping to run into you.'

Emma smiled up at him, then at Grace. 'Nice to meet you too. We've had a lovely morning.'

'I don't how I'd manage without this young man here,' Mrs G told Emma. 'He's taken good care of both of us since my Bernie died. I broke my hip last year, and I can't get out like I used to.'

'Afraid I can't stay,' he said, with an apology in his grin and handing the leash to Mrs G. 'Got work.'

Grace shook her head. 'You work too hard. You and this lovely girl here should be out enjoying yourselves.'

Emma smiled at him. 'Work comes first.'

He knew Emma understood. She believed it as much as he—something some of his other lovers hadn't. But he was also working on the playtime her life had been lacking. The idea of convincing Emma to let him take the rest of the day off with her was tempting, but he had to meet the new club owner and go over the books.

They farewelled Mrs G, then picked up his car. He dropped Emma home first. But he lingered over a long hot kiss before letting her go. 'See you tonight.'

On Tuesday Emma had a rostered day off—and her first luncheon date with Jake.

Since Jake had clients all morning, she was meeting

him at his office. His *real* office, which he shared with two other professionals. In a respectable building in the commercial heart of the city.

She rode the elevator to the fourteenth floor, smoothed the lapel on her black jacket as she stepped into a bright reception area with wide windows and glimpses of the Harbour Bridge between the skyscrapers. A dark-haired woman with exotic eyes that hinted at her Asian heritage greeted her with a professional smile at the desk. So different from the first time she'd met him at his place of work—and in so many ways.

Emma smiled back. 'I'm Emma Byrne and I'm here to see Jake Carmody.'

'Oh. Emma, hello.' Her professional smile widened to friendly interest. 'I'm Jasmine. Jake told me to expect you. He's with someone at the moment. Can I get you a coffee or something while you wait?'

'Thanks, I'm fine.'

'And thank you for sending in the soaps. They're a real hit. I'm making a list of people wanting to buy more.'

'That's very kind of you.'

'Are you sure I can't get you a coffee?'

She shook her head, smiling back. 'I'll just admire the view.'

'It's not nearly as spectacular as where you're going for lunch. I booked the table.' She lowered her voice to a conspiratorial whisper. 'Oh, and I probably wasn't supposed to tell you that.'

Emma had expected to grab something in the little café downstairs, and was pleasantly surprised. 'I didn't hear a thing.'

'Don't plan on getting any work done for the rest of the afternoon. I— Excuse me a moment,' she said when the phone rang. 'Carmody and Associates.'

Ten minutes later Jasmine was still handling what seemed to be a complex call. Emma glanced at her watch and flicked through another magazine. Maybe they should postpone their lunch for another time. He was obviously busy.

Even as she considered it, she heard a door open and Jake's voice in the corridor. '...Any time—and don't worry. It's all going to be fine.'

'Thank you, Jake,' a woman's voice said. 'For everything.' Her voice trembled. 'You've given me a chance to start over and I'll never forget it.'

'Just put it all out of your mind for now, and concentrate on spending some quality time with Kevin while I get things rolling.'

The woman appeared first, in jeans a size too big on her too-thin frame and a faded black top slipping off one shoulder. Her hair was scooped into a knot on top of her head and she carried a thumb-sucking toddler on her hip.

Familiar...Emma racked her brain, trying to place her as Jake followed close behind. He walked the woman to the elevators on the other side of Reception, squeezed the woman's bony shoulders as she entered the lift.

Then Emma remembered where she'd seen her. The waitress from the Pink Mango. Cherry.

Obviously a woman like her couldn't afford to be paying Jake for his professional services, yet he was treating her with the care and respect he'd offer any fee-paying client.

Then he turned and saw her, and his frown cleared and his face lit up. 'Emma. Sorry to keep you waiting. Unexpected delay. Hang on a sec, I have something for you.' He disappeared again into his office.

Jasmine, still on the phone, smiled at Emma and rolled her eyes as she spoke to the caller.

Then Jake returned with a fluffy black-and-white stuffed dog. 'According to the tag, his name's Fergus.'

'Oh…' A warm squishy feeling spread through her body. 'You got me a dog.'

'I hope you like stuffed animals.'

'I did, I do. I guess I never grew up.' She'd mentioned never having pets and he'd bought her the next best thing. 'Thank you.'

He jerked a thumb at the busy Jasmine to indicate they were off, then walked Emma to the elevator. It was crowded with office workers headed out for lunch. He flagged down a cab, then they took a short ride to the Centre Point Tower.

She stared up at the famous landmark, as high as the Eiffel Tower. 'We're going up there?'

'I know you hate heights, but I'm sure you'll enjoy the food,' he said as they shuffled towards one of the elevators that shot sightseers to the observation deck, the Skywalk and other adventures Emma had never felt the urge to discover. 'Don't look till we're there.'

She slipped her hand in his and looked up at him. 'Maybe it's time I did.' Steeling her stomach muscles for the inevitable drop, she let out a nervous laugh. 'I might even surprise myself and enjoy it.'

And she didn't shut her eyes once all the way to the top—which seemed to take for ever. The three-hundred-and-sixty-degree revolving restaurant afforded magnificent views of Botany Bay and as far away as the Blue Mountains. She was so proud of herself she even ventured to the slanted window for a quick dizzying glimpse to the street way below.

Jake's hand on her shoulder and his 'Congratulations' made it even more special. She might never have had the nerve to try if he hadn't been there to encourage her. But her legs were still shaky as she set Fergus on the edge of the table.

Jake ordered white wine and a shared seafood platter for starters. He'd made the right decision about the venue—seeing the almost shy pleasure in Emma's eyes when she'd faced her natural fear was worth it.

'Any other plans for your day off?' he asked, setting the menu aside.

'I have an appointment with a potential client at two-thirty.'

'New client?' He leaned forward, interested. 'That's great, Em. Where?'

'It's a new natural products shop in the mall where I work.'

'So we've plenty of time.' He raised his glass. 'Cheers.'

'Cheers.' She tapped her glass to his.

'Emma, I've been thinking about you getting your products out there. Letting people sample them. Why don't you ask one of the shops you supply if you can set up a display one Saturday morning or during late-night shopping hours? I'll give you a hand. You might sound out this place this afternoon, since they're new, and see if they're interested.'

The seafood platter arrived and she selected a prawn. 'That's an idea.'

'We'll need to set up a website first, in case customers ask, and get some business cards printed so they can contact you.'

'You really think my products are good enough for all that hoopla?'

'*Hoopla?*' Had no one ever encouraged her to aim for the stars? 'Are you kidding? After that sensual demonstration the other night?' He pointed the crab claw he was holding her way. 'You'll never know if you don't give it a go. Honey, have a little faith. In yourself *and* your products.'

'I'm trying to. I *do*,' she corrected, and gave a half-laugh. 'Force of habit. I'm not used to others sharing my enthusiasm, and I'm still getting accustomed to the different mind-set.' Setting her palms on the table, she leaned forward with a grin. 'Of *course* you have confidence in my products; why wouldn't you? They're the best you ever tried, right?'

'Right.' He grinned back. 'We'll make a start tonight,' he decided. 'I'll come over when you get home and we'll make plans.'

Emma took another sip of cool fruity wine while she thought about his ideas. She didn't want to let him—or herself—down, especially when he was so busy. Surely she could try it on her own? Even if she just let him help her with the IT side of things? 'You're very generous with your time, Jake. As if you haven't got enough to do with your practice and winding up the club. Are you sure?'

'Of course I'm sure. I want to help you any way I can.'

'Cherry obviously thinks you're pretty wonderful too.'

He looked slightly stunned. 'You know Cherry?'

'I recognised her from the club. I didn't know she had a child, though. I guess you don't think of people in that industry as being mums and having otherwise ordinary lives. She looked pretty down…' She waved a hand. 'Sorry, it's none of my business.'

'Cherry and her kid were evicted from their accommodation a couple of weeks ago. She came to me for help.'

Emma understood that feeling, that desperation, all too well. She'd had to work after school to help pay the bills when her mum had been too depressed to get out of bed for weeks on end. 'That's a horrible, gut-wrenching feeling, and even worse with the added responsibility of a child. What about women's shelters?'

'Do you have any idea how many homeless people there are in Sydney?' His expression changed, and his eyes met hers with an understanding she'd not expected. 'Maybe you do.'

Emma nodded. 'It wasn't that desperate with us, but it so easily could have been. So Cherry came to you?' She remembered the woman's tremulous and relieved voice outside Jake's office. Cherry saw the kind of man Emma saw. An approachable man, an honest man, someone she could trust to help her and her child in a time of desperate need. A man who was generous with his time and expertise. 'It shows how highly she thinks of you.'

But he shook his head as if it was nothing. 'She needed a place for the night, for herself and Kevin. I told her there was a room at the back of the club she could use until we sorted something out. She's staying there for the time being.'

'If anyone can help it'll be Jake Carmody.'

They didn't talk for a moment while they sampled more of the delicious food. 'So...who looks after Kevin when Cherry's working?' Emma asked between mouthfuls.

Jake chose a prawn, peeling it carefully while he answered. 'The girls take shifts. They're a tight bunch. Protective. Mostly they're just people trying to make a living the best and sometimes the only way they know how.'

Emma didn't miss the slightly defensive tone. As if he had a personal interest or understanding. She speared a piece of pickled octopus. 'So what happens next? Obviously that can't work for ever.'

'I've bought a place. It needs some work, but I'm using the sale of the club to finance it. Temporary accommodation for people like Cherry to stay until they get themselves on their feet. I've asked Cherry if she'll run it. It'll get her out of the club scene.'

She took a moment to consider his words before she answered. He seemed so sure—as if he'd thought this through over a long period of time. 'This is very important to you.'

Jake nodded, selecting another crab claw, snapping it open. Damn right it was. It was the only good thing to come out of his inheritance: an ability to make a change for the better. If he only helped one person it would be worth it.

'I've been around that strip club for a big chunk of my life, Emma. Seeing women and their kids come and go. Seeing their lack of power over their own circumstances, the hopelessness in their eyes. Wanting to do something to break the cycle. That's why I went into law. I may not have had the world's best upbringing, but I've turned it around, I think.'

He saw her shift closer, elbows on the white tablecloth, her fresh, clean fragrance wafting towards him. 'I reckon you have,' she said softly. 'You should be careful, Jake, a girl could fall hard for a guy like you.'

His head shot up. Her eyes... Maybe, just *maybe,* there was a hint of those for ever stars in that blue sparkle? He shredded another prawn while his heart tumbled strangely. 'Not a girl like you, Emma. You're too smart.'

The little crease dug between her brows as she popped an olive in her mouth. 'Why not a girl like me?'

Careful. The last thing Emma needed right now was another crack in that heart. 'We're both career types, you and me,' he said, avoiding her gaze. 'Work hard, play hard.'

But were good times all he really had in common with

Emma? He'd never discussed the club or his upbringing or his reasons for his choice of career with anyone. Not even Ryan. Though his mate knew of his father's business they'd never talked about it. Yet he'd talked about it with Emma. But she didn't need to know his whole life history.

Shaking the thoughts away, he lifted his glass, drained his wine, then said, 'Tell me more about this shop you've discovered that's going to help send your new career soaring...'

Emma drove home, her mind abuzz. The new shop was happy for her to promote her products with a display—this coming Friday evening, no less, to coincide with their first week of trading.

Jake was the only one who'd ever shown an interest and inspired her to take the plunge. Jake's encouragement and support had lifted her spirits and caught her enthusiasm. With his help she might just be able to make it work. Correction: she *would* make it work.

With his help so many people were better off, she thought. She thought too, how he'd chosen a career so he could help people like Cherry—the girls and their plights had made a lasting impression on him.

Because he'd grown up around the strip club. For how long? she wondered. Had his mother been a stripper? How long had it been since he'd seen her? She remembered the fleeting expression in his eyes when he'd spoken of her, just once, on the night of the hens' party—at odds with the casual indifference in his voice.

She hadn't let herself become interested in his past because what they had was based around the present. But now she simply couldn't ignore it. His past had shaped him into the man he was. He might be fun-loving, casual and outgoing but there were shadows there too.

She switched direction and headed for his place. There was so much more she wanted to know.

CHAPTER THIRTEEN

EMMA pressed the intercom on the wall outside Jake's home. 'It's me,' she said, when he answered. 'Let me in.'

The gate slid open and by the time she'd reached the door Jake was waiting for her, naked but for a towel low around his hips. 'I thought we arranged to meet at your place, but if you've come to share my shower...' His sexy grin faded when he realised she wasn't smiling back. 'Something wrong? Didn't it work out with the new clients?'

'No, no, nothing like that. It went well, really well, and I'll tell you about it later. But...' She waved a hand. 'Can we talk?'

He gestured her inside. 'Let's go to the living room.'

She followed him, then went to the window and looked out at the sea while she took a calming breath. She didn't know how it was going to go. Whether he'd resent her for what he might see as an intrusion on his privacy. But this was too important to ignore.

'I've been thinking about what you said this afternoon,' she said slowly. 'About Cherry and the place you've bought. How important it is to you.'

'It is, yes. Is that a problem for you?'

'Of course not.' She turned to face him. 'But why buy

a place? Why be personally involved? Why not give to a homeless charity instead? *Why* is it so important?'

Jake listened to her rapid-fire questions while he dragged in a slow, slow breath. Having Emma come into his life was one of the most life-changing events he'd ever experienced. To his surprise, he discovered he wanted to answer them, to have her listen and understand. His only concern was if once he started he might not be able to stop.

He crossed the room, gripped her shoulders loosely and steered her towards the couch. 'Sit down.' He sat down beside her, fisted his hands on his thighs. Took another breath. 'I lived there, Emma. The back of that strip club was home sweet home. So I know first-hand what it's like to be powerless.'

'Oh…Jake.' She lifted a hand, thought better of it and drew it back. 'How long?'

He shifted a shoulder, always uncomfortable with sympathy. But that wasn't what she was offering. Just support and a willingness to listen with an open mind. He'd never realised he'd needed it until now.

He gazed through the windows into the deepening twilight. 'I was five when Mum left in the middle of the night. I hadn't started school yet. I had no friends. Can't blame her, Earl cheated on her as regular as clockwork. She worked late-night shifts cleaning offices, so I saw all sorts come and go at our apartment. One night she just didn't come home. It was like losing an arm.' Or a heart.

Emma didn't speak, but he felt her reaching out to him with streamers of warmth that touched the dark, secret places inside him.

'It was lonely and isolating—after all, I could hardly ask schoolmates to come over and play. As I grew up I understood what had happened, and I swore I'd never be like *him*.' His fists tightened against his thighs. 'But the one person I'd counted on, the one person I'd loved and trusted, left me there. She didn't take me with her and it hurt like hell.'

He felt her hands cover his fists and looked into her moisture-sheened eyes.

'Your mum stayed in a loveless marriage, Emma, but she stayed. Even a mum who gives you grief is better than no mum at all—at least yours had some compassion, some sense of loyalty. But then, that's my opinion. We're always going to see it from our own perspective.'

'How do you know she went to South America?' she said softly. 'Did she come back for you?'

'She sent a postcard once, when I was ten. New continent, new husband, new life. Anyway, after she'd left Earl didn't see the point in paying rent on two places and we moved in to the back of the club. At least I had a roof over my head and food in my belly.'

'A child living in the back of a strip club?' Her eyes changed—ice over fire—and she exhaled sharply. 'The authorities? Didn't they ever catch up with Earl?'

He shrugged, remembering times when he'd been ferried to some stranger's home in the middle of the night. 'Earl was clever. Always one step ahead. It wasn't so bad,' he went on. 'The girls used to make me breakfast sometimes before they went home. They helped me with my homework. Substitute mums of sorts.'

'Your young life must have been very confusing. How did you cope with it all?'

He wrapped a hand around the back of his neck. 'Kept to myself. Studied. Swore one day I'd get out. I was seventeen when I left and found a part-time job and a room to rent.'

'I'll never understand a mother leaving her own flesh and blood.'

He remembered the despair and heartbreak he'd seen too often in his mother's eyes. The guilt that had tormented his youth. The pain of that rejection and abandonment he'd never really got past. 'Because when she looked at me she saw him.'

'Ah…' She shifted closer, the fresh, untainted scent of her skin filling his nostrils. 'But you're *not* him. And she's missed out on knowing someone amazing.' She combed her fingers over the back of his hair. 'You're kind and generous and thoughtful. You're also a man of integrity, and don't let anyone tell you different or make you feel less or they'll have me to deal with.'

A band tightened around his heart. Even knowing his past, she didn't judge. 'Using my inheritance to pay for a safe house is one way of addressing the injustice. My mother didn't benefit, but others will.'

'You're one special guy, you know that?' Her compassionate blue gaze cleared and brightened, and she touched the side of his face with gentle fingers.

He hauled her against him so he could feel her generous warmth against the cold. 'I need that shower.' He needed the water's cleansing spray and her caring hands to rid himself of unwanted memories. Memories that no longer had a place in his life. He closed his eyes. 'You want to wash my back?'

'Does that mean I have to get naked too?'

He drew in a breath and opened his eyes. She was smiling. He touched her hair. 'Unless you want to drive home dripping wet or wearing my bathrobe.'

'Yeah, there's that. Whatever would I do if the car broke down on the way?'

Or you could stay here…

Only he didn't say it. She might be ready to hear it now,

but he didn't want rejection of any kind tonight. He undid the top button of her blouse. 'You *want* to get naked too?'

'Try stopping me. You know what?' She pressed her lips to his chest. 'I even have some spare soap left over in my bag from this afternoon's meeting.' She opened her mouth and flicked out her tongue, leaving a damp trail as she worked her way up to his Adam's apple then his chin. 'There's a new fragrance I'm trialling…' She let her hands wander over his hips, drawing tight little circles through the terry towel with her fingers. 'Eygptian nights. Musk and sandalwood.'

'First Tahiti. Now the East. A round-the-world tour, huh?'

She grazed her fingers over his hardening erection. 'More like a journey of discovery,' she whispered, drawing the towel away. 'Just the two of us.' She reached behind her neck, unfastening her zip and sliding it down so that her dress slipped to the floor. Stepped out of her panties and unsnapped her bra, tossed it away. 'One back scrub coming up.'

At Emma's place later that evening, Jake worked with her on a website design for Naturally Emma. They drank instant coffee and ordered business cards and composed her website pages. It helped take their minds off the earlier conversation. There was a new understanding, a comfortable silence between them as they worked.

Emma took shots of her products for Jake to upload to her computer. She was literally bouncing off the walls with enthusiasm. And nerves. 'Where will I put the extra stock?'

'You'll find a place. I have an empty room under the house if you need it.'

'What if this thing explodes? How will I keep up?'

'Now, *that's* the confidence I like to hear.' He smiled at her, the computer screen's glow reflecting the encouragement etched on his expression. 'You'll give up your day job and employ someone to help you.' He stretched his arms over his head, then reached out to take her hand. 'You'll be fine. If you need help I'm here.'

She breathed deep. 'You don't know how much it means to have you in on this with me, if only to get me started.'

As usual, he shrugged off the praise. 'No worries. I'll have the website ready for you to look at tomorrow night.'

When Jake left, she worked on into the wee hours. She made a start on some mini soap samples and selected a collection for display.

The following day Emma took off in her lunchbreak to slip further down the mall and make arrangements with the shop, collected her business cards from the printer, then caught up with Jake in the evening and approved the website.

Naturally Emma. She stared at the screen, biting her lips, hardly able to believe it was really happening. The lavender background with elegant flowing script and artistic design. The photos. The little piece about her background and qualifications that she'd composed.

'Only two nights to go,' she said, hugging her arms.

'I'll be here to pick you up,' he said, rising. 'But I need to get going. I've got some of my own work to catch up on.'

'I'm sorry. I've monopolised your time.'

'Not at all. Glad I could help.' He pulled her up for a quick kiss. 'Get some sleep.'

The mall was bustling with late-night shoppers when Emma and Jake carried her boxes in at five-thirty on Friday evening. Lights gleamed on the shiny store windows, the smell of roasting nuts and popcorn mingled with perfumes and hair treatments. Elevator music tinkled in the background, along with the ever-present underlying tide of urban chatter.

Kelsey, the shop's proprietor, had set up a table for the products just inside the entrance, and was serving a customer as they arrived. She smiled and waved when she saw them.

'I've got a severe case of killer butterflies,' Emma told Jake as she pulled stock from her box and began arranging it on the table. Her hands weren't steady, her pulse was galloping, and she really, really wanted something to moisten her dust-dry throat. 'What if no one stops by?'

'Looking at you, why wouldn't they?'

She glanced at Jake over her box. He was smiling at her, his eyes full of encouragement. He believed in her, she couldn't let him down. She couldn't let herself down. 'I'd rather they look at the products, but thanks.' She swallowed. 'Would you mind getting me a bottle of water? I forgot mine.'

'Sure.' He put down the box he'd been emptying. 'Back in a moment.'

Kelsey, with curly red hair and moss-green eyes behind her rimless glasses, stepped up as Jake walked away. 'Your guy's a superstar.'

Her guy. Emma started to deny it then stopped. Her heart took a flying leap. Yes, she realised. He was. 'None of it would've happened without his support.' She drew out a cellophane-wrapped basket full of soaps and held it out. 'This is for you. You can take them home, give them to friends. Whatever. I hope your new venture's a success.'

'Oh, Emma, thank you. It's beautiful.' Kelsey admired the basket with a smile, turned it in her hands. 'I think we'll both do well. People look for natural products these days. I'll leave it here for now, so customers can see it. Thanks so much. Oh, I've got a customer...'

Jake slowed as he arrived back, then stopped, watching Emma talk to a couple of elderly ladies. The shop's down-lights glinted on her glossy dark hair. She wore the same white top she'd worn for the hens' night, with a slim white knee-length skirt. Tasteful, professional. A chunky gold bracelet jangled on one wrist as she gesticulated.

She'd ditched the nerves, obviously, and was deep in animated conversation, smiling, eyes alive with friendly interest. Calm, in control, and the sexiest girl in the mall. In all of Australia. How different was this Emma from the Emma he'd seen wearing that top only two weeks ago?

He felt a twinge around his heart—he seemed to be get-ting a lot of those lately—and his fingers tightened on the red foil balloon with its twirling ribbons he'd purchased on impulse after remembering her edict about no flowers.

He shook his head. No matter what she said, Emma was a woman made for hearts and flowers and pretty words, and he was discovering, to his surprise, that he wanted very badly to give them to her. Because, unlike with his previous lovers, with Emma they would mean something more than traditional and often empty gestures.

He watched her pack soaps into a bag, pass it to one of the women with a smile as they handed over their cash. They continued down the mall. Then a guy in a snazzy business suit stopped at her table.

Jake watched Emma smile some more. Watched her flick back her hair as she talked. Pretty boy leaned closer, head tilted to one side, listening. Nodding. He picked up a soap flower and held it to his nose.

Jake scowled and wasted no time making his way to her table. 'Sorry I took so long, honey.' Slight emphasis

on the endearment as he handed her the balloon and her
water, then nodded at Mr Businessman. 'How's it going,
mate?' He stuck out his hand. 'Jake Carmody. Emma's accountant.'

The man shook his hand. 'Daniel McDougal.'

Beside Jake, Emma made a noise at the back of her
throat, setting water and balloon aside. 'Thanks.' Then she
darted him a disconcerted glance. 'Jake, Daniel is from
Brisbane. He owns a large health food chain and is interested in trialling my products up there.'

'That sounds great.' Jake nodded again. 'I'll let you two
get on with it, then.' He dropped a firm hand on Emma's
shoulder, let it linger a few seconds longer than necessary.
'If you need me, my phone's on. I'll be back to help you
pack up.'

'My accountant?' Emma said on the way home.

'Yeah.' Why the hell had he got so proprietorial back
there? He didn't *do* proprietorial. He dismissed the unsettling notion from his mind and concentrated on the traffic.
'Because I'm coming over on Monday night to look over
your financial records,' he said. If this was going to take
off, Emma needed someone she trusted from the get-go
to help her manage the financial side.

'Oh. Okay. Thanks.' She bopped her little balloon
against his arm. 'And thank you for tonight.'

'Pleasure.'

He glanced her way. She had a dreamy expression on
her face. He looked away quickly. *Accountant? Sure.* She
knew exactly what had gone through his mind.

On Saturday Emma caught up with all the things she
hadn't been doing, such as grocery shopping, washing and

cleaning. In the evening Jake took her to a little out-of-the-way café where the pasta was hot and the jazz was cool.

She was thrilled when Jake asked her to share dog-walking duties the following morning. They took Seeker for his walk before Jake went in to the office to catch up on his own neglected work.

Emma spent the afternoon looking forward to seeing him again at dinner while she put together a gourmet beef casserole and whipped up a batch of Jake's favourite lemon poppyseed cakes.

But how long would this thing with Jake last? How long before he tired of her? The way her father had tired of her mother and taken a mistress. The way Wayne had tired of her and found Rani. A guy like Jake with good-looks and all the charisma in the world could have any woman he wanted.

He'd never mentioned anything lasting. *Don't look too far ahead,* he'd told her. *Enjoy the ride.*

And it was one amazing ride.

She could handle it if—when—it came time to let go. Whatever happened, she'd be fine. Because he'd changed her, made her a confident woman who could meet life head-on. She loved him. But a wise woman knew if her love wasn't returned there was nowhere for it to go. She hoped she was strong enough now to let him move on. At some point.

She needed to stand on her own two feet with this business. And she could. He'd given her the belief in herself to give it a really good go. After he'd shown her what to do with the accounting side of things she was going to say thank you very much and be her own businesswoman.

When Jake arrived after work on Monday night, Emma was looking more than a little harassed.

At the front door they spent a moment with their lips locked before she broke away with a sigh. 'This is impossible,' she said, walking to her work spot at the dining room table. She flicked at an untidy pile of papers, sending a couple sailing to the floor. 'I can't do figures. It's a mess.'

'First off—calm down.' He took her hands in his. 'I'm in business law. That makes me a figures guy. Brew us a coffee while I look over your books.'

She stared up at him, eyes panicked. 'Books? I don't have books. I have paper. Piles and piles of paper.'

'Okay. Why don't *I* make us coffee while you gather them together? Then I can take a look. And don't worry. That's what I'm here for.'

'But it's *not* your worry. I have to be able to do it on my own…'

She trailed off, but not before he heard the hiccup in her voice. A sombre mood fell over him, a dark cloud on a still darker night. He squeezed her hands that little bit firmer. 'I'll be available for however long you need my help.'

She looked away at the clutter on the table. 'I'm not a complete moron. I should be able to handle it myself.'

'You're not and you will,' he reassured her. 'I'll sort it, show you how it all works, then you can take over.'

A few hours later he'd organised her paper filing system into some sort of order. He'd set up an accounting program on her laptop and entered her details. All he had left then was to show her how to manage it.

He'd hardly been aware, but at some point she'd finished packing and stacking and made another coffee. He sipped his, found it stone cold. Stretching out the kinks in his spine and neck, he turned to see her zonked out on the couch, fast asleep, a book on the Pitfalls and Perils of Small Business still open on her stomach.

He didn't get nearly enough time to watch her in that state, so he took the opportunity while it presented itself. Turning his chair around, he straddled it, resting his forearms along the back.

Her waterfall of glossy dark hair tumbled over the side of the couch. Her long, dark eyelashes rested on pale cheeks. Her mouth…a thing of beauty, full and plump and turned up ever so slightly at the corners, as if waiting for one chaste kiss to awaken her…

Her eyes would open and that glorious sapphire gaze would fix on his and he'd kiss her again…not so chaste this time…

His lips tingled with sweet promise. His heart beat faster, re-energising his bloodstream, reawakening sluggish muscles. Desire unfurled deep in his belly. Amazing—this feeling, this need for her, never waned. In fact, it was stronger than ever.

But he touched only her silky hair. She needed her sleep. She looked pale, worn out. He should leave, let her rest. They'd catch up tomorrow. But he couldn't leave her to finish the night on that spring-worn couch.

Gathering her in his arms, he carried her to bed, laid her down, and for his own peace of mind pulled the quilt right up to her chin.

She stirred and looked up at him through sleepy eyes…

And it was as if he saw all the days and nights in a fantasy-filled future when he'd wake and lose his heart over and over every time he gazed into those captivating blue depths—

When I saw my children in her eyes…

A bowling ball rolled through his chest. His throat tightened as if the air was slowly being squeezed out of him by an iron fist, and for a few crazy seconds he thought he might black out.

But his moment of panic slid away like an outgoing tide over hard-packed sand, replaced by a shiny and unfamiliar warmth which seeped deep into his heart.

Love.

It had to be love. What else could it be? He'd not recognised it before because he'd never experienced it. Never believed in it. Not for him. Love had always been an unknown. His childhood had been one of rejection and indifference. His entire adult existence had revolved around relationships that never lasted. The women in his life had been about fun and good times. He'd never really taken the time to get to know them on a deeper level. Hadn't wanted to. Maybe he'd been afraid to.

But he knew Emma. And she'd opened his eyes and his heart to a different world. A world where life held more meaning than he'd ever imagined.

'Jake… Wha…?' Her drowsy murmur drifted away.

'Sleep, sweetheart,' he murmured against her temple, and she snuggled into her pillow, eyes already closed again.

He woke before dawn, still fully dressed on top of her quilt, his eyes snapping open to the fading sound of a car's tyres screeching in the distance. Emma was spooned against him as warm and soft as a kitten. He shifted carefully off her bed and let himself out into the pearl-grey of early morning.

He hurried to his car. He had plans to make before his working day started.

CHAPTER FOURTEEN

JAKE was wearing a groove in the floorboards in Emma's studio. He'd left the office at lunchtime, dropped by Emma's workplace and asked her for a key so he could work on her computer. She'd told him she'd be home by six.

It was now twenty minutes past.

The mustard chicken and orzo casserole he'd ordered from his favourite gourmet kitchen was in the oven. A bottle of her favourite bubbly was chilling in the fridge, along with a couple of his favourite gourmet cupcakes.

He'd cleared the work from her table and covered its scarred surface with a cream lace cloth he'd found in her kitchen drawer, placed on it a bunch of red poppies he'd bought.

Should he have taken her to some fancy restaurant instead? No. He didn't want a bunch of strangers intruding. He wanted to share the moment with her. Only her.

A beam of light arced through the window and the familiar engine's sound had him reaching for gas lighter and candles.

Grabbing the plastic carry bag of fried chicken and a bottle of fizzy stuff from the passenger seat, Emma swung her bag over her shoulder and almost danced down the steps.

She couldn't wait to tell him her news. She hadn't phoned. She needed to say it in person.

'Honey, I'm home,' she sing-songed as she pushed the door open.

She was met by some herby, aromatic fragrance. On the table, tall red poppies speared out of a jar alongside two squat red candles already lit.

Jake was pouring fine pink champagne into two glasses that were far too elegant to have come from her cupboard. *He* looked too elegant, in slim-fitting black trousers and a snowy-white shirt that looked as if it had just come out of a box.

'Seems you beat me to it.' She set down her own cheap bottle of fizz on the sideboard and admired the candlelight reflecting on crystal and silver. 'This looks wickedly romantic.'

'I thought it was time I took a chance on the romance bit. You don't mind, do you?' Hands occupied with wine and glasses, he grinned and leaned forward so that she could plant an enthusiastic kiss on his lips. He smelled of some exotic new fragrance.

'I don't mind. Taking chances is what it's all about, right?' Overflowing with excitement, she sashayed over to the oven, peeked at the delicious-looking meal inside. 'And I bought take-away. You should've let me know you were planning a seduction.'

'I wanted to surprise you.'

'You did. And I've got—'

'Everything's ready. Sit.'

He didn't appear to hear her. Okay, this wasn't the moment, she decided. He'd obviously gone to a lot of trouble. 'It smells yummy.'

'It tastes even better.' Pulling out her chair, he waited till she was seated, then walked to the oven. He removed the casserole, set it on the table, then sat down opposite her.

'You okay?' She studied him. 'You seem a little…' she circled a finger in the air '…preoccupied.'

His mouth kicked up at one corner as his gaze drifted over the front of her shirt. 'If I am, it's your fault for looking so sexy after a day at work.'

'And don't you know just the right things to say?' While he spooned the meal into shallow bowls, she fingered a poppy. 'I didn't know poppies had blue centres.'

'These do.'

'Made-to-order poppies? Hmm. You *have* put thought into this.'

'They remind me of you in that sexy red coat of yours. Tall, slim. Blue-eyed. Gorgeous.' He raised their glasses, handed her one. 'To happiness.' Did his eyes look different tonight? Deep and dark… Maybe she was imagining it.

Because everything looked different tonight. From the sunset to the sea, even her old studio apartment. Everything *felt* different tonight. Her life was about to change.

'To happiness.' She took a sip, then set her glass down. She was bursting to talk but she squashed it. She didn't want to spoil his evening's plans. She wanted him to see her make time and enjoy the meal he'd obviously taken so much thought with first. The crystal flutes were sparkly new and very expensive. He'd used her best silver cutlery and china and her grandmother's tablecloth.

She spread a matching cloth napkin over her knee. 'Did you cook this yourself?'

'It's from a gourmet shop in Bondi. I shop there so often the owner's thinking of making me a partner.' He passed her a bowl. 'I'd have cooked, but today's been a bit of a rush.'

So while they ate she asked him about his day. One of his colleagues in the office was taking on a high-profile case. He'd almost finished entering her data on the computer.

How was it going with Cherry and Kevin? He'd driven Cherry to the safe house and they'd chosen paint for the walls. Cherry and a couple of the other girls were starting that job next week in their spare time.

When they'd polished off the last cake crumb from their plates and were enjoying their filtered coffee, Jake decided the moment was right now. He took a gulp of coffee to moisten his throat and steady his nerves. His fingers tightened on the little box in his trouser pocket.

'Emma, I—'

'I have some news—'

Both spoke at the same time.

She was clutching her hands together beneath her chin. Her sapphire eyes shone like stars, reflecting the candle-light.

A premonition snaked down Jake's spine and his breath snagged in his chest. Why did he suddenly feel as if the floor was about to give way? He nodded once. 'You first.'

Her shoulders lifted and she leaned forward. Her familiar fragrance curled around his nostrils.

'You talked about taking a chance earlier—on romance. And it's been lovely. Everything. Thank you for making the evening so special.'

He acknowledged that, but didn't speak.

'I've taken a chance too. I've been offered work in Queensland. *Real* work. Work I love, work I've wanted all my life but never had the opportunity to do.'

Jake was having trouble processing the words. *Queensland.* He was grateful he was sitting down because his legs suddenly felt like lead stumps. 'Queensland?'

'I know. Isn't it exciting? I can't believe it.'

Neither could Jake. 'Where? Who? You've made plans?' *Without discussing it with me?*

'You remember Daniel McDougal? From the mall last week? Well, he was so impressed with my products he had them analysed and everything, consulted with his partners, and rang me this afternoon. He wants to invest in my product line *and* take me on as a consultant to liaise with his client base all around the state.'

Daniel McDougal. Mr Pretty Boy. 'But what do you know about him? Aren't you jumping in without the facts? God, Emma, you can't just—'

'Turns out he's Kelsey's cousin. You know—the owner of the shop? I talked to her, and checked him out on the internet to make sure. Danny's a real success story up there.'

So it was *Danny* now? Jake clenched his jaw. 'You don't have to make a decision right away, Emma.' But she didn't seem to be listening.

'He's got stores around Australia. He's booked me an airline ticket for tomorrow morning to meet the staff and look over the factory before I commit to anything. He emailed me the information. I have a copy right here. Since you're the expert, I'd be grateful if you'd check it out?' She reached into her bag, pulled some papers out, set them on the table.

Damn right he'd check it out. He picked them up with a restraint he was far from feeling. 'This isn't something you simply say yes to, Emma.' He flicked through the first couple of pages. 'There are other considerations to take into account.' *Us, for starters.*

'Of course, and I know that. Jake, put those pages down and look at me.'

He did. He'd never seen her so happy. That sparkle in her eyes, excitement glowing in her cheeks.

'We've got something special,' she said. 'But it was only ever temporary, I'm realistic enough to know that. I'm a career girl, you said so yourself. This chance to do something meaningful with my life is what I've been waiting for. And if it wasn't for you I'd never have had the courage to go for it. I have to try or it'll all have been for nothing. Do you understand?'

His fingers clenched beneath the table. 'Yes.' She was thinking with her head, not her heart—she was doing the right thing. He knew she had to give it a shot. Because if he told her he loved her and asked her to stay and she missed out on her big opportunity he'd never forgive himself. He forced himself to smile. 'I'm proud of you, Emma. You've come so far.'

Her answering smile and the dancing sapphires in her eyes faded a little. 'It's such a big decision, and I have to make it on my own, but… Oh, Jake, I…' She bit down on her lip. 'I…I almost wish I could ask you to make the decision for me. *With* me.'

Damn. Her heart was bleeding into the mix, threatening to sabotage everything. He needed to leave soon, because he didn't trust himself not to try and change her mind—and that would be the worst thing he could ever do for her.

'That's the old Emma talking. Don't listen to her. You know what you want, so go for it.'

A memory of his mother flashed through his mind. She'd left him too. The circumstances were at opposite ends of the spectrum but the hurt was the same. All these years he'd never allowed a woman into his heart, and in a couple of weeks Emma had managed to do what no other woman had.

'Emma. You're a very special woman and I've enjoyed being with you. But circumstances seem to have made the decision for us. And I want you to go. I want you to have that opportunity to shine because I know you will.'

Rising, he swiped his jacket that hung over a chair, shrugged it on—he'd never felt so cold. He picked up her papers. 'I'll look this over and get back to you.'

'Jake, wait.' She pushed up, eyes wide. 'Why are you leaving so soon? Didn't you have something you wanted to tell me just now? You let me have my say—it's your turn.'

He shook his head. 'I was going to tell you I'm flying out too—tomorrow morning. A client's set up a new business in Melbourne and wants my advice.' He waved a hand over the table. 'The meal was to…sweeten things.' He smiled again but it felt as if his lips had turned to stone. 'Turns out it was a celebration after all. And if I know anything about women, you'll need the rest of the night to sort what you're taking and pack.'

He took her in his arms, kissed her beautiful lips just once. Inhaled the scent of her shampoo, drifted his fingers over her silky cheeks as he stepped back and looked into her eyes one last time.

'Go, Emma, and make me proud.'

CHAPTER FIFTEEN

EMMA yawned as the taxi pulled into her driveway at ten p.m. on Thursday evening. She paid the cabbie, jumped out to key in the gate's security code, then collected her cabin bag from the footpath.

As she rolled it across the pavers she saw her mother exit the back door, the old cardigan she'd wrapped around her shoulders flapping in the breeze as she came to meet her.

Just what she didn't need right now, but Emma pasted on a smile. 'Hi, Mum. You're back.'

'Yesterday. I got your text. How was Brisbane?'

'Warm and sticky.' And lonely.

'Jake dropped by this afternoon to drop this off for you.' She held out a large envelope. 'Said he'd rather leave it with me than in the letterbox.'

'Thanks.' She frowned. 'I thought he was going to Melbourne.' It must have only been an overnight stay. Emma knew she should wait until she was alone, but she needed to see what Jake thought of the offer of employment. She so needed to see his handwriting. Anything. Something of him.

She slid the documents out. A green sticky note was attached to the top page.

Hi Em. Looks OK.
Remember, go with your gut—if you think it's right,
do it. And good luck.
J.

'My offer of employment.'

Emma blinked back tears as she slid the contents back into the envelope. Forty-eight hours ago she'd thought it was worth more than gold. Now she knew it wasn't. A successful career was an empty one if she couldn't share it with the man she loved.

Rubbing the chill air from her arms, she reached for the handle of her case. 'I hope you were pleasant to Jake?'

Her mother pursed her lips, but then seemed to relax a little, and something like a smile twitched at her lips. 'Bit of a charmer, that one. Done all right for himself, hasn't he?'

'Yes. He has.'

'Come inside for a few moments.' She turned and began walking the way she'd come.

The kitchen, when Emma entered, was warm and smelled of fresh-baked cinnamon cake. She hadn't smelled that comfortable homey aroma in this kitchen in years.

Her mother pulled a carton of milk from the fridge. 'Would you like a hot chocolate? I could do with one myself.'

'Thanks.' Emma sat down at the kitchen table. 'You've been baking.'

'Stan's coming up to Sydney tomorrow.' She put milk in the microwave, then set slices of fresh buttered cake on the table. 'Try this and tell me if I got it right. I tried a new recipe.'

Emma took a slice and broke a piece off, bit into it.

'Mmm—yum.' She dusted off her fingers. 'So how long will Stan be staying?'

'Not sure yet.'

'He's staying here?'

'Yes.' Her mother stirred chocolate powder into the hot milk and poured it into two mugs, then carried them to the table and sat down.

Emma cupped her hands around the mug and blew on the steaming surface. 'This smells good.' Almost as good as the old milk and honey fix. 'So…things are going well for you two?'

'We have a lot in common.'

'That's great, Mum. What are you planning while he's here?'

'We'll take it as it comes. What about you and Jake?'

Emma could feel her mother's eyes on her and stared into her mug. 'He… We…' She swallowed the lump that rose up her throat.

'He was the mistake you thought he might be?'

Still staring at her mug, she said, 'It was one of those get-it-out-of-your-system things…' Only she hadn't.

'So you're going to Brisbane to work?'

'I thought I was. But I've changed my mind.'

She flashed Emma a look. 'Why?'

'Mum, why did you stay with Dad when you had so many reasons not to?'

'I had two children.'

Emma's jaw tightened. 'And you made us pay for your unhappiness. Every day of our lives.'

She saw her mother flinch, then she put her mug down and folded her arms on the edge of the table. 'Yes. I did. I'm sorry for it. I was wrong.'

Emma studied her, thoughtful. Jake's mother had abandoned her child and he'd suffered the consequences his whole life. Emma's had stayed, even if it would have been better for all if she hadn't. But maybe her mother had been too afraid to leave—afraid of the changes it would bring. The way Emma had been afraid.

Basically her mother had made what she'd thought was the right decision, and it wasn't Emma's place to judge.

'Sorry, I shouldn't have said that,' Emma murmured.

'It needed to be said. I needed to hear it. But a good man, a man who takes the time to look beneath the hard shell and find the woman inside screaming to be let out...' Her mother's voice softened. It was a tone Emma hadn't thought her capable of, and an unexpected smile brightened her whole demeanour. 'Well, he can change your life.'

Emma nodded. 'Yes. He can.' Stan had instigated the change in her mum without Bernice even being aware of it. And wasn't that what Jake had done for Emma?

Friday

'Good afternoon, Carmody and Associates.'

'Hi, Jasmine, it's Emma Byrne.'

'Emma, hi.' There was a smile in Jake's PA's voice that wasn't only professional courtesy. 'What can I do for you?'

Emma's fingers tightened on the phone and she rolled her lips together before saying, 'I was wondering...is Jake there?

'Yes. He's free at the moment. Do you want me to put you thr—?'

'No.' She swallowed. 'Thanks. I wanted to know... I want...' She sucked in a deep breath. 'Actually, I was hoping you could help me...'

Jake checked his watch, then pressed the intercom. 'Jasmine? Looks like your friend's a no-show. Why don't

you give him a call, tell him to reschedule? I'm knock-
ing off early—'

'She'll be here,' she assured him. 'Do me a favour and
wait a few more moments.'

Jake was already shutting down his computer with
his free hand. Jasmine hadn't mentioned her friend was
a woman. The only woman he wanted to see walking
through that door was a million miles away.

'I gave her my word you'd see her tonight,' Jasmine continued. 'Hang on…' He heard a muffled sound then, 'I can
see her from the window. She's walking into the building
now.'

Emma refused to let the nerves zapping beneath her ribcage win. She was a woman on a mission and nothing was
going to stand in her way. So she wasn't afraid of walking
into an office high-rise to face the most important meeting of her life.

Six p.m. on a chilly autumn evening in Sydney's CBD
and the business day was over. Workers were trickling out
of the building on their way home.

Her work was just beginning. The most important work
she'd ever done. The most important work she'd ever do.
She'd promised herself she'd talk to Jake Carmody, and
she would. She could.

Shrugging her bag higher, she marched inside. A couple of men in snazzy business suits exited the lift. She
clutched the miniature hat box at her waist as she passed
them. Did they know her life was on a cliff's edge? Could
they hear how hard her heart was pounding? She hit the
button for the fourteenth floor and watched the numbers
light up while her stomach stayed on the ground floor.

The doors slid open smoothly and she stepped out.
Jasmine looked up and smiled, collecting her bag from

her desk on her way out. 'Go straight in. He's getting a little impatient.'

'Thanks.'

Emma heard him on the phone before she reached the open door. That deep, lazy voice that rolled over her senses like caramel sauce. Only three days, but she'd missed hearing that voice. She loved that voice. She loved the man it belonged to. It was time she took the big, scary leap and let him in on that fact.

She took a fortifying breath, then knocked and entered.

He was sitting behind his desk and looked up sharply, eyes widening when she closed the door behind her.

'Something's come up. I'll speak to you tomorrow,' he said into his mobile without taking his eyes off her. He disconnected and set the phone on the desk. 'Emma.'

'Hello, Jake.'

'I'm expecting a client…' He studied her face. 'I'm guessing it's you.'

'Jasmine told me you'd be here. She asked you to wait, so thank you.'

His eyes raked over her coat and she felt a flush rise up her neck. Heat, desire, longing. Her body reacted to his gaze as if it had been programmed for his exclusive use, and her nipples hardened beneath her finely woven cashmere jumper. She wished she knew what he was thinking, how he felt about her turning up without calling first.

He checked his watch. 'I was about to leave. I need to get home.'

Her heart clenched so tight she wondered that her blood still pumped around her body. Her fingers tightened so hard on the little box she wondered it didn't implode. 'A… date?' She had to force the words out.

He stared at her with those beautiful, dark, unreadable eyes. 'What do you think, Emma?'

'I think…if it was…I'd try to talk you into cancelling because I need to talk to you first.'

'No need—there is no date.' He was turning his mobile over and over in his hands. Watching her. 'How was Brisbane? Is the new job everything you wanted?'

'Yes. And no.' She focused on those eyes. 'It's everything I wanted in a career. Double the income I'm making at the call centre. A spacious office with my name on the door. The chance to build my own business on the side. A chance to travel.' She sucked in her lips. 'But it's not enough.'

'Not enough.' Rising, he came around to her side of the desk, leaned his backside against the edge. 'Why isn't it enough, Em?'

He enjoyed being with her, she knew that. He made love to her as if she were a goddess. He believed in her. But did he love her? How would he respond if she asked him? There were no guarantees in life and love, but wasn't taking that leap of faith what it was all about?

She tightened her fingers on the little box and sucked in a lungful of air. 'It's not enough because I want more. I want it all. What's the point in being successful if you're lonely?' She pushed her gift into his hands. 'I love you, Jake. I need you in my life. No matter what else I do or don't have, I need you.'

He shook his head slightly, as if he couldn't believe what he was hearing, then looked down at the box. Back to her.

'Open it.'

She forgot to breathe as he lifted the lid. He met her eyes. A slow smile curved his lips and her breath whooshed out. He lifted out the cupcake with its red heart piped on top.

'It's not soap. It's chocolate—you can eat this one.'

'I'm not so sure I want to. It's too special.'

She twisted her trembling fingers together in front of her. 'Jake…do you love me back? I really, really need to know if I'm making an idiot of myself here…'

'Emma.' He set the cake and its box beside him on the desk, then covered her hands with his. 'I know that when I'm with you, when I look at you, I have this feeling inside me that makes Everest seem like an ant hill. It makes me want to go out and climb its highest peak with my bare hands. It gives me a reason to get up and watch the sun rise and thank the universe for bringing you into my life. I'd say that's love, wouldn't you?'

'Yes. Because that's how you make me feel too.' She was beyond terrified that she might have let this chance slip through her hands. It gave her strength to continue. 'I came here to say…to ask…Jake, will you marry me?' The last words rushed out on a trembling breath.

His eyes darkened, warmed. And his slow smile was the most wonderful, heartbreakingly beautiful sight she'd ever seen. 'That's going to be one hell of a story to tell our children some day.'

Our children. Her heart blossomed with all the possibilities of a future together opening up inside her. 'So…is that a yes?'

He brushed the back of his hand over her cheek, the side of her neck, leaving a shimmer of heat, the scent of his skin. 'I'm not planning on having our kids out of wedlock, sweetheart.'

He bent his head towards her and she rose on tiptoe, slid her arms around his neck and pressed her lips to his with all the pent-up emotion and love she had inside her. He kissed her back without hesitation, without reservation, dragging her close so that she could feel the fast, hard beat of his heart against hers.

Finally she drew back so she could see him, cupped

his treasured face in her hands. 'I was afraid to love you. Afraid of its power. It can lift you up, but it can bury you so deep you can't see a way out. I saw what it did to my mother. I saw how she let it destroy her.

'But when I went to Brisbane I realised I wasn't like her. You showed me that, by pushing me out of my comfort zone and allowing me to see another side of myself. And I want to thank you for the rest of our lives.'

He smiled down at her. 'And I want to let you.' Then his expression sobered. 'I was afraid too, but wouldn't admit it—even to myself. I've never let anyone close. It was easier to play the field and move on. But with you I couldn't seem to let you go. Until you told me about the new job. I wanted you to have that career you worked so hard for. That success. I had to let you go and find it for yourself, even though I knew I loved you.'

'It's not enough. Not without you.' She tugged his hand. 'Can we get out of here?'

'Sure thing.' Tightening their clasped fingers, he headed for the door. 'I've got a surprise for you.'

Jake handed his address and a healthy wad of notes to the parking attendant on their way to pick up Emma's car. 'Find someone to take care of it and there's enough cash for a cab back,' he told him, then, slinging his arm around Emma's shoulders, he hustled her along the street. He wondered that his feet touched the ground. Half an hour ago he'd been at the lowest point in his life and now he was flying.

A short time later he kissed her on the front door step. 'Welcome home. I love you, Emma, and I'm never going to tire of hearing myself say it.'

'I'm never going to tire of h—' A long, low whine interrupted, vibrating through the door, followed by a whimper and a series of sharp barks. '*What* is that?'

He unlocked the door and a flurry of paws and joyous barks greeted them. 'Meet Scratch.'

'You bought a dog? So *that's* why you had to get home.'

'He's the abandoned dog I told you about.'

'And you rescued him.'

'I just couldn't bring myself to leave him at the shelter, so I picked him up yesterday.' He bent to scratch behind his silky ears. 'I think we rescued each other—didn't we, boy?'

'We were all in need of rescue,' Emma murmured. 'Hey, there, you little cutie, you.'

Jake watched her wasting no time getting acquainted, crouching down so Scratch could sniff her and approve. With a joyous yelp he rolled onto his back, his tongue lolling out, adoration in his eyes.

Jake squatted beside Emma to scratch the dog's tummy. 'So what do you think—you and me and a crazy pooch? You didn't know he was part of the deal—you sure you still want to marry me?'

'Are you kidding? He seals the deal absolutely.'

He looked at Emma, his heart overflowing with that mysterious thing called love. It had eluded him all his life but now... Now he had it all.

A few moments later, with Scratch tucking into his dinner, Jake put the little velvet box into Emma's hands. 'To make it official.'

Her eyes widened. 'What's this? How...?'

'I was going to propose to you the other night. Until you told me your news.'

Realisation dawned in her bright blue eyes. 'So *that's* why you went to so much effort. Oh, Jake. I was so focused on myself I didn't—'

He placed a finger on her lips. 'Just open it.'

'Oh, my...' she breathed. 'It's beautiful.'

Three diamonds on a platinum band winked in the light. 'One for you, one for me, one for the kids we're going to make,' he told her, sliding it onto her finger.

He lifted her off the floor, twirled her around and around until they were both dizzy, then waltzed her to his bedroom the way he'd waltzed her to bed that first time they'd made love.

He tugged on her belt. 'I'll have you know the first time I saw you in that coat I wondered what you were hiding beneath it. Now…take it off and let me see.'

Later, Emma cuddled against him in his king-size bed. Scratch snored doggy snores in his basket nearby. 'I think I'd like to stay right here for the rest of the weekend.' She stretched, feeling satisfied, in love, and entirely too lazy.

'Sounds like a plan. But I doubt Scratch will agree.'

'Our house by the sea and a dog,' she murmured. 'This really is home. What a wonderful life…'

'And what do you want to do with that life…' he nuzzled the sweet taste of her breast '…besides making love endlessly till dawn?'

'I want to concentrate on Naturally Emma. Danny's still going to market my products in Queensland, and I might go up once a month to see how it's going.'

'Maybe I can accompany you sometimes. As your accountant.'

'Nuh-uh. If you accompany me it'll be as my husband.'

'Even better.' His hand created a warm friction over her belly. 'I'm shifting some of my office work home. When I decided to take on a dog I made the commitment to be home more.'

'We'll neither of us ever get any work done.' She drew a line up his shin with her toes and draped her top half over him like a scarf.

His laugh was more of a choke as his arms went around her to pull her all the way on top. 'Reckon you're right.'

She buried her face in the musky warmth of his neck and breathed in his scent. 'I'm always right. I asked you to marry me, didn't I?'

'So…how does a wedding as soon as Ry and Stella come back from their honeymoon sound?'

She lifted her head so she could look into those warm coffee eyes and see his love for her shining through. 'Perfect.'

* * * * *

MILLS & BOON

THE HEART OF ROMANCE

A ROMANCE FOR EVERY KIND OF READER

MODERN

Prepare to be swept off your feet by sophisticated, sexy and seductive heroes, in some of the world's most glamourous and romantic locations, where power and passion collide.
8 stories per month.

HISTORICAL

Escape with historical heroes from time gone by. Whether your passion is for wicked Regency Rakes, muscled Vikings or rugged Highlanders, awaken the romance of the past.
6 stories per month.

MEDICAL

Set your pulse racing with dedicated, delectable doctors in the high-pressure world of medicine, where emotions run high and passion, comfort and love are the best medicine.
6 stories per month.

True Love

Celebrate true love with tender stories of heartfelt romance, from the rush of falling in love to the joy a new baby can bring, and a focus on the emotional heart of a relationship.
8 stories per month.

Desire

Indulge in secrets and scandal, intense drama and plenty of sizzling hot action with powerful and passionate heroes who have it all: wealth, status, good looks…everything but the right woman.
6 stories per month.

HEROES

Experience all the excitement of a gripping thriller, with an intense romance at its heart. Resourceful, true-to-life women and strong, fearless men face danger and desire - a killer combination!
8 stories per month.

DARE

Sensual love stories featuring smart, sassy heroines you'd want as a best friend, and compelling intense heroes who are worthy of them.
4 stories per month.

To see which titles are coming soon, please visit
millsandboon.co.uk/nextmonth